# Schea

# About Greg Judge

Greg Judge has had careers as a military officer, a meteorologist, a project manager for a large corporation and a university adjunct professor. He travels extensively and has visited all continents, except Antarctica. Greg is retired now, lives in Seattle and can be found at www.facebook.com/gwjudge1948. He has three daughters and 6 grandchildren.

# Customer Reviews of <u>Schea</u>

"A page turner thriller…"

"Keeps your curiosity going wanting to read more…"

"Look forward to the sequel…"

"Twists and turns that keep you reading…"

"Could not put it down until the end…"

"Gripping action novel of one girl's journey from tragedy to triumph…"

Greg Judge

# Schea

Schea

Cover Design by Daleen Smit, daleen@spiritofthecape.co.za

ISBN: 13:978-1548173180

Fiction/Action & Adventure

To my mom, Kathy, an avid reader who passed on her love of books and stories to me.

# ACKNOWLEDGEMENTS

I would like to thank all of those family and friends who supported and encouraged me through this whole process. They do not necessarily know how important they were in helping me stay motivated and excited about my writing projects.

I would like to single out and thank my friend Pam for reading my manuscript, and for providing encouragement, support and suggestions that helped me to make a better product.   I would like to thank my daughter, Stephanie, for being my most enthusiastic cheerleader during this project.

I would like to offer special thanks to my brother, Mike. He read each section of the manuscript as I completed them and not only stayed an enthusiastic supporter of the entire project, but also provided numerous helpful suggestions, corrections and ideas for me to consider.

Additionally, I would like to offer thanks to my cover designer, Daleen Smit, who read the manuscript and brought the image of Schea in my mind to life in a beautiful visual for the cover.

# Contents

# Schea

## 1 Mission Seven: Rahim

Schea took a breath and held it for 5 seconds. She then let it out slowly as she sighted her target through the scope 250 yards away in his hotel room. He was a high ranking leader in the Taliban and has been proven to have been involved in several recent terrorist incidents in Europe and Asia. As he passed by the window, she relaxed her breathing and gently pulled the trigger on her H&K sniper rifle. The bullet shattered his skull, but before she saw this result she had already sent a second bullet into his chest. Within a minute of the second shot, she had broken down her rifle and packed it away. Someone would come to the small room in the abandoned building to pick it up later. She then walked calmly down to the street with her head covered and cast down as she made her way to the train station.

Sahid al Rahim was now a deceased Taliban terrorist.

She stepped off of the train in Ankara after the hot, dusty 3 hour train ride. She continued to the curbside just outside of the station and entered a black limousine that was waiting with its engine running. The driver did not know her, but he knew how to recognize his passenger. She was wearing the uniquely designed headscarf that she was told would be worn by his passenger. She entered the limo and sat silently for the 45 minute ride to the embassy.

After arriving at the embassy, she was escorted to the basement 3 floors below and handed her packed travel bag. She opened the bag and began to change into western style attire for her long trip back to the United States. The same limo and driver took her to the airport. Again, they rode silently and he didn't even look her way when she exited.

Her flight landed at Dulles Airport a few miles outside of Washington, DC. She passed through customs and immigration without incident and was met at the curbside by another waiting limousine. The driver was young and serious looking. She was driven to a modest hotel just outside of the Washington DC beltway and knocked on the door of the room number that she had been given by the driver. Chuck Halvorson met Schea and asked if she would like the usual. She nodded and he went to the mini-frig.

Chuck was the head of a new unit that he and the President of the United States were putting together. This unit would be staffed with resources that could be used for unique missions around the world and the President, Jameson Bankcroft, had asked Chuck to form it. They had heard about, then met Schea Tailor several months ago, decided she would be the first member of the small special unit and this had been her first mission for the unit. Nothing was said until she and Chuck were comfortably seated. Chuck finally asked how the mission went and she said the mission went well then took a sip of her usual drink, a Diet Coke. Chuck had a McCallum on one ice cube.

He asked a few questions, Schea answered them and confirmed that the target had been eliminated. Chuck nodded, told her to get some rest and to call Todd who would do the detailed debriefing. She knew this had only been a test for her since the shot was easy and the planning details were straight forward. The President and Chuck simply wanted to see how she handled herself on a mission. They already knew that she was good based on the missions she had completed for Todd, but had still asked for a test.

The President learned of Schea after she saved his son's life from a suicide assassin in Brighton, England. Her current employer, Todd Groden, had been called in to meet with the President and that is when Chuck asked for his help staffing the new unit with highly skilled operatives. Chuck asked him to provide his best operative who would set the standards for future members. Todd told him to start with Schea since she was his best operative. They were stunned at first because they had thought that she was just a young and pretty office assistant. Todd assured them that she was not just some young kid and, after reviewing her previous missions, they asked to meet her.

When they finally met Schea, and got over the fact that she was a 17 year old teenage girl, they asked her if she would like to join their unit and Schea readily agreed.

# 2 The Good Life

If Schea Tailor were a regular teen, she would still be in high school. However, Schea is anything but regular since becoming a highly paid special operative. But, in order to get to this point in her life, she has had to live a life that few could have survived, mentally or physically.

XXXXX

After meeting with Chuck, she went to her rented home in Annapolis, Maryland, undressed, showered, crawled under the thick warm duvet on her canopy bed and slept soundly for the next 7 hours.

She awoke the next morning, dressed in her running gear and went for a 6 mile run at an easy 7 minute per mile pace. After some light stretching, she showered and walked to her favorite coffee shop.

Her home was on the waterfront off of a picturesque side street, and she loved walking along the paths that bordered it. As she sipped her tea, she reflected on how she had gotten to this point in her life.

She had already eliminated, meaning killed, over a dozen targets and regretted none of them. She was confident that each and every one of the bastards deserved to die.

XXXXX

Schea had been born into a home that was full of love and laughter. She had loved her parents and idolized her older brother and sister. They lived in a beautiful cabin style home in the small town of North Bend located in the picturesque Cascade Mountains of Washington State.

Her dad, Jason, had been a Navy SEAL while her mom, Sharon, had been an outstanding and well respected, professor at the University of Washington in Seattle, about an hour's drive from their home.

She had given up teaching once she and Jason started a family. She wanted to be home with her children and decided to home school them. Both parents had been prudent investors and managed to create a small fortune in property and equities. This gave them the means to create this idyllic lifestyle for their growing family.

Schea, her brother, Rob, and her sister, Allison, loved being homeschooled. One of the benefits for Schea in particular was that she didn't have to continue to explain to the other kids how to pronounce her name. It was pronounced as though the letter c were not there or that it were silent. People were always saying something like S-chay but it is actually pronounced like Shay.

Sharon schooled them in the basics that any kid would get in a public school, only better, and Jason schooled them in the woods and mountains around their home. They learned how to find food, build a shelter, start a fire, and survive on their own. Jason also taught them how to hunt and fish. Schea was able to shoot a small rifle by age 4 and could hit a target 100 yards away 10 out of 10 times by the time she was 5 years old. She seemed to be a natural shooter with a keen eye and nerves of steel. She learned to box by age 8 and could handle people bigger than her by age 10. All three kids were expert trackers and hunters before they became teenagers.

On one occasion Schea, aged 10 at the time, and her brother were out bow hunting while he was home on a short leave from the army. Rob was about 10 yards in front of Schea as they followed a known deer path through the woods being exceptionally quiet so they didn't spook a deer. Suddenly, they heard some crashing to the right of the path, and as Rob turned to look behind him, a bear leapt onto the path between them and looked straight at Rob.

Rob had not nocked an arrow so he had no time to swing his bow around to take a shot. Schea had the perfect shot, took it and hit the bear in the side. She quickly nocked a second arrow and put it into the back of the bear's neck. The bear collapsed onto the path and breathed his last. Rob looked at her with a stunned look on his face then smiled, came over to Schea, hugged her and said, "Good shot pipsqueak."

She grinned back at him and said, "Thanks bro."

XXXXX

Her brother was 8 years older and had joined the Army right after being certified by the state school board that he had completed all of the requirements for a high school diploma at the age of 17. After basic training, he applied and was accepted into Special Forces training where he performed exceptionally well and was recommended for the Delta Force.

Her sister was 4 years older and had decided to go into the public school system when she was 14. She loved it and loved the exposure to a regular teenage life. She did well in almost all of her classes, especially her computer class and had been labeled a computer nerd by her classmates. But, she was not the typical nerd. She was beautiful, funny, smiled almost all of the time and could charm a room within 5 minutes of entering.

But as sometimes happens, Schea's life changed dramatically.

# 3 Life Takes A Dark Turn

Shortly after returning to his unit from his home visit, Rob completed Delta training and was sent to Afghanistan. While on a routine patrol in the mountainous northeastern region of the country, his unit was ambushed. Everyone in his patrol was killed but he was captured. After a month of brutal torture and beatings, he was executed by the Talban group that had ambushed his unit. Schea was only 11 years old and the family was devastated when the army officers came to their door with the news. Schea was particularly devastated because she had always thought that Rob was indestructible.

Unfortunately, this was not to be the end of her loses.

XXXXX

Her parents were both marathon runners and frequently ran races together while the kids cheered them on. As a tribute to their son, they started a charity that raised money to help pay for the education of the children of fallen military men and women. One of the ways they raised money for their charity was to seek sponsorship for the marathon races they ran.

A year after Rob's death, they started a pledge drive for the New York City Marathon and planned to run the race together. It is a wonderful marathon that takes runners through New York's 5 boroughs. It starts just across the Verrazano Bridge in Staten Island and winds through each borough before finishing in iconic Central Park.

Security had become increasingly tight over the years following several high profile attacks at sporting events around the world. Packages, large purses and backpacks were no longer permitted along the marathon race course, and spectators are watched and randomly searched during the event. Since the race started on Staten Island, most runners had to be transported to the start area by buses.

Schea, her sister and parents were staying in downtown New York City within walking distance of the finish area. Schea and Allison went with their parents to the staging area for the bus transportation to the start area. Only runners were allowed to enter the staging area where the buses were queued, and they were not permitted to take bags onto the buses. Most of the runners had to wear several layers of clothing in order to keep warm in the chilly fall air at the start area overlooking the bridge. Most of the runners would simply discard these layers along the race course.

Schea and Allison gave their parents hugs and kisses and wished them a great race. Just before stepping onto the bus, they turned and blew kisses to the girls. It took about 10 minutes to get the first few buses moving out of the area to the start line and they were on the 5th bus in line. As the buses headed out, Schea and Allison headed back to the hotel but would return to the finish area with another couple who were friends of the Tailors and had a son running in the race.

After they had been in their room for about 45 minutes, they heard a loud noise outside and went to the window to see what it was. They were on the 10th floor of the hotel, so they had a good view of the area but could not see anything out of the ordinary nearby.  As they looked farther into the distance toward the area of the Verrazano Bridge, they saw what they thought was smoke.

As they continued to stare they were startled by loud banging on their door.  When Allison opened the door, the other dad started talking about bombs, buses, runners, and Schea could only stand transfixed.  She didn't understand everything that he had said, but she immediately knew that this was bad, really bad, and would probably get worse.  Slowly she realized that Allison was pushing her towards the door and telling her they had to go.

XXXXX

There had been two explosions and investigators eventually determined that two of the runners had been suicide bombers.  They had come to the United States from Kosovo 2 years ago and their histories and contacts were still being investigated.

They had gotten onto different buses, 2 buses apart and triggered the bombs as their respective buses were crossing the Verrazano Bridge.  Each bomber had sat in roughly the center of their bus in order to cause maximum carnage.

Three people survived on the first bomber's bus and only one survived on the second bomber's bus.  There were multiple injuries and 4 deaths on each of the nearest buses.  Jason and Sharon did not survive.  They were on the bus with the second bomber.

Schea and Allison had lost their brother, mother and father in just 2 years and felt completely lost and abandoned.  Schea was only 12 and Allison had only just turned 16, and now they were alone.  They were both smart, tough and could survive in most harsh situations, but none of their training prepared them for this.  Schea withdrew completely into herself.  *What would she do?  Where could she go?  Who would care for her now?*  Allison handled it better.  She was the older sister and, since it was just she and Schea now, felt that she had to take charge of their lives.

# 4 Hope

Friends and family took them in, but none of them could care for both girls at the same time, thus they became separated and each went to live with different families. Schea was horrified when this happened. Allison, ever the stronger one, took her aside and talked quietly and calmly to her. "This is only temporary and we will be together soon."

Luckily, a year after the death of their parents, Schea and Allison were finally reunited. They were taken into a foster home in Raymond, Washington which is a fairly rural area located 3 hours south of Seattle and close to the Pacific Ocean. The foster family included a mom, Crystal Watson, dad, Drake, and 2 bothers, Rod, aged 17, and Hank, 19. At first it seemed like the ideal situation, the kids got along well and the parents were caring and provided well for the girls.

However, after about 4 months, Schea noticed that Allison seemed to be withdrawing from social interaction. At first, she thought that maybe Allison was just feeling the pain of the losses they had suffered. She guessed that this was likely because Allison had not had time to mourn, since she felt the need to take care of her sister.

A month later, Schea went to her sister's room to talk, found it empty, and figured that Allison was downstairs or outside. The Watsons owned a large tract of land, with several out-buildings because the place had been a farm many years before. The mom and dad were in town shopping and, since it was a Saturday, all of the kids were home.

As Schea wandered the property calling Allison's name, she thought she heard a muffled shriek come from an old work shed a little distance away. She figured that Allison and the boys were hiding and would jump out as she walked by trying to scare her. She smiled and decided to turn the tables on them. Using her hunting skills, she walked a little distance away and stopped calling for Allison.

After about 5 minutes she silently made her way to the back of the shed, thinking that she would suddenly burst through the back door and scare the would be attackers. As she approached the back of the shed, she could hear muffled sounds and figured they may be hatching a new plan to surprise her. She came up to the back of the shed and peeked through a small grimy window.

What she saw horrified her. The boys were naked, as was her sister, and Hank had his back to the window. Allison was lying face down on the floor while Rod crouched down behind her. Schea saw that his private part was stimulated and he was leaning into Allison. Schea could not make sense of what was happening.

She knew what they were doing because she was old enough to have learned about sex and how it was done, but this didn't make sense. This was her sister, Allison, who was about to do it with the younger brother. Now, she debated whether to barge in or let them be. After all, Allison was old enough to know what she was doing and maybe she wanted to have sex with him. But, Hank was there watching. This didn't make any sense to Schea!

Suddenly, she heard Allison cry out and say, "No! Please stop!"

Schea's decision had just been made for her. She flew through the back door screaming. As she came in, she grabbed a shovel that was leaning just inside the back door, held it slightly above her head and yelled at the boys, "Stop! Get out."

The boys quickly jerked backwards away from Allison. They looked scared at first, probably because they were caught in the act as well as being naked, but then they did the most shocking thing. They smiled. Both boys slowly picked up their clothes and began to get dressed, all the while smiling at Schea.

Just before they left, the boys looked at each other, then back at Schea. As they looked at her, their eyes slowly began to scan every inch of her body. They looked lustfully at her budding breasts and young legs. It had been a warm day, so she had on shorts and a tank top. She did not wear a bra yet and began to realize what they were thinking. The boys scanned back to her face, smiled again then turned to go out. As they left, Hank turned around once more. He looked at Allison with no real interest, but did look back at Schea, gave a slight nod, grinned and left.

It took a moment for Schea to collect her thoughts after the door closed then she bent down next to Allison. Allison was crying softly and mumbling. Schea helped her to get dressed then they walked out the back door and into the woods.

They went to a small clearing where they knew they could be alone, and once Allison had composed herself, Schea quietly asked what had happened.

Allison told her.

# 5 Hope Lost

Allison told Schea that several months ago Hank had come across her in the wooded area beyond the back yard. She had gone there to find a quiet place to try to think about what she was going to do after she finished high school the following year. At first, Hank seemed to be fine just talking quietly. He could be charming and kind when he wanted to be. Allison finally asked him about his plans for the future and he talked about the military being a possibility since his grades were not good enough for college.

All seemed to be going well, when he suddenly put his arm around her waist. She gently moved away and smiled in a way that said she wasn't really interested in something like that, but he persisted and she became scared. He was a big kid, and about a foot taller and 100 pounds heavier than she. Suddenly, he grabbed her. She screamed, but they were too far out in the woods for anyone to hear her.

She began to fight him off, when she was suddenly grabbed from behind. At first she thought it was someone who had heard her scream and was there to help. When she was pulled away from Hank, he just stood there. No fear and no panic. She turned and saw that it was Rod who had pulled her away. She became confused and scared because both boys were now grinning at her. Before she knew it, the boys pulled her down and began pulling off her pants and shirt. They also pulled their pants off, while holding her down. They seemed adept at this, as though they had done it before.

They both raped her, first one boy then the other several times. It lasted for over an hour and, since she had been a virgin, she bled quite a bit, which they seemed to enjoy even more.

When they finally finished and got dressed, they stood on both sides of her and looked down at her back since she was lying face down. After a minute or so of gawking at her, Hank leaned down near her head and quietly asked, "Do you think your little sister might like to join us sometime?"

At this, she rolled over and tried to yell, but her voice was raspy and strained since she had been shouting when they had first started. She finally said as loud as she could, "Leave my sister alone".

Hank smiled and said, "It's too bad you feel that way. But, I will agree to leave little Schea out of it on one condition. You cannot tell anyone about this and you have to submit to either of us at any time." She was horrified at this, but felt she had no choice. She gave a slight nod.

Hank smiled, stood, and the brothers wandered off.

It took Allison about an hour to pull herself together. She finally got dressed and cleaned herself as best as she could in a nearby stream. When she got back to the house, Crystal saw that she seemed to be having trouble walking. When asked, Allison told her that she had taken a longer walk in the woods than normal and had had a hard fall down a small ravine. Crystal wanted to take her to the doctor, but she said she was fine and that nothing was broken or damaged. She was just sore and bruised, and would be fine in a few days.  Schea remembered this same excuse, but thought nothing of it at the time.

Allison continued, "After that incident, one or both boys took me in my room if no one was home or out in the woods or in an out-building.  They did this to me at least a couple times each month and I learned from their conversations that they had done this to about 3 or 4 other girls over the years. They started when Rod was 14 and Hank was 16."

# 6 Escape

Schea couldn't believe what she was hearing from her sister. Her immediate reaction was anger and wanted to beat the crap out of both boys but Allison cautioned that the boys were too big. Schea said they should tell the parents and the police. Allison reminded her that if they did that, then the boys would come after her too.

Schea tried to argue that they would be protected but Allison merely responded, "Even if we are moved to a new home, the boys will probably not serve much, if any, jail time. Then, they will likely track us down for turning them into the police and once they do, they are evil enough that they would not stop at just raping us. They would likely beat us or worse."

Schea knew then that the answer was to find a way to get as far away as possible from them and reasoned with Allison, "If we can simply get away, yes, the boys might think about looking for us. But, as soon as they realize we did not tell anyone about what they had done, they will feel safe and merely move on to another unfortunate girl."

Allison reluctantly agreed to try to escape, and they began to work on an escape plan. They felt somewhat guilty that they were not doing anything to stop the boys from doing the same thing to other girls, but they were in survival mode and could only concentrate on getting far, far away from them. Maybe they could try to do something about the boys once they felt safe.

They figured that their best option for escape was through the woods because it was familiar territory for them. They had meager possessions, so a small backpack for each would suffice and they didn't even need to hoard food and water since they knew what was edible in the woods and could both hunt, plus water was plentiful in the good old rainy Pacific Northwest. Schea did not want Allison to have to go through another ordeal, so they had to leave soon. They decided to leave in 2 days once everyone had gone to sleep.

XXXXX

It was a Monday evening two days later when they put their plan into action. The parents normally stayed home in the evenings during the week, but another couple had invited them over to meet a new family who had moved into the area a couple of weeks earlier. The new couple had teenagers, 2 girls, 15 and 16 and a boy, 12. While the parents were telling the four kids about the new family and that they would be out for the evening, Allison and Schea gave each other a quick look, as did Rod and Hank. But, the mind meld completed by each pair of siblings was decidedly over contrasting thoughts about this new family with 2 teenage girls.

Drake and Crystal left at 7 pm and said they would be back at around 11 pm. The boys wandered off to their friend's house a short time later, where they were supposed to spend the night. After they all left, the girls met in Allison's room, discussed their plan and decided not to leave until after the Watsons got home and were asleep. They didn't want them to find out that they were gone until the next morning, which would give them more time to get as far away as possible.

They would meet again in Allison's room at about 1 am because her room had a large tree just outside the window. They figured it would be much easier to leave from her room without being noticed. There was no easy way out of Shea's room other than into the hallway, down the stairs and out the front door.

They packed their backpacks with the supplies they felt they would need and reviewed the plan several more times looking for any holes that might exist in its logic. This had been something their dad had drummed into them years ago. At about 10 pm, just before the parents were expected to be home, Schea went back to her room. She and Allison wished that they could lock their doors, but none of the bedroom doors had locks.

Schea heard the boys come in at around 10:30 pm, which was odd since they were supposed to stay the night at their friend's house. The parents arrived about 15 minutes later and she heard muffled talking then the family made their way to their respective bedrooms. Schea was tired from the tension of the last couple of days but wanted to stay awake until it was time to go. However, exhaustion set in and she fell asleep.

She woke with a jolt at 1:15 am and wondered why Allison had not woken her. She frantically got her stuff ready and peeked out the door. Allison's room was directly across from hers. Once she saw that there was no one about, she quietly slipped out and across the hall. She slowly and, as quietly as possible, opened Allison's door.

What she saw almost made her sick. Allison was lying on her back on her bed. There was blood everywhere and she seemed unconscious. Schea tried to revive her but to no avail, so she screamed, ran to the Watsons' bedroom, and started banging on the door.

Drake quickly opened the door, told Schea to calm down and tell him what was wrong. She couldn't talk so she grabbed his arm and, with more strength than he thought she had, dragged him up the stairs to Allison's room.

When Drake saw Allison, he stood stunned then started moving quickly. He checked Allison's pulse and found that she was still alive. He told Schea to go downstairs and tell Crystal to call 911 then he covered Allison. When Schea ran back into the room, he told her to watch her sister and ran downstairs to see if Crystal had called 911. She did, so they ran back upstairs, entered the room and started trying to keep Allison warm and comfortable.

Schea did not speak. She simply looked at Allison's face with an intensity that could mean anything from horror to confusion to impassion.

# 7 What Now

Medics arrived about 10 minutes later and took Allison to the hospital in the nearby town of Aberdeen where she was stabilized and cleaned up. She fell into a coma shortly after.

The boys had, in fact, gone to their friend's house last night but came home and told their parents that they needed to pick up a few things. The parents said that it was okay so the boys got the items and left again.

The theory adopted by the police about what had happened to Allison was that someone had snuck into the house, maybe through Allison's window, in order to rob the place while everyone was asleep. The person, or persons, must have woken Allison while she slept and beat her to silence her.

Schea thought. *Why then had she been raped? Why didn't the thief continue with the robbery once he had silenced Allison?*

The detective's theory was that the person decided to rape Allison first, and then continue his thieving ways. But, when she had fought back, he had beaten her and raped her again, leaving before anyone heard anything.

*Why didn't they do a rape kit? Take DNA and blood samples?* The explanation was that they were a small town and didn't have forensic crime equipment or expertise. They did take blood and smears but, unfortunately, they took them after Allison had been cleaned and bandaged, reasoning that they were trying to save the girl before trying to solve the crime.

Schea knew better. She knew but could not prove what had happened. She knew that the boys had gone out and, perhaps, may have even gone to their friend's house, but she doubted it. At any rate, whether they waited nearby or came back later, it didn't matter. They had hatched a plan. They climbed the tree outside Allison's window, the same tree they were going to use to go the other way, and silently crept into Allison's room.

The boys must have cupped her mouth quickly and, with 2 of them, it was easy to immobilize her but she had fought back, and fought back hard. Her response prompted them to use brutal force and, once she was beaten to near unconsciousness, they took their turns with her. Schea couldn't be sure if they had done it before the parents got home or after they left the second time, but it was probably the latter. They were not worried about their parents because their bedroom was downstairs and near the back of the house. They weren't worried about Schea walking in on them either because, frankly, that might have been an added benefit for them.

The boys probably then left the way they had come figuring any investigation would likely focus on a robbery and believe the person must have entered in the same way they did. Therefore, they didn't worry about a scuffed window sill or broken branch or matted down grass near the base of the tree. They also knew that the police might even lose the files.

XXXXX

The boys eventually came to the hospital. When Schea saw the look on their faces, she knew they had done it and cursed herself for falling asleep. If she had heard them go to Allison's room, maybe she could have done something to try to stop them - scream, rouse the parents, anything. Maybe she would have ended up in the same condition as Allison, or worse, but at least she would have tried to do something to stop them.

Her goal now was to do whatever she could for her sister's recovery. She stayed with her as long as the medical staff allowed and, when she had to leave, she went back to the house but stopped interacting with anyone in the family, especially the boys. When she was in her room, she blocked the door to keep everyone out. It wasn't much, but she felt a little better for the effort. She slept but would wake up startled at the slightest sound.

Over the next month, Schea spent most of her time at Allison's bedside. She ate little, stopped going to school and never spoke to anyone in the family, or anyone else for that matter.

Then, one night while she was sleeping, she heard the phone ring. She heard the soft sounds of Drake shuffling to pick up the phone but didn't hear what was said. She looked at the clock, saw that it was 3 am, and knew for sure that this was not going to be good. She heard footsteps coming up the stairs, then down the hall until they stopped at her door. Drake knocked and called her name. She didn't respond, so he called again and added that they needed to go to the hospital right away. She moved the stuff that she had piled in front of the door, opened it and saw the look on his face. She knew things were about to get a whole lot worse for her.

Drake quickly said, "The doctor on duty said that Allison has taken a turn for the worse and we should come as soon as possible."

Schea almost refused to go. She knew what she would see, would find, would witness and did not want to do any of it. But a voice in her head said, *Allison needs me to be there*. She was already dressed so she grabbed a light jacket and left with Drake and Crystal. They arrived at the hospital an hour later and the doctor started to explain Allison's situation, but Schea heard none of it.

As they entered Allison's room, Schea could not take her eyes off of her sister. She walked over to the bed, held Allison's hand and noticed it was cool to the touch. She watched Allison's chest go up and down very, very slowly - too slowly. The machines told it all. All of the numbers were either too high or too low. She didn't need to know which was good or bad. She knew what was going to happen and she just wanted to be with her sister.

As she looked at Allison's face, she knew somehow that she was leaving and would be going to be with Rob and their parents. She wasn't raised religious but she believed that God existed and didn't know much else. As if out of a thick fog, she saw that someone had come to stand next to her and the person was moving their mouth and looking very sincere about what they were saying. She didn't need to know what they were saying. She knew Allison was gone and was once again the lovely, happy sister Schea had always known. So, Schea sighed, turned and left.

Schea guessed that they were all talking about what to do with the body because that is what it was now. Allison was no longer there and the body was now a shell that used to house Allison but now it wasn't needed. Schea also supposed that they were talking about her. *Will she be okay? What should be done for her? How can they care for her? Should she be crying? And, if she wasn't, what should they do for her?*

*Well*, she thought, *let them wonder.* At his point she didn't really care. She had one objective: *The boys would pay dearly for this and there was no doubt in her mind that she would make it happen. It was only a matter of when and how.*

# 8 A New Family

Schea was so lost in her thoughts about the past that she didn't hear the waitress ask if she wanted something else. "Excuse me, miss, would like some more tea?"

Schea quickly recovered and said, "No, thanks. May I have the check, please?"

The waitress left the bill on the table and moved on to another customer. Schea put cash down and left.

She walked past the City Dock with its shops, bars and restaurants then headed up Randall Street to the US Naval Academy, cleared security and wandered onto the campus. It was a beautiful and historic campus. The residential streets just inside the main gate were lined with old stately homes for the various officers at the academy. Most of the academy buildings were built in Greek revival architecture with open areas, benches and lots of trees. The academy also bordered on the Severn River and she enjoyed wandering the campus and relaxing in the green belt areas or looking out over the river.

The midshipmen were busy rushing off to classes or training or various athletic endeavors but she was always noticed by the guys when she was on academy grounds. After all, she was pretty, had a nice figure, and moved like she owned the place.

Schea was a little small for her age, never more than about 100 to 105 pounds and just shy of 5 feet 2 inches tall. She had long, dark hair, at least at this point, since she sometimes had to change the color, style and length for certain missions. She had hazel eyes that were always wide open and searching. It may have been tactical searching from her perspective, but it also made people feel like she was looking at them in a friendly and open way. This was a great benefit for her and she smiled as she thought about her training nickname, the Ghost. She could hide in plain sight, which came in handy during her missions. She was always underestimated by bad guys.

Her lips were full but not puffy and seemed to always have a slight smile on them. Her skin was tanned because of the amount of time she spent out running, swimming, and hunting. She had an alluring figure and was well proportioned - not too big here and not too small there. Some would say that her best feminine features were her butt and her legs because of her training regimen.

She decided to sit for a while in the park across from the academy chapel and John Paul Jones Crypt, the famous naval hero of the American Revolution. Her mind and thoughts returned to the years after Allison had passed when she had become alone.

XXXXX

By the age of 13, Schea had lost her entire family, but she was making plans, and that made her feel better. She could do nothing to change the past and she was certainly not going to try to live in it.

She would continue to move forward. She had plenty of money since the family trust was now hers. The money was comfortably tucked away in various well managed investments and would now be allocated to her in small monthly payments but, because of her age, she needed a guardian until age 18, when the money would be hers to do with as she pleased.

About a month after Allison had died, Schea went to stay with an uncle and his family. They had been at the funeral and had suggested to the Watsons that she should live with family. They had readily agreed. The boys acted suitably sad that she was leaving them and Schea figured they were probably somewhat sad, but not for the same reason as their parents.

She stayed with 2 of her uncles and their families over the next year. She wasn't hard to care for since she was self-sufficient, went to school regularly, did her chores, never got into trouble and treated everyone with respect. She got along well with, and even liked her cousins, especially the younger ones.

But, she rarely said anything about what she was thinking, how she was feeling and never allowed anyone to get close to her. The 2 families had taken her to various counselors to see if they could find a way to get through to her. All of the counselors said she was respectful and answered all of their questions but only with short, clipped responses. They knew she was holding back but could not find a way to get to her well-kept secret places.

Schea was grateful that they were trying to help her, but she didn't need their help. She really didn't. She knew what had happened to each of her family members. She knew that they were all now together somewhere and that they were happy. She knew each of them was gone and she was now developing plans to deal with those responsible.

What more was there to do in her life? She didn't need a job or a way to make money. Her parents had taken care of that as they had always promised. She knew she needed a legal guardian until she was 18 and she sort of understood why. She was studying hard at school and was always on the honor roll. Again, her parents had prepared her well for the world she now faced.

She liked computers, but was not as skilled as Allison, and she really enjoyed math and science like her mom. She was an accomplished shot with most weapons and could track just about anything in the woods, including people, thanks to her dad. And finally, she was becoming much better at planning and at being patient. Her family - all of them - had prepared her very well for her future. She didn't really understand why there was so much fussing about over her.

XXXXX

She was now living with her aunt, Melissa, and her uncle, Peter, in Edmonds, Washington. But, sadly, shortly after Schea turned 14, Uncle Peter had a stroke. He survived, but needed a great deal of care and her aunt was frantic about what to do about Schea. Melissa had grown to love Schea but was becoming overwhelmed.

She called her brother-in-law, who had moved across the country to New York City. Unfortunately, he was leaving shortly for an overseas business assignment in Tokyo with the whole family and, even though it was a promotion for him, it was still going to be difficult to budget for his family in the very expensive city of Tokyo.

One day, while her aunt was caring for her husband, old friends of Schea's father came around for a visit. He and his wife were known to both Schea and her uncles. They had come to her brother's, her sister's and her parents' funerals. They had heard about her uncle's stroke and wanted to see if there was anything they could do to help.

Jim and Grace Samuelson lived in Bend, Oregon, located in the middle of the state. Melissa and Jim and Grace eventually sat in the living room talking for quite some time. Schea went to her room to study for a math test she had the next day at school.

She knew Jim and Grace, of course, and was pleased when they came to see her aunt and uncle. Schea's family had taken several trips to visit them over the years. Central Oregon area is a mecca for all things outdoors, including hunting and fishing, which both Jim and her dad loved.

She remembered her dad and Jim sitting for hours out on a boat on the lake near Jim's home. They never caught anything or, if they did, they threw them back, but they would come back to the house all smiles with their arms around each other's shoulders. The two of them would each grab a beer and sit out on the porch, sometimes never saying a word, just looking out over the lake, often watching the sunset. Jim had been a SEAL around the same time as her dad so they were probably reminiscing about those days.

She liked Jim and Grace. They did not have children of their own but they occasionally fostered a child. As a result, they loved to dote on Schea, Rob and Allison whenever they visited.

After the adults had chatted for a couple of hours, Melissa came to Schea's room and asked if she would mind coming downstairs to say hello to Jim and Grace. Schea had finished studying and had been wondering if she could go downstairs to do just that, but they had seemed to be in such a serious discussion she decided to stay in her room to read. She followed her aunt to the living room, and both Jim and Grace stood and gave her a big hug. Then they all sat.

They mentioned how sorry they were about her uncle's stroke and asked how she was doing. Schea gave her usual stock answer by saying that she was doing well. There was brief silence then Grace mentioned how difficult it must be now for her aunt to try to care for her husband and the kids. She didn't mention Schea, which Schea immediately picked up on but remained passive and listened while Grace talked.

Finally, Grace cleared her throat, looked at Schea and asked, "How would you like to come to our place for a visit and, possibly, to stay for a longer period. Your school term is close to finishing, so you can probably finish your classes online. We recently accepted a girl to foster and you would make a wonderful big sister for her."

Grace took a quick breath then continued. "The girl is 9 and lost both her parents in a boating accident and there appear to be no other relatives. Her dad was an only child and his parents passed

27

away many years before. The girl's mom was Korean and met her husband when he was stationed at Osan Air Base in Korea, where she was born. The mom told everyone that she had no living relatives but, in that culture, it is common for a family to disown a daughter who marries someone who associates with military men."

"The girl's name is Jenny and will be arriving in about a month once all of the paperwork is complete. After her parents died, she was put into a foster home that was more-or-less a transition home for kids who will be eventually going to a permanent foster home in the United States."

Schea remained silent during Grace's explanation and could see the logic in all she said. It was obvious that her aunt was becoming overwhelmed with normal household duties, while caring for her husband and managing the 3 children. She also saw the logic in what Grace was now proposing regarding Jenny. Jenny's loss was something that Schea had gone through, so she might be able to help her. Logically, this was a no brainer, and knew she should go to Oregon and stay with Jim and Grace.

But, she was also beginning to feel the stress of moving from one household to the next and starting the process of making her way in a new family. She knew Jim and Grace but not all that well. Then there was Jenny, and she could probably be of help to her. But, she had always been the youngest kid in her family and in each of the families that she had lived with over the past 4 years. *How would Schea know how to be a big sister?*

*And then there was Jenny*, she thought again. Jenny had been only 9 when she lost her parents. Schea had been 11 when she lost her brother and 12 when she lost her parents and sister. She was only a few years older than Jenny when she found herself all alone. At least Schea had had some relatives and friends that she was able to count on. Jenny had no one. Schea remembered how alone she had felt.

Schea could, if she wanted to, be her big sister. *What do big sisters do?* She had no idea, except that she did in fact know. She had had a big sister - a loving, caring, funny big sister – a big sister that had died protecting Schea. So, yes, the decision was in fact an easy one.

Schea told Grace and Jim, "I would like to come to your place to visit and to maybe stay. I am also excited to meet Jenny."

XXXXX

It all happened pretty quickly. Schea was an excellent student, so the school did not have a problem with her completing her studies online. Schea didn't have much, so there was no need for any type of moving van or truck since it all fit into the back of Jim's SUV. There was a guest bedroom in Melissa's house, so Jim and Grace stayed there while everything was finalized. Schea's aunt had to sign over the guardianship to Jim and Grace but that could be done without them there. If the court needed to see them or they had to sign papers, much of that could be done electronically. In the remote chance they had to be physically present for some reason then they could drive back to Edmonds, Washington.

They left on a Saturday.  Schea said good-bye to her cousins and Melissa in the living room then went to her uncle's bedroom where he was recuperating.  He had trouble talking and would often start moving his mouth as though talking but no sound came out.  Schea leaned over to give him a light kiss on the forehead, touched his shoulder and told him that she loved him and that she hoped he got better real soon.  He forced the side of his face that still worked into a half smile and winked his one good eye. Schea smiled and left the room.

A short time later, they all climbed into the SUV and were off to Bend.

# 9 Jenny

Bend is an outdoor paradise. If you like golf, it's there. If you like skiing, it's there. If you like boating, hunting, fishing, camping, hiking, they are all there. Schea was looking forward to doing all of that and more because she knew that both Jim and Grace were outdoor people. They owned an outdoor adventures travel company and Jim took the guests out on their adventures while Grace did everything else.

They had about 10 small cabins that could be rented by guests staying in the area for extended periods, but many of the guests came in for one day adventures and were often local or within a few hundred miles of Bend. Guests coming from farther away, like Seattle or Portland, were usually on their way somewhere else and only stayed one night.

Jim and Grace loved what they did and guests saw that immediately. A good number of guests returned to the adventure company year after year. They also never had to advertise because guests recommended them to every one of their friends and family members. They even had guests coming in from all over the world, especially Asia, Australia and New Zealand.

Jim had several full-time employees who helped him with the running of the adventures. They were experienced guides and often had certain areas of expertise, such as white-water rafting or hunting. Jim asked a couple of them to look after things while they were away and they were happy to do so. After all, most of them thought that it was amazing that they had a job that paid them to do stuff they loved doing.

Jim, Grace and Schea arrived at 3 o'clock on Saturday afternoon. There was a hunting trip group just returning, so there was a lot going on as they arrived and Grace quickly showed Schea to her room to get settled in. Schea didn't seem to mind the frantic activity since it helped time to go by. She had also forgotten how beautiful this area was and was getting excited about her future for the first time in many years.

Here, everything revolved around doing fun stuff outdoors and Schea enjoyed all of it - cleaning equipment and cabins, packing up camping gear for a weekend trip, helping Grace in the kitchen and helping Jim and the other guides get the guests ready for one of the adventures. She even began going along on some of the adventures to help the guides.

The house was a two story 5000 square foot structure. The rustic exterior was just for show since the house itself was solidly built, completely wired for all kinds of electronics, including internet, Wi-Fi, and satellite TV. The cabins were likewise wired and whatever the guests needed, they could find it here. The house had 5 bedrooms, 4 were normal size, while Jim and Grace had a typical master bedroom. Much of the downstairs was taken up by Grace's office, the living room and the kitchen. There were also a few storage areas for Jim's various adventure gear. The larger items, such as small boats, skis, et cetera were stored in two large out-buildings.

Guests had access to the office so they could complete the registration process and the kitchen on days when Grace hosted a group meal. These kitchen days were always a favorite event because Grace was an excellent cook.

Schea could hardly take it all in. She did not remember most of this from the times that she had visited but she was probably too busy running around outside with her brother and sister.

Thoughts of her sister reminded Schea that she was going to be a big sister in a few of weeks and the nerves started to set in. *How would she be as a sister, let alone a big sister? What should she say? What should she do? How should she interact with a 9 year old girl?* She didn't know any of it, but kept coming back to Allison. Schea decided to think about what Allison would do and then do that. *That should work!* In the meantime, she set about getting all settled in and finishing her school exams and papers. She needed to be ready for Jenny.

XXXXX

Jenny was waiting at Travis Air Force Base (AFB) 3 weeks later. Jim, Grace and Schea drove to Travis, located just outside of Sacramento, California, to pick Jenny up.

After the accident, Jenny was flown to Travis Air Base accompanied by a military assigned guardian. Jenny had been devastated by the loss of her parents but another military family at Travis had agreed to take care of Jenny while the military determined where to place her. Jenny knew the family, because they had also been in Korea and had come to Travis about 2 months before the accident.

As Jenny settled into their home, she slowly became more understanding of what had happened to her. She was an American citizen and her dad was a United States Air Force veteran, so the military was required to take care of her until the courts could decide what should be done.

The family she was staying with had a couple of girls near Jenny's age and thought it would go well since Jenny had met the family's children while they were in Korea. It did and it didn't. Jenny was a good kid, but she rarely spoke and had trouble adjusting at school.

Unfortunately, the couple was only going to be at Travis for a month longer. He was leaving the service and moving back to Florida where they would be staying with relatives temporarily until he could find work and a place to live, and they would not be able to take Jenny. Something would need to be done, and quickly.

Travis Air Force Base is an out-processing point for many military members who have completed their time in the service and Jim had processed out at Travis many years before. One of the sergeants, Master Sergeant Richards, who was also involved with some of the out-processing paperwork for Jenny's temporary family, had kept in touch with Jim. As a matter of fact, he had gone up to Jim's place a few years ago with his family to go on a hiking adventure that Jim had guided. He knew Jim and Grace sometimes took in foster kids so he took a chance and called after hearing about Jenny's plight.

When Richards told Jim about Jenny's situation, Jim said that he would talk it over with Grace and call back. Jim called back within the hour and they said they would love to have Jenny come to live with them. Jim was told that it would probably take 4-6 weeks to get all of the paperwork done and ready. Richards also asked Jim if they could come to Travis a few times to help complete the paperwork and to meet Jenny. They said, "Of course. We would love to meet her."

It was a week after that phone call that Jim heard about Schea's uncle's stroke and her plight, so he talked to Grace. "Could we become foster parents to 2 girls within a matter of a month? We know Schea, so that wasn't a problem and we have heard good things about Jenny."

They were getting to the age where handling kids could be tough, especially girls who were in their early teenage years. On the other hand, they had plenty of room and were both robust due to the type of business they were in. Besides, they had always wanted kids, but could they take on 2 at once?

Finally, after some discussion, they decided they could and had headed up to Edmonds in order to broach the idea with Melissa. When Melissa agreed and Schea agreed, Jim called Travis to make sure there wouldn't be a problem with Jenny's situation. Sergeant Richards said that he will check, but thought that it would be a great idea for Jenny to have an older sister, especially one that might be able to relate to her. A week later, Jim and Grace got the news that they were going to be foster parents to 2 girls in a month.

XXXXX

Jenny had met Jim and Grace twice during the process of completing all of the paperwork and knew her situation warranted she should stay with them. She had no place else to go, but she was still nervous and a bit angry. *Where was her family?* She knew that her parents were gone, so she didn't mean them. *Where are the other people that are normally in a family? Why didn't any of them come for her?*

The nice sergeant had told her that the official records her dad had filled out declared that he had no living relatives to declare as beneficiaries of his military insurance and survivor benefits. The sergeant wasn't familiar with Jenny's mom's family history, but there were none listed in any of the official and unofficial records that he, or anyone else, could find.

Jenny kept thinking that there must be someone. She remembered some of her friends having dozens of family members, from siblings to grandparents to uncles, aunts and cousins. *Where were hers?*

Jim and Grace had told her on their second visit that Jenny was going to have an older sister. They explained briefly that Schea had also lost her parents, who were well-known to Jim and Grace and explained that they knew Schea very well and that she was nice and a lot of fun. They asked Jenny if she would like that and Jenny said that she would.

But now, standing here waiting for this new family to arrive, she became nervous and began to feel some doubt about all that was happening. It was one thing to meet people but another thing to live

32

with them.  Schea sounded nice, *but what would she be like back at their house when Jenny asked questions or wanted to play or needed help with school work?  What would she be like then?*

Jenny finally saw the SUV pull up to the curb outside of the Travis AFB recreation center.  The sergeant was with her, as well as a court-appointed child advocate.  She watched as Jim, Grace and Schea got out of the car.  She had seen Jim and Grace so there were no surprises there but she had not seen Schea before and was surprised by what she saw.

Schea wasn't much bigger than she was.  She had dark hair that was pulled back into a pony tail and was wearing a blue t-shirt with the words *"Seattle Seahawks"* on it and a pair of blue jeans.  She had a nice smile and walked towards the building with a self-assured stride.  As they all entered through the door, Jenny suddenly got really nervous and was about to run out the back door, when Schea confidently walked straight towards her.

Schea stopped a few feet in front of Jenny, gave her a huge smile and told Jenny, "I am really happy to meet you."  Jenny mumbled something and then the most wonderful thing happened.  Schea gently reached out, took her by the hand and said, "Let's go play foosball!"  *How did she know that was one of her favorite games?*  Jenny simply said okay and off they went into the recreation center play area.

The adults watched all of this transpire smiling.  They thought that there would need to be time taken by all concerned in order to introduce the girls.  They figured that they would ask questions of each girl to try to get them to open up so they could get to know each other.  Well, not these two girls.  They seemed to have handled the situation just fine.

XXXXX

When Schea walked into the recreation center, she had no idea what to expect.  She had seen pictures of Jenny and knew most of her family background and history and had been saddened by what had happened to her parents.  She wasn't necessarily excited about this quick change in her life, but she was getting used to dealing with change.  Besides, she was beginning to like the idea of being a big sister.

As they had first walked into the room, Schea saw Jenny standing with MSgt Richards.  Jenny had been hanging back a little and it seemed she was trying to hide behind Richards' leg, which was big enough for her to do so.  What Schea also saw was that Jenny was beautiful.

Jenny had inherited her mother's small frame, slightly angled dark eyes and silky black hair.  She had also inherited her father's handsome, symmetrical facial features, not his masculinity, but the soft, kind, open and ready friendliness.  Jenny would probably grow to be taller than the typical Korean woman, but she would maintain her beautiful exotic looks.  Schea was pretty and Allison was beautiful, but Jenny would be a *knock-out*.

Schea had talked to Jim and Grace about Jenny in order to get a better idea about what she was like. *What did she like to do? Did she like school? Did she like the outdoors? What kind of things did she like to do with friends?* From this, she knew that one of Jenny's favorite games to play was foosball.

Schea reasoned it would be best to approach Jenny directly and didn't think that they needed to stand around and chat. They also didn't need the adults to help them to learn about each other. She and Jenny simply needed to push forward with this new life they were being thrown into. So, that is what Schea did and Jenny responded just the way Schea had hoped.

XXXXX

Schea and Jenny walked into the recreation room and spotted an available foosball table. They knew they would be leaving for their new home in an hour or so as soon as the adults finished whatever it was they had to do. They didn't talk as they walked to the table and, when they got to the table, they each took a side, and Schea dropped the little white ball onto the table.

Jenny immediately scored. She looked at Schea and gave her a somewhat blank look as if asking whether she was mad that she had scored so fast. Schea looked up, smiled, and told Jenny, "That was an amazing shot. I didn't even see how you got the ball into the goal."

Jenny gave a shrug, smiled and said, "Well, when you are good, I guess you are just good!" They played for about an hour and Schea only managed to score 3 goals, mostly by luck, and had no idea how many goals Jenny had scored.

After about 10 minutes of playing, they started light chatter as they played, rarely looking up at each other. They found out that both loved school and learning new stuff. Jenny enjoyed the outdoors, but not nearly as much as Schea. Jenny also had never held a weapon of any type and did not know anything about self-defense. Jenny was an avid reader and good at many of the computer games out there.

The one thing they did not mention at all was their past tragic loses. Schea knew about Jenny's, but she didn't know how much Jenny knew about hers. Besides, that could all be covered later, if at all. The most important thing right now was to simply concentrate on helping Jim and Grace form this new family into a loving and well-functioning unit.

On the long drive to Bend, Jim and Grace asked the girls a few questions, nothing probing, just things like what did they want for dinner, do they want to go to a movie tomorrow evening, or if they wanted to stop for food or a bathroom break. The girls sat next to each other in the back seat and chatted quietly. They would giggle every now and again or just sit quietly looking out of the window at the passing scenery.

When they arrived at the house, the girls grabbed their stuff from the back of the SUV and went upstairs to their rooms. Schea showed Jenny which room was hers and then took her to her own room. Neither girl had many personal possessions, so there wasn't really much for either of them to look at. They eventually went downstairs and Grace gave them a tour of the house.

34

Finally, Jim took them outside and gave them a tour of the property. Jenny was not as good a swimmer as Schea, but she had no fear of the water. Even so, Jim suggested that she not swim alone until she was older and more confident. She said that was fine, especially when Schea offered to go with her anytime she wanted to go for a swim. Jim was glad that Schea had made the offer since she was an excellent swimmer and could become an Olympian, if she really wanted to.

XXXXX

Jim recalled that a day after Schea arrived he suggested that she should go for a swim. It was a sunny warm day, so Schea was all up for it. Jim hung out on the dock as Schea came out of the house wearing a green one-piece suit with a small fish logo on the front near the top. Jim said he would watch just to make sure she was okay and suggested she not go too far out, since the water was still pretty cold and she could tire. Schea said that was fine and would stay close to the shore and the dock.

She stood at the end of the dock and executed a perfectly straight dive into the water with barely a splash. She came up then began swimming freestyle from the dock along the shore to the right. She went about 100 meters, turned and started swimming back along the shore past the dock. She swam to the left of the dock about 100 meters, turned then swam back again and did this 3 times without a break. Jim figured she'd be coming out soon since she had just swum 1200 meters, but she didn't!

Instead, she flipped over and did the same with the back-stroke, the breast-stroke and the butterfly stroke. When that was completed, she finally got out of the water. Jim handed her a towel and Schea said, "That felt great. Thanks for suggesting it."

He told her that she was welcome to go for a swim any time she wanted and after that first day, all he said as she exited the house to go for a swim was to not go too far out into the cold water. She never did and he never worried about her going for a swim.

# 10 Normalcy

Both Schea and Jenny told Jim and Grace they wanted to go to a regular school. What Schea did not say was that Jenny wanted to continue going to a regular school and she only wanted to go because she wanted to be near to Jenny.

Jenny was new and Schea worried about her as any big sister would and, more surprisingly, she really liked feeling that way. Schea didn't really care one way or the other about a regular school.

She knew she was good with school subjects and could take care of herself. What she did not know was how she would handle all of the teenage drama that seems to go on at school. Allison had told her about some of it and her advice had been to stay immune to it by never reacting to it and staying clear of it when she could. If not, she could always just walk away.

Schea wanted to make sure that Jenny was protected from any of it. She had grown attached to Jenny and felt that the feelings were mutual. They laughed a lot and told each other all kinds of kid secrets. Schea enjoyed helping Jenny learn to swim better and to enjoy the great outdoors, while Jenny taught her how to play foosball and computer games, and to open up and be more involved with those around her. She also felt that Jenny was really making a difference in how she remembered the past.

She was still devastated about losing Rob, Allison and her parents, but she was spending more time now thinking about the fond memories they had had together, rather than the events that took them away from her. Schea also felt she was helping Jenny cope with the loss of her parents. They had talked a couple of times already about those loses, how they happened and how they felt about them. They seemed to grow less and less weary of the losses as they shared them. Schea felt she and Jenny were going to grow to love each other like sisters and be lifelong friends. Schea also vowed secretly that she would not fail to protect Jenny the way she had failed Allison.

XXXXX

As they planned for school, Schea knew they weren't going to be in the same class or school this year. Jenny would probably be placed in 5th grade, which meant she would be in elementary school which wasn't too far away from the high school where Schea would be.

Because Bend was not a large city, the high school Schea would attend had grades from 7 to 12. Schea had thought about continuing with home school or even online school until Jenny entered 7th grade in a couple of years. Then, once Jenny was in the high school, Schea would start there too.

However, she decided to start now so she could see what high school was like and what obstacles Jenny might have to face. Schea had no idea what grade she would be put into but Jim told her she could be tested, and the school would figure that out, which sounded fine to her.

Grace drove her to the school and they met with the school counselor who would administer the test. Schea was escorted to a room where she would take the proficiency test. Jenny had come along too, so while Schea was being tested, Grace and Jenny explored the town. Jenny wanted to see the elementary school where she would be going and Grace had some shopping to do. The counselor had told Grace to come back in about 4 hours since Schea should be finished by then.

After their quick exploration of Bend, Grace took Jenny back home then returned to the school to meet with the counselor. Schea and the counselor were already in the office as she entered. The counselor said that she thought that Schea probably did well, since she had finished every part of the testing process faster than the counselor had ever seen. As a matter of fact, when Schea indicated that she was finished and the counselor saw that there was still time left, she encouraged Schea to use the time to go over her answers. Schea told her she had already done that - twice!

The counselor said the results will be back in about a week so they headed back to the house.

XXXXX

A week later, the counselor called and asked Grace if she and Schea could come into the office to review the results. They arrived, met in her office and once seated, the counselor looked at Schea and smiled. Schea sort of smiled back but was a bit wary of exactly what was going on.

The counselor finally looked over at Grace and said, "Schea did not just do well but had some of the highest scores I have ever seen. She scored in the genius bracket on all parts of the test and could join Mensa right now if she wanted to." She explained. "In order to get into Mensa, you generally must have scores higher than 132. Schea scored 161. Einstein would have been impressed!"

"As far as I am concerned, Schea can have her high school diploma right now, but the school system requires students to take certain classes in order to graduate. I suggest that Schea could simply test out of some and finish the others online. Once she has filled those requirements and has her diploma, Schea could probably apply to any major college or university and be accepted with open arms."

Grace was stunned and had a huge smile on her face when she turned to look at Schea but what she saw, surprised her. Schea had a determined expression on her face while looking intently at the counselor, and she wasn't smiling. The counselor asked, "Isn't this wonderful news?"

After a few seconds, Schea finally asked, "Do I have to?"

The counselor asked, "What do you mean?"

"Do I have to skip school?"

The counselor sat back in her chair, looked at Schea and said, "You could still go to school if that is what you really want to do."

"Good, because that is exactly what I would like to do."

37

The counselor looked stunned and it took her a moment to say something. "Okay. What grade would you like to enter?"

"Tenth. At that grade level, I will be near the same size and age as the rest of the students, which will make life at school much easier. The courses will be easy, of course, but since I have never attended a regular school for very long, this will be a better way to learn what it is like at school. I can also learn how to interact with people my own age, both boys and girls."

The counselor could not argue with her logic, so she said okay and filled out the paperwork for Grace to sign.

After hearing about Schea's scores, Grace had decided that she was not going to make the decision for Schea. This was going to be her decision and hers only. However, as they were walking to the car, Grace's mind raced through what had just transpired. She was right to let Schea make the decision and could not argue with the logic once Schea presented it. But, even though she had only had the girls in her care for a few months, she had been a foster parent enough times to be able to read the signs that told her a child was leaving something unsaid. And Schea was leaving something unsaid.

She felt she knew Schea well enough to believe it was probably best to approach her directly. Schea could evade or refuse to answer her, but beating around the bush or trying some off-hand way to get Schea to tell her what was unsaid would probably result in the same thing anyway. *So, why not just ask.*

She did and she was correct. Schea told her why she wanted to go to school.

"What I said in the counselor's office was actually all true. But, what I didn't tell the counselor is that I also want to be as close as possible to Jenny as she makes her way through school. I want to be there for her. I have plenty of time to advance my schooling and go to a fine college, but Jenny represents the here and now and that is exactly where I want to be."

When they arrived home, and right before they entered the house, Grace stopped, looked at Schea and gave her a big hug. As she hugged her, she told her, "You are a wonderful person, a blessed daughter and the best sister that Jenny could have ever hoped for."

XXXXX

At school, life went well for both girls. They earned excellent grades, made friends, which Jenny seemed to be much better at doing than Schea, and were happy at home. They helped around the house with a variety of chores and Schea helped on more of the adventures. She could help on all of them, but Jim focused on those that might have kids participating, especially those around her age and younger. He worried a little about putting her into all-adult groups or in groups that had older boys.

Schea would be 15 soon and was developing into a young woman with all that that entailed. Schea never flaunted her looks or body and always wore conservative clothes and swimwear. She never wore a two-piece swimsuit or short-shorts or halter tops. One reason for this was that she was serious about what they were going to be doing on the adventures and the clothing she wore had to be appropriate for the adventure. Skimpy clothes and outfits were not appropriate for any of the adventures. Even when she went to school, she always wore blouses or sweaters that were never tight along with long pants or jeans or the occasional skirt at or below the knees.

Several times when there were groups there for an adventure, Jim saw the men - both teenage and older - glancing with interest at Schea as she walked by or while she was packing equipment for a trip. And, she definitely got the stares when she went for a swim but seemed to be oblivious to it all.

XXXXX

The following year, when Schea was 15 and Jenny was 12, the girls really felt they were truly sisters. They loved doing things together and having secret talks in one or the other's room. Both had a great school year, but for different reasons. Jenny's grades were excellent and she had made a ton of friends. She was well liked by students and teachers alike.

Schea's grades were also excellent, even though she rarely read any of her textbooks or studied and usually finished any homework within 15 to 20 minutes after arriving home. She would then do chores or go help Jenny with her homework and, sometimes when they were done, the two would head outside for a swim or a hike in warm weather, or skiing and snowshoeing in the winter.

It was now mid-summer and the girls were actually looking forward to the coming school year since they would now be in the same school together. Life was good.

But change is inevitable, it seems.

# 11 Jenny Leaves

One day while the girls were swimming and Jim was taking a group of hikers on a 12 mile hike, someone came into the office while Grace was working on paperwork. She assumed this was a potential guest and asked him what she could do for him.

He was not in uniform and introduced himself as Major Dennis Welman. He said that he was from the army's Provost Office at Joint Base Lewis McCord located near Tacoma, Washington. He asked if there was someplace where they could talk, so she showed him to the living room and asked if he would like something to drink.

He politely said, "Thank you but no, I am fine. I need to talk with you about something important. Is your husband here?"

Grace sat down across form him. "No, but he will be back in a couple of hours."

"Okay. Do you have a girl living here named Jenny Kennedy?"

"Yes. We are fostering her, but hope to adopt her in the future."

He was quiet for a few seconds and seemed to be collecting his thoughts. What he said next, would always be remembered as the shock of her life.

He cleared his throat and said, "A relative has come forward and would now like to have Jenny come to live with his family. He will accept full guardianship for her and, if she desired it later, he and his wife would like to adopt Jenny."

Grace said nothing and just stared at him, but inside, she was thinking. *This had to be a joke and he will start laughing or Jim will suddenly come through the door and they will all start laughing. But, if this was true, then it is a very cruel joke and Jim would not do that. She also didn't see this serious looking US Army Major as being a jokester. No, this was the truth and it wasn't just important, it was a nightmare.*

"How can this be? When we took Jenny in, we were assured that there were no living relatives on her dad's side and none of her mother's family wanted her."

"This relative has provided proof that he is the half-brother of Randy, Jenny's dad. They share the same father and his name is Jeffrey." He proceeded to tell her what had transpired.

XXXXX

Randy's parents had gotten divorced and his dad remarried, but his mother did not and died of breast cancer a couple of years later. Randy was only 4 years old at that time and was told that his mom had passed away.

His father's new wife had been his mistress for 2 years before he and his wife divorced. She and he had had a baby boy a year into their affair but decided to give the baby to the woman's brother to raise. Randy's dad and the woman had no idea at the time where their relationship was going, but they also did not want to abort the baby or give it to strangers.

Her brother was a few years older and had a wife and 2 kids. They were doing well and were happy to take Jeffrey into their home. All went well for many years. Randy's dad and his step-mom were great to him and he thought that he was an only child.

Jeffrey did well so they were reluctant to pull him away and disrupt his life. When the two families got together, Jeffrey simply thought of Randy as his cousin but never knew they were half-brothers. Over the years, as the two families stabilized, the truth just stayed a secret.

Jeffrey's siblings both got involved with drugs and the wrong crowds and it was a miracle that Jeffrey did not. One was killed in a gang shooting and the other became involved in the sex trade, at first as a participant then as a recruiter. She was killed by one of her "girls". Jeffrey's parents were, of course, devastated by all of this. Randy's parents felt horrible about it all but did feel right about asking for Jeffrey back, so that is the way it stayed out their entire lives.

Randy's parents died in a plane crash while on a 20th anniversary trip in Brazil. Jeffrey's parents died separately, the father of a heart attack while chopping wood at their summer cabin and his mom a year later by a drunk driver. By then, Randy had gone into the US Air Force so, at 18, Jeffrey decided to enlist in the US Army.

Over the years, with military moves, address changes and new families, they simply lost touch with each other and Jeffrey had no idea that Randy and his wife had been killed until he came back to the States to process out at Lewis-McCord.

He and his wife, Mary, have a boy, 10, and a girl, 14. They met her in Honolulu where Mary is British, and was teaching there. They started dating, eventually fell in love and got married.

Her parents, in Newcastle, England divorced, and moved on to different lives. They disowned Mary for marrying a Yank and have never been a part of their lives.

Now, Jeff and Mary are back in the states and he is getting ready to start a job with a security firm in Virginia.

Lewis-McChord is a joint Army and Air Force base and all personnel are handled in the same service areas. While Jeffrey was getting some paperwork done, he overheard one of the Master Sergeants talking about a case that he had handled while he was stationed at Travis AFB. Jeffrey was not paying attention until he heard the name *Kennedy*.

He finished his paperwork and was about to leave when he began to think about Randy and wondered if this could be a relative. He had hoped to eventually find him once they were settled in the States. He figured Randy might be back in the States since he had been in the military longer. He approached Master Sergeant Richards, excused himself, and asked about the Kennedy case he had mentioned.

MSgt Richards had no reason not to tell him the high-level details, but he did ask why he was interested. Jeffrey mentioned Randy's name and how they had lost touch over the past 20 years. Richards knew right away what was about to transpire. He told him the story and Jeffrey immediately told him that he was almost positive that Randy and Jenny were related to him. Richards asked if he had any documentation and Jeffrey said that after all these years he had nothing.

Military folks can find it difficult to keep track of lots of documents and family stuff after so many moves. Richards suggested that one way might be to compare DNA samples. They have both of their samples on file since the military started collecting it from all service members in order to help identify remains. He asked for Jeffrey's permission to do that but did not need permission for Randy's since there were no living relatives other than Jenny who is a minor. Jeffrey agreed.

Jeffrey left and decided to check some old files he'd had a friend store for him while he was overseas. He contacted his friend, had the items sent to him and reviewed them when they arrived. In a stack of old papers that his dad had kept, he found a letter addressed to him that he had never opened.

He opened it and it outlined what had happened those many years ago. He was now positive that he was indeed Randy's half-brother.

XXXXX

A few minutes later the girls came running in from their swim and saw the man sitting there. They were used to guests being around all the time, so they simply slowed down and said a polite hello. Major Welman smiled back and said hello as they scampered off to their rooms.

He asked, "Is the little one Jenny."

"Yes."

He smiled and said, "She is very pretty and seems to be having lots of fun with your daughter."

Grace was too overwhelmed to try to correct his assessment of who Schea was, so she said nothing.

At that point Grace heard Jim in the office. Before he could head back out to help the guests get ready to leave the camp, Grace asked him to join her in the living room. He could see by the look on her face that this was important so he leaned out the office door and told Doug, one of his guides, to take care of the guests and he'd be out as soon as he could. He entered the living room and Grace introduced Major Welman as they all sat.

Grace gave Jim a quick summary of what the Major had told her. Jim's expression went from mildly curious to a grimace then to pain. He and Grace realized that there was no argument or justification for fighting this. From what Welman told them, they knew that the Kennedys were a good family and definitely relatives of Jenny's. They had only had her with them less than 2 years, but the bond was so strong they felt their hearts break. *What could they do? How would they tell Jenny? How would they tell Schea?* This was a nightmare.

Jim asked Welman how long before Jenny would have to go to the Kennedys. Welman said the paperwork and court documents would be completed by the end of the month, but the Kennedys had asked if they could come as soon as it was convenient to start to get to know Jenny.

"Sure. We will contact you next week in order to set something up."

Welman replied, "Normally, the court would insist on Jenny being handed over immediately to Child Services while the process was underway but Richards told the Kennedys about you and how well Jenny has adjusted to her new home and having a sister, so the Kennedys emphatically vetoed that. They do not want to upset Jenny's life any more than it has been already, especially now that she seems to be so happy. They are willing to let you have some time to talk to Jenny about the change that is coming, and to allow Jenny some time to digest it all."

"But, Jeffrey's new employer wants him on location in Richmond, Virginia in 6-8 weeks. The Kennedys also know that Jenny and your daughter may have already formed a tight bond over the past couple of years and want them to be able to maintain it for the future. They suggest that Schea could visit them any time and Jenny would be allowed to visit here as well. They want this change to be the final disruption in Jenny's young life and are hoping you feel the same way."

Jim and Grace insisted they did and wanted this to go as smoothly as possible, too.

Welman gave them a warm, sad smile and said, "I hope to hear from you next week."

After they escorted Welman out, they both sat back down on the couch and stared at the floor for a few minutes, each trying to come to grips with this news. They had feared this after they had taken Jenny in, but those fears had receded over time and they never really thought about it anymore. Now, they had to figure out how to tell the girls and decided to speak to the girls together as a family.

Doug came in at about this time. Jim said that he'd be out later and asked Doug to just handle the guests. Doug saw right away that something serious was going on, so he said sure, and went back outside. Grace went up to the girls' rooms and found them both in Schea's looking at one of Jenny's textbooks. Grace interrupted and asked the girls to come join her in the living room and Schea sensed that something was up.

The girls followed Grace to the living room and sat on the sofa next to each other. Jim and Grace each took one of the chairs facing the sofa. Grace started by telling them who the Major was and what he had told them. Jenny seemed confused, asked questions and Grace answered as best as she could.

Jim smiled as Grace went through all of this. He occasionally glanced at Schea but she sat quietly and he almost thought she seemed bored with all of this. Then, he reminded himself of what she was hearing and how this was probably affecting her. He knew how perceptive Schea was so he figured she had probably figured out what the end of the story would be and was now trying to figure out how to deal with it.

He was right. Schea knew as soon as Grace mentioned that Jeffrey was Jenny's father's half-brother what was going to happen. Jenny was going away. Her new sister was going away and yet another family member was leaving Schea. She was hearing Grace explain the details and what was going to happen and heard Jenny start to cry and ask why, but she knew that there was nothing that could be done to prevent any of this from happening. *She had not been able to stop what happened to Rob or her parents or Allison, so why should this be any different? Jenny was leaving and that was that.*

Schea quietly rose, stole a quick look at Jenny, walked away and went out the door. She walked past Doug and the guests he was helping and didn't seem to notice any of them. By the look on her face he knew something bad had just happened and figured the best thing he could do was to concentrate on taking care of the guests and not burden Jim with any of it.

A few minutes later, Doug saw Jim come through the front door and start looking left and right. He figured he was looking for Schea so he walked over and quietly said she had headed for the trees behind the canoe storage building. Jim gave a nod and headed in that direction.

Jim found Schea about 100 meters into the trees sitting by a small stream. He knew she had heard him coming, probably as soon as he entered the tree line, so he was not worried about startling her. He sat down next to her and they both simply stared at the water coursing down the stream towards the lake.

After a few minutes, all Jim could think of saying was that he was sorry about what was happening.

Schea stayed quiet for another few minutes then said, "I know that you're sorry and none of this is anyone's fault. This was inevitable. As soon as I developed a bond with Jenny, I knew in the back of my mind that Jenny was going to go away and that it was only a matter of time. After all, everyone I care about eventually leaves." She glanced at Jim and said, "In fact, I know that you and Grace are going to be leaving me too one of these days."

At this point, Jim could take no more. He gently put his arm around Schea and pulled her to him. She did not resist. Once he had both his arms around her, and he could feel her fluttered breathing, he whispered in her ear, "That will never, ever happen. If anyone tried to take you away against your will, then they will have to kill me and Grace in order to do it." He felt Schea let out a little sigh and lean in closer to him. They stayed that way for a few minutes, then slowly separated.

Schea looked into Jim's eyes and said, "We should go back to the house. Jenny needs all of us to help her get through these next few weeks."

When they got back to the house, Grace was still sitting on the sofa. She quickly ran over to Schea and embraced her tightly. Schea had trouble breathing but she hugged her back just as hard. They eventually pulled away and Schea saw that Grace's eyes were puffy and red from crying. Schea gave her a small smile and asked if Jenny had gone to her room. Grace nodded and her eyes strayed up the stairs. Schea turned and headed that way.

Jenny's door was closed, so Schea knocked softly and slowly opened it. Jenny was lying on her bed with her head buried in the pillow. Her back was moving up and down quickly, so Schea knew she was crying. Schea went over, lay next to her and drew her gently into her arms. Jenny did not resist. As a matter of fact, as she got closer to Schea she suddenly turned into her and held Schea as tightly as she could. Schea did the same and both girls quietly cried.

They stayed this way for, what seemed a long time, but was probably only a few minutes. Finally, seemingly by unspoken mutual agreement, they slowly separated and sat cross legged on the bed looking at each other. Schea reached over and took both of Jenny's hands in hers, smiled and told Jenny, "No matter what happens, we will always be sisters and I will always be there for you. I know that this is a hard thing to understand now because it has all happened so quickly. But, it doesn't sound too bad."

"From what I heard, this family really, really wants to care for and love you, Jenny. Your new dad is your dad's half-brother, they have 2 kids near your age and, since the girl is older, you now have 2 older sisters to watch out for you. The boy is a year younger than you, so you will have someone that you can be an older sister to. However, the best news is that you can cause all kinds of trouble for him, just like sisters are supposed to do." Jenny giggled.

Schea and Jenny talked about the change, how it will happen, when and how many times Schea could come for visits and Jenny could visit. Pretty soon they were giggling and talking about how much fun it will be when all of the kids are together with Schea as the big, big sister.

Schea laughed when Jenny told her that the one rule that Schea would have to abide by was that only Jenny could cause trouble for her brother. He was off limits to Schea because Jenny was his big sister and she was going to watch out for him.

At some point earlier in this exchange, Jim and Grace decided to go up to see how the girls were doing. At first, they stood about 10 feet from the door since they weren't ready to disturb them. Then suddenly, they heard some talking and then a few giggles and then laughter. They both looked at each other with eyes wide then smiled. They quietly went back downstairs and hugged. As they pulled away, Grace looked at Jim and said, "Thank God for Schea." Jim smiled and nodded.

# 12 Transition

There was much to discuss concerning what needed to be accomplished over the next several days. They needed to discuss the visit by the Kennedys then contact the Major. Grace also needed to contact the school and withdraw Jenny. Jenny wanted to see some of her friends in order to tell them and insisted that Schea come with her. Schea had no problem with that.

Jim explained briefly to the guides about the move. They were all surprised and expressed their desire to help in any they could. Jim contacted the major and discussed a date for the Kennedys to visit and, after some discussion with Jeffrey, it was agreed they would drive down the following week. This gave Jenny 4 days to get ready.

It was also agreed that this would be the first of two visits before the day that Jenny would actually leave for Richmond. It was also agreed that Jim, Grace and Schea would drive Jenny up to Lewis-McChord on the day they would fly out of SeaTac Airport. They would not go to the airport, thinking that it would be best to say all of their goodbyes at Lewis-McChord.

On the visit date, Jenny and Schea took extra time to spruce up their rooms and Grace spent time getting the house in order. Since Jim would be largely unavailable, he made sure that all of the guides and staff were ready to handle all of the guests, unless there was an emergency. Everyone knew what was going on and they assured Jim that they could handle anything that came up.

The plan was that the Kennedys would drive south on I-5 to Portland, Oregon, then head east along the Columbia River. They would spend the night in Hood River, Oregon so that they would be well rested when they arrived. The following morning, they planned to arrive at Jim and Grace's between 9 and 10 am. They'd spend the day with the girls then return to Lewis-McChord. Jim, Grace and the Kennedys would discuss the next visit and final departure date sometime during that visit.

Jenny and Schea sat outside on the porch waiting for the Kennedys to arrive. It was felt that until this first meeting, all communications back and forth would go through the major and, after this visit, they could decide how best everyone should communicate. They had received several family pictures in emails from the major, so they knew what Jeffrey, Mary and the kids looked like.

The dad was good looking and Mary was pretty. The girl's name was Izzy, short for Isabel, and the boy's name was Archie, short for Archibald, after Mary's granddad. The girl was pretty and the boy had a little bit of a pudgy face. Everyone was a little nervous, except Schea, who was calm and did all she could to keep Jenny in good spirits. At about 9:15 am, they saw the car turn and head up the driveway. The driveway was gravel and about 300 meters long so they could see a trail of dust as the car got closer. Jenny reached over and grasped Schea's hand and Schea took it into her lap, patting it with her other hand.

Their vehicle came to a stop and the Kennedys started to pile out. Mary was out first then Jeffrey from the opposite side. The boy came out of the passenger side and the girl came out the other side behind her dad. Schea and Jenny both stood and came to stand next to Jim. The Kennedys approached as a unit and they all started saying hi and shaking hands seemingly at once. Only Grace and Mary gave each other hugs.

They finally moved apart and Grace suggested that they all go into the house. They started up the stairs with Grace in the lead then Mary, Jeffrey, and Jim. Once the adults were in, Jim glanced back to hold the door for the kids. When he turned, all he saw were the kids heading down to the dock to look at the water and the boats. They seemed to already have started chatting away and, not surprisingly, Schea was in the lead. He smiled.

As he entered the living room, Grace was asking if they would like some coffee or tea. Mary and Jeffrey were placing their orders and Grace turned to Jim to ask what he would like then saw a huge smile on his face. She looked behind him and asked where the kids had gone. He didn't say anything and just pointed out the front window. They all came over to look and saw all 4 kids down near the dock pointing and laughing.

Jenny and Izzy moved over toward the end of the dock, leaned over and it seemed that Jenny was pointing at something in the water. Schea had taken Archie off of the dock and was pointing towards the canoe house and the building that held the tents, skis and other adventure gear. He looked at her with huge puppy-dog eyes - clearly impressed, if not a little smitten - with this new girl. The adults all watched and smiled until they finally turned to sit.

Before Grace could go to get the coffee and tea, Mary said, "I am amazed that they all just seemed to take off together and get along so well."

Grace and Jim looked at each other, then back at the Kennedys and said, "Let us tell you about Schea."

But first, while they sat with their coffee, Jeffrey went over their story and mentioned some of Mary and Jeffrey's history that probably wasn't in any of the documents that they had seen. It was nothing earth-shattering, just personal stuff like how they met, where they got married, the birth of the kids and their eventual move back to the states.

Jim and Grace took their turn and did much the same thing for their lives. They didn't have to say much about Jenny since Mary and Jeffrey knew the same things that they knew. Then they got to Schea.

The Kennedys knew Schea was not Jim and Grace's daughter since that had come out during the first phone call to the major, along with a brief history that included only the basics - no family, some foster care then to the Samuelson's. But, Jim and Grace felt that, if they were going to stay involved in Jenny's life and since it was agreed that Schea could visit her in Richmond and that Jenny and the

Kennedys were welcome to visit here any time they wanted, then Mary and Jeffrey needed to hear more about Schea's life.

Jim and Grace took turns relating her story. They told them about her brother, parents and sister and what they were like. They told them about her brother's death, then her parents, and finally her sister. They did, however, leave out the rapes that her sister had suffered, and only related the official story about a botched robbery.

They told them how Schea ended up with them and about her life here. They also told them about her outdoor skills and all of the training she had received from her dad. Finally, they told them about her school tests and that she didn't even have to attend school but stayed in school because she wanted to be near Jenny to watch over her. All through their telling, Mary and Jeffrey would exchange looks, and at times, their mouths would open, and their eyes would grow wide.

When they finished, Mary looked over at Jim and Grace who sat quietly and said that she was amazed that someone could live through all of that and appear to be so normal. "How is she doing now?"

Jim pointed out the window and said, "You can see for yourself how she is doing."

Jim added one last comment, because he felt that it was important for them to know. "Jenny has been a Godsend not just for us, but also for Schea. They bonded immediately and have become like sisters over the past 2 years. When they were told about the change, Schea went to Jenny's room and within 30 minutes she had Jenny giggling and laughing about life again."

"Over the last 10 days, we have been checking in with Jenny to make sure she is going to be fine with the upcoming move. At first she simply said she was okay. But, after some *Schea time*, Jenny started talking about how exciting it will be for her to be a big sister just like Schea has been to her. She also said she wasn't really losing a big sister but will now have two big sisters – one here and one in Richmond."

At this, the Kennedys shook their heads. Mary immediately told them that Schea was always welcome in their home for however long she wanted to be there. She also reiterated that, if it fit everyone's schedules, then they would love to bring the kids out here, especially during the summers.

They chatted about Jeffrey's new job and the adventure business. Finally, Grace asked if they wanted to get a tour of the house and property, and they readily agreed. After wandering the house and pausing a little at Jenny's room, they headed outside. They couldn't see the kids, but they heard some yelling and laughing coming from the area behind the house. Jim talked about the activities they provided and they went to the outbuildings to check out the equipment, then finally headed behind the house.

The kids had apparently started a game of hide-and-seek. It seemed that Jenny was 'it' because she was the only one they could see. When she saw them, she gave a quick wave and continued her search. She found Archie first and he tried to run but she caught him so he would be 'it' on the next go-round. The adults smiled at this, probably due to some long-ago memories of the same game.

At noon, Grace and Mary went inside to throw some lunch together while Jim and Jeffrey continued to sit on the porch. They both talked about their military service and their current work.

The kids suddenly came running around the corner of the house and asked if they could go swimming. Jim asked Jeffrey if the kids had bathing suits because if they didn't, they always kept a supply of various sizes and colors for any guests' child who forgot to bring their own. Jeffrey smiled and said that they had come prepared. The kids ran in, changed and flew out the door to the dock. Jim asked if Izzy and Archie could swim and Jeff said yes and that they were good swimmers. Jim told him that Schea was pretty good and had spent a lot of time helping Jenny fine-tune her techniques and endurance.

After about 30 minutes, the kids started wandering out of the water and began playing on the beach but Schea continued to swim. Jeffrey watched as she rolled onto her back and began the back stroke. She did that seemingly forever. Then, she rolled onto her stomach and started the breast stroke. Finally, she switched to the butterfly and did that for about 15 minutes. But, before she started the butterfly, Jeffrey turned to Jim and said, "Wow, she was really good."

Jim smiled and said, "Yup, really good."

As they watched, Schea suddenly went under the water. Jeffrey watched for about half a minute and then glanced at Jim who wasn't even looking. After a minute and still no sign of Schea, Jeffrey turned to Jim and said, "Schea hasn't surfaced yet. Someone should go make sure she's okay."

Jim said, "Nah. She's fine."

Finally, after 3 minutes, Jeffrey couldn't stand it. He stood and started for the water but, before he got 10 feet, Schea broke the surface about 300 meters from where she had gone under. Jeffrey stopped, stared at her then turned back to look at Jim.

Jim smiled and said, "I did the same thing the first few time she did that. She can easily stay under for 3 minutes and swim 250 to 350 meters. I have no idea how, but she can!"

Jeffrey shook his head and sat down again.

Lunch was called, so the kids came running in and changed. Grace and Mary decided to make it a buffet style, so everyone grabbed a plate and filled it with sandwiches, salads, fruit and several side dishes. The conversation was lively and funny at times, especially due to some of Archie's comments. He loved to tell silly jokes and every time he did, the parents chuckled, but the girls just rolled their eyes. When they were done, the kids helped clear the table while Grace and Mary cleaned the dishes, and Jim and Jeffrey dried and put everything away.

The afternoon proceeded happily for everyone until finally at around 4 pm, Jeffrey announced that they had to hit the road. There was a chorus of "do we have to" from the kids, but they dutifully got their stuff together and, after some hesitant hugs, climbed into the car. As the car drove off, Jenny and Schea waved from the driveway, while Izzy and Archie waved through the back window.

Jim, Grace, Schea and Jenny were somewhat quiet during the rest of the afternoon. They ate some of the leftovers from lunch then Schea and Jenny went upstairs to Jenny's room. Jim and Grace gave each other a knowing look and began moving around the house doing simple and mindless tasks. They knew what was going to happen in a few weeks, and wouldn't like it, but there was nothing they could do about it, so there was no need to talk about it.

Meanwhile, Schea and Jenny sat in Jenny's room and talked about how much fun they had had. They both thought that Jeffrey and Mary were very nice and that Izzy and Archie were fun to hang out with. About an hour after they had gone into Jenny's room, Schea said she was pretty tired and was going to go to her room to get ready for bed. They hugged and Schea went across the hall to her room. She entered, sat on her bed for about 10 minutes then curled up on her bed and fell asleep.

The Kennedys next visit went much the same as the first. There was lots of talking, laughing, playing and food.

XXXXX

The day they were expected to leave to take Jenny to the Kennedys at Lewis-McChord arrived. Everyone was pretty quiet while they packed bags, got the SUV ready, and helped Jenny pack her stuff. Much of Jenny's things would be shipped later since there wasn't enough room to take it on the plane to Richmond. Jim asked if she would like her bed shipped and she said yes. Jim and Grace told her that she could have whatever she liked and they were sure the Kennedy's wouldn't mind. She asked for most of the stuff in her room as well as her bike.

When Jenny's stuff was all packed and they were about ready to leave the room, Schea came over to Jenny and gave her a hug. She pulled away and told Jenny that they would see each other often and to not be sad. Schea gently took Jenny's hand, put her hand over it and placed a beaded bracelet onto her palm.

Jenny looked at it and her eyes grew wide. She looked at Schea and started to shake her head but Schea smiled and told her that she wanted Jenny to have it. Jenny knew what this cheap little bracelet meant to Schea. Allison had given this to Schea when the family was on a car trip to some of the western states. They had stopped at a gift shop while visiting the Wounded Knee Battlefield site and Allison had bought the bracelet at the gift shop.

Schea was 8 at the time Allison gave it to her. Allison told Schea that this bracelet had special Native American powers, and if Schea ever needed her, then she should close her eyes and concentrate on sending Allison a help signal. Allison told Schea that she would sense that she was needed and come

50

to Schea. Both girls knew this was just a story, but Schea had never forgotten how serious Allison was as she told her this tale and knew she meant every word of it.

Schea had kept it all these years as a reminder of how much Allison had loved her. Now she wanted Jenny to know the same feeling and refused to take it back. Jenny looked at the bracelet and scrambled into Schea's arms. They stayed that way for several minutes then pulled away smiling. They were still smiling when they came downstairs and took their stuff out to Jim to be put into the SUV. Jim and Grace did not expect that they'd be smiling but figured it was better than lots of crying and groaning.

They had to get to the base by 8 am, and since the drive was about 5 hours, they left a day early and spent the night just outside of Olympia, Washington. This meant they would only have an hour drive to the base in the morning.

XXXXX

They arrived at the base and were met by Major Welman at the gate. The Major arranged for them to have a guest pass for the day, so that they could enter the base and proceed to the Kennedys' temporary quarters. As they arrived, the Kennedy's were all outside waiting. No one was overly sad or happy. Everyone moved in an efficient, almost robotic manner taking care of bags, packing the Kennedy's rental car, making sure all of the paperwork was completed, asking if anyone had forgotten anything and doing double checks of the SUV and the temporary quarters.

Finally, everything seemed to be in order and they started to say their goodbyes. It was a somber affair and even the kids had a sense that this was a serious point in their lives. No one cried, but there wasn't much levity either. Jim and Grace were standing by the SUV and all of the Kennedys were in their vehicle, which left just Schea and Jenny facing each other.

Schea smiled first, then Jenny did the same. They hugged and while embraced, Schea whispered to Jenny to remember the magic bracelet. As they pulled away, Schea gave Jenny a kiss on the cheek and turned to get into the SUV. Jenny did the same and both vehicles pulled away towards the base gate. Once they had proceeded out of the gate, the Kennedys turned north to SeaTac Airport, while Jim, Grace and Schea headed south to go back home to Bend.

# 13 Todd

Schea did not go back to school. She tested out of her classes or finished them online and received her high school diploma about 3 months after Jenny's departure. Life, at first, was pretty subdued around the house. They were pretty busy with summer guests and Schea enjoyed helping the guests. Jim started giving Schea more groups to manage on her own. Schea seemed to be able to handle any overly friendly young men quite easily so he worried less but still kept a watchful eye on her.

Everyone seemed to handle Jenny's departure better with time. Jenny emailed often, as did Schea, and they talked over Skype once a week, schedules permitting. It was sometimes difficult to link up because of the time difference, school and other activities but they also used Facebook and Twitter.

It seemed that Jenny was adjusting well to her new family and had already made friends in their new neighborhood. Izzy and Archie often got on Skype with Jenny so they could chat with Schea too. They also talked about possible visits but they all agreed that a visit should not be made for at least 6 months in order to give both families time to adjust.

Jim and Grace noticed that outwardly, Schea seemed perfectly normal and seemed to have had no adverse reaction to Jenny's departure. But, they also sensed that something was going on inside her that needed to be addressed. They discussed possible approaches to take in order to help Schea with whatever she was trying to deal with and finally decided that, even though Schea usually liked the direct approach, this was not one of those situations where it would likely work.

XXXXX

As the Thanksgiving holiday approached, Jim suggested to Grace that they should go on a camping trip to Crater Lake, Oregon. The snows had been light and random, so the road leading up to the lake should still be open. Jim suggested that this might be a good opportunity to try to get Schea to open up about what might be troubling her and Grace agreed.

When they told Schea, she was excited because she loved Crater Lake, especially the sunsets. So, a few of days before Thanksgiving, they closed up the business, packed their camping gear, and headed to the campground on the south side of the mountain.

Crater Lake is the deepest fresh water lake in the United States and was formed about 8000 years ago when the Mount Mazama volcano collapsed. It is almost circular in shape and has 2 small islands in it. There is a very difficult marathon held there every year which makes it even more special to Schea because her parents had run that marathon.

They arrived late on the Monday before Thanksgiving, quickly set up their tents and made their camp-site nice and livable. It was almost dark when they arrived, so they made a fire and cooked dinner. Later, they sat around the fire after the pots and dishes had been cleaned and stowed. They also made sure that there was no food, even small scraps, left around since these would draw certain unwanted critters into the camp at night. They enjoyed a few hours of small talk around the campfire before turning in for the night.

XXXXX

The morning air was crisp as Schea exited her tent. She could see white puffs of her breath as she exhaled the fresh, chilly air. She truly loved it here. During breakfast, Schea turned to Jim and Grace and told them that she was so happy that they had made this trip and thanked them for suggesting it. They smiled and Schea smiled, but they could see that her inner voice was starting to talk to her again.

They cleaned up the area and went for a hike around some of the trails that head up the mountain to the lake. Grace packed some food and Jim brought along some warmer clothes and tarps in case the weather turned on them. They spent the day checking out the beautiful vistas and all of the interesting animals and plants they saw. The following day was spent in much the same way.

On Thanksgiving Day, Jim pulled Grace aside to talk while Schea wandered off to check out a nearby stream. He suggested that he would go with Schea to watch the sunset over the lake that evening and try to see if she would tell him what might be going on.

XXXXX

As the afternoon wore on, Jim suggested that they go up to the lake to watch the sunset and Schea was all up for it. Grace said she was a little tired and would stay in the camp while they went. Schea didn't think anything of it so at 3 pm, she and Jim set off for the lake and the sunset.

After arriving at the rim and selecting a spot, Jim and Schea sat quietly for about an hour watching the sun do its magic. Schea finally turned to Jim and, just as Jim and Grace had hoped, opened up.

"What do you think I should do in order to make my parents, brother and sister proud?"

Jim replied. "Well, what do you think your parents would like you to do?"

Without hesitation, Schea said, "I think they would want me to help make sure that their lives were not given up in vain."

"How do you think you could best accomplish this?"

She quietly responded. "I want to help prevent bad people from being a threat to innocent people."

Jim nodded. "I think that is an excellent goal." And, he began thinking about a friend of his who might be able to help Schea accomplish her goal.

XXXXX

They left for home on Saturday and things started getting back to normal.

53

Jim told Grace what Schea had said the night they got back and Grace only nodded but didn't offer a solution or suggestion. She knew what Jim was probably thinking.

It so happened that Jim's friend started an organization, whose mission statement was to do just what Schea wanted to do. They hired men with experience in units like the Special Forces to accomplish the kinds of things that Schea had mentioned.

Jim contacted his friend, Todd Groden, and suggested that he consider Schea for a possible role in his organization. When Todd heard her age, he immediately said no, which Jim expected. So, Jim explained Schea's situation, how she came to this point and her skills.

"Todd, you need to make an exception. Trust me. You will not be disappointed once you meet her."

"Okay, I'll consider her for training and get back to you." A few days later, Todd called Jim and asked him to bring her in for an interview.

XXXXX

Schea walked into Todd's office alone. Jim had figured that if these two people were to eventually trust each other then they needed to meet one-on-one.

Jim told her about Todd and what his organization did. "What do you think? Is this something you would like to do? Before you answer, you need to know that you will be the youngest amongst a bunch of guys. You will train with them and there will not be special treatment because you are a young girl. They will expect you to do your share and handle all tasks assigned."

Schea paused, walked a short distance away, stood for a second or two then turned, came back to Jim and said, "I want to join Todd's group."

Todd had watched her approach from about 20 yards away when Jim dropped her off. What Todd saw impressed him. She walked confidently with cat-like strides.

He estimated that Schea was only about 5 feet 1 inch and 100 lbs. Her hair was dark brown and pulled back into a neat pony tail and figured that it would fall to her shoulders, if loosened. As she got closer, he could see that she had blue-green eyes, a nice pert nose, slightly pointed chin and wore no make-up.

Todd had already been told about her intelligence, her athletic achievements, her prowess in the woods and her abilities with various weapons. She was physically one of the better applicants he had ever had for his organization, but what he did not know and needed to determine, was whether she was mentally ready for this type of work. And that meant dealing with horrible conditions, horrible people, and killing people.

Todd interviewed Schea for about 2 hours and figured she was doing the same with him. *Good. That will come in handy when sizing up opponents or friends while on the job*. She was soft-spoken but

54

firm in her belief that she wanted to join his organization.  He asked her why and she told him about the various loses in her life, how they happened and how they made her feel.

She didn't know why, but she also told him what had really happened to her sister and not the official story.  He asked her what she planned to do about the boys, since he figured that she was not going to let them get away with what they had done.  She gave him a tiny smile and told him that she was working on it but she would never let it affect her work for him and he acknowledged this with a simple nod.

At the end of the interview, Todd knew he wanted her on his team and said so.  "However, because of your age, I will not take you on just yet.  The truth is, you are one of the best candidates I have seen so I'd like you to come back when you are 16."

"I can do that.  Can you tell me what I can do to make myself ready for the training?"

He smiled at her and said, "Train, train, train and, when you get so tired you think you can't possibly do more, tell your mind to shut up and do it all over again."

She looked him directly in the eyes and said. "No problem."

Todd called Jim and said that Schea was ready to go.  Jim arrived back from the coffee stand and was sipping his coffee when Todd and Schea walked out of the office.  Todd told Jim he was very impressed with Schea and asked who her legal guardians were.  Jim said that he and his wife had been appointed her guardians.  He told Jim that he needed to know this just in case he needed to get approval for any medical care that she might need when she is training.  At this, he turned to Schea and smiled.  She smiled back and winked.

Todd was hooked.  Because of her age, he told Jim to bring her back when she was 16.  At that time he would reassess her and consider taking her in for training.  In his own mind, he had no doubt she would make his team and that he'd probably be smiling for the rest of the day or longer.  As they drove off, he shook his head and thought, *Schea is a hoot!*

XXXXX

Todd had started his organization about 15 years ago when he and several of his fellow Special Forces and SEAL buddies started talking about the need for a group of operatives who could handle jobs that no government agency could deal with.  They figured that wealthy people, large corporations, certain non-governmental agencies and maybe even some governments might pay to have these special situations handled.  Some of the examples they thought of were hostage rescues, targets that could only be accessed using deep-cover assets and hits that could not be linked to any government agencies.

Their plan was to recruit from the ranks of former elite military units, police forces and other agencies with well-trained people for this type of work.  They would be assessed for acceptance based on the intelligence, physical fitness, weapons skills, and other skills, which might include self-defense, hunting, tracking and technology.  Their training would be set up to help them hone these skills and not to give them these skills. Their training would focus primarily on their ability to plan operations and to improvise when needed. They would also be assessed on their mental ability to handle the types of missions that they were expected to take on.

Todd thought about Schea's age and gender. He had only had one female in the unit and that was 10 years ago. She had come to him from the Air Force's Search and Rescue unit, was highly recommended and met all of the assessment criteria. She had been 30 at the time and stayed in his unit for 3 years. The youngest male had been 25 and he didn't last long in the field. Schea would have her work cut out for her to make it through the training and gain the acceptance of the other trainees, trainers and anyone she may work with in the field.

XXXXX

In the car, on the way home, Jim asked Schea, "How did it go? Do you still want to work for Todd?"

"It went well and I know now more than ever that this was what I want to do."

Over the next year Schea increased her training with weapons, hand-to-hand combat and survival. She also increased her fitness regimen. She swam, non-stop, for hours, both above and below the water and ran at least 100 miles a week. Jim and Grace told her that she did not have to worry about helping with the adventures anymore but she did anyway and would take a group out 2 or 3 times each month. She felt that this helped her to continue to build her socialization and people-reading skills.

# 14 Getting Ready to Meet the Guys

As Schea remembered her last days with Jim and Grace, and her first days with Todd's unit, she noticed one of the young midshipmen wandering along the path and heading toward her. She had met a number of the young men from the academy and they were all generally polite, nice young men but she has not dated anyone even though she has been asked out frequently.

This midshipman stopped in front of her and said, "Excuse me, miss. Are you visiting the academy? I'd be happy to give you a tour."

Schea looked up at him, smiled and said, "Thanks, but I live here in town and have wandered around the academy often, so I know the campus fairly well."

But, he was not a quitter, they usually never are. "Then may I buy you a cup of coffee?"

Schea hated doing this, but she responded with a lie and said, "No, but thank you. I am meeting someone over in the City Dock."

"Lucky guy! Maybe another time." He walked on!

Schea decided to head back into town before she had to lie to another guy. It wasn't that she was against dating and she had even thought about getting together with a couple of the guys, but she always seemed to stop before saying yes to a date.

Two guys had actually tried to kill her while on missions and she had originally thought they were nice, but they weren't, and she eventually had to kill them. She figured that she'd say yes when she was ready to say yes.

Even if the guy wasn't trying to kill her, what could she tell him when asked about what she did? She'd have to lie. What would she say if asked where she was going or how long she would be gone? Again, she'd have to lie. Her life was just not fit for dating.

She headed home and made some lunch. It was a very nice September day and it would be great to eat out on her deck overlooking the water. She threw together a salad and half a sandwich, grabbed a Diet Coke then headed out onto her deck. She began thinking about that year of training with Todd's unit. She smiled as she thought about the day she met the guys at the camp.

XXXXX

When Schea turned 16, Jim took her back to Todd's and Todd told Schea he would take her into his unit for training but it would be a trial period. If she proved herself, then she could join if she still wanted to.

Todd turned to look at Jim and said that he and Grace would still have to provide their approval. However, she could, if she chose to, file a petition with the court to be manumitted from the requirement for a guardian. If it is approved, then she could make all of her own decisions but that

57

could be decided at a later time. Jim looked at Schea and smiled. He told her that it was completely up to her to decide what she would like to do. He and Grace would support her 100%.

Jim asked Todd if Schea would have time for visits home or if he and Grace could come to visit her. Todd told him that there could be no visiting at all for the first 3 months, but after that, Schea could spend one weekend every three months at home.

"However, if she did not return or if she was even one minute late arriving back, then she would be immediately dropped from the training program and not given a second chance. In this line of work, no one can ever count on a second chance."

Schea said, "That's fine with me."

Jim hugged Schea, hopped in his car and drove away. He and Grace cried a little after he had gotten home but they quickly realized that this was what was best for Schea.

Grace had already said her goodbye back at the house and had used the quiet time while Jim was outside getting ready to drive Schea to Todd's to tell Schea how much she loved her. Schea told Grace that she had grown to really love her like a mother. This comment, of course, brought both of them to tears. Jim had been ready to open the door at that moment, but when he saw them crying and hugging, he quietly stepped back onto the porch and waited.

On Schea's last visit to see Jenny and the Kennedys, she told Jenny about her plans. Jenny stared at her wide-eyed with fear at the thought that Schea would be putting herself in dangerous situations but Schea pulled her into her arms and quietly told her that she would be fine. She said she would always be well prepared and would not take any unnecessary risks.

Schea knew that she probably should not be telling Jenny as much as she had, but she wanted Jenny to know why she might be gone for long periods of time with no contact. She also told Jenny that it was extremely important for Jenny to never talk about what she was doing, even with the Kennedys and especially not with Archie and Izzy. Jenny promised and they hooked their little fingers together.

As Schea and Jenny were getting ready to do something fun with Archie and Izzy, Schea turned and reminded Jenny about the bracelet. Jenny smiled and showed her that she wore the bracelet in a little velvet bag around her neck. Schea laughed and told Jenny, "You will probably have to find a better place once you start to get boobies."

At this, they both started giggling and kept it up as they walked into the room where Archie and Izzy were waiting. They, of course, asked what was so funny and Jenny said, "Oh nothing."

# 15 Preliminaries

Todd took Schea to the training camp. It was located on some property that he had acquired after leaving the CIA and, like Jim, he had invested wisely and lived frugally. He was a confirmed bachelor at age 55, but had, and still has, girlfriends. However, in his former line of work, he could not seem to find the right woman for his life style. This was unlike Jim who had found Grace during the last few years of his service.

Todd's official office was located in a small corner of a strip mall in Bend and his training camp was located near Redmond, Oregon with lovely views of the Three Sisters Mountains. He spent most of his time at the camp and only used this office as a front for his Project Management and Security Company. He had a Master's Degree in Project Management from USC and his PMP designation from the Institute for Project Management. He had all of the right materials in his office on his desk and in a couple of bookcases. These included textbooks, various business magazines, professional journals and the latest edition of the Project Manager's revered bible, the Project Management Book of Knowledge.

He gave her a brief outline of the camp. It was a sprawling complex of buildings and training areas. It had a shooting range, an obstacle course, a fully equipped gym and an indoor Olympic size pool. There was lots of land to practice running, jumping, playing hide-and-go-seek and getting really dirty. Todd's camp office was also his home and was located in a building just past the entrance. He had a small kitchen, bedroom, bath and living room. It wasn't fancy and it looked like a single man's hovel.

There were several storage buildings for various types of equipment and one building used solely as the armory. It was a well-constructed, concrete-and-steel structure with no windows and one massive locked steel door. There were numerous backup electrical generators that were all regularly tested and always full of fuel. One of the buildings was a two-story dormitory that housed up to 20 people. Each person had their own room with a small bathroom, and everyone ate communally in the dining hall on the first floor.

The only people Todd used for trainers were former operatives that he had personally recruited, who wanted to come in from doing field work. There were few assigned roles - trainees did all of the cleaning, dish washing, trash hauling and general maintenance. Anyone with certain skills, like construction, helped with repairs. One of the staff was a former medic, so he handled routine cuts, bruises and other injuries. Serious medical attention resulted in a quick helicopter ride to the nearest facility.

Todd drove up to the facility and stopped just outside of his office/home. On the drive from downtown Bend, they exchanged mostly small talk - where they were born and where they had gone to school. They each had deaths in the past that they mentioned, but did not elaborate upon. There was no discussion of Todd's work or jobs he managed. That stuff would need to wait. Schea liked Todd's manner and seemed to be getting a good feeling about him. Todd was also warming up to Schea's teenage innocence. But, the one question that he needed to get answered soon was could she turn from that innocent teen and kill a person?

They went into his office and he quickly showed her around his small quarters. When finished, he asked if she'd like a cup of coffee, but she politely turned down the coffee and said she wouldn't mind a Diet Coke. He smiled, went to his kitchen and came out with a cup of coffee for himself and a Diet Coke for her.

He sat down at his desk and she sat in a chair facing him. He was wondering where to begin, she was wondering when he'd begin. Todd started with a simple question. "Could you kill a person?"

Without blinking or glancing around for some help, she answered, "Yes. I have seen enough killing to know that it can be done and quite easily by bad people. If they can so easily kill some innocent stranger, or even someone they actually know, then I see no reason why the reverse should not be true. I don't actually feel hatred toward those who killed my family but I do feel the need to stop them from doing it to someone else."

Todd watched as she spoke: Her eyes were focused. Her expression was neutral. Her body language was relaxed and he saw no little twitches and tells. She simply answered his question. Todd now had the answer to his question. Schea would kill someone whom she believed needed to be killed in order to save someone else's life.

Todd rose from his chair, asked her if she would like a tour of the camp and they walked out to the dorm. As they walked, Todd told her that he had 6 trainees and 4 trainers in the camp at present.

"All of the trainers and trainees are out in the field for a 2 day exercise and will be back tomorrow afternoon. I planned your arrival this way so that you could become acquainted with the camp on your own."

Todd suddenly stopped and turned to face Schea. He looked down at her since he was 6 feet 4 and she was a little over a foot shorter. He was also about 240 pounds of muscle. She almost bumped into him because he had stopped so abruptly, looked up at him and waited. It appeared that he was collecting his thoughts or struggling with some particular thought that he wanted to get out.

Finally, Todd said, "I really struggled with my decision to take you into training. One reason is that you are female and all of the rest of the group are male." Before she could respond, he held up his hand for her to wait until he was finished. "I also struggled with the fact that you are so small. Even my other female was almost 6 feet tall and had been a former weight lifting competitor. But, what I really struggled with is your age. The youngest person I have ever taken into training was 25 and he hadn't made it through. The mental side is the hardest part of the training because we focus so much on how to find and kill someone. I have found that the older, more experienced trainees have the least difficulty with this and tend to do better in the field."

Raising his hand again to stop her from saying anything, he continued. "But, I am getting more and more requests for jobs that required people with the skills, temperament and look that only a young operative can satisfy, or they at least can pass for a young operative. I have had to turn a number of jobs down because I couldn't satisfy these requirements. I felt bad that I couldn't help a client and worse because they might never get the right person for the job."

"I figured that an operative like that would be too young and inexperienced, and would probably end up getting killed. It was also likely that no one would be assigned and the target would simply go on doing what they were doing. When I met you, my initial reaction was to say no but, as I talked to Jim and then to you, I realized that if I was ever going to find someone for these types of jobs, then I had to give you a try. I hope you are that someone."

When Schea figured he was finished, she gave him a reassuring smile and told him, "Do not worry. I am 100% sure that I am the right person for this work and you will not be disappointed. Your clients will get what they want and the target will get what they deserve."

They entered the dormitory and Todd showed her to her room. He made sure she knew she could lock the door from the inside and that he had installed, in her room only, an alarm she could set off using a special code word. All she had to do was to say the word itself and the alarm would sound around the camp. She didn't ask why because she knew what he was trying to do and appreciated it.

He pointed out the other rooms and then they went to the dining room. Todd grabbed 2 Diet Cokes from the refrigerator and brought them to one of the tables. He handed one to Schea and they sat across from each other. "No one knows that you are the new trainee or anything else about you, even the trainers do not know. Everyone simply thinks that I was looking for someone and assumed that the person would be the typical newbie: male, around 30, former military or SWAT."

"I did that because I don't want them to start second guessing me about bringing a young female into the group. But this means that you will have to start proving yourself right away. They will see a cute girl, begin to smirk and think how stupid I am to bring someone like you into the group."

She smiled and guessed what he was trying to do to the group. He smiled back because he recognized that she knew that he was trying to get them to underestimate her and this would make it a lot easier for her to prove them wrong. They would look at her and never think she had the physical or weapons capabilities to handle the training program. It also meant that some might try to go easy on her and others might try to force her to quit by making things exceedingly difficult.

As they walked back to his office, Todd was still worried about the psychological side of the training and the emotional toll it could have on people. He told her this and mentioned, "You will likely be subjected to verbal comments at times. Some might even try to ambush you mentally with sudden outbursts of foul comments specifically about you and what will happen to you in the field. Can you handle that?"

"I admit that it will probably be more than anything I have heard, but I am sure I can handle it. Some of the comments and language that I had directed at me on a few of the overnight adventure experiences I helped conduct were pretty annoying. And, when Jim or the guides were not around, some of the men would try to touch me or make suggestions of what we could be doing. I chose to ignore them and they usually just gave up after a little while. If anyone touched me, I did comment that if they tried anything again, then they would regret it and most never did it again."

"A couple of times, some young guy would think that he was tough enough to handle a little girl and try touching me a second time. My reaction was always quick and painful for the culprit. A knee or elbow or hand chop would get them to back off."

"Once, a particularly annoying and disgusting young guy did try a third time after the first and second warnings. After I finished with him, one of the guides came over to where I was in order to help with one of the boats. He found the disgusting guy holding his arm and could see that he was in obvious pain. He asked what happened and I turned to the guy, raised my eyebrows and suggesting that he should tell him. He simply mumbled that he had slipped and fallen on some rocks. The guide took him to the camp and patched him up." Schea smiled at the memory.

Todd smiled too, but he still warned Schea that all of these men were a lot rougher and stronger than that young man. She said she knew but was ready for the challenge and saw it as useful training for her when she was in the field.

They talked a bit more about the training and what Schea should expect. He knew most of it was going to be no real test for her but he did caution that some of it might require strength or height that she did not have. He said that he would work with the trainers to make sure that they took this into account. But, Schea made sure that he knew she expected no special treatment.

Todd helped Schea get her stuff to her room and gave her time to sort things out then he went back to his small office to check on notes, emails and some other paperwork.

After about 2 hours, Schea knocked on his door and he told her to come on in but then reminded her that she could enter the office at any time. He said that only the individual rooms were off limits to anyone without permission.

They ate a quick meal that Todd prepared and discussed the overall schedule for her training. There were no specifics because those would be worked out with the trainers. He told her that everyone would be returning at around noon the following day and would be given a few hours to get cleaned up, take care of personal business and get ready for lunch.

He said that other than his smart device, there were no phones or computers of any type allowed in the camp. This was for safety as well as training discipline. After all, many missions were conducted in far-flung areas where devices might not work or the operative could not take the chance of it giving away their position.

He also told her that Facebook, Twitter and other social media were strictly forbidden. He said she needed to close the accounts and he would have his tech specialist erase any evidence of their existence. This was for safety and security reasons. If she became an operative, then he would help her set up some fake accounts that could not be traced back to her and she could use these to communicate with friends and family.

He said she will wait in his living room the following day while the others arrived and got cleaned up. At about 3 pm, he would call for a meeting to go over how their training went in the exercise and, once everyone was present, he will come into the dining area with her. They both smiled. Schea smiled because she was excited to get started. Todd smiled because he couldn't wait to see the reactions of his trainers and the trainees.

# 16 The First Day

Schea got up the following morning and went for a 10 mile run. When finished, she changed and swam laps for about an hour. She ate a light breakfast then went to the gym to workout with the weights. Finally, she showered and went to the office to check in with Todd. "You have been a busy young lady."

At that moment, they heard laughter and idle chatter in the area of the dormitory, and Todd said that they should head into the living room. He suggested she read anything she found in the bookcases or take a nap on the sofa. She assured him that she'd be fine and was looking forward to meeting everyone. He smiled, closed the door and went to meet the group.

The trainees and trainers headed for the dormitory as soon as they entered the camp complex. This training exercise had involved tracking various targets at night and they had not been given anything to do this. All they could use were their tracking skills and stealth. They deposited their packs in the hall and went to their rooms to shower and change.

Todd waited for them in the dining area where they would eventually come back to. Two of the trainers arrived first then slowly the trainees and other trainers arrived. Everyone said a quick hello to Todd and went to the refrigerator for a beer. They gathered at various tables chatting about the exercise and speculated on what was next for them. A couple of the trainees were close to graduating and were wondering what their first assignment might be.

There was a lot of joking, laughing and cat-calling, and Todd enjoyed the good natured camaraderie amongst all the trainees and the trainers. After about an hour, Todd rose and told them that there would be a meeting and a debriefing in 30 minutes then left.

Todd entered his living room and found Schea curled up in an oversize chair reading a book. He looked at her and couldn't believe he was going to put this 16 year old girl through his training program then send her into the field after sick bastards. As he looked at her, she looked even smaller because the chair was so big and she had her legs curled up under her. She looked like a big beach ball sitting in the chair, except with hair coming out of the top of it. She put the book aside and smiled.

He asked, "Are you ready?

"Yup. I can't wait to meet the guys."

She had her hair in a ponytail as usual and was wearing an Oregon Ducks t-shirt, a pair of jean shorts and sandals. She looked pretty, almost sexy with her firm body and tan legs. He almost suggested she change, but then thought better of it. He wanted them to see her for who she is. He also wanted them to get over the fact that she was not just some very cute girl. She is a new trainee and a tough one at that, which, he was sure they would learn the first time they had to compete against her.

Todd nodded. "Let's go."

They walked into the dining room side by side and stopped about 10 feet from the group. As they had approached, the first few who saw them started to elbow the guys around them and nodded their heads in Todd's direction. Very quickly everyone became quiet and stared at them. Todd knew he didn't have to worry about what Schea would be doing.

She was grinning and surveying the group. She was evaluating each of them to determine whether they were a trainer or trainee and what their particular skill set might be.

They stopped and Schea stood casually about 2 feet to his side. She stood relaxed with one leg slightly out to her left side with her hands folded together and hanging down in front of her.

Most of the guys had little smiles on their faces, while a few leered. Some of the guys leaned into the guy next to them and softly whispered something. Finally one of the trainees said to Todd, "I didn't know you had a kid."

Someone mumbled and commented, "Or a grandkid more likely," which got some laughs.

Todd continued to smile then started. "I'd like to introduce everyone to Schea Tailor."

A few guys said hi or mumbled hey. To which Schea responded with a polite hello. However, most were simply staring at her and trying to make some sense of her presence at the camp. There had never been a woman, let alone a girl, in the camp.

Finally, Todd dropped the bombshell and announced in a clear voice, "Schea is our new trainee." You could have heard the old preverbal pin drop. No one said anything for about 5 seconds while Schea continued to smile at them.

Then, suddenly it seemed that everyone was talking at once. Schea heard comments like, "You've got to be kidding?" "This is ridiculous." "She's a girl." "She's just a kid."

Then Schea heard someone comment, "She'll never be able to handle it." And, the smile vanished from her face.

Todd started to say something, but she put a restraining hand on his arm and he stopped. Schea walked toward the men and politely asked, "Who said that I will not be able to handle this?" No one said anything at first because they were so stunned with her bold and sudden appearance in their midst.

Finally, one of the trainees said, "No offence, but I just don't think you'll be able to handle it."

She had noticed him earlier when she was scanning the group. He had been one of the few who frowned at her. She estimated him to be in his mid-thirties. He was a big guy, so his skill-set would include hand-to-hand combat and the knife would be his probable weapon of choice, since she figured he liked to be up close and personal when he took out a target.

Schea proceeded to tell him then asked, "May I ask your name?"

He looked around then said, "Gus." He quickly looked at Todd and said, "He probably told you about each of us."

Before Todd could say anything, she walked up to Gus and said, "I do not need to ask anyone about any of you. I can get the measure of any man, here or elsewhere." Then she stepped back a little and asked him loud enough for everyone to hear clearly, "What would you like to do in order to prove that you are right."

Gus quickly looked at Todd who simply shrugged and said, "You started this, so you might want to answer her."

Gus had lost some of his bluster at her challenge but then looked at her and asked, "What would you prefer?"

She kept staring at him. "I asked you first."

The men were getting confused - some were shaking their heads, some were smiling and finally one of the trainers said, "We should stop this and get back to business."

Schea turned her attention away from Gus and asked, "What is your name?" He said Lester. Schea looked at him and said, "You are a little younger than Todd and prefer stealth because you are an excellent tracker. Your weapon of choice is your brain, but if that isn't working, then you prefer a sniper rifle." Lester smiled and nodded. Schea politely thanked Lester for trying to help but said, "I demand respect from not just Gus, but from everyone in this room. And, if I want to earn that respect, then it has to start right now."

She walked back over to Gus and said, "Well, what's your answer, Gus?"

Everyone, including Todd, was now looking at Gus, expecting him to answer. Gus was thrown completely off guard by her which, of course, had been part of Schea's plan. Finally, Gus sighed, straightened up to his full 6 feet 3 inches and said, "Fine. I choose hand-to-hand fighting in the ring, no-holds-barred."

Todd almost stepped in at this point but was stopped with what Schea did next. She smiled and told Gus, "That is an excellent choice." She then politely asked Gus, and all of her focus was now on him, "Would it be okay if I went back to my room to change into something more appropriate for our exercise?"

He mumbled, "Sure, whatever."

Schea scampered away to her room like a girl who had been asked to go to a dance for the first time.

As Schea changed, she remembered a story she had once read on a summer afternoon. It was a story about the real or fictitious character in British lore, Robin Hood. His best friend was a man named Little John and he was huge. It was said that he was around 6 feet, 6 inches tall and at least 240 pounds.

At one point, while Robin and his men were serving with King Richard's army in the Holy Land, he had challenged a man named Sir Nicholas. Sir Nicholas was a member of the Order of Knights Hospitaller, a military order charged by the Pope with defending the Holy Land.

Sir Nicholas was about half of Little John's size, but he was well trained and relied on speed, quickness and his brain to beat his opponents. The challenge was accepted and they fought with shields and swords. Sir Nicholas defeated Little John by engaging him with his skill set and not with Little John's. Schea decided to use the same tactic with Gus and left her room smiling.

When Schea had left for her room, all of the men started talking and telling Todd not to let this go on. Others were telling Gus to let this go. Todd finally put his hands up for silence. Once he had their attention, he told them, "I appreciate your concern, but I am not going to stop this." He then looked at Gus and very firmly said to him, "If you think this is going to be a cake-walk, then you had better quit now. You'd better give it your all or Schea will hurt you."

Everyone was stunned to hear this last comment. What could he mean by *hurt you* and why would he even think that could be the result of such an obviously mismatched fight? They knew he only recruited the best, but this seemed like a crazy-bad idea.

Just then, they heard Schea's door open and close. She eventually walked out to the dining area to face the men. She had changed into her one-piece bathing suit, but had put on a pair of full length nylon running pants and trail-running shoes.

She stopped and asked Gus, "Do you need to change or do anything to get prepared?"

He stared at her, harrumphed and said, "No. I'm ready."

Schea replied, "Cool. Me too."

Still no one moved.

She finally looked around and asked, "So, where is the ring?" even though Todd had shown her the gym during their tour of the camp. "We should probably get going since dinner will be starting soon." She looked at Gus and waited. The smile vanished from his face and he scowled at her.

Schea smiled back, but it was a different kind of smile from the one she had given him earlier when she asked him to decide. This smile was frighteningly scary. They finally headed for the door and everyone else trailed behind like ducklings following their mom and dad.

As Schea followed Gus she watched him from behind. She noticed that he favored his right side ever so slightly. She also noticed that he had a slouch to his posture - maybe this indicated an old injury. She stored that information away in case it might come in handy.

They entered the gym and Gus climbed into the ring while Schea did the same and everyone else gathered around. One of the trainers made an appeal to Gus to quit this but, before Gus could say anything, Schea glared at the trainer and gave him the same smile she had given Gus earlier. "Don't worry. I won't hurt him too badly." The trainer smiled and backed off.

Todd climbed into the ring and looked at the two competitors for a few seconds. He reiterated, "This is a no-holds-barred contest, but I may choose to stop it at any time if I think real damage or injury could occur." He climbed out and said, "You can start when ready."

Schea could tell that Gus was a bit unsure how to proceed and might even be thinking that he shouldn't be trying to beat up a little girl. He was probably figuring that even if he did win, no one would give him any credit for it. He was in a no win situation. He should have backed out from the very beginning and apologized to Schea for his comment. That way, if she washed out of the program, he could simply say that he knew she wouldn't make and, if she graduated from it, then great. The main lesson was that he had to learn to keep his big mouth shut.

Gus looked over at Schea and saw that she was giving him that smile again. He finally pulled himself together and decided to just get this over with quickly and take his licks from the guys over some cold beer. He started rocking back and forth and began moving around the ring.

Schea figured Gus would not take Todd's advice and would underestimate her. He would probably try to end this quickly then go off with his buddies. So, she decided that the kindest thing she could do for a potential fellow field operative was to help him to achieve his goal of going off with his buddies quickly.

She moved with Gus. Every move he made, she mimicked. If he moved to the right, then she did. If left, then so did she. If he moved toward her, then she moved toward him. If he brought his hands up, then she did. She did nothing but what he did and could tell that he was getting confused, but then he started to get angry. It was like when you were a kid and your little brother would do everything that you did. It was cute at first, but it becomes pretty annoying quickly. She was annoying him. *Good.*

Gus thought. *What a waste of time this whole thing is?* He wanted this over. He moved quickly to his left then back to his right then came at her. But she wasn't there. She didn't copy him this time. When he went left, so did she and kept going even when he moved to the right which he favored. He then suddenly saw her coming straight at him.

She was so fast. She hit him in the left kidney then drove her foot up into his crotch. He was tough though and didn't seem to be bothered with either hit. She was now across from him again, staring at him and mimicking him, again. She was infuriating Gus.

This time Gus decided to come straight at her and back her into a corner. As he slowly approached her, she didn't move. As he got closer, he thought he had better be ready for one of her lightning moves. He was now only 3 feet from her and she still just stood there. He finally charged.

What he hadn't noticed was that Schea had been slowly slouching a little at a time. She had also braced her feet by moving them a little side to side on the hard mat. Just as he charged she ducked and drove straight at him with her head aimed at his belly. He was ripped, but the head can be a pretty powerful weapon when used correctly. It can be used to plan a mission or as a battering ram, and she decided to use it as a battering ram.

She caught him squarely in the stomach just below his diaphragm. All of the air in his lungs was forced out in a split second but he still managed to get one hand on her left ankle as he doubled over. She reached up, grabbed his balls in her right hand and squeezed with all her might.

He finally let go of her and she shot out from under him. She scrambled to the far side of the ring and thought. *That was close.* She had to stay out of his reach.

Schea had done some real damage this time. He was winching from the pain in his crotch and the blow to his stomach, but he was not out of it yet. She had not been touched other than the brief grasp of her ankle and she could see that he was really furious now. She guessed he was going to try to punish her the next time he came at her, so she decided to go after him.

Schea started to dance around in the ring. She would go this way then that way. She would stop and sway left to right. She would dance from one foot to the other. She kept moving. As she did all of this dancing, she slowly got closer to his right side. Since he was also planning his next move, she decided to go first and end this now.

As she danced around a little closer to his right side, she suddenly dropped to the floor of the ring and rolled toward him. He tried to step back so that he could jump on her, but she was so damned fast.

She was suddenly at his right side, quickly got into a crouch and rammed her shoulder into the side of his right knee. She heard a slight snap and moan from Gus. She continued around behind him, jumped onto his back and wrapped her arms around his neck. She had to keep ducking the wild punches he was throwing at her from above and the side.

She took a second to steady her hold then jammed her right knee into his right kidney and began pulling to the right with all her strength. Gus struggled mightily and began landing weak punches to her right leg and arms, but she held on. It seemed like forever but, like watching a slow-motion video, Gus slowly began to topple to his right. Just before they hit the floor, Schea scrambled around behind again and put a choke hold on his neck. She tightened her grip and Gus slowly lost movement then passed out.

Schea held on for a few more seconds then slowly got off of Gus. As she moved off of him, she quickly checked for a pulse and found a slow but steady one. She stood up, shook some feeling back into her arms, wiped her brow on her bare arm and looked around. All she saw were stunned faces, some with their mouths hanging open, and some with slight smiles. Mostly, there seemed to be disbelief in what they had just seen happen.

Todd let the moment last a bit then he climbed into the ring. He looked around and quietly, but firmly, asked if anyone doubted his decision to bring Schea into the group. No one said anything for a few more seconds and then they all started saying, "Nope." or "No way." or they just shook their heads. He could tell that some still harbored a little doubt but that was good. He wanted to keep challenging them to accept her and for Schea to keep proving her worth and merit.

Todd told a couple of the trainers to take care of Gus and to see to his injuries then Todd, Schea and the rest of the men went back to the dining room. As they walked over, several of the men came up next to Schea and said that she was amazing. One guy asked her if she could teach him how to fight like that and she said she'd be happy to.

As they entered the dining area, most of the guys went to the refrigerator for a beer. One guy came boldly over to offer one to Schea but then he seemed to remember that she was too young and looked embarrassed. She gave him one of her warmest smiles and said, "Thanks, but I'd prefer a Diet Coke." He went back quickly and got one for her.

When he came back he introduced himself as Jack Choi. They shook hands and Schea said, "It's nice to meet you, Jack." Gradually, they all came over and introduced themselves to her. Besides Gus and Jack, there was Bret Shea, Michael Kelly, who had a lovely Irish Brogue, Glen Miller and Randall King. Two trainers also came over and said hello, congratulated her and told her their names, Kevin Doyle and Lenny Yankovich. Lester was helping Andy Benson with Gus.

It was near dinner time, so Glen and Todd volunteered to cook up something. They made a big kettle of chili, warmed up a bunch of rolls and everyone dug in. There was idle chatter and some laughter. The guys sitting near Schea would ask a question or two and might volunteer a bit about themselves, but Schea could tell that no one had any idea what to make of her.

Todd sat at the table where his trainers were sitting. Gus and the other 2 trainers came in during the meal and Gus was silent and sat alone.

At about the time it seemed things were winding down and before people started to clean up or leave, Schea stood and walked to the end of the tables so that everyone could see her. She looked around and gave everyone a warm smile then began to speak.

"I'm sorry about the contest that I had to have with Gus." She looked at Gus and told him, "I hope you are okay and that we will be able to work together." He looked at her and gave a slight, less than enthusiastic, nod.

She then focused on the group, including Todd and the trainers. "I am glad and feel lucky to have this opportunity. I lost my entire family at the hands of horrible people. Before they were taken from me, my father, mother, brother and sister gave me extensive knowledge of weapons, martial arts, hunting, tracking and surviving in harsh environments."

"But, I know that I need to learn more and hope to do just that here. I also know I can learn a great deal from each of you. I don't expect friendships, but it would be nice. However, I do expect respect and will do everything I can to earn it." She sat down and they all mumbled agreement and began finishing their meals.

As Schea rose to leave, Todd asked her to come to the office once she had a chance to shower and change. As she walked to her room, several of the trainees told her they were glad that she spoke up and they were looking forward to working with her. Jack was one of them and he seemed to be the most accepting. A couple of others simply smiled at her as they went to their rooms.

About an hour later, Schea walked into Todd's office and saw that all of the trainers were present. She looked refreshed and had on a t-shirt, blue jeans and sandals. She had on a different Oregon Ducks t-shirt and one of the trainers, as she walked by, said that he was a Washington Huskies fan and asked if she would stop wearing that damned Ducks t-shirt. He smiled and she smiled shyly and shrugged.

Todd suggested that they go into his living room. After everyone had gotten a beer, a coffee, or a Diet Coke, they all sat. Schea sat on the overstuffed chair she had occupied just a few hours earlier.

Todd looked around the room at his trainers for a second then said, "You all saw what can happen when Schea is underestimated. We had both warned Gus what would happen if he did, but he ignored both warnings and acted like the contest was about showing this little girl what the real world was all about."

Todd asked, "Have any of you seen Gus fight so carelessly?" No one responded. "Gus is a much better fighter than that, although, I'm not sure if he would have prevailed over Schea even if he had taken her seriously." He glanced at Schea and she had a wistful smile on her face while playing with her hair.

Todd continued by saying, "Schea is probably a better runner and swimmer than anyone at the camp and her endurance is remarkable. Based on what I know, she is probably one the best shooters, archer and knife handler I have seen. I'd compare her sniper skills to Lyudmila Pavlichenko, the Russian WWII female sniper credited with 309 kills. Lyudmila was also small and said to have had the coolness of a viper. Schea might also be as good as Chris Kyle, America's most successful sniper."

"The point I want to make is that her physical abilities and her skills-set are not at question here, although she could still continue to learn. What I want to know is if she can handle the emotional side and mental toughness needed for this job? She is young and that worries me a little for this type of work but," and he emphasized this point, "keep in mind, it is not her specific age or her gender or her looks that I am concerned about."

Lenny looked at Schea and asked her, "If you are in the field on assignment and had to kill a target, could you do it?"

She uncurled herself on the chair and sat forward. She looked Lenny in the eyes and told him, "I would not have taken the assignment if I thought for a minute that the target did not deserve to die. So, yes, I would kill the target and think nothing of it."

She had delivered the response with such cold conviction that Lenny actually felt a chill run up his spine. Lenny, Todd and the other trainers realized at that moment that if Schea had a sign while on a mission, it was her eyes. When they went cold and piercing, she was about to strike.

Todd repeated what Schea had said at the meal. "Schea doesn't want and should not receive any special treatment. Although, because of her height and size, some accommodations might need to be made for certain tasks that require a taller reach than she has, or when lifting extremely large loads."

As they filed out, Todd called after Schea. When she turned, he said, "Get a good night's rest. Training begins tomorrow."

# 17 Training

The training was tough but fair.  No special considerations were given to Schea and she did not ask for any.  Even in one-on-one training, she held her own.  The trainees had seen the fight with Gus, so they knew that they could not take anything about this girl for granted, except that she would beat the crap out of them if they got lazy.  She lost several one-on-ones, but took it as a lesson and tried to learn what she had done wrong.  The trainees and trainers admired and respected her attitude.

No one could match her running and swimming prowess.  She could run and swim farther than anyone and her endurance was remarkable.  She was about equal to them at the shooting range, except when it came to marksmanship.  She seemed to have a real knack for long range shooting.  She wasn't as good as Kenny or Glen when it came to tracking, but she was much better than all of them when it came to stealth.  Todd figured that it was mostly because of her size.  She was capable of hiding in the smallest of places and seemed to be a ghost moving through underbrush.  As a matter of fact, that became Schea's nickname at the camp.  She was *The Ghost* and she liked it.

Everyone was friendly toward her, even Gus.  He was even friendly with her at times when no one was around.  Jack was the friendliest trainee with her and she seemed to respond to him a little better than the others.  He would sit with her at meals and they would laugh or quietly talk about stuff unrelated to training.  Jack knew that friendship was the limit of his interaction with Schea since they all knew what would happen if they tried any unwanted advances towards her.

About two weeks after Schea started, Todd had to let Bret go.  Bret took it well and, before he left, he made sure that he shook everyone's hand and thanked them for their help.  When he got around to Schea, he smiled and told her that he really admired her and wished her good luck.

Schea really liked the training and always gave it 100% which the trainers and trainees respected.  Whenever there was a team competition, the team leaders always chose Schea if they had first pick.  She was flattered by it but knew she had to work for that honor as well.  Her team didn't always win but that was part of the learning process.  The trainers and Todd never held back when it was time to review Schea's performances on a team or in individual tasks.  If she screwed up, they told her, as they did all of the recruits and always took the time to demonstrate what they had done wrong or could have done better.

XXXXX

One training session was on weapons, specifically the use of close order weapons, like knives.  The trainer was Lenny who is just shy of 50 years old and had emigrated from Eastern Europe after the fall of communism in that region.  He has never revealed from which country, but that's his little secret.

He was talking about the use of a knife in a fight.  He knew that Schea was the most accurate with one, so he asked her to help him demonstrate.  Schea got up and he gave her a throwing knife.  It had the perfect weight, and an easy-grip handle.  He pointed to a target about 10 yards away and asked her to try to hit it. She stepped up, tossed, and hit the target dead center. "Excellent throw, Schea." Then Lenny handed her a butter knife and told her, "Now, hit the same target with this knife."

Schea looked at him questioningly and he simply pointed to the target. She stepped to the line, tried to get a good feel for the butter knife's weight and balance, set herself and tossed. She hit the target, but not dead center.

He said, "Good toss, but you may not have stopped the attacker with that and might need an additional weapon. Assuming you got the butter knife from a kitchen drawer, maybe you might reach in for another weapon and pull out this." He handed her a fork. "Now what do you do?"

"My point is that you must learn how to use anything and everything that might be found within reach as a weapon." From then on, they had to practice with butter knives, forks, spoons, chopsticks, screwdrivers, letter openers, staplers and all kinds of objects that might be found in homes, offices, on the street or in a store. It was actually enlightening and quite fun.

XXXXX

Schea understood Todd's reasoning for allowing some accommodation when it came to extreme heights and loads but none of the trainees ever complained or made a remark about it. However, it frustrated her that this had to be done. If she was on the team, then heavy loads were handled by one of the men and if there was a height obstacle that needed to be scaled, someone would boost her up and over it.

In her spare time or during a long run or swim, Schea would think about how she might overcome the height and load limits she had. The load limits were a puzzle. She knew she was strong for her size, but her size limited the load that her frame could support.

On one long run as she was sprinting to the finish area she thought that she might have come up with a way to overcome the height limit. She knew there was a team competition coming up and there was usually a height barrier to deal with sometime during exercises. *Maybe I could try my solution at that time.* She secretly practiced it a few times when no one was around.

On the next team competition, she was on a team with Jack and Michael. None of them was very tall, so this might be a good opportunity for her to try it. The competitions were generally a mix of obstacles, escape routes, planning scenarios, and teamwork challenges.

Each member of Schea's team was an excellent shot, so this should be a good match with Glen, Gus and Randall, who were much better at tracking. The tipping task was probably going to be the obstacles they would need to get past. Schea's team had teamed together before and had worked well. But, no matter what team she was on, it took a little extra time to help her over high obstacles.

The competition started with each team on a separate course in order to avoid too much competition and possible conflicts. Each team was given an envelope with a description of the course and its layout. The trainers made sure that the courses were as similar as possible.

The trainers and Todd were out on the courses watching and evaluating. They moved around so a team never knew if a trainer was around the next turn or hiding in a tree. Kevin was the trainer at the start line and, once he felt that the others had enough time to get into position, he told the teams to start. Schea's team headed into the wooded area and encountered a couple of obstacles to crawl under then each had to hit a target with a pistol from 50 yards away. No problems so far.

They started running up a slight hill for about 2 miles and then headed down towards a small stream. They never slowed and simply leaped other the 8 foot-wide stream bed. After crossing the stream, there was another target to hit with a light-caliber rifle. As they left the area and went around a short curve, they saw a 12 foot wall they were required to get over.

Jack shouted to the team that he would plant himself at the base then lift the other 2 over. Michael would then reach down and pull him up and over.

Schea looked at Jack and said, "Watch this." And, she took off in a sprint.

At about 50 yards away, Schea quickly scanned the area near the front of the wall and saw what she needed. She made a slight turn away from Jack and Michael and headed towards the wall at a 45 degree angle.

Just as it seemed that she was going to slam herself into the wall, Jack and Michael watched dumbfounded as she suddenly seemed to rise into the air in front for the wall with her hands straight up from her body. She was moving along the wall then her feet came in contact with the wall and, unbelievably, she started running up the wall. The next thing they saw was that she had disappeared over it.

Jack and Michael scrambled to the wall and Jack lifted Michael up so that he could scramble to the top then lift Jack to the top. As Michael reached up to the top to get a firm hold, he felt someone reaching for his hand and pulling him up. He looked up and there was Schea.

She looked back down at Jack and told him, "Get your ass moving up the wall so that Michael and I can pull you over."

They continued the competition and eventually won. At the finish area, the team members were enjoying beers, while one was enjoying a Diet Coke. Jack and Michael were telling the other trainees what Schea had done while the trainers and Todd were talking quietly. Once, as Schea was looking at the trainers, she saw Todd turn his head and look right at her then smiled and turned back to the trainers.

After about 10 minutes, the trainers came to the two teams and told them that they had all done a good job. Andy looked at Schea and said, "I was watching your team as you approached the wall and I couldn't believe what you did to get over it." The other team looked surprised since they had thought Jack and Michael were telling tales.

Schea told them, "I have been thinking about and practicing how to get over high obstacles without help for weeks. When I saw the log wall, I knew it was time to give it a try. I think anyone could probably do it, once they know what to look for and how to approach the wall."

"I remembered watching a collegiate track meet on TV several years ago. One of the commentators said that the Fosbury Flop approach had been a radical change to how one high jumped back in the 60s and 70s and showed an old video of how it was done before the flop. He then explained how the Flop came about and how it was done. So I reasoned that maybe an approach like that would work for me when scaling high walls. I figured that in the field, I may not have anyone to hoist me up over a wall."

"When I approach a wall, I look for something near the front of the wall that I can use as a little springboard. I make sure I get as much speed as possible when approaching the wall at a 45 degree angle and, as soon as I hit the springboard, I leap with all my strength and throw my arms up to get more momentum. As I come at the wall and my feet make contact with it, I continue running up. When I come close enough to the top, I make one last leap and throw myself to the top. In the exercise, I could have made it all the way over, but I knew I needed to secure my position on top in order to help Jack and Michael."

When she finished, she looked around and said, "It's pretty easy to do if you practice a little." She looked at Jack and said, "It should be a piece of cake for you!"

She looked at the trainers and said, "There are probably limits depending on the person's weight and height, and I figure that I can probably handle up to 10 feet without a springboard. From 10 to 12 or 13 feet I need something to spring off of. Above that, I would probably not succeed, but a taller person might if they can get enough speed and aren't too heavy." Then she smiled at everyone and took a swig of her Diet Coke.

Todd smiled and thought. *Here is this 16 year old girl teaching 10 experienced and fit men how to get over a wall with no help. What will she do next?*

# 18 A Break with Jim and Grace

Jim and Grace visited her for the first time shortly after the wall-walk incident. Todd met them first and told them how well she was doing. "Schea has earned the respect of all of the men and they really seem to enjoy having her as a part of the group." He, of course, did not tell them about the fight with Gus. "Schea is out on a training exercise and will be back in about an hour."

Todd showed them around the camp, took them to the dining area and then to Schea's room. "If Schea wants to show you her room, then that is okay, but everyone's privacy is rigorously observed at the camp, so even I will not enter Schea's room without her permission." He hoped that he made both Jim and Grace understand that Schea was respected and well cared for.

They were in Todd's living room when they heard a soft knock on the door. Todd opened it and Schea came in. He had left her a note telling her to come to his living room when she returned but did not tell her why.

Schea quickly moved to them and gave each a big hug. When they finished, Todd told them to stay and help themselves to anything in the kitchen, then he left to check with the trainers on the day's exercises.

Jim, Grace and Schea sat down, Jim on the chair and Grace and Schea next to each other on the sofa. They asked, "How are you doing? Do you like it? Are you eating?" All of the things parents would ask their kids when they came home from summer camp. Schea reasoned that this was sort of like summer camp and smiled inwardly. Jim filled her in on the adventure business and updated her on how the guides were doing.

Grace updated Schea on Jenny and told Schea, "Jenny is doing well and having a good time with her new brother and sister, mostly the sister! Jeff and Mary treat her just like a daughter and dote on her often, but not too much because of the other kids. Jenny asked us to say hi once we had a chance to see you and that she remembers your caution about not mentioning any of this to anyone."

After about an hour, they walked over to the dormitory. Schea introduced Jim and Grace to anyone who was around and they all said hi. She then took them to her room. Grace and Jim looked around and saw how neat and organized it was. Her bed was made and her things were either neatly organized on her desk or dresser, and a small bookcase had 15 books neatly placed on the shelves. Grace was thinking that this was a little new for Schea. She had never been a messy kid but had also never been a *neat freak*.

As they went back through the dining area, they were met by Todd. He walked with them out to their car and told them that they could visit again in the next 3 months for a few hours or Schea could visit them for a weekend, but they needed to contact him first in order to make sure Schea would be in camp. He said good-bye and left them to their hugs and kisses. There were no tears, only sighs of wishing it could have been longer. *Maybe next time*, she thought. Schea waved as they drove away then, once they were out of sight, she went up to her room.

Grace and Jim were quiet as they drove away. Grace was thinking again about how neat Schea's room had been. She reasoned that this might be Schea's way of getting some kind of order in her life after all of the turmoil she had gone through these past 6 years. Finally, she turned to Jim and asked what he was thinking. He thought a moment then said, "I thought she looked great and that this was definitely the right thing for her."

"I agree." Grace replied. But she also knew that she would be really worried once Schea became an active operative in Todd's business.

# 19 Finishing

Training progressed well over the next several months. Jack and several others mastered Schea's *Wall Walk*, which is what they started to call it. When Todd told Schea that he and the trainers were going to insert this technique into their training manual, she said, "Cool!"

Schea continued to excel in the physical exercises, and with a little additional training, she could easily qualify for the United States Olympic team in running, swimming and shooting. She also improved her tracking skills with Kevin's help and added several more moves and punches to her martial arts skills thanks to Jack. Lenny focused on her small-arms shooting skills since she was already a highly skilled sniper.

And, she lived up to her nickname. On some of the exercises, her team won because Schea could never be found in order to be taken down. On a couple of occasions, even after the exercise was over, she stayed hidden. The first few times, Todd got worried that something may have happened to her but then she would suddenly appear, seemingly emerging out of thin air.

Todd had harangued her for doing it but eventually gave up. Instead, he told her that when an exercise was over, she needed to come in. If she didn't, everyone would head back to camp and just leave her. She smiled and said okay.

After the next exercise and after Schea did not emerge from cover, the group went back to the camp. When they came in and went to the dining area, there was Schea, sitting in her usual spot with a Diet Coke. She had also laid out snacks and cold beers for everyone. They all smiled and said, "Thanks, Ghost!"

An area where she needed lots of help was driving large vehicles. She was good on two-wheeled vehicles, like motorbikes, scooters and motorcycles. She could also handle 3-wheelers pretty well, mainly because they were so much fun to ride. However, 4 large-wheeled vehicles could be a problem for her since her legs were often too short to reach the pedals. Adjustments could be made for her but only if time and materials were available. Unfortunately, neither of these would generally be available in the field.

Schea was comfortable around technology and could quickly learn just about any of the smart devices with little instruction but didn't seem interested in expanding her knowledge in the area. Todd talked to her about this at one point. "Schea, technology can be your only friend in some situations. It can help you find someone or, more importantly, how to get away from a particular place."

Schea listened politely then pointed out, "But, the reverse is also true, right? I mean, if you have a technology device and are using it, someone else can find you and track you."

He agreed but said, "Yes and there are ways to avoid that like removing SIM cards and batteries or using burner phones."

Another area Todd worried about was her lack of social interaction skills. When not involved with training, she might sit with various members of the group but not fully engage herself with anyone. She'd answer questions but rarely asked them. She could talk about running, tracking, and martial arts, but knew little about sports, music, movies, TV shows and various entertainers. On one visit to her room to answer a question she had about a training task, he noticed how organized everything was in her room. He also knew from his discussions with the trainers and other trainees that none of them had ever been invited into her room. He needed to get her to work on this.

At the six month point, Randall left. At 7 months, Todd introduced the group to a new trainee. He was another young recruit, 28, and his name was Frank Katts. Frank was 5 feet 8 inches, 180 pounds and had been a champion wrestler in high school and college. He had been about to try out for the Olympic team, when he injured his shoulder. It was fine now, but he had missed his chance. Frank had also spent a few years in the army and had been recommended to Todd by a friend.

Todd proceeded to introduce everyone and got to Schea last. Frank smiled and said hello. He then asked Schea to come over to his office for a minute to go over the *Wall Walk* wording for the training manual.

After they left, the group started chatting to Frank and he with them about where they were from and what they did before joining the camp. At one point, Frank glanced towards Todd's office and asked if the little girl was Todd's daughter.

When he looked back at the group, all he saw were smiles and several chuckles. Gus was groaning as he remembered the day that he thought that she was just a little girl. Finally, Frank asked, "What did I say?"

Lester came over to him and smiled as he said, "No, she is not Todd's daughter and she is not related to anyone here. She is a trainee like you."

He couldn't believe it so he smiled and said, "Stop fooling around. She can't be a trainee. Tell me who she really is."

Frank glanced around and everyone was smiling.

Gus said, "Go ahead and tell him what she would do if he ever made that comment in front of her."

Frank looked even more confused and turned back to Lester.

Lester was feeling a little sorry for Frank, but was still not going to let him off easily. So he put his arm around Frank's shoulder and calmly said, "If you ever tell Schea that she is some little girl and couldn't handle the training then she will rip something personal off of your body and make you eat it."

Frank looked back in horror then he smiled again, still thinking that this was some kind of initiation thing that everyone had to go through. However, he was also getting a little nervous because there were no giggles and no one seemed to be indicating that this was some kind of joke. He finally shrugged and said, "Okay, whatever you say."

XXXXX

After a month of training and watching Schea perform, Frank was glad he had kept his mouth shut. He was amazed at some of the things she could do and decided to try being friends with her.

Frank, like Jack, easily learned the *Wall Walk*. After he learned it the first time, he commented that this was a really nifty skill. He asked one of the trainers how it had come about. The trainer said Schea invented it. Schea was working on something nearby and Frank glanced over and said, "She is pretty amazing."

One afternoon, Todd walked into the dining area to see one of his trainers. As he walked over to him he noticed Schea and Frank sitting at a table talking. They would laugh at times and overheard him say that *Les Miserables* was one of the best movies he had ever seen and that the music was amazing. She said that she had never seen it so he said he'd ask Todd if they could rent it and watch it in the dining area on Todd's laptop.

When asked, Todd thought it was a good idea. Schea was learning how to open up to people and seems to be gaining social skills because of Frank. Todd would have to watch them during the next month to see how this progresses.

XXXXX

On one training exercise, Frank was supposed to be searching for a hiding place in order to store weapons. The others were searching as well and they would all meet in 15 minutes. He quickly went to the edge of the camp property and dug through some underbrush where he found a phone. He opened it and hit a button that dialed a pre-stored number. When the call went through he said, "Contact", took out the SIM card and battery and broke the phone apart. He threw all of that over the fence.

He made it back to the others a minute late but no one said anything.

XXXXX

Todd knew he was approaching decision time with regards to Schea because it would be a year in a couple of months since she had come to him. Gus and Glen had already departed and Michael and Jack would depart next month while 2 new trainees would join the group in a few weeks. This was a busy time for him and maybe he used that as an excuse to not think about Schea's upcoming departure. But, he had to start now because it was important to her and, frankly, to him.

The one sticking point for him was always her age since she would be barely 17 when she was finished with her training. *Could he or should he send someone her age out to the field to kill bad guys. Well that has been what all of this training has been about.* He had specifically taken her on because he felt she could be involved in a lot of field work where others could not. He had to decide, but not now.

81

The 2 new recruits were doing well and had been told the same story about Schea as had Frank. The only problem is that one of them did not believe it.

As they were heading out on a training exercise 2 days after they had arrived, one of them shouted at Schea that if she needed some help, then he was her man. She had smiled and asked him what he meant by that. Unfortunately, the idiot actually told her what he meant by his comment and, just like Gus, he found out that, not only did Schea not need his help but he would probably be the one asking for help over the next week or so while he healed up from the pounding she had given him in the ring.

A year after Schea had entered training, Todd asked her to come by after she helped clean up the dining area following dinner. He was sitting in his office when she stepped through the door. He asked her to sit and if she wanted something to drink. She said no so he went to the kitchen to get a beer. He knew she knew she was finishing up her training and probably figured this was the meeting to discuss what is next.

"You have exceeded all of my expectations. You mastered all of the weapons training requirements, the survival scenarios and the planning exercises. As a result, now that you are 17, I want to know if this is still what you want to do. Do you in fact want to go into the field to kill bad people?" He put it bluntly because he wanted her to clearly know what she would be expected to do.

Before she could answer, he continued. "This is not a desk job. You will be cold, hungry and alone most of the time. You will probably be chased by lots of really bad people who will likely try to kill you. You will possibly have to interact socially with despicable people in order to get the job done. You will probably be touched or even groped in many situations and be assaulted. You will be away from family and friends for unknown periods of time with absolutely no contact with them. You might lose family and friends while working and never know it until the job is done and you get home."

"So, do you still want to be accepted into this organization and be sent on missions that could result in some or all of those things happening?"

Without hesitation, Schea told him, "Yes, I still want to do this. This is exactly what I want to do, even more than when I arrived."

"I love Jim and Grace and have come to love the Kennedys as well. I also, of course, love Jenny with all my heart. The thought of any of these people being taken from me by rotten, conniving, sick bastards like those that took my brother, parents and sister scares me. If I can prevent even one of these bastards from hurting one more person, then that is what I want to do, and the sooner, the better."

Todd sat back, looked at her for a moment then said, "Okay, you now work for me and I will have an assignment for you soon. In the meantime, continue with your training like nothing has changed, because it hasn't. Tomorrow evening, we will meet again and I will go over some rules covering your assignments and who you will be while in my employment."

# 20 The First Mission

Schea arrived home after the coffee shop, had lunch and set the dishes in the sink to be washed later. She wandered into the living room, and grabbed her laptop to contact Jenny. She had emails from her friend Alice who is a friend and lives near Portland, Oregon. She responded to Alice and as she finished, her phone rang.

She answered knowing it was probably Todd. He said, "Welcome back! How was the Turkish hospitality?"

Schea replied, "Thanks, and it was most pleasant. Are you coming to my place?"

"Nothing like jumping to the point, but then, what else would I expect from my best operative?"

She laughed. "Just answer the question, buddy!"

"Okay girl, I'll be there in a couple of hours and you will take me out to dinner. And, it better be someplace nice."

"Oh, don't worry. I have several special places in mind to take you."

"That's what I am afraid of. See you in two hours. Be ready to deploy for sustenance." He hung up before she could come back at him.

She smiled and was actually looking forward to seeing Todd. He had become such a good friend to her these past 2 years and was like a father figure in some ways. She made herself a cup of Earl Grey to take out to the deck. She recalled the day she got her first assignment from Todd.

XXXXX

Schea came into Todd's office after dinner the day after he had told her that she now worked for him. They sat in his living room and he grabbed a beer for himself and a Diet Coke for her. The coffee table separated them and Todd had placed several folders on it. He took each and reviewed what was inside with her.

The first one was a court order for Schea to be manumitted from the need for guardianship. It gave her access to her trust fund and the phone number of the trust's manager. He said she should change the number as soon as she meets with the manager so that only she and the manager have the number but, he said, she might want to consider sharing it with someone she absolutely trusts. If she did this, then she and this person could create a code word which would tell the friend that Schea needed access to her account but couldn't do it on her own. This person could then contact the manager and give him her instructions for how to get the particular amount of money to her.

The next item was her job description at Todd's Security Firm. She was designated as a Research Assistant. She had a salary of $65,000 per year with 21 days of paid vacation and 2 weeks of paid sick time. Her hours of work were unspecified and she must be prepared for extensive and lengthy overseas traveling. She looked up at him after she read all of this and smiled. "Welcome to the company." He explained that this needed to be on file in case an audit of his books was done or a certain government agency wanted to know about his business expenses.

"The salary is real and will be deposited monthly in an account that you should set up. I would suggest you use the money on a regular basis because we don't want anyone who might look at that account to get suspicious. Also, avoid linking Jenny to any accounts, transfers, or other transactions because they can be monitored and traced."

"The client will pay my company for any missions you handle. It is usually 50% up front then the remainder once the mission is completed. I will put your share, which will be 80% of the total, into an account that you control. All of your fake passports, accounts, IDs, drivers licenses and other documents are different, but they all indicate your age as being at least 21, some as old as 30."

The last item was the key to her lock box. "You have been assigned a lock box at a small bank in downtown Portland. You need to specifically ask for the manager and tell him you have important documents to retrieve for Todd Groden. The manager will then show you to a secure room where the lock box is located. My key will remove the lock box and your key will open it. You must wait until you are alone in the room before you open it. Inside the box, you will find your various passports and documents, as well as cash in a variety of currencies for you to use until you begin getting paid for your assignments."

"You are lucky because, since you are so young, your DNA and finger prints are in no one's files. You've never been in trouble or in the military or in any position where your samples needed to be taken, however, wear gloves when possible and to try to keep your DNA out of any mission environments, if possible." Before she could say anything, he smiled and said, "I understood that can sometimes be hard to do, but you should keep it in mind anyway."

He recommended that she continue to try to learn more about popular topics, such as entertainment, sports and politics and to remain current on the trends in these areas.

When he finished, he asked if she had any questions. She told him no and said she would get started on the manumitting process and bank stuff right away.

He smiled and said, "Well, you are now officially out of training." She grinned broadly.

XXXXX

Todd lent Schea a car and she left the camp after packing up her things and saying bye to anyone around. She then spent a few days with Jim and Grace where Jim helped her with the legal process and bank stuff. He did not ask any questions and only provided the moral support, if needed. When they weren't doing this stuff, they relaxed at the house and talked about some of the clients they had over the past year. Jim also told her some funny stories about several misadventures with the clients – falling off horses was a common habit for clients.

One client and his son had hired Jim to take them on a weekend camping trip. The boy was 14 and the father figured they'd probably only get one last chance to bond before the boy got into his teenage mindset. One night the boy wandered away from the camp where they had pitched their tents and the dad told him not to go far.

Pretty soon they heard loud screaming and what sounded like a bull elephant charging through the trees. The next thing they saw was the boy racing towards them screaming, slapping his face and flapping his arms. Then they heard what he was yelling - bees! They all jumped into the truck after closing up the tents. The bees finally got bored with the whole thing and went home.

Schea was laughing during the whole story and, right before Jim got to the part about jumping into the truck, Grace got up and went into the kitchen. Jim knew she was probably having a hard time dealing with what Schea would be doing with her life soon.

It was a nice three-day visit, but it eventually came to an end and Schea drove back to the camp. As she headed back, Schea thought. *One of these days I need to get my own car.*

# 21 Mission One: Mendoza (Part 1)

Upon returning, Schea went into Todd's office. Todd picked up the last folder, opened it, set it down and looked up at Schea who sat quietly. He could tell she was nervous and desperately wanted to know what her first mission was going to be.

He began by reminding her that she needs to remember why he selected someone like her, a young girl, to work for his company. She nodded. "One of the main reasons is that these targets are mostly men who like young girls and the younger the better, and your first mission involves one of our." He hated to have to put her in the company of these creeps but he also knew that she could handle it and would not be deterred from completing the mission. He gave her the background on the target of her mission.

"Your mission involves this man," and he put a picture in front of her. It showed a middle-aged man, probably Mexican by the look of him. "This photo was taken in secret by an informer working for their client." He reminded her that she would never know the client unless absolutely necessary. She nodded and continued to stare at the photo.

"This is Alvarez Mendoza and he is a leading drug dealer and member of a Mexican drug cartel. He is known to be responsible for numerous revenge killings, but none have been proven. One of Mendoza's small side businesses is kidnapping. He kidnaps only young women or small families with young girls. He holds them for ransom, but whether the ransom is paid or not, he always kills the victims. Unfortunately, not before he repeatedly sexually assaults the women."

"Three months ago he kidnapped a young family of four while they were vacationing along the Pacific coast of Mexico at a villa they owned. The husband was the son of a very wealthy Mexican industrialist. The father refused to pay the ransom and hired a well-known security firm that specializes in hostage rescue, but they failed to get there in time."

"Mendoza somehow found out about the planned rescue, and had all 4 members of the family murdered and left in a nearby garbage dump. He also left a video at their vacation residence addressed to the father. The police found it, watched it and advised the father not to watch it, but he insisted."

"All of the men in the video wore stocking caps that covered their faces. The video showed 5 men standing to the side of the family. The father and mother were tied to chairs that were bolted to the floor. The 2 daughters, age 13 and 15, were each being held by one of the kidnappers. They were crying and the father was yelling at the kidnappers to leave them alone."

Todd took a deep breath and looked straight into Schea's eyes. "The men began assaulting the 2 girls in front of their parents. Both of the parents begged and screamed for them to stop. They did not. The girls screamed at first, but then they seemed to start losing their minds and just kept mumbling."

"After an hour of this, both girls simply stopped moving and lay on the concrete floor bleeding from various cuts and covered in bruises. The mom looked as though she had passed out. The father simply moaned over and over saying, please stop."

"At this point the men held both parents' heads up so that they could see the 2 girls. One of the men stepped over the prone girls, pulled out a long machete and slit the girls open. Then, they untied the mom, assaulted her for an hour in front of her husband and slit her open. The father was simply killed. The bodies were put in garbage bags then dumped on the town's garbage heap. The video ended with that."

During the whole time Todd told Schea this gruesome story, she only blinked once. When he finished, she only asked one question, "Where's Mendoza now?"

Todd told her to wait a bit more. He said, "The authorities investigated the deaths of course, but only found one match to the DNA that was left behind. It was Mendoza's because he had been held over-night at one point several years before and they had taken his DNA. The other 4 men did not seem to have DNA on file or maybe the Mexican databases are not that well maintained. The latter is more likely the case."

"Mendoza's lawyers convinced the jury that his DNA had been put there by the ruthless killers. He also had people testify that he was with them so he couldn't have done this terrible crime. Nothing happened to him and the other 4 men could not be identified so that appeared to be it."

"The father of the young man hired his own security team to hunt down the 4 men and kill them, plain and simple. They found out where the 4 unidentified men were hiding out and, sometime later, they were found in several places around Mexico, dead from various causes. The authorities blamed the deaths on drug violence."

"Mendoza's security is fairly good so the father's hired security team had to finally tell him that Mendoza was untouchable. The father has now come to us." Todd paused and waited for Schea to say something and she did. Again, she asked where Mendoza was now, a little more firmly this time. He figured he had better wrap this up soon and get Shea on her way before she starts pounding on him.

"Mendoza is staying at his expansive villa located about 75 miles south of Monterrey. It is well guarded and has walls surrounding the compound." He handed her a picture taken from above the compound by a drone that the father purchased.

Schea thought for a few minutes and Todd said nothing. "The road leading up to the villa appears to be the only one," and she looked at Todd.

"Yes, it is the only road and it leads directly to the villa from a small town located about a mile away. Some of the guards go to the town for drinks when off duty. It is suspected that they are also keeping an eye out for any strangers that show up and seem overly interested in the villa."

"All of the guards have quarters on the villa grounds. The staff of the villa numbers about 15, which includes the cleaning staff, kitchen help and gardeners, and they all live in the village. Mendoza is married, but his wife is currently traveling in Europe with their son for the next 2 months looking at potential schools for him."

"Mendoza's mistress stays in the villa with him while his wife is gone. He stays there all of the time now and we suspect that he might be waiting for the father to give up hunting for him, which he will not do, or Mendoza is expecting something nasty to happen to the father because he may have initiated a plan to have the father disappear. All of this means that we do not have much time to get to Mendoza. We want to have him eliminated before Mendoza's wife returns and before something happens to the father."

Todd waited a minute while Schea digested the information. Schea asked, "The household staff gets to and from the village by some form of transportation provided by the villa, right?"

"Yes. A truck drives to the village every morning at about 7 am, they all climb into the back of the truck and the truck takes them into the compound. We presume that the guards do a quick search of everyone before they head for their respective jobs."

"Later, at about 4 pm, the truck brings all but 3 people from the kitchen staff back to the village. We presume that the 3 people left behind stay until Mendoza and any guests have completed eating, and everything has been cleaned and put away for the next day. They probably prepare snacks or light breakfast fair in accordance with Mendoza's instructions."

Schea finally outlined her plan. "I will enter Mexico along the coast east of the villa and travel at night to a position near and slightly above the village. I will observe the workers going to and from the village to the villa, as well as the actions of the guards who are with the truck. I will then move to a position near and slightly above the villa where I can observe the guards and their routines along with the staff."

"I am hoping I might be able to observe some of the internal movements through a window, if possible. I want to observe Mendoza and his mistress as much as possible. I will try to determine a way to hide on that truck as it goes into the villa and, once inside the villa, I will make my way to a point where I can be unseen until nightfall then I will sneak into the house and wait for the staff to leave."

"Once the kitchen staff has gone and everyone seems to be sleeping, I will make my way to Mendoza's bedroom. I will try to make sure the mistress is not hurt and once he has been eliminated, I will make my way out of the villa and back to the coast. I'll stow a small bag in some rocks where I originally landed that contains a phone or other device that I can use to get extracted."

Todd thought a minute and asked, "What will you do if you cannot find a way to hide on the truck?"

"Another option will be to waylay one of the staff and pose as them or as a replacement. If that isn't possible, then I can play up to one of the guards while he is having a few drinks in the village and try to convince him to take me up to the villa for the boss to enjoy."

Todd was about to say something about the last option, but stopped himself. He realized that it could work because, after all, that was why he had hired Schea. She was trained to pull off that role.

Instead, he asked, "Once inside, what will you do about the mistress?"

"I hope the mistress sleeps in another room but, if she sees me, then I will not allow the mistress to cry out and alert Mendoza or the guards. The mistress will have to be silenced either before or at the same time as Mendoza. If it's before, and it is reasonable enough to gag and tie her up, then I will do that. Otherwise, she will have to be collateral damage."

Todd nodded. "Do you think you need some type of backup escape plan?"

Schea thought for a moment and said, "I might but I won't know what it should be until I actually need it."

"Okay, contact me as soon as you realize it. I will arrange for your delivery and pick up on the coast. I know several current and former operatives that can handle that job nicely."

Schea told him she would need a few weapons and a pair of high powered night vision binoculars that could also be used in the daytime. She also wanted a burner phone with a solar charger, in case it died before her return. She would go through her clothes to make sure she had the right attire for each phase of the operation. Todd gave the key to the weapons storage room to her and told her to pick whatever she wanted.

She left and chose a suppressed 45 pistol with a 15 round mag. She then moved to the knives. She wanted 4 just in case she had to throw one or two. She selected 2 small knives for throwing and 2 good sized serrated killing knives. She wasn't going to have a lot of room on her person for much more than these. Since she had already cleaned out her room and had placed her stuff in Todd's living room, she searched through her clothes there and found what she needed.

Todd told her that after she left, all of her clothes, books and other miscellaneous items will be put into a storage locker in Portland. Instructions will be placed in her lock box, so she should take her key and give it to Jim to hold.

XXXXX

She borrowed Todd's car, drove to Jim's and left the key. She only told them that she had to go to work. Jim nodded, Grace smiled, gave her a hug and Schea returned to the camp a short time later.

Once she had all her items packed and ready, they drove to Redmond, Oregon and went to a private airstrip outside of town where a small plane was waiting for them. Schea had her items in a backpack.

Todd looked at Schea, smiled and said, "Have a nice trip."

She smiled and said, "I'm looking forward to a little down time from all of this training stuff."

Todd grinned and she turned, walked to the plane and handed her bag to the pilot who put it into a storage compartment near the plane's tail. She climbed in with the pilot and he started the engine. As they started to taxi, she took a quick glance at Todd who looked back at her then walked to his truck. She was now on her own.

XXXXX

The flight lasted 4 days since they had to stop for fuel and rest. They only spoke of mundane things and never talked about anything personal, and certainly nothing about her mission. Schea spent much of the time enjoying the views from the plane. She figured that the pilot had done this type of thing a number of times for Todd. The only thing that she noticed was that he seemed to be surprised when she was the only one who climbed into the cockpit. When they rested, it was at cheap hotels located close to the airstrips. There was always someone waiting to take them to the hotel and back to the plane.

They finally ended their journey on a small airstrip near Corpus Christi, Texas. The pilot taxied the plane to a deserted area off to the side of the landing strip, turned off the engine and got out as did Schea. He went to the storage hold, got her backpack and handed it to her. She said thanks, but he said nothing and went back to the cockpit.

She walked toward a waiting car near the side of an old hangar. She didn't turn, but she heard the plane takeoff. The man waiting in the car put her bag in the trunk, opened the rear door for her then headed away from the airport.

He said nothing during the 2 hour drive and, when he finally stopped, Schea saw that they were at a small pier. The driver opened her door, handed her bag to her, got back in and drove away. Schea surmised that this appears to be the way things operate in the field. No one talks or interacts with the operatives. That way, if asked, they can truthfully say that they know nothing about the person or what they were doing.

Schea walked down to the only boat that was at the dock. A man came out of the cabin of the boat, looked at her and asked if he could take her bag. Schea handed him the bag and let him guide her by the arm onto the craft. There was no one else on the boat and he told her that he would stow the bag in a compartment that was well hidden. This was in case someone wanted to search the boat.

He asked if she would like something to drink. He said he had beer, coffee and water and she asked for water. He got her the water and told her that the trip would take about 2 days depending on weather and sea conditions but, if all goes well, they should be at the destination around midnight 2 days from now. She nodded and he returned to his position at the helm. He started the engines, deftly pulled away from the dock and headed out to the open sea.

As with the pilot, the trip went fine and they only talked about mundane stuff. Schea was curious about the boat, so she asked a good many questions about the boat, navigation and what some of the instruments on the boat were for. The captain appeared pleased that she was interested in his little craft, so he delightfully told her all about his boat and the joys of sailing.

There was a small sleeping compartment forward under the deck off the boat and she slept there. During the 2 mornings they were together, he always welcomed her to another beautiful day and handed her a bottle of water.

Late on the second day, he told her they were getting close to their landing point. He told her to get her stuff ready in case someone got nosy. If they did, then she would need to decide to stay on the boat to explain what she was doing or she would need to quietly go into the water and swim to shore. If she decided to swim, then he would tell her where they were and make sure she knew which direction to go. But, he hoped that she would not have to do either. She smiled at him and said that she hoped so too.

At around midnight he told Schea they would be at the drop off shortly. He had already told her about what to expect in the area for homes, villages and people. He asked if she knew how to get where she was going and she said yes. He nodded and looked back towards the shore. After about 5 minutes, he told her to get ready and that she would feel a slight bump which was her signal to get off of the boat. He told her that the water was about 3 feet deep, so she would have to wade ashore. She nodded and thanked him for his help.

Suddenly she felt the bump, went over the side and waded to shore. By the time she walked onto the beach and turned around, the boat was nowhere to be seen. *Alone again!*

# 22 A Camp Break-In

Todd sat in his office 10 days after he had taken Schea to the airport. He knew she had made it to the coast because the pilot and boat captain had called in the code that told him their part of the mission had been a success. He figured she was probably at her observation post above the town or possibly at the villa. Based on the plan, she should be attempting to enter the villa in the next few days.

He had silently prayed for her when she had left and had decided to send along another prayer today. He told himself to stop worrying about her, but he had trouble doing it. He had to keep reminding himself that she was one of the best trained operatives he had and that he had hired her for the very reasons that she was now on this particular mission. Hers were going to be some of the most difficult missions and involve some of the vilest targets he would be asked to eliminate.

He hoped that she was utilizing her 'Ghost' skills well on this mission. She would certainly need them.

XXXXX

Todd was now concerned that someone seems to have snuck into his office when he was not around. When he came back from dropping Schea off at the airport, he noticed that one file drawer was slightly open. He didn't keep any data on the people at the facility except for an emergency contact number and some basic stuff just in case some official wanted to check on who was at the camp and what they were doing there.

His cover for the camp was that it was a sportsman's club. They also held training sessions on shooting, hunting and fishing. He and one of his trainers were certified to instruct in those areas, while all the rest were called guests.

He was glad that no one came around while Schea was here. It might have looked a bit strange to some people. After all, a 16 year old girl, living and training with a bunch of men, some twice her age, might have raised one or two eyebrows. He could have relied on Jim and Grace to back him up if any alarms were raised but it was still better that no one had come snooping around.

But now, it appeared that someone might be snooping around. He had the area where the buildings are located electronically secured against bugs and signaling devices, but he had no cameras anywhere. He didn't want any of his operatives caught on *Candid Camera* at some later date.

Maybe he would install a small camera in his office temporarily to make sure there was no threat. If after 3 or 4 months there was nothing on it, then he could remove and destroy all video footage.

It might be someone in the camp or outside who infiltrated the camp. The camp was well protected but it wasn't high level stuff, which might look really suspicious to an outsider.

He really needed to find out who was snooping around and what they might have been after.

# 23 Mission One: Mendoza (Part 2)

Schea had made good progress that first night after getting on the beach. She traveled about 20 miles then rested during the day in a small shelter she put together in a stand of trees well away from any roads or buildings. She rested for about 10 hours, sleeping for 6 of those. She had been a little stiff from all the traveling she had done the day before but last night's easy 4 hour jog helped her to loosen up. Now that she was loose and well rested, she figured that she would be looking at the town by early morning in 2 days.

The countryside she was traveling through was hilly and covered with mostly small trees, bushes and grasses. She was carrying several bottles of water and a bunch of MREs but knew she would eventually need to find additional food and water.

The village she was going to was a few miles from the slightly larger town of Linares and she didn't even know if the village had a proper name. Maybe it had grown there when they were constructing the villa and simply continued on after all the construction was completed. She hoped she might be able to buy or find some additional water and food outside of Linares before arriving at the village.

She approached the village just before sunup 2 days later. She had hidden during the day and snuck food and water from homes, shops and huts but no one seemed to notice she had been there.

After arriving, she found a small hill just south of the village to observe from. She set her pack aside, pulled out her binoculars to watch the early-morning activities, and saw people moving about just as the sky was brightening. After about an hour she noticed a small group of people congregating near what looked like a small café and figured these were probably the people who make up the villa's staff.

Sure enough, a short time later, a large pick-up truck rumbled along the road from the villa and stopped in front of the café. No one exited the truck, but there was one guard sitting in the back watching the people climb in. The people just jammed into the back and sat on the sides or floor of the truck. Once they were all loaded up, the guard in the back did a head count then banged the side of the truck. At that point, the truck drove off toward the villa.

Schea figured, if this was how it went each morning then she would not be able to hide somewhere on the truck. Besides, even if no one stayed with the truck, she didn't see any places she could hide. She settled in, waited until nightfall and watched again as the truck returned. The guard counted them as they left, and when he was satisfied the people who had gone into the villa had all departed the villa, the truck drove back to the villa.

She continued watching the village to see if she could determine where the staff and the guards might hang out in the evenings. It seemed that most people out in the evenings were hanging at a building located on the opposite side of town from the café. She didn't see anyone that looked like a guard, but she did believe that several of the people were from the villa staff. As it got closer to midnight, the village seemed to shut down for the night.

The next morning, the same loading routine occurred. She was now focused on option 2 to get into the villa. Maybe she could pose as one of the staff. She tried to watch each person more carefully this time as they walked to the café, milled around and climbed into the truck. She did the same when they returned. She really did not think that there was anyone she could replace physically, and worse, it seemed that they all knew each other quite well which would make it impossible for her to sneak into the group as one of them.

She was now looking at option 3. She watched the clubhouse, as she decided to call it, for any signs of some of the guards. The truck never came back on either night, so she figured that any guards coming to the town would either have their own vehicle or would have to walk.

She finally saw one guy who was probably a guard walk to the village. She reasoned he was a guard because he walked directly to the clubhouse and was a bit larger than any of the other men in town.

XXXXX

She decided to go out to the villa and arrived there 2 hours before sunup. She located a hill with a clump of small trees and bushes nearby, and decided to wait there. After she dozed briefly, she started watching the villa. There wasn't much activity that she could see until just after the sun came up over the eastern horizon. It was at her back, so that made watching the morning activities a bit easier.

She finally saw movement around several of the buildings that were near the outer wall of the compound. They were all men and looked to be guards. They all seemed to be smokers and most carried coffee cups. Most went into one of the buildings, stayed then came out eating rolls or other items they hadn't quite finished. *Must be the kitchen*, she thought.

Many also went into and out of a larger building and, since many could be seen fixing their pants and belts, she figured it must be the bathroom. Finally, she heard an engine rumbling and a truck came around the side of the compound. It stopped at the villa exit, a guard climbed in the back, the gate was opened, and they headed out to the village.

As Schea watched the compound during the day she saw other guards carrying weapons, mostly AK-47s, but there were also a few who carried shotguns. Each of them also had a handgun strapped in holsters around their waists.

As she observed the house, the first movement she saw was a young woman pulling open the curtains of a window directly in front of Schea's position. She was stark naked, beautiful and seemed to be fit. As the woman peeked out of the window and yawned, a man came up behind her, also naked, and wrapped his arms around her waist. It was Mendoza. *Good.* Schea figured this must be the bedroom and now knew where to find Mendoza at night.

XXXXX

The staff arrived in the truck a short time later. Most went into the house, while a few started clipping branches, cutting hedges, et cetera. Some of the inside staff would occasionally come out to get something from one of the buildings or to talk to a guard.

Mendoza never came out and she only saw him a couple of times during the day as he passed by a window on her side of the villa. The mistress came out once to tell a guard something while she pointed toward the village. He seemed to understand, nodded then left in the direction of the town.

The daytime activities seemed to be routine. The guards patrolled, the gardeners took care of the outside, and the indoor staff generally stayed inside. Late in the afternoon, the truck came around to the front, the staff loaded up then the truck pulled out of the compound and headed for the village.

Schea kept watching because she wanted to see if any guards went down to the village. Her patience was rewarded at 9 pm when one of the guards came over to the guard at the gate and said something to him. At one point he half turned and pointed back toward the house. The other guard seemed to understand and proceeded to open the gate. Schea recognized the guard that was leaving as the same one who had been in the clubhouse the night before.

She knew from the briefing material that the walls were 12 feet high, which was just about the limit for her to wall-walk over them. She decided that the only way for her to get in was through the front door which meant that option 3 was how she would do it.

Schea made her way back to the village and watched the clubhouse. At around midnight, she saw the guard begin to make his way back to the villa and decided that when this guard came to town again, she would wander into the clubhouse pretending to be a runaway from Texas.

XXXXX

The next evening, Schea waited and hoped that the guard would show up. Just after 9 pm, she saw two guards appear and one was her new "friend", although he did not know it yet. She had to decide whether to risk dealing with 2 of them or to wait until the following evening. She decided to risk dealing with 2.

She changed into jeans and a t-shirt, hid the knives but left the gun in the backpack then walked into the village and headed for the clubhouse. There were only 5 people in the place, all men, and 2 of them were the guards from the villa. There was also a guy at the bar who dispensed the beverages.

Schea was playing a vulnerable girl seeking help. She had a desperate and helpless look on her face and kept fidgeting with her hands. She eventually walked over to the table where the guards were sitting and said, "Excuse me. Do either of you speak English?"

They had seen her come in and seemed to be wondering what this strange young girl was doing in a place like this. The guard that she had seen before looked at her and said, "I speak a little English."

She stood shifting back and forth on her feet. "Um, I need help. I ran away from home in Raymondville, Texas because my dad was always drunk and beating my mom. He also slapped me around." She hesitated a little then continued. "Lately, um, he has been looking at me in a funny way." She looked down as she said that and the guards seemed to get her meaning. "I'm only 14 and don't like the way he looked at me. It was creepy." The guards frowned as though they were sympathizing with her.

She took a breath and continued. "I hitched a ride from a very nice old guy, who told me he was heading to Mexico. I told him that would be fine, but asked how we would get across the border. I don't have a driver's license or passport. He told me that the crossing he used was really lax on discipline and he had a friend who could get them across."

"At first, he was really nice and we crossed the border without any problems. As we drove along, he asked if I was hungry and I said sure. But, when we stopped it was just an old abandoned shack so I asked what was going on, but before I could get out of the car, he grabbed me and started trying to kiss me and touch me."

"I finally got away and hitched another ride with a group of men and women who seemed to be going to work at a farm. After that, another ride dropped me off near this village, so I decided to see if I could get some help. I really want to go home. I didn't bring my cell phone so I am hoping you will let me use one."

Her guard buddy said, "Sorry, but our phones are in the room at the villa where we work."

"I think I saw it, but the villa was so dark I decided to try here. It looked really big and fancy."

The guard said, "It is very big and owned by a very wealthy and important man. Please sit until we finish our beer then we can go to the house to let you use a phone."

She looked unsure but then sat down and the other guard brought her a beer. "I am only 14 and not allowed to drink. Me and some friends tried some beer one time but I didn't like it."

"Don't worry. You're old enough to drink in Mexico." The guard assured her.

She shrugged, thanked him and took a sip. She smiled and said, "It's not bad."

She avoided eye contact as much as possible but, at one point, she stretched as though she was tired, but it was so they could get a good look at what was under her t-shirt. She had purposely not worn a bra and they liked it.

Finally, they finished their beer and asked, "Are you ready to go? It's only a short walk to the villa."

"Okay, but I need to go to the bathroom first."

She went around to the bathroom and quickly moved two knives into the back waistband of her jeans then pulled her t-shirt over them. The other two were strapped to the inside of each leg and left the gun in her backpack. She suspected that she was not supposed to make it to the villa with these guys. In that case, when she was done with them, she was going to have to figure out a way to fool the gate guard into thinking that she was there for Mendoza's enjoyment.

If these guys did take her to the villa, there was only a 20% chance that they would turn her over to Mendoza still chaste. They would want her for themselves and it might even turn into a romp with all of the guards. She steeled herself for what was to come and went out to the table where they sat patiently.

As she approached, and before they saw her, she noticed that they had their heads together and were softly whispering. As soon as they saw her, they stopped and smiled at her. She gave them a sweet smile and thanked them again for helping her.

The guard said, "No problem." He then pointed to the other guard and said, "He will follow later. Are you ready?"

She nodded and they walked out the door.

She guessed they were not going to wait until they got to the villa. This guard would pretend to take her to the villa then his buddy would jump her from behind. They would both assault her and take her to the villa for the rest of the guards to have their way with her.

She actually thought their plan was better for her. She could take them one at a time pretty easily, but 2 at the same time might be a little more of a problem. *Yes, one at a time was better for me*, she mused.

They strolled toward the villa. They chatted and he told her how sorry he was that her father was such a mean man and she nodded thanks. About 100 yards from the village, he turned to face her and said that she would need to wait here while he peed. Schea said nothing.

She watched his eyes and sensed that he was going to move on her so she whipped a knife out from the back of her waist and jammed it into his neck. He had no time to react and couldn't have yelled if he had wanted to since his voice box and everything around it were now just mush. He slowly collapsed.

She used his shirt to wipe the blood off of her face but left a little on her shirt. She dragged him into a nearby ditch and covered him up with whatever she could find. She had to move quickly because she figured guard number 2 would be along shortly.

When she finished with him, she walked about 10 yards back towards the village. This way, she could intercept number 2 as he snuck up from behind. She lay on the gravel road and rolled around a bit to get dirty as though she had been struggling. She tore the front of her t-shirt and exposed one side of her chest. She also undid her jeans and pulled them down a little so that he could see her panties. She laid there waiting.

He arrived a few minutes later and she guessed he was pretty anxious. As he walked to her and looked down, she moaned and mumbled, "Why." He looked around for number 1 and must have figured that he had gone off to piss. He kneeled down over her, and began to paw at her chest.

As he started to tug at her panties, she quickly pulled her hand from behind her back and jammed the same knife number 1 got into number 2's neck. He jerked up and grabbed at his neck, but it was too late for him as well. As with number 1, the knife created a path of destruction all the way up to his brain, and he slumped over on his side.

Schea dragged him to the same ditch as number one. She laid him on top of number 1 and covered them with debris. She didn't want them found too soon. No one seemed to travel this road at this late hour and, if all went well with the next part of her plan, she would be in and out of the villa within the next 2 hours. That would put her on her escape route at least 4-5 hours before the excitement started tomorrow morning.

Before she left, she decided she needed something to show the gate guard that she was sent to the villa by number 1. She uncovered the guards and pulled number 2 aside. She scanned number 1 and saw what might do the trick. She noticed that number 1 was wearing the most ridiculously elaborate belt buckle she had ever seen. As she looked more closely, she noticed that the design in the center of this 3 x 4 inch thing showed a naked girl and guy. *Gross.* She removed the buckle, covered the guys up and walked towards the villa.

When she was about 50 yards from the villa, she moved off the road into a clump of bushes. She put on a clean shear blouse, removed her jeans and put on a short, but not too tight skirt. She showed just enough of her upper legs to make it interesting. She removed the knives from her waistband since they might raise an eyebrow or two. Instead, she hid the two throwing knives under her skirt, secured to the front of her thighs.

She left the two hunting knives and gun in her backpack knowing she could not take the backpack into the compound since it would surely be searched. She also hoped that the guard in the villa would not search her too thoroughly. If he did, well, then she'd have to develop a new plan. She hid the backpack in the bushes and strolled towards the gate.

For this role, she would not be a poor, shy little American girl. Instead, she would be a confident teenage hooker and had to convince the guard that she had been sent by number 1 specifically for Mendoza. She hoped the belt buckle would prove that she had been sent by number 1. She strolled to the gate and knocked on the big door. She only wanted to attract the gate guard's attention and not the whole compound. It didn't open, so she knocked again a little louder. Suddenly, she heard the bar on the other side move then the gate opened about a foot. The guard had to look down to see who it was.

He was pretty tall, so Schea looked up at him and gave him one of those lascivious smiles that she hoped would take his mind off of being cautious. She also put her hand on her breast and slowly rubbed it as though she might have an itch there. It worked. He opened the door wide and let her in a few feet.

He was probably hoping that this pretty little thing was just wandering around trying to earn a few bucks here and there. But, before he could say anything, Schea smiled, pulled out the belt buckle from the pocket on her skirt, held it up to him, and asked if he understood English. Still staring at her breasts, he said he did so she gave him her little speech.

"The master of the house asked this guard", and she wiggled the buckle, "to find him some play thing for the night. I am it. The guard told me that the lady of the house was away and his personal assistant wasn't feeling well and would not be unavailable tonight."

As she talked she kept looking around like she was bored with this whole thing and just wanted to do her job, get paid and leave. She even pretended to chew gum and looked at him impatiently. She could tell that he was thinking what his boss didn't know wouldn't hurt him.

He finally gathered himself up and asked where Hector was. She hoped that he was talking about number 1. She shrugged and said, "He was getting busy in the village and told me to go up to the house and show the guard at the gate his buckle."

She smiled at him, leaned in close and told him, "Maybe if you are interested, I could stop by after I am released by the master. I will only charge you half the price." She gave him a big smile and opened her eyes nice and wide. She also gently took his hand and placed it on one of her breasts. He squeezed a little too hard and Schea winced then gently removed his hand. As she did, she winked and said, "Later. The master is waiting."

He sighed, smiled and nodded okay. "I am the only guard at the gate tonight so when you come back out, just stop here and I will take us to a quiet spot."

She smiled at him conspiratorially.

# 24 Mission One: Mendoza (Part 3)

The gate guard closed and bolted the gate then led her to the front door, opened it and took her over to the guard inside the front hallway. They spoke in Spanish for a short time, the door guard nodded and the gate guard left, but not before he gave her a little wink as he went by her. She smiled sweetly at him.

Schea understood enough Spanish to know that the gate guard had not told the door guard about this being something that number 1 had been asked to do. Maybe he didn't believe her or maybe he wanted to take some of the credit - either way it seemed to work. She stood awkwardly while the door guard closed the door. She could feel his eyes on her back but did not turn to look at him. He told her to follow him.

They walked up the stairs and down to where Schea figured the master bedroom was located. Schea wasn't sure what she was going to do if the mistress was there. If the mistress was then she would have to take care of the guard, the mistress and Mendoza, which could be a challenge. She guessed that she would just have to see what was on the other side of the bedroom door and proceed accordingly.

When they got to the door, the guard knocked and waited. It took about half a minute but then Mendoza opened the door. He had his bathrobe open and it looked to Schea that he might have been busy. He seemed grumpy about this interruption but, as soon as he glanced at Schea, a neat little smile came over his face. He looked at the guard and asked, "What is this about?"

They spoke in Spanish, but it seemed to Schea that he was telling Mendoza the same story the gate guard had told him. Mendoza kept glancing over at Schea and she would give him a sweet smile in return. When the door guard finished, they all just stood there a few seconds then Mendoza dismissed the guard and opened the door for Schea to enter.

Schea did not see the mistress anywhere but she could just as easily be in another room or maybe the bathroom. She walked toward the bed then turned to look at Mendoza and he was looking at her with a great deal of interest. *Good. That would occupy his mind for a bit and he will not be thinking he is in danger.*

Mendoza switched to English and asked her to sit on the bed. She did. He came over and stood a few feet in front of her. "What is your name."

"Lisa."

"How old are you?"

She looked aside as if thinking about what to say then sighed and quietly said, "14."

"Where are you from?"

"I'm originally from Portland, Oregon but now …." She trailed off and shrugged.

"How long have you been doing this?"

She looked up at him with hard eyes and said, "Ever since my father raped me 2 years ago." She then looked away.

He sighed and sat next to her.

He put his hand on her shoulder and said, "I'm glad that you came to my house. You will be safe here and I will take good care of her." He moved his hand to her knee and gave it a little squeeze then started moving it up her thigh.

Schea was afraid that if she let him move his hand up her thigh much more, he would find the knives. But he stopped and leaned down so that he could look at her face.

"Would you like to live and work here?" he asked softly.

Schea looked at him, shrugged and said, "I guess that would be okay. I promise that I will be a good worker. I can clean and don't mind outdoor work either. I'm pretty strong for my size." Finally, she looked down again and mumbled, "I can do other things too."

He put his arm around her shoulders and gave her a little hug. "You will be a great addition to my staff."

He stood and removed his robe. He was naked and was obviously anxious to move on to the next activity.

Schea guessed that their conversation had moved his thoughts from one head to the other so she smiled and asked, "May I use the bathroom first?"

"Sure." He pointed to it.

Schea could see that the door was open so the mistress was not in there.

She got up, moved into the bathroom and closed the door. She leaned over the sink and ran the water. She splashed her face a couple of times, but did not dry it with any of the towels. She removed her blouse, took off her skirt and removed the 2 knives but left her panties on.

Schea calmed herself and picked up her 2 knives. She held one behind her back and opened the door with the hand that held the second knife, but only about an inch. She wanted him to anticipate the fun he wanted but would not have. She moved both hands behind her back and gently nudged the door open with her foot.

Schea stood there for a moment and shyly looked at Mendoza. He was lying on the bed and, at the sight of her, he pushed up onto his elbows and gave her a smile, but his eyes told a different story.

They held pain and she knew whose pain he thought it was for, but she had other plans regarding, and they did not include her.

Schea stepped in and walked around to the foot of the bed keeping her back turned away from him. His eyes followed her with rapt anticipation. She put one knee up onto the foot of the bed and then the other, still holding her hands behind her. As she did this, she leaned down a little so that he could focus on the breasts. She slowly knee-walked up to his feet, placed one knee on one side of him then the other knee along his other side.

It seemed to Schea that he couldn't decide which he wanted to look at, her breasts or her panties. His eyes kept moving up and down between them. *Good. This meant that he wasn't looking at my face.*

When Schea's knees were finally on either side of his knees, she started to lean in closer to him as though she were going to settle into his arms. She was watching his eyes and, when it looked like he had decided to place his arms around her, she struck, and the knife in her right hand came around from behind her.

The movement didn't seem to register in his mind and he realized too late what she was about to do. The knife entered just below his chin then moved into his brain. His body stiffened and he stared straight at her. Schea quickly moved to his side. Still holding her eyes on his, she took the other knife from behind her and proceeded to cut him open as he had done to those little girls.

His eyes seemed to suddenly realize what was happening to him because they instantly went wild with fear. She smiled and said, "Now you know how those poor little girls felt." She had no idea if he could hear or even understand her, but it felt good to just say those words to the sick bastard.

She left both knives in him for the moment and watched as he seemed to begin to realize what she had said but, just as quickly, his eyes turned blank. She got off of the bed and turned to go to the bathroom but then stopped. She turned and looked at him again as if her mind were working on something.

Schea walked back over to Mendoza and pulled the knife out of his neck. She glanced down at his now flaccid penis, reached over with one hand, grabbed his package, sliced it all off with one flick of the knife then proceeded to stuff them into Mendoza's mouth. It didn't fit well but she shrugged and pushed as much in as she could.

Schea walked into the bathroom, set the knife down on the sink and washed the blood off as best she could. She wiped the counter and anything else she had touched, put her clothes back on and secured the knife against her thigh again. She walked back into the bedroom and looked at the dead Mr. Mendoza. She pulled out the knife that was still stuck in his chest and wiped it off on the bed sheets.

Schea was about to put that knife into its sheath on her thigh, when she heard the doorknob turning on the bedroom door. She knew she had to kill whoever it was before they had a chance to

103

sound an alarm. She moved behind the door as it opened, and watched the mistress walk into the room. At first, it seemed as though she was trying to figure out where she was then she saw Schea and quickly glanced at Mendoza.

Schea saw at once what she was about to do and could not let that happen. Before any sound came out of her mouth, Schea jammed the knife into her throat. The mistress stiffened and fell backward with a thud, and Schea hoped that it wasn't loud enough for the guard to have heard. She quickly wiped the knife clean but did not put it away. She would likely need it again.

Schea's escape plan was to sneak by the door guard and deal with the gate guard. It was about 2 am, so there shouldn't be much going on. She went down the stairs, saw the door guard dozing in his chair and quietly exited the house. As she walked toward the gate, she noticed two guards just coming from behind the house. The gate guard had apparently told them to expect her in the early morning hours because they hardly gave notice.

Schea had turned her blouse inside out to hide the blood and to make it look to him like she had to leave Mendoza's room in the dark. As she walked up to the guard, she lightly stroked her thigh up and down, showing more of it for his delight. She came up to him and smiled. He smiled back and motioned for her to follow him to the side of his little guard post. She saw that he was apparently in a hurry. *Good, because so am I*, she thought. She noticed that they would be under the stars and lying on the damp grass.

The gate guard took her hand, leaned her against the wall, and started to feel her breasts. As he reached down for her crotch, she swung her arm around from behind her back and slit his throat from right to left. He gurgled up blood, stared at her then fell to the ground. Schea shoved him as far as possible into his little love nest, moved along the wall to the gate, lifted the locking arm, opened it and left.

Schea made her way to where she had hidden her backpack. She grabbed the backpack, moved behind some small trees, put on her running shoes and stuffed the sandals she wore for her rendezvous with Mendoza into her backpack. She took off at a run.

Schea wanted to be as far as possible from the compound by early morning. She could run a marathon easily in 3.5 hours, so that should put her one-third of the way to the coast. The plan was to go back to the coast the same way she had come and, when she reached the spot where she had landed, she would grab her burner, charge it and make the call to be picked up.

Schea arrived on the coast about 18 hours later after encountering no problems along the way. She found her burner but had to wait until daylight in order to charge it. She squeezed herself into a little group of rocks up from the beach and waited. She was nervous and excited at the same time.

Schea wanted to get back home, wherever that was going to be. Todd was finding a place for her to live but where exactly it would be, she didn't have a clue. She guessed it would not be far from the camp and his office, but she was pretty new to this operative business stuff.

She also had no idea what she would do or how to have a normal life. She would finally be really, really on her own and would be free to live where she liked, do what she wanted and make friends. Of course, this would all need to be within the limits of her job. *Wow, lots to think about. But not now. I need to get out of Mexico, and quickly.*

XXXXX

After the sun had been up for a few hours and the phone was charged enough to last a few minutes for the call to be made, she dialed a number and entered a code. Then, she sat and waited.

That evening she heard a faint distinct whistle, walked down to the water's edge, and looked out to sea. Slowly a boat emerged from the darkness. It bumped into the beach and Schea climbed aboard. Nothing was said and the boat headed back out to sea and to America. After the boat was about 100 yards from shore, Schea broke up the burner, disassembled the gun and tossed everything, including the knives, into the water.

Schea would burn her clothes, backpack and everything else she had taken with her, once she got to Texas. The captain had a new backpack waiting for her in the small cabin in the boat. She went into the tight space and changed into the clothes from the backpack. There was also a new burner, a purse with $3000 in cash and some makeup. She looked at the makeup and thought. *What is wrong with Todd? She never wore makeup, but she had to admit with a smile, it was still a very thoughtful gesture on his part.*

# 25 Dreams

Todd arrived at her house two hours after he had called about the Rahim mission. Schea invited him in and they sat on her deck - he with a beer and she with a Diet Coke.

Todd asked, "So, how did the mission go?"

Schea recounted the details about the trip over, Rahim, the shot and the trip home. When she finished that, she asked, "How has it been at the camp?"

"Oh, the usual stuff."

Schea smiled and nodded. "Yeah, secret stuff always makes for a short conversation."

Todd laughed. "Right. Secret stuff! Come on, let's go eat. I'm starved. I hope you are paid up on all your credit card bills because this could be a big charge."

Schea smiled, "Oh, don't worry. I just made a killing in my other job that earned me a big paycheck."

XXXXX

They had dinner at Pusser's Caribbean Restaurant and had fun reminiscing as much as they could, given that there were a lot of people around. One of the things they could talk about was when she got her first apartment, her first car and her first driver's license. She had not even had to take a driver's test to get it.

When they got back to her place, they hugged and he told her to take some time off. He didn't see anything coming her way for at least a month or so.

Schea made some tea and checked her emails. Alice had answered, said she was happy and hoped that Schea might be able to make some time to come out to Portland for a visit. Schea responded and told her she had some time off for a little while and would definitely try to get out to Boring.

She smiled because Boring is the small town where Todd had found a place for her after the Mendoza mission and she had given the apartment to Alice when she moved to Annapolis. Schea remembered when she'd first gotten to the apartment in Boring.

XXXXX

She sat in the little living room of her fully furnished apartment looking around at her own place. The apartment was just off of Meadow Creek Lane in Boring, Oregon, which is located 30 minutes east of Portland. The name suited this little, sleepy town quite nicely, but Schea didn't care. The last thing she wanted was a bunch of people and lots of traffic.

Todd rented the place for Schea and paid for one year in cash up front. The manager was thrilled and didn't ask him to sign some type of lease, which was exactly the point. He left the address in Schea's lockbox.

In the lockbox, she found a set of car keys and directions to where it had been parked for a month. He had also provided a valid Oregon driver's license in her name. The car turned out to be a Honda Civic and was only a few years old. It had GPS, which she had used it to get to her apartment.

When Schea first entered her place, she saw that all of her stuff had been brought in and placed in the middle of her living room. Todd also stocked the refrigerator with lots of Diet Coke. There was no food because he had no idea how long she would be away when he rented the place, and figured that she'd want to stock it herself.

XXXXX

Todd was now sitting in the living room, and had arrived about 2 hours ago. When she opened the door to let him in, she could see that he seemed happy to see her and they had spent most of the two hours going over the Mendoza mission. As she related all she had gone through and what she had had to deal with, he listened intently. Occasionally, he smiled or told her "Good thinking."

When she finished, he congratulated her and asked her to tell him what she had learned and if she had any regrets about the killings. She related some things about her preparations and some of her decisions which could have been better thought out. He nodded but didn't say anything. She also mentioned that she had been over weaponized because she had only needed the 2 knives.

He said she could have left the 2 hunting knives out of her kit, but it wasn't a bad idea to have a gun just in case the knives had to be thrown and couldn't be retrieved. Then he reiterated his question about regrets for the killings.

She thought a moment and said that the only one that bothered her was the mistress.

Todd told her, "Operatives will almost always have a kill that they think wasn't necessary or could have been avoided. It is for that very reason we do debriefings and reviews after every mission. No one is second-guessing, it is just part of the learning process." She nodded, but didn't say more.

He told her to take some time off and visit Jim and Grace but should put off visiting Jenny until they are sure that there will be no blow back from Mendoza's demise. He didn't think so, but it is always best to be careful.

As he got up to leave, he turned and said, "The client was extremely happy with the results. After reading the accounts in the official news releases, the client decided to get hold of the official report from his contact in the police department. He read it and was so happy with your special treatment of Mendoza that he gave you a 20% bonus for a job well done."

Before Todd opened the door, he turned and asked what she was thinking of doing. She smiled. "I will definitely visit Jim and Grace and send Jenny a short email." Then, she grinned. "I might also check to see how the boys are doing."

Todd nodded and said that he pitied the boys, but not too much! However, he reminded her, "Don't do anything that will jeopardize your identity."

XXXXX

Schea sat for a while staring at the door after Todd had left. She knew Todd had been trying to get her to be honest with him about her feelings and tell him if she was having a problem with what she was being asked to do. The only feeling she had about her job was that she wanted to keep doing it. She felt great knowing that Mendoza would not be able to hurt any more little girls.

Schea also knew she would be getting lots of jobs exactly like this one. She would be going after some of the worst people and knew she would have to get close to them and let them do some gross things to her. She would never let herself be raped, of that she was positive. If stopping it was impossible then she, and as many of them as possible, would die.

The problem she was dealing with now, were the dreams. She had had bad dreams for several years after her brother, parents and Allison had been murdered but, with time and the life that she had built with Jim, Grace and Jenny, the bad dreams had gone away. Now, they were back, they were different, but they were scary.

The current dreams were about her. In some of them, she is running but can't seem to get away. Just as the bad guy grabs her, she wakes in a sweat and screams or jumps from the bed. In others, she is trying to help someone, usually a young girl, but is always too late. She didn't tell Todd because she knew, or at least hoped, they would go away after some more time had passed.

# 26 Mission Six: The Boys (Part 1)

Schea visited Jim and Grace staying with them for a week. She helped Jim with several client outings and kept up her physical training. When she left, she bypassed her place and headed north to Aberdeen, Washington about 30 minutes north of Raymond and got a room in a cheap hotel, paying cash.

The morning after arriving, Schea drove to Raymond. She was going to make this a quick trip around the town, and would stay in her car, wear sunglasses and a floppy sun hat. She did not want to be recognized and have the boys warned of her presence in the area.

She entered town on Highway 101 which splits the town in half. The residential area is on the east side and the business area is on the west side. The huge Weyerhaeuser lumber mill is on the northwest side of town adjacent to the Willapa River. Not much had changed since she had last seen it 4 years ago, which is pretty much as she figured. Not much changes in the sleepy little town of Raymond.

She decided to drive through the business side of town first. What little there is of the town, lies basically on one main street. She turned onto Ellis Street from 101 and, a short way along, she turned left onto 3rd. The lumber-yard was down Ellis to the right and the Pitchwood Alehouse was to the left on the corner where she figured the workers at the yard spent a lot of time. She bet that the boys probably worked at the yard by now and frequented the Alehouse.

She continued along 3rd, passed the theater, the Legion Hall and finally turned in front of the Carriage Museum at the south end of town. She drove back across 101 into the residential area and passed by the Watsons' place. She noticed that it still seemed to be occupied, but looked like a dump. It needed painting and the yard was a mess. There were no vehicles parked there at the time but everyone may have been out running errands or working.

Schea drove to the corner and turned toward the back of the property. She noticed that all of the outbuildings on the Watsons' property were gone and there was now a rundown chicken wire fence bordering the back yard. She guessed that maybe they had sold off all of the land behind the house, maybe to a developer. The developer probably tore down all of the old buildings and was waiting for funds to begin developing the land. For what, she couldn't guess. *Who would want to come to a rundown town like Raymond, Washington.*

She didn't linger and drove past the high school, where Allison had attended, and the elementary school, where she attended, was right across the street. She decided to head out of town before someone mentioned to the local sheriff that there was a stranger driving randomly around town.

As she headed back to the 101, she passed Slater's Diner, which used to be a popular place for kids to hang out. As she glanced over she saw 3 girls walking and talking animatedly and giggling. Schea knew all 3 of them. Two had been classmates of Allison and the third had been in school with Schea. They had all grown out of their little girl bodies and were now young women.

Schea wondered if they knew the boys.  She hoped they didn't, at least in the way she knew them.  It was a good thing that Schea had not walked around town openly since she might have been recognized and the boys would likely hear about her visit.

# 27 Boring Life

As Schea headed back to Boring, she realized she would need some help with her mission to get the boys. She knew she could ask Todd but she did not want to force him into a difficult decision, a decision which could jeopardize his organization. She would have to take more time to think this through. The boys will just have to wait for now.

Schea remembered how much fun she had watching the *Les Mis* movie with Frank and listening to him talk about the various singers and performers he enjoyed. She wasn't ready yet to go down the sports fan path but she would probably enjoy seeing some shows and movies. She also decided to start listening to popular music using CDs. She shied away from possessing any smart devices.

Schea used cash for her personal expenses. Todd had suggested this approach but also cautioned her to not be too obvious when she pulled out cash to pay for the more expensive items.

xxxxx

A week after returning from Raymond, she decided to spend the weekend in Portland to do a little shopping, sightseeing, and to see a play at a local theater. She reserved a room for 3 nights at the downtown Hilton, mainly because it had free parking and was only a couple of blocks from the theater. As usual, she paid cash for the room but needed a credit card to reserve the room and cover any additional room costs. Her credit card could not be traced and the bank always accepted whatever charges were placed on the card.

After checking into the Hilton, she walked to the ticket window of the theater. Schea walked up to the window and said, "I would like the best single seat you have for this evening's performance." The ticket seller found a single seat in the fourth row near the left side of the stage and showed it to Schea. "That sounds fine," pulled out the money, counted out the cost of the ticket, and handed it to the seller who handed her the ticket and her change. Schea put them into her purse and wandered off.

She suddenly remembered what she had done at the hotel and at the theater after walking about 2 blocks from the theater. She quickly looked around, but didn't see anyone who appeared to be following her. She reminded herself to be more careful.

It was a warm sunny day, so Schea decided to spend the afternoon walking along the river. She really wanted to have a *normal person* afternoon and evening. She wore a flowery skirt, sandals and a short-sleeve V-neck pullover. She walked along the river a good way to the north and had some lunch. She also stopped a few times and sat on the benches that lined the walkway watching the people. She saw young couples walking and holding hands, families with kids, and groups of teens joking and laughing together.

At first, these scenes made her sad because she didn't - and probably wouldn't - have any of that for a long time. She also thought about how much her parents, as well as Jim and Grace, loved each other. She wondered if that would ever happen for her. Then she thought about children and how

111

much she loved being around Jenny. *Will I ever have children? But, I can't think that way, at least not right now. I am doing something important and know that what I do is probably helping to ensure that the people I am watching can do what they are doing now.*

It was late in the afternoon and Schea needed to get back to her room to shower, change and eat before heading to the theater. She started back and elected to take the shortest route back to her hotel. She walked a few blocks then turned down a small side street which would take her directly to the hotel.

Schea was thinking about the play she was going to see and hoped she'd enjoy it, when suddenly, as she passed an alley, strong hands grabbed each arm and she was dragged into the darkness of the alley. She was pushed behind and up against a large dumpster, and was now facing away from the street while looking into the eyes of 3 young men.

Schea knew she had seen one of them before, but couldn't place him. Her senses were in rest mode since she was not on a mission. She quietly stood with her hands to her sides and waited for one of them to say something or make a move. She didn't really want to hurt them, at least until she knew what they wanted from her, and she certainly didn't want to create a scene.

The guy in the middle finally told her, "Hand over your purse." She thought that was a reasonable request, so she did. She stood watching as he searched inside her purse. Finally, he pulled out a wad of $500 in cash and showed it to the other two.

The guy on the right asked, "Where would a young girl like you get that kind of money?" She said nothing. He turned to his buddies and suggested, "She must be either a thief or a whore and I vote for a whore." He looked at her and asked, "Are you a whore?" She said nothing.

They all looked back at Schea but she stayed quiet. The same guy asked her again where she got the wad of cash. This time she answered that it was an inheritance. He looked at his buddies and said that she must be lying and is probably a whore.

At this point, Schea could see where this was going and didn't like it. She also did not want to be late to the theater. So, she told them, "Look, keep the money and I won't say anything to anyone. Now, I would really like to go, okay?" The guy with her money said not yet and had the look that told Schea he was going to be trouble.

Schea had had enough. She needed to end this before it got worse. She gave a sigh and got all sad and said, "Please don't do this." As she was saying this she bent over a little like she was going to cry. The guy on the right who had been challenging her story started to reach for her.

He didn't get a chance because Schea quickly reached into his crotch and grabbed on tight while she gave it a yank. At the same time, she kicked out with her left foot, struck the knee of the guy on her left and heard a snap. The guy in the middle caught the right knee in his crotch as her leg came back from the other guy's knee and he bent over and moaned.

None of the guys had seen any of this coming. The guy on the left was down on the ground moaning. She let go of the crotch of the guy on the right, and he turned and ran. That left the guy who used to be in the middle, but was now alone, moaning with tears in his eyes. He was about a foot taller than Schea and kind of chubby but, because he was bent over, Schea could look at him at eye level.

Schea smiled and said, "I am going to take my money back now." He quickly reached into his pocket and, with a shaky hand, gave her the money. She thanked him, picked up her purse, brushed her skirt off and told him, "Have a nice evening." She stepped over the guy on the ground and walked out of the alley to her hotel.

XXXXX

Schea enjoyed the play and spent Sunday checking out some of the museums and local landmarks. She checked out of the hotel on Monday morning and headed for the elevator with her suitcase. She pushed the elevator button for the garage level and waited. As the elevator doors opened, she saw an elderly couple, and a young guy who was leaning in the corner. He had a bellhop's uniform on and appeared to be helping the elderly couple take their bags to their car.

Schea looked at him then remembered where she had seen him before. He was the guy on the left in the group that tried to assault her on Saturday. She smiled to herself and walked in. He wasn't looking as she got on because his head was down, and he seemed to be in some pain.

The correct garage level button for her was already pushed, so she turned her back to him and faced the front. When the doors opened to the garage, she stepped out and turned to help the elderly lady out while she blocked the door from closing with her bag. The bellhop still had not looked at her. The lady thanked her and the old man smiled as he exited.

As the bellhop moved to exit the door, Schea stepped in front of him. As he looked at her, the recognition jumped out at him and he stopped. She smiled and said, "You look like you are in some pain." He just kept staring at her, almost pleading for her to not do anything more to him. She smiled, took the couples bag from him and let the door close on his leg before he could scramble back. She heard a loud moan from behind the closed elevator door. She smiled, turned and helped the couple to their car.

XXXXX

Over the next month, Schea went to the theater regularly and found she really enjoyed the escape from reality that it gave her. She saw a couple of musicals, a few comedies and one drama, which she didn't enjoy as much as the musicals and comedies. One weekend, she even drove down to Medford, Oregon to see a couple of Shakespeare's plays performed.

On one weekend visit to Portland for a play, Schea decided she wanted to help the theater by giving them a donation. She came around to the theater the next morning after a particularly fun musical and asked if she could see the theater manager. She was directed to his office and he asked her in.

113

As Schea walked in, he thought that this pretty young girl probably wanted a part in one of the upcoming plays. He would have to direct her to the producers for that kind of decision. So, he asked, "Please have a seat and tell me what I can do for you?"

"I would like to make a donation to the theater."

He looked at her in surprise and felt a little bit annoyed. He thought. *She could have just left her donation at the ticket window and didn't need to be bothering me.* But, he decided to play along and asked, "That's very generous of you. How much would like to donate?"

"Would $100,000 dollars be helpful?"

He was stunned and just stared. But then he thought that this must be some kind of joke or prank. He told her, "It would help us a lot. It is quite a large amount though and I am wondering where you would get that kind of money?"

She said, "Right here," and pulled out a thick wad of $100 dollar bills. He almost fell off of his chair.

He quizzed her for a while trying to make sure this was not a hoax and that it was for real. Schea continued to assure him that it was real and that he could talk to her bank manager to confirm that this was not stolen money or drug money or worse.

She called her bank manager. When he answered, she said, "Hello Marvin." She listened, smiled and then asked about his daughter Mary. She asked if she was still in Cambridge attending Harvard. She listened a bit, smiled and said, "I have someone here who would like to talk to you about my financial trustworthiness." She said good and handed the phone to the theater manager.

The manager said hello and told the bank manager about his concern. He listened, saying "Okay" a few times and occasionally glanced at Schea with wide eyes. Finally, he said thanks and hung up.

After he ended the call, he folded his hands on the desk, looked at Schea, smiled and said, "I am very grateful for your generous donation."

"I have a few conditions." Schea told him that for the near future donations would always be in cash and that all donations must be listed as anonymous. Her name was never to appear in any of the theater's materials, brochures or lists.

She explained that since she was so young, someone might try to take advantage of her. She gave that wide-eyed, innocent, slightly afraid look she hoped would placate him. It did. He agreed to all of her conditions and told her that her privacy would be respected at all times. She stood and looked at him, "If you faithfully follow these conditions then I might consider setting up an automatic donation to an account that you would like to be used for the theater. I will, however, require an accounting report of how the donations are being spent."

He looked at her and knew that she was serious.  He also knew this was a reasonable request, so he said, "Absolutely.  I will provide the details at any time and in any format you ask for."

She thanked him and left.

He stood, staring at the pile of money on his desk.

She smiled as she left the theater.  The conversation with her bank manager was all bogus statements and none of them were true.  His name was not Marvin and he did not have a daughter at Harvard.  The words and phrases were an elaborate method for them to use in order to be able to communicate whether she was indeed who she said she was and if she was under duress.  The scheme changed every 4-6 months when she and he had time to get together to create a new one.

XXXXX

Two and a half months after she returned from her visit with Mendoza, Todd called.  He had a mission and asked her to meet him at his office in 3 days.

# 28 Mission Two: Pirates

Schea shook her head as she recalled the incident with the three guys in Portland. She wished that they had just taken the money and left, but guys can be very stupid when they get around girls. Of course, she counted on this very fact in order to ensure the success of her missions.

XXXXX

When Schea walked into Todd's office, she was surprised to see Michael there too. They said hi and she sat. Todd began the mission briefing.

"This is going to be a 2 person mission. You will be posing as a young couple on a sailing trip in the waters off the Horn of Africa."

"The client is a wealthy Arab and he is hiring us to take out a particular Somali pirate. All pirates kidnap people, however this kidnapper's specialty is not the wealthy but the almost wealthy. He goes after people who look like they have a good amount of money but are not part of the *Super Rich*. He chooses these people because they have money to extort and will almost always pay. The *Super Rich* sometimes pay, but they almost always hire someone to attempt a rescue and to make restitution on the kidnappers. They might also be able to get their government's support for action against the kidnappers. The almost rich were not able to do either."

"The really nasty thing about this pirate is that he rarely returns the captives alive after the ransom is paid. He rapes the females, kills everyone, and dumps them in the desert. They are usually found by locals several weeks later."

"However, he made one big mistake with his recent kidnapping. This wealthy Arab is part of the *Super Rich* crowd. The pirate chose his grandson who was a bit unconventional for our client's liking. He enjoyed partying and drinking and spending his family's money. On one of his excursions, he rented a modest boat and invited a girl that he had met a few weeks earlier in a London club to go sailing with him. She had been only too happy to go."

"Unfortunately, as they passed through the international waters off the coast of Yemen, the really bad pirate captured them and demanded a ransom. He thought that they were just some well-to-do Londoners out on a boat ride. The ransom was paid and the pirate did what he always did."

"The bodies were found a month later. The girl's body was sent back to her parents in Bath, England, while the boy's body was returned to his parents. The boy's father went to the grandfather and pleaded for something to be done. In their culture, something like this had to be avenged. The boy's grandfather agreed and has contacted us."

"Our client will spare no expense to have this done but he wants proof. I argued this last point because this is not something we have ever done. He explained, if he cannot show the family proof that this act has been avenged and that the pirate is truly dead, then the family will continue to want revenge and might go after others, who might be innocent fishermen. So, I acquiesced to his request.

The client wants the head of this piece-of-shit pirate. I will do the packaging and will pay for the postage, so you just need to bring the head back to me."

Schea and Michael looked at each other, shrugged and said, "Okay, boss." Then they proceeded to discuss the best way to complete the mission.

XXXXX

The final plan calls for Michael and Schea to be flown to Oman. The client will ensure that someone picks them up and delivers them to a secluded port where they will find a boat. The client will also ensure that whatever we need in terms of weapons and supplies will be there. We just need to send him a list. The client has spies currently trying to make sure they identify this particular pirate. A description of him and his boat will be with those supplies.

They will pretend to be a young couple out enjoying a week of sailing. The client has actually bought a drone and will use it constantly to patrol over them. It will send video back to their command center and Todd will contact them when the pirate is seen. If the pirate sees them, then they will wait for the pirate to come to them. If he doesn't, then Todd will guide them in the direction of the pirate.

Once the pirate's crew boards them or takes them onto their boat, they can take them out. "And, don't forget the pirate captain's head." Todd reminded them. When the mission is complete, they are to notify Todd and a helicopter will be sent to retrieve them. They must stay in international waters and must not be taken onto land.

They agreed, talked about what they would need and Todd sent their shopping list to the client. They left for Oman 2 days later.

XXXXX

Schea and Michael arrived at the boat and saw that everything they had ordered was neatly stacked inside. It was a good-sized boat with twin inboard engines, electronics and a nice cabin that could convert into a sleeping area for 8 adults. There was a small, fully stocked galley. They stowed the gear they had brought with them and made ready to sail.

Michael was experienced with boats because his dad had been a fisherman off the coast of Galway, Ireland and he had been sailing on boats since he could walk. Schea had sailed a good deal on the lake near Jim's but had never sailed in something of this size. But, she was a quick learner and Michael was a patient teacher.

They were a good team and there was no friction between them. They had gone through much of their training together, so they already knew each other's strengths, weaknesses, and personalities. They reminisced about the training, laughing at some of the hijinks and goof ups that had gone on. Most importantly, they had the utmost confidence and respect for each other.

117

They ate, slept, and dressed in front of each other but always kept it professional and turned away when the other needed privacy.

XXXXX

A week after Schea and Michael left, they were sailing off of the coast of Somalia. Michael had on a pair of shorts and a t-shirt. Schea was lying on the deck sunbathing in a tiny bikini. They had been notified an hour ago that the pirates were approaching them fast and would probably be there in 90 minutes. They had quickly retrieved their weapons and hid them around the boat. They had also changed into their current outfits.

Schea wanted to draw their attention to her. Michael smiled when they discussed this and said they'd be gawking like school-boys who suddenly found themselves in the girl's shower room after gym class. Schea chuckled and reminded him that he was not to be looking at her at the same time. He had work to do. He smiled and said he would do his duty, just as she was doing hers in her itsy bitsy bikini.

They figured the captain and his crew already had their eyes on them. They knew from the report Todd had provided that there would probably be 6-8 pirates on their boat. They would likely come aside of their boat and send a couple of men over. They might push them around and threaten them, but mostly they'd leave them under guard while they ransacked the boat. They would eventually force them onto the pirate's boat and tow their boat with them.

When the pirates were about 100 yards away, Schea walked around in her bikini to make sure they got a good look at her. After doing that for a short time, she pulled on a pair of baggy shorts but left her bikini top on to make sure they would still be distracted. She then discretely hid 2 knives on her thighs under the shorts. She placed a machine pistol into a small backpack she would grab if they sent her to the pirate boat. Michael had already hidden 2 knives under his shorts and had a gun taped to his lower back under his shirt. They looked in the opposite direction of the pirate boat and waited.

When Michael figured they were close enough to know he and Schea could hear them, he turned, looked back at them and attempted to speed away. He thought they'd send a few warnings shots, which they obligingly did. Once they did, he stopped the engines and they looked back at the pirates fearfully. As the pirates came along side, he protectively pushed Schea behind him, which any brave man would do for his little lady.

Two pirates jumped onto their boat and started pushing them and yelling at them. Neither of them was the pirate captain, then Schea spotted him. She nudged Michael and slightly nodded her head in the pirate captain's direction. Michael recognized him too. The captain was standing at the wheel of their boat with three more pirates and they were all gawking at Schea. She knew what they were like, and it wasn't a bunch of school-boys.

Their extra weapons were well hidden, so the rampaging men only managed to find some cash and a laptop, which they quickly handed across to the other pirates and it all ended up with the captain. Michael and Schea stood to the side and tried to look scared.

118

The pirate captain yelled something to the guys on the other boat and they moved quickly toward Michael and Schea. One of them grabbed Schea's arm and started pushing her toward the pirate boat while the other man stood in front of Michael pushing him back. Schea and Michael started yelling and protesting, but not too much.

They had discussed this possiblility, and decided, if it happened, then the pirates were probably going to leave a least 2 guys on the boat with Michael and take Schea to the pirate boat. Separating them was strategically a good idea for the captain but, more likely, they probably just wanted some fun with the girl.

As Schea boarded the pirate boat, the captain came over, grabbed her bikini top and ripped it off. If he also went for her shorts, then they would have to act right away. If not, then Schea would try to isolate the captain away from the remaining 3 men. As soon as he yanked her top off, Schea screamed and covered her chest. Michael started yelling at the captain and pushing the men with him, but not too hard.

The captain forgot about the shorts and glanced at the men with Michael. He yelled something at them and one guy punched Michael in the stomach. Michael pretended that it was a crushing blow and doubled over. Schea almost started to laugh. His acting was pretty bad. But then she quickly got back to business because the captain had now turned his attention back to her.

Schea had already backed away from him when he started yelling at his men. She stood about 3 feet behind him and was slowly inching away. She had dropped her arms behind her like she was trying to steady herself. He was now concentrating on her breasts which he seemed to like very much. She breathed deeply as though afraid but it was really just to make sure her breasts moved up and down in a little hypnotic dance.

Schea hoped that the captain was grateful for all that she was doing for him in his last few moments on the planet. *Well, screw him if he didn't.* Her booby dance also caused the 3 men on the pirate boat to turn their backs on Michael and stare at her. The captain had probably told them to be patient, and they will get their turn later. Schea would have told him that she disagreed, but that would have ruined this pleasant moment for him and his mates.

Oh yes, the captain was indeed enjoying her breathing quite a lot. He smiled as she found herself braced against the side of the boat. He probably figured she was trapped now but Schea had other ideas. *Well, that's about as isolated as I am going to be for the good captain.* As he was about to reach over and grab Schea, shots and shouts rang out. The captain quickly looked back towards Michael and the two men. Both men were now down then one of the men on his boat went down.

As the captain started to turn back toward Schea, she put a knife into the back of one man, while Michael placed a bullet into the head of the last pirate standing. Now, there was just the captain. As Schea reached for her other knife, the captain grabbed her and spun her around in front of him. He held her around the upper chest and pointed his gun at Michael, who was crouching down behind the side of the boat. He yelled at him to throw his gun out and stand up. Michael, of course, was not about to do either of those things. So he just started to yell crazy threats and other stuff back at him.

Schea started pretending to struggle with the captain. While he was looking over to where Michael was hiding and yelling at him, Schea continued her little wiggly struggle and slowly inched downward until she was finally able to reach under her shorts and grab the other knife. The captain had his gun pointed at Michael, so his interest was now diverted from Schea and her breasts.

Michael continued his yelling back at the captain and would fire a shot at him every now and then. This kept the captain struggling in his mind as to how to handle this unfortunate development. He had to keep the girl in front of him so that Michael would not be able to shoot him, but he was now trapped. Neither adversary could do much of anything to the other, except the captain had forgotten about the little adversary entangled in his arm. Big mistake.

Schea turned the knife in her hand so that it was pointing at the captains left thigh. As she continued her struggles, she suddenly gave a mighty push backward, momentarily causing the captain to lose his balance and drove the knife deep into his thigh. This caused him to lose his grip on Schea.

Schea darted away from him to the left just as Michael stood and shot him in the chest. He died instantly, but now he was leaning back against the side of the boat and fell over into the sea before Schea could grab him. She immediately jumped in after him.

He was sinking fast due to the weight of his clothes and shoes so she went under water to find him. She found him about 5 or 6 feet below the surface but couldn't pull him up. She made a quick decision and reached down to the knife she had stuck into his thigh. She pulled it out and moved up his sinking body to his head.

Schea positioned herself behind him and started slicing into his neck. The knife was sharp, but the human neck has lots of bones and muscles that can hinder a good clean cut with a knife, especially while holding your breath under water and trying to hold onto a man to keep him from sinking while hanging on his back. She had to concentrate. There was work to do.

Schea was pretty close to the limit of her ability to hold her breath. She had cut through the tissue and was now slicing away at the neck bone but she needed to finish this quickly. She stuck the knife into his shoulder - no sense losing a perfectly good knife - grabbed his head, wrapped her legs around his waist and twisted with all her strength. The head snapped off into her hands and, before the good captain could sink and steal her knife, she yanked it out of his shoulder.

Michael had watched in horror as the captain fell backward into the water. He thought, *Well there goes the head we needed.* But, then to his surprise, Schea went in after him. He checked to make sure the pirates on his boat were dead, scrambled over to the pirate boat and made sure the other pirates were also dead. Then, he ran to the spot where the captain and Schea had gone overboard, looked down into the water and saw blood.

He knew he had hit the captain, so this blood must be his. Everyone knew Schea was a superior swimmer on or below the water, but he wondered if he should go in to help her. He hesitated for a minute then decided to make the rescue call in order to get more help.

Just as he was getting ready to go into the water to help, the captain's head appeared at the surface. He almost fired his gun, thinking that maybe the captain was not dead. But before he could do that, he noticed that there was a hand holding the head, and watched as a sputtering and gagging Schea appeared at the surface.

Schea spit out some water and took several deep breaths. Then, she looked up and smiled at Michael. "It's a nice day for a swim. Will you join me?" At that, she held up the captain's head. "Look what I found!"

Michael grabbed a length of rope, tied it around a grommet on the side of the boat, looped the rope around his arm, and jumped over the side. Schea was treading water easily by this time and handed the captain's head to him which he tossed into the boat then helped Schea climb up the rope onto the deck. He followed her up and they both sat on a crate that was sitting on the pirate ship's deck.

After a bit, Michael got up, took off his t-shirt and handed it to Schea. She pulled it over her head and settled it over her naked torso. She nodded a thank you to Michael and smiled. Finally, Michael looked at her and said, "Dumb-ass broad."

She looked back at him, "Yea, well, sticks and stones may break my bones, but names will never hurt me."

He laughed and she smiled. It had been a good mission and they had made a good team.

The rescue team arrived about an hour after Michael made the call. In the meantime, they moved the 2 dead pirates from their boat onto the pirate boat. They poured gasoline from the fuel tanks on the pirate boat all around then moved over to their boat and pushed away.

When they were about 20 feet away, Michael went to the bridge and started the engines. He left them in neutral, while Schea loaded the flare pistol, took aim and shot a flare onto the pirate boat. Michael gunned the engines and they sped away as the boat caught fire.

When they were about 100 yards away, the pirate boat exploded into flames and gradually sank. They changed into fresh clothes then placed their weapons and other supplies into a pile in the little cabin. The only item they planned to take with them was the captain's head.

The helicopter arrived and lowered a ladder for Schea to climb up into the bay with the captain's head in a pillow-case. Once she was on board, Michael set the timer on a small, but powerful, explosive charge in the middle of the cabin. Michael quickly ran to the waiting ladder, hooked his arms securely into the webbing, and waved for the pilot to get moving.

The pilot moved away from the boat, and when they were about 200 yards away, the charge went off, and the boat sank within seconds. The pilot hovered while Michael climbed up into the bay where he sat next to Schea, and they gave each other a thumbs-up. They wearily settled back in the cramped area for the ride back to Todd and his command center.

Todd had been called once the team was on its way and was waiting for them when it landed. Without saying anything, the three of them, along with the captain's head, went to a small briefing room. There was coffee, beer, Diet Coke and snacks waiting for them. Todd and Michael each grabbed a beer and Schea grabbed a Diet Coke.

They were still a little too wound up to eat, so they sat at the table while Todd debriefed them. He stared wide-eyed when Michael told him how Schea had retrieved the captain's head. When Michael finished, he looked at Schea and smiled.

"Well we needed the head, right?"

What could Todd say? They did indeed need the head.

He congratulated them on a good mission and left with the head. Michael and Schea were given a couple of rooms where they could rest and get cleaned up. After showering, they both took a nice long nap.

# 29 Boring Again

Schea went back to her Boring life, both literally and figuratively. She liked it that way. Missions were so full of tension and action, it was nice to just kick back and be, well, bored.

She continued to go to the theater, got to know several of the actors and stage crew and they started asking her to go out with them after performances. She declined at first but then figured why not. After all, she felt she deserved a life too! Several of the guys hit on her but all of these advances were politely declined. She was happy on her own but, when she was alone at home, she wondered if she might try dating a little just to see what it might be like. She promised herself that she would give it a chance at some point.

When they asked Schea to go to bars and clubs, she explained that she was only 17 so she could not go. She actually had an ID that said she was over 21, but she chose not to use it. A couple of people told her they would sneak her in, but she refused that too. They accepted her decisions about bars, but still invited her to their apartments for parties. If Schea was offered a drink, she always refused.

No one seemed to mind her choices, so people started to have soda available for her. She enjoyed their company and had fun listening to their stories about plays they had done and stuff that happened behind the scenes. There was also a lot of talk about various hookups people initiated.

The difficult situations were when they started asking Schea what she did. Did she have a job? Was she going to school? Where did she go when she wasn't around? She told them that she had graduated from high school early and a friend of the family hired her as a researcher for his security company. The job paid good money and she traveled a lot. She said that sometimes she would be sent on a job quite suddenly.

When asked about what kind of jobs these were, Schea would say that she really couldn't talk about them because her friend's company was hired for various high profile security situations. Some asked if she was one of those that actually provided the security. She laughed and said, "Me? Goodness no. I'm no fighter and I hate guns. I simply do the research on places to stay, help set up command centers and do other random stuff." They seemed to buy the explanation but were still impressed that she got to travel to so many cool places. She thought. *Yea, like the waters off of Somalia and the deserts of eastern Mexico. Very cool places indeed.*

XXXXX

On one sunny day, Schea was out on a run along the waterfront in downtown Portland and passed one of the actors she knew. She slowed, said hi, then ran with him. He was surprised to see her, but was happy to have the company. They chatted about theater stuff, finally finished the run along the waterfront, got some water and sat in the park.

The actor's name was Gary and he mentioned that Schea seemed like a pretty good runner. She shrugged and said she guessed she was okay. He told her about the Rainier to Pacific Relay Race that was coming up in the summer. The race was run by teams of 11 people. There were 33 separate legs to the race, so each runner ran 3 times, alternating with the other runners. The race started on Mount Rainier and finished in Ocean Shores on the Washington coast. He told her that the theater company always had a team and used the race to raise money for charity. He said that one of the members on the team had gotten a big role in a play being produced back in Chicago, so she would not be able to run, and asked Schea, "Would you be able to take her place?"

Schea looked away as if considering but she was really trying to come up with a good way to decline. *What if she got an assignment? What if something materialized during her planning for what to do about the boys?* Finally, she shook all of those thoughts off and decided. "Sure, but with the condition that I could get called away." He said that was cool and they would deal with it if it happened.

Well, it didn't happen, and she really enjoyed the race and the fun time they had sleeping in sleeping bags in fields or the van. What she really enjoyed was the cheering that everyone did for each other during the race. Some of the runners on the team were really good but most were only casual runners. It didn't seem to matter how fast or slow anyone ran. Everyone was cheered and told that they had done a great job on their particular leg of the race.

The team finished somewhere near the middle in terms of overall time for all teams and they stayed one night in Ocean Shores before heading back to Portland. They were all impressed with Schea and asked if she would like to be a member of the team each year. She said she would as long as she was in town.

# 30 Mission Six: The Boys (Part 2)

Todd did, in fact, rack up a huge bill at dinner that evening with Schea. He must have ordered all the highest priced items in the three main areas - appetizer, main course and dessert. The man loved his desserts. She didn't care. She could certainly afford it and she always enjoyed spending time with Todd.

The day after Todd left, Schea decided to spend some time exploring along the Chesapeake Bay. She hadn't gotten around to exploring the area, even though it was located just outside her door. She figured that today would be a good day to start. She especially wanted to visit the many fabulous restaurants that she was told were there. She had tried crab cakes on the first day she had arrived in Annapolis looking for a house. They were delicious and told the waitress this, but her waitress said that the best crab cakes were found south along the bay.

She didn't want to spend all of her time driving around, so she headed out of Annapolis on Highway 2 south. After about 30 minutes, she saw a sign for a place called Galesville and thought, *Why not!* She pulled into town, parked and began walking. The weather was nice and the town had the look of a seaport. She walked for a good 90 minutes before stopping at a Starbuck's for some tea.

When the barista gave her the tea, Schea asked, "Can you direct me to a nice restaurant where I can get some delicious crab cakes?"

The barista didn't even have to think on it. She said, "You should head down to the bay and go to Thursday's Steak and Crabhouse."

It sounded good to Schea, so she said, "Thanks. I'll do that!"

She was sitting there now and had enjoyed a delicious lunch of crab cakes. She was just finishing up her Diet Coke when she looked over at one of the tables and saw a group of 4 elderly ladies sitting and talking. She remembered the day she had spent as a little old lady in Raymond, Washington.

XXXXX

About a week after meeting Gary on her run, Schea decided to pay another visit to Raymond. She actually planned it out while she was coming back from her pirate adventure. One of the people she met at the theater was a makeup artist and that had given Schea an idea. She contacted the theater manager and asked if it was okay if she asked the makeup artist to help her create a disguise in order to play a joke on an old friend. He told her to go right ahead.

Schea went to the theater a day later and found the makeup artist arranging her stuff and replacing old products with new ones. Her name was Alice. They knew each other from the theater parties they both attended so, Schea walked in, said hi and Alice did the same and told her the manager had called and asked her to help Schea with whatever she wanted.

125

Schea smiled and told Alice, "A rich uncle of mine somehow heard I was involved with the theater and gave quite a nice donation to the theater. He probably thought I worked here or had become an actor or something like that."

Alice chuckled and said, "What he doesn't know, won't hurt him, right?"

Schea chuckled and said, "Oh yea!"

Schea explained what she wanted to do. "I'm going to meet an old girlfriend from high school and want to play a joke on her. We were constantly doing stuff like this to each other in school."

Alice nodded knowingly and smiled.

"I want to look like an old woman, maybe around 70 years old," she said. "I also need to dress and act that age."

Alice nodded. "That will be quite easy. Many plays require a young person to play the part of someone much older, so I have all the right makeup and clothes you will need. I can even help you to act like a 70 year old since I sometimes play one if the role isn't too demanding and doesn't require singing. You should come by about 2 hours before you leave to see your friend."

XXXXX

Schea arrived at the theater at 8 am the next day and went to see Alice. Alice had everything ready and began to apply makeup. She only needed to apply it on areas that would be exposed, such as her hands and face. After applying the makeup, Alice placed a wig of grey hair on Schea's head and asked her to look in the mirror. She was amazed. If she didn't know that it was she looking in the mirror, she would have thought that she was looking through a window at someone else - someone much, much older.

Alice then selected a couple of dresses that looked to be the right size and, after a few tries, finally decided on an ankle-length brown and white, flowery dress with long sleeves to cover her arms. She had Schea put on a pair of stockings and a pair of black flats. Alice then spent about an hour showing Schea how to walk and talk like an older lady would. Schea could not believe the transformation. Alice made sure that Schea knew she had to always be in character, even if she went to the restroom.

Finally, Alice stepped back, gave Schea the once-over, smiled and nodded satisfactorily. She told Schea that when she was done, she could just wash all the makeup off, and bring the clothes and shoes back to her. Alice wished her luck.

Schea got into her car and headed for Raymond. She figured she'd arrive around noon and would go straight to Slater's for lunch. She would linger there for a couple of hours, striking up conversations with folks and asking questions about the Watsons.

Shea's cover was that she was an elderly aunt who lived back East. She would say that she had decided in her later years to get back in touch with Drake and Crystal Watson. She'd tell them she had inherited a sizable amount of money when her husband died and wanted to make sure in her will that it went to the right people. That should open up some mouths.

Schea arrived in Raymond at 12:20 pm and headed for Slater's Diner. The exterior was plain yellow and the inside was ivory. There were about 20 small, square tables with 4 chairs at each and a counter with 10 round seats. She entered and walked to a table using a cane. She had added the cane to her disguise at the last minute.

She sat in an area she figured would eventually have lots of people sitting and eating. The waitress came over, handed her the menu and asked, "Would you like some coffee?"

"I'd like tea, if you have it, thank you."

When the waitress came back with the tea, Schea ordered a small salad and a bowl of chicken soup. The waitress took the order and went off. By then, about a dozen people had come in and were sitting relatively near Schea's table. *Good. I want them to hear my conversation with the waitress.*

The waitress brought Schea's order and before she could leave, Schea asked, "May I ask you a question."

The waitress smiled and said, "Sure."

"I'm from the East Coast and a relative of a family who used to, or maybe still does, live in Raymond. I'm trying to contact them." She said it loud enough for the others to have heard her.

"Who are you looking for?"

"Drake and Crystal Watson."

The waitress sighed and got a sorrowful look on her face. Schea saw the look and asked, "Did something happen to them?"

The waitress nodded her head and said, "Drake passed away 2 years ago. He had gotten drunk and tried to drive home. He attempted to speed across the 101 while a logging truck was approaching and was struck in the driver's side. He died instantly."

She continued. "Crystal was so distraught that she stayed closeted in the house for several months. She finally couldn't stand it here any longer and moved to stay with relatives in Texas. She said that every time she thought of the 101, it reminded her of Drake and the crash."

Schea put on a sympathetic face and said, "That's so terrible. I feel horrible that I was not here to help." She asked, "Do you know where Crystal is in Texas?"

The waitress said, "I do not."

Schea said, "Drake is the son of my dear sister who passed away 5 years ago. I hadn't known Crystal's family very well back then and have no knowledge of them now, I am sad to say."

Then Schea asked the question she really wanted to know the answer to. "What about the boys, Hank and Rod?"

The waitress grimaced a little and said, "They are still living in the house and work at the lumber mill down by the river."

"I only have a short time to stay in town and would like to try to contact them before I go. You see, I have a sizable fortune and they appear to be my only living relatives."

The waitress nodded in understanding, but quietly told her not to leave any of it to those boys, emphasizing *those*. Then, she walked away.

Schea slowly worked on her meal and waited. After about 10 minutes, a lady who had been sitting at a nearby table leaned over and excused herself to get Schea's attention. Schea turned and smiled. The woman got up, leaving her companions, and asked if she could sit with Schea. Schea said sure and indicated the seat across from her. The woman didn't understand Schea or ignored her. It was probably the latter. The woman sat in the chair next to Schea on her left. Schea smiled.

The woman introduced herself as Mrs. Jefferson and said that she lived down the street from the Watsons' house. Schea now remembered her. She had been a nice lady but seemed to be a little bit of a busy-body. *Good. I need a busy-body.*

Mrs. Jefferson began by telling Schea that she was so sorry about the loss of Drake. Drake drank too much, but he never hit or hurt Crystal or the boys. "Although," she said, "the boys probably should have been disciplined much more than they were. They had always been trouble in the neighborhood when they were young - knocking over trash cans, stealing other kid's toys and starting little fires."

This made Schea think that maybe she had been wrong years ago to have assumed that no one would have believed that the boys could have been involved in Allison's death. But, she couldn't worry about that now. She had work to do.

"I also thought, but couldn't prove, that they may have stolen and tortured some of the neighbor's pets. The pets would disappear and everyone would search for them, even the boys, but I sensed that their concern was far from genuine." She continued, "As they got older, they would get beer and go out in the woods behind their house to drink, sometimes with some other boys. I also noticed that every now and then a girl might go with them. I don't know what went on out there, but I don't think that it was anything good."

"A few years ago, two girls came to live with the Watsons. They were in their early teens and seemed like nice girls. Crystal had always wanted a girl but couldn't have children after Rod was born. The girls were sisters and they didn't want to be separated again after their parents had died."

Schea could feel her heart breaking as she said this.

"Anyway," continued Mrs. Jefferson, "the following year, the older sister was killed in a botched robbery, or so they said." She looked at Schea intently, leaned in and whispered, "But I never believed that story. I was sure that something bad had happened, but again, when it came to the boys, as usual, there was no proof that they had anything to do with it. The youngest girl left soon after to live with some other relatives and never returned. That is when Drake's drinking started to get excessive."

Schea waited until she seemed finished and had no additional information before she gently grabbed Mrs. Jefferson's hand and gave it a light squeeze. She thanked her for sharing the tragic story of her relatives.

Mrs. Jefferson smiled back and nodded. She seemed to get a little thoughtful. Finally, she leaned over again and told Schea she agreed with the waitress. "Do not leave any money to the boys. You ought to try to find Crystal in Texas and give it to her. She was the nicest of all of them." She got up and moved back to the table with her friends.

Schea paid the bill and left Slater's Diner. She was pleased with her disguise. Even though Mrs. Jefferson had probably seen her many times going to and from school or playing in the neighborhood, she still did not recognize her, which was good because now she was going to go see the boys.

She drove over to The Pitchwood Alehouse and parked in the lot behind the bar. She left her cane in the car and walked around to the front of the bar. She stopped, steeled herself and walked in. It was 3:30 pm, so the workers were still at the mill, but the shift at the mill ended at 4 pm for most of them, so the bar should begin to get busy shortly.

The exterior was rough brown wood planks. The name of the bar was cut into a large wooden board and posted to the upper left of the door. The interior was dark wood paneling and had several bar stools at the bar. The bar had a long Formica top that extended from wall-to-wall. There was an opening to the far left so the waitresses and bartenders could move in and out from behind the bar. The tables and chairs were randomly spread around the interior as though no one cared to establish an organized setting. Schea sat at a table in the far corner to the right of the door.

There were 5 men seated at the bar and looked like regulars. The bartender came over to her, asked what he could get her and she ordered a glass of white wine. He brought a glass and went back to his regulars. She slowly sipped the wine and waited.

About an hour later, the place was pretty busy, but she still had not seen the boys. Schea thought she might have to leave and try again another time, but then the boys came through the door. They barked hellos to a couple of guys then sauntered up to the bar. The bartender knew their preference and had their beers ready by the time they reached the bar. They grabbed their beers and sat at a table just to the left of the bar.

The bar now had 3 waitresses working the customers seated at tables. The waitresses would take their orders and pick them up at the left side of the bar. Sometimes they needed to go behind the

129

bar to get a customer's drink and used the hinged part of the counter to get through. The waitresses ranged in age from about 22 to 26 and were attractive.

Schea now knew why the boys sat at the table just to the left of the bar. This was where they could get the best views of the waitresses. The boys would sometimes make crude remarks to them, who would only glance and continue working, but the boys would just laugh and continue their drinking. About 20 minutes later, 2 more guys came in and sat with the boys. The waitresses took their drink orders and brought them back to the table.

Now, all 4 were making crude remarks, and it was becoming crowded and rowdy. Schea was taking up an entire table so she decided to leave and watch from outside. She paid for her drink and headed out the door. As she started to leave, she heard someone shout and ask, "Can I buy the lady a drink?" and then laughing. Schea recognized Hank's voice and smiled as she exited.

She walked to her car and debated whether to stay there or drive around to the front. She figured that since she did not know what kind of car they had, she would need to be in front. She drove around to the front and parked on the opposite side of the street about 50 yards down. She was in front of the now-closed Bridge's Fine Dining restaurant, and had a good view of the front of the Pitchwood in her rearview mirror. She scrunched down and waited.

The boys eventually came out at about 10 pm and walked around the back of the bar. Schea started the car and slowly pulled away from the curb. She figured that they would head east on Ellis, cross 101 and head home. She went to the end of 3rd, turned left, crossed 101 and headed up Commercial Street to 14th. At 14th, she turned left and parked a block away from the Watson's house.

The boys arrived home shortly after and Schea watched the house while various lights came on then off. The house finally went dark around midnight.

She had taken a room at a small motor inn in South Bend, Washington, located about 20 minutes south of Raymond and went there. She slept lightly and, the next morning, she tried to re-apply her disguise. The results were not nearly as good as Alice's, but it would have to do.

She drove back to the Watsons' at around 6 am, and waited for the boys. They left at around 7:30 am and headed to the mill. She followed them and watched as they entered the Weyerhaeuser parking lot then decided to head back to Boring.

She didn't know this, but two days after she left Raymond, it was all over town that some rich old lady had a fortune and wanted to leave it to the Watsons. The busy-body network in Raymond had worked well. The boys found out and remembered the old lady from the bar. After that, they were on alert every day for her. They planned to be on their best behavior for her if she ever came back in order to win her trust and, oh yes, her money.

Satisfied with this reconnaissance mission, she made several more trips to Raymond in disguises that she created for herself. She rented a different vehicle each time in case the boys were looking for the one she drove on her first visit and stayed in her vehicle all the time. All she wanted to do was to get a good feeling for the boys' movements and activities.

Schea wasn't exactly sure what kind of revenge the boys deserved or what she really wanted to do to them. She could try to solve Allison's murder and accuse them or she could just kill them. The fact that she thought of the last option scared her. She knew after what happened to Allison, she wanted them dead but, even so, she didn't really know if she would do something like that.

But now, after what she has been doing in her job, she wasn't all that concerned about killing these perverts. They deserved it. *Isn't it my job to eliminate deviant bastards from the world?* she wondered. But, she wasn't so sure that this situation warranted their death.

# 31 Mission Three: Vincent (Part 1)

Schea decided to spend the night at a small hotel she found outside of the town of Nutwell on Herring Bay on her Chesapeake tour. It had started to rain, but her hotel balcony had a roof over it so she made some tea and sat out on the balcony bundled up in a jacket and pajamas.

Schea recalled that it was about a month after the recons to Raymond when she got a message from Todd saying he had a mission for her. The timing was good because she now felt she had enough information to form a plan for dealing with the boys.

This mission had evolved into one of her more complex missions. It was also the mission that ended up having a totally unplanned mission that led to her job working for the President of the United States and move to Annapolis.

She remembered how the mission had gotten started.

XXXXX

For her 3rd mission, Schea was told by Todd that her target was an Eastern-European man from Serbia, but that he didn't have a home there. His name was Vincent Nicoleyev and he had homes in London, Berlin, Bratislava and Varna, Bulgaria. He dealt in guns and human trafficking. His specialty in trafficking was young girls from 12 to 16 that he found all over Eastern Europe and he was to be eliminated.

Schea went onto a website that was known to be used by men like Vincent to find young girls. She placed a post on the site and included a slightly sexy picture of herself, which did not show her face, along with some slightly racy details about what she liked to do and the kind of man she wanted to meet. She had learned from her first 2 missions that men like Vincent seemed to favor young American girls, so she didn't hide the fact that she was American. Schea also said she was 15 and her name was Michele.

It wasn't long before Vincent, and hundreds of other men and women, contacted her. With help from the information in Vincent's file, she was able to sort through the replies and identify Vincent. She responded to his reply and immediately deleted her profile from the website. If he asked why she had deleted her profile so quickly, she would say that she had selected him after reviewing most of the others, and didn't want to be annoyed with more contacts. He didn't, but asked her to meet him in London. She said okay and she'd be there in 2 days.

She had given him her phone number so he called her a day after she arrived in London. They talked for about 15 minutes then he asked if she could meet him in Brighton the next day. It is a small, lovely seaside town just south of London. She said that worked perfectly and agreed to meet at Molly Malone's Pub on West Street at 3 pm, which is a popular bar about half a block from the boardwalk.

She had been staying in Hounslow, just outside of London, when he called. Hounslow is near Heathrow Airport and on the Piccadilly Tube line into London. So, she checked out after his call, took

132

the Tube into London and made her way to the Waterloo train station. She bought a ticket to Brighton and left about an hour later. After arriving, she checked into the Jury's Inn located across from the train station.

Molly's Pub is a fun place to meet, if you like music, noise and lots of young people. She walked into the bar, took a seat at one of the tables near the back of the bar and ordered a Diet Coke. She wore a pleated white mini-skirt and a thin, clingy red cashmere sweater. Vincent arrived about 30 minutes after she did and she instantly recognized him based on the picture she had seen in Todd's file. She did not approach him but simply sat at her table looking around at the bar patrons.

He noticed the cute young girl sitting alone, walked over to her table, and stood. She looked up and smiled. He said, "I am Henri. Are you Michele?" She said yes and he sat down to her right.

She turned slightly so that they faced each other. She watched him give her the once over, moving from her face to her legs so she slowly crossed her legs so that her skirt slid up a little. He seemed to appreciate the gesture.

She continued to play the sweet 15 year old role and told him, "I am so happy that you contacted me. I didn't like any of the others who responded to my post."

He asked Schea what she would like to drink and she said a Diet Coke. He went to the bar and ordered a bottle of Smithwick beer and a Diet Coke. He sat back down, opened her soda and poured a glass for her. Vincent held his beer up, Schea raised her glass and they toasted to their new friendship.

"Well, Michele, where do you live?"

"I have always lived in Los Angeles and my parents are movie producers. I just finished my freshman year in high school and told her parents I wanted to do online schooling from now on. They never pay much attention to me and simply agree to whatever I want. I also told them I decided to go to Europe for a month and they said okay. My parents gave me a credit card in my name when I turned 14 that doesn't seem to have a credit limit and they have never scolded me for charging too much."

Henri smiled then asked, "How did you know about that website?"

"Well, one night while I was in my room lying in bed, I found that website about men looking for girls. I decided to try putting a post on it to see what would happen. It was crazy. I think I received well over a hundred responses but most were really nasty. Some, like yours, were cool and suggested some fun things to do. I mean, I guess I'm a little experienced but have kind of wondered lately what some of those things might be like."

"My girlfriends and I talk, you know, about boys and sex and our bodies and what some girls are doing." She could see that Vincent was really getting worked up hearing all of this. She decided to push it a little more. "I like to sleep in the nude with my window open and sometimes, I walk by or stop at the window or like I am looking for something. It gives me these really exciting feelings. I also like to have fun trying to make myself get those feelings using my hands and occasionally do it in front of the window."

Schea acted embarrassed and said, "Oh gosh, I am so sorry. I shouldn't be talking like this to you. You are probably thinking I am a bad girl." She looked at her lap and thought. *Boy that must have really gotten him worked up.*

Vincent was impressed with her boldness and for taking charge of her own life as she talked about her actions regarding her parents. But, after that last stuff, he could hardly think straight. He wanted to take her right there in the pub on the floor. Instead, he decided to keep calm. "I am very impressed with your independence and your interest in controlling your own life."

She smiled, glanced away and said thanks. He told her that he ran a number of businesses in Europe and had several houses, but preferred Paris.

At about this time, the song *La Vie En Rose* started playing. Vincent became quiet and asked Schea to listen to the song. It started with a trumpet solo then a beautiful slightly sad vocal performance in French. When it finished, Schea said it was beautiful. Victor told her, "It was written by a famous French singer, Edith Piaf, in 1945 and I have always loved that piece."

"I recently heard a new version of it with an American trumpet player, Jumanni Smith, doing the trumpet solo and the first part in English. The second part is sung in French by a famous young American singer named Jackie Evancho. I am hoping that one day you might get to hear it."

Schea said she'd love to hear and maybe even see it performed.

He finally suggested, "Let's go to my hotel. There is a nice, quiet little bar and it is only a short walk from here." Schea said that sounded great.

They left the pub and turned right on the boardwalk. They walked along the boardwalk a short distance and entered The Hilton Metropole Hotel. As they walked along, he would 'accidentally' brush his hand along her butt. She would just smile and occasionally step in a little closer to him.

As they entered the hotel, Schea noticed that there seemed to be increased security in the lobby. There were several men who looked out of place, and she saw that they had intercoms. This was either high security or an elaborate robbery. She didn't think that it was a robbery so she figured that either Vincent or someone else was the focus of this security.

Vincent suggested they have another drink in the bar before heading to his room. She smiled and said she'd love to. As she walked into the bar ahead of Vincent, she reasoned that it was someone else who was the focus of this increased security because the security guys were not paying any attention to them.

Her instincts told her to stay alert.

She and Vincent sat at a table located near the window. When the waitress came over, he ordered two glasses of champagne and, as the waitress moved away, he laid his hand on Schea's thigh and smiled as she put her hand over his. She gave his a light squeeze.

He was sure that he had found a nice, hot, young girl for the evening.

She was sure that he would be an easy kill since he was so easily distracted.

But, things never seem to be straight forward in this business.

As she scanned the bar area and chatted with Vincent, she noticed that security personnel were now entering the bar. Two security personnel came in and scanned the area. One positioned himself near the lobby entrance and the other went to the exit that led to the rooms. Soon after, a young man and woman entered followed by 2 additional security personnel who moved to each end of the bar.

The couple sat at a table near a bookcase that lined the wall across from the windows between the 2 exits. She didn't recognize the young man but she immediately knew he was the person of interest for this security detail.

Vincent was too busy trying to get busy with her to notice any of this. He slid his hand up and down her thigh then casually put his arm around her shoulder and drop his hand to her breast. The cashmere was soft and her breast was firm. She moved a little closer to him, but was hardly interested in what he was doing. She was thinking about her mission and, now, the other mission that seemed to be unfolding in the room with them.

She inwardly chastised herself. *Pay attention to your mission. Stay focused.* So, she got back to her business and heard him saying, "You are so beautiful and I really want to get to know you better. Let's go up to my room for a drink and more privacy."

"I'd love to but I need to go to the restroom first."

Vincent started to say that she could use the one in his room but then his phone buzzed and he excused himself. He walked out into the hotel lobby, glanced back and smiled as if to say, "Do not go anywhere. I'll be right back." Schea smiled.

Schea was still puzzled by the need for all of this security for the young man and woman, then she noticed a women enter the bar area. Schea wasn't sure why but she suddenly felt tensed. The woman was taller than Schea, but most women are. She looked about 30 and was attractive, had an athletic build and wore a light jacket over a pretty blouse with a knee-length skirt. All very well matched for color and style.

The woman seemed to glance briefly at the young man then turn away. However, that look spoke volumes to Schea and she immediately knew that this woman meant trouble. The woman's eyes had pierced the distance between her and the young man like knives. *Dammit.*

The woman went to the bar, ordered a glass of white wine and stood at the bar sipping the wine.

Vincent came back and sat. He leaned over and put his hand on her thigh and began rubbing it again. "I have to leave for an important business meeting but want to know if you would like to come to see me in a couple of days when my business is concluded?"

Schea put on a pouty face and asked him if he really had to go. He said yes, and she gave a big sigh. She looked at him and asked, "Where is your meeting?"

He said that he couldn't tell her but, "I will meet you in Chamonix, France in 2 or 3 days, if you like and I will pay for everything." He looked at her and smiled.

She smiled back and said, "Sure. Call me when you are ready for me." She knew he was already ready but she wanted to tease him a little. She smiled sweetly.

He seemed to lose track of his thoughts then called the waitress over, told her to give Michele anything she wanted, and put it on his tab. He kissed her on the mouth and gave her leg a rub all the way up this time. As he left, Schea thought. *How do I ever make it through these kinds of meetings without laughing or puking on these dirt-bags?*

XXXXX

When Vincent got to his room, he started to undress to get ready for his trip. His bags were still packed so there wasn't much to do. When he was ready, he pulled out his phone and made a call.

"I have to leave for a meeting in Moscow." Pause "Yes, I want you to continue to watch her. If she leaves, follow her wherever she goes." Pause "I'll be calling her in 3 days to make arrangements for Chamonix and you can follow her there too."

He put his phone in his pocket and smiled. He thought. *Man. That little sweet piece of ass is going to give him all of her body over and over until, well, until the end.*

# 32 Mission Three: Interruption

Schea asked the waitress for a diet cola and turned her focus back to the woman at the bar. The woman didn't turn around to look at the young couple because she didn't have to. She could keep an eye on them by watching them in the big wall mirror behind the bar. The woman also glanced at the security personnel around the room.

As she watched, Schea noticed that the woman was beginning to move ever so subtly. Her legs were beginning to straighten, her arms were flexing, and her focus was narrowing. Schea also saw her hand slip slowly into the small handbag hanging off of her shoulder and knew that she was going to make her move on the couple.

Schea calmly stood and started for the restroom. Her path would take her directly in front of the woman, and place her between the woman and the couple. She paced herself so that she would be at that point at the same time the woman came within her reach. A she walked, she looked straight ahead toward the restroom but kept the woman in her peripheral vision. As Schea reached the midpoint, she saw the woman start to withdraw her hand from her purse. If there was nothing in it, then Schea would simply continue to the restroom. If there was, then Schea would act.

There was something in her hand. Schea saw the grip of a small handgun come into view from her purse just as she walked in front of the woman. The woman may have been hoping that Schea would shield her from the security personnel, and what she was planning to do, and she was right. They had no clue what was about to happen.

But, Schea did.

When the woman had the gun fully out, but still pointed at the floor, Schea reacted. Like a flash, she grabbed the woman's wrist just above the gun hand, twisted it down and back inside toward her body until she heard a snap. Before she had completed breaking the woman's wrist, she was already coming up toward her throat with her palm. Schea caught the woman full in the throat, and the woman gasped.

In the meantime, Schea had let go of the wrist and was swinging her arm around behind the woman to drag her down and away from the couple. They landed in a pile on the floor and the woman started screaming in some language that Schea didn't recognize. She was also flailing her broken arm and good arm wildly. Schea stood quickly and wrenched the woman's broken arm straight out. She twisted it at the shoulder and heard another snap. For good measure, she stomped her foot down on the woman's throat and the woman went limp.

All of this happened so fast, that the security detail didn't realize what was happening until Schea had the woman on the floor. They finally reacted and two of them ran over just as Schea broke the woman's arm at the shoulder and stomped on her neck. Those two pulled their guns, and ran toward Schea and the woman, while the other two of went immediately to the couple and pulled them out of the area.

The two that ran over to Schea, yelled at her to get down on the floor so she let go of the woman's arm, which fell heavily to the floor, and got down on the floor and waited. She also thought. *Now what did I get myself into. Todd is really going to be pissed.*

One of the guards found the woman's gun under her, along with additional rounds and a knife in her purse. One of the two guards, who had taken the couple away, came back and told the first two that the young man had seen what happened.

"He told me that the girl saved their lives. He said he looked up as the crazy woman approached and saw her start to pull out a gun but the girl knocked the woman down and beat the crap out of her."

The men looked at each other and finally asked Schea to get up, which she did.

They asked, "Who are you and what are you doing here?"

She answered, "I'm Schea Tailor and I am here on business for my boss' company. His name is Todd Groden and the company is a high-end personal security firm."

"Is that where you learned those skills?"

She smiled. "Oh, no. I am too young for that stuff. I am a research assistant and go to where a command post is needed for an upcoming job to make reservations and other arrangements. I learned that stuff from my older brother. He was in the Special Forces and taught me a bunch of moves so that I could defend myself against groping boyfriends."

They seemed to buy her story and one of them, who probably had daughters, smiled knowingly. "Who was the man you were sitting with?"

"He is a business contact that I had to meet with." She smiled and said, "I almost had to use those moves on him. He was getting way too friendly but then, luckily, he had to leave for some kind of meeting."

They apologized for treating her the way they did at first, but said they weren't sure initially *who was who*. Schea smiled and said, "Don't worry about it. I am unhurt and just happy that I happened to be in the right place at the right time."

The young couple was guided back in and the man walked over to Schea. He shook her hand and told her how grateful he was for her help. She smiled and shrugged. He asked if he could buy her a drink or some dinner but she said, "No. Thanks. I really need to get going."

Schea said bye and waved as she went out of the bar and the hotel. When she got to the street, she thought. *Oh boy. I need to call Todd right away.* And went quickly back to her hotel room at the Jury's.

XXXXX

After Schea left, the couple and the men were silent for a moment. Then one of the detail asked if anyone could believe what they just saw. He couldn't believe how fast Schea was. One of the men said that she looked to be around 15 or 16, but after seeing what she had done, he thought that she had to be at least in her mid-twenties. No one had a ready answer for how she could have done what she had done.

The lead security guard finally turned to the young man and said, "Sir, we need to get you out of here quickly in case there is another attempt. After all, the president wouldn't like it if 4 well-trained Secret Service agents let something happen to his son, especially after a girl had already saved him."

They left the hotel and headed to their limo to take them back to London. The young man's date was dropped off at her home in Hampstead, while the president's son, Jacob, was taken back to his room at the Ritz Hotel on Piccadilly Street. Once Jacob was in his room and the agents were posted outside his door, he went to the minibar, grabbed a scotch and drank it straight from the little bottle then grabbed another one, and sat on the sofa.

Jacob thought about what had happened. He knew why he happened to be looking over at Schea just as the attack had occurred. He was checking her out. In fact, he had been doing that since he had arrived in the bar.

He was surprised when the agent had suggested Schea was only 15 or 16. He had thought she was closer to his age, 24. *Oh well, if she was that young, then she would be off-limits for dating, but he still wanted to see her again. She seemed to lead a pretty interesting life.* And, he really craved something more interesting and exciting in his life.

Jacob's dad had been a senator when he started at Oxford 4 years ago. At that time, there had been no need for high security and such a controlled life. He had hoped that this experience would be his chance to have some fun and adventures in Europe. But then his dad won the presidential election 2 years ago and all of those hopes were dashed.

Now, he had to request permission to go anywhere and everyone around him had to have a security clearance conducted. He was proud of his dad and happy for him and the family, but he was getting a little tired of all of it. He finished his drink, fixed another and sighed. He would be back in the States in a few months after graduation and would need to think about his future.

XXXXX

The attacker was taken to London, where she was interrogated by British and American security officials. The bar had cleared out so quickly when the fighting started that they were pretty sure no one knew exactly what had happened, nor did they know who any of the people involved were.

The manger had been told, of course, by Britain's intelligence people, that they should expect a special guest and that all video equipment must be off. The ever proper British hotel owner made sure that the entire staff knew they had to be discrete and that all filming would be terminated at precisely 6 pm. They were also told to stop anyone from taking photos or videos inside the hotel. This, unknown to them, also assured Schea that she would not show up on any videos in the hotel or bar.

XXXXX

Vincent had gone directly by limo to London's Heathrow Airport to catch his flight for his meeting and heard nothing of the ruckus in the hotel bar. The only thing he was thinking about was Michele and her young firm body. He really wanted her and would definitely call her in 3 days for a little adventure in Chamonix.

As they approached the airport, his phone chimed. He picked it up and listened for a minute then said, "What? She did what?" He listened some more then hung up. *Well, that is certainly interesting.*

XXXXX

Schea called Todd as soon as she got to her room. It was near midnight and he had just gone to bed. Schea told him clearly and succinctly all that had happened. She also told him that she did not ask for names because that might seem a bit too inquisitive and listened without interruption.

When she finished, he told her, "You were right to give your name, my name, and where you work. I also agree that you should not have asked for any details about their client but they are probably American based on your description." He suspected that they would be calling him and he would need to be prepared.

"How do you feel about the odds of success in your current mission?" He asked.

She thought a moment then explained, "Vincent left about 10 minutes before all of the excitement, so he had to have been well away. I don't know where he is going but he said he will call me in 3 days and we will be meeting in Chamonix. I believe I should wait for his call and continue with the mission."

Todd thought a moment, decided that he trusted her judgment and agreed to allow her to continue with the mission. However, he suggested she get rid of her weapons. "I'll figure out a way to have weapons made available when you arrive in Chamonix and send you the instructions. You ought to leave Brighton and go up to London. Greenwich might be a good option since it is outside of central London."

# 33 Mission Three: Vincent (Part 2)

The following day Schea left for Greenwich. She arrived in London and took the Tube out to Greenwich, arriving at 1 pm. She found a small hotel, The Mitre, near the Tube station and booked a room for 3 nights. She placed her bag in her room then decided to check out the town.

Schea liked it right away. It had quaint shops and cafes and a nice view of the Thames. She also enjoyed touring the *Cutty Sark*. This ship used to hold the record for the fastest circumnavigation of the globe, and still does among schooners. She had dinner in the Gipsy Moth pub near the *Cutty* and sat next to a window so that she could continue to see its sleek lines and structure.

She slept well and went for a 15 mile run the next morning along the Thames Path. The path runs on both sides of the river and goes east and west for many miles. It is a great place to run, except that it can get pretty crowded later during the day with tourists.

After her run and shower, Schea went out for breakfast and tea. She found a nice café - The Hola Paella - inside of the Greenwich covered market. The weather was a little chilly, so she sat inside at the café enjoying a warm tea. She suddenly felt, before she heard, someone approach and turned as a young man reached her table.

He asked if he could join her. This was definitely a first for her and she didn't know what to say or do, which was also a first for her. He was cute and looked to be in his early twenties. He asked again with his eyes not his voice. Finally, she thought. *Why not?* "Sure." She pointed to the seat to her right.

He sat and said, "My name is Greg." He waited for her to tell him hers but she only smiled. "It looks like it's going to be a nice day." She mumbled that she agreed.

He was British based on his accent and asked, "Are you enjoying your visit to London."

She said, "Yes." Then, continued to look at her tea.

"Why did you choose to visit London?"

"I thought it would be a nice place to visit." She could tell that he was getting a little dejected.

He finally sighed. "Well, have a nice day," and started to leave.

As he stood to leave, Schea turned and said, "I'm sorry. Would you mind staying a little longer?"

He smiled back and said, "Of course. I would love to stay for a while." He sat back down.

Things went much better after that. Schea said, "I'm sorry for my earlier silence, but I have some things on my mind. My name is Michele and I am here on a European holiday and I am 17."

He reintroduced himself as Greg, that he lived in Chester, and that he had come to London to visit some friends in Camden Town, which is on the north side of London. He told Schea that he was 19.

They continued to chat and ordered more coffee for him and tea for her. She, of course, only told him about her cover life. He said that he was surprised that a girl of 17 had, what seemed like, an important job. She shrugged and said that her boss knew her family years ago and seemed to accept that.

About an hour later, he asked if she'd like to walk along the river and she said sure. They spent the next couple of hours walking and talking along the Thames. They walked past the Naval College with the Royal Observatory sitting high up on the hillside. He finally asked her if she would like to have dinner with him later. Schea asked about his friends and he told her that they were not meeting until the day after tomorrow. She hesitated a minute and then said sure. He suggested they meet at the Globe Theater next to the Tate Modern museum at 7pm.

They parted and Schea decided to walk up to the Royal Observatory. She enjoyed the tour of the observatory, and the museum and was especially fascinated by the Harrison clocks. She walked down river to the Tower Bridge and crossed over to check out the Tower of London. She ended up taking the Beefeaters' guided tour of the Tower. The Beefeaters are retired military veterans and live at the Tower with their families. They recently accepted the first female Beefeater.

Schea eventually went back to her room to change at about 5 pm. She checked her phone for voice or text messages, but didn't have any then headed to the Globe at 6:30. Greg arrived at 7 pm and they walked a short way along the river to the Founders Arms Pub. It sits right on the river so they had great views of the tourist boats and other craft sailing up and down the Thames. They also had a wonderful view of the dome of St. Paul's Church on the other side of the river.

She ordered a Diet Coke along with the fish and chips. He ordered a pint of the London Pride and the bangers and mash. They talked about London and Schea asked about his home in Chester. They had a nice evening and, as they walked out, he asked her if they could hang out tomorrow, and she said okay.

Greg suggested that they meet at the Globe Theater again since they both knew how to get there. She paused a moment then said sure and that she'd meet him at 10 am. He said okay and gave her a hug. She returned the hug and they headed off in different directions.

When she got back to her room, she sat on the bed and thought about what had just happened. Then, she smiled and thought. *Cool, I just got picked up by a cute British guy. That's pretty neat. He seemed to be nice and respectful, so why not have some companionship for the next day or so?*

She got up the next morning early and went for a 10 mile run. After she showered, she went to a small café near the hotel and had a bagel with cream cheese along with a glass of water. She met Greg at the Globe at 10 am and he suggested that they head to Westminster. As they crossed the Millenium Walk Bridge, he stopped and told her, "Look east along the river." He pointed to their right.

"The bridge you see down the river with the tall towers is not the famous London Bridge. It is actually called Tower Bridge. London Bridge is the next one up from Tower Bridge toward where we are." He pointed to the left of Tower Bridge, "The castle-looking structure is the Tower of London." She didn't tell him that she had taken the tour of it yesterday.

He spent several minutes telling her some of its history and Schea really enjoyed the *standing-on-the-bridge* tour he was giving her. She also enjoyed, for the second time, hearing the story about how the Tower had to always have 7 ravens or crows in residence so that the monarchy would not fall. In order to assure this, they clipped their wings so that they couldn't fly away.

They continued across the bridge towards St Paul's, headed past the church and up to the St Paul Tube stop. Before heading in, he asked Schea if she was hungry and she said she was. They turned to the left of the Tube entrance and walked about 100 meters to the Paternoster Pub. They went in and ordered a light lunch. She had a Diet Coke and he had a London Pride. After lunch and a nice conversation, they left and walked east to the Bank Tube station.

As they headed for the train, they heard one of the many performers singing a sweet song called *Walking In The Air*. They paused to listen and, before continuing, Greg dropped a couple of pounds into the singer's cup. As they continued to the train, Greg said, "I love that piece. I'm a space exploration junkie and watch a lot of videos put out by NASA. Mostly, I watch videos of the pictures taken by the Hubble Space Telescope or by the International Space Station."

"One that caught my attention several months ago was a NASA YouTube video of various short clips taken by one of the missions to the station. It showed numerous scenes of night and day over all parts of the Earth and the song Walking In The Air was playing in the background. That version of the song was sung by a famous young American singer named Jackie Evancho. I really think that her voice is fantastic."

This caught Schea's attention because Vincent had mentioned this same singer. If this singer was so famous, then many people around the world would know of her. Schea did not but that was only because she never really listened to the radio or watched much TV. She would definitely have to check her out.

They bought their Tube tickets and made their way to the Circle Line. They got off at Westminster and spent the rest of the day in much the same way as they had the day before. They walked over to the Westminster Bridge and stopped partway across while Greg gave her history of the sights they could see. He told her about the London Eye, the history of the nearby bridges, Parliament, Westminster Abbey, and Big Ben. He seemed to know a good bit about the history of London, so he talked and Schea listened. He told her that the clock tower that everyone called Big Ben was not really Big Ben. Big Ben is the name for the great bell in the tower that strikes on every hour.

At about 4 pm, her phone rang. She smiled and said she should get this since she was expecting a call from her boss. He smiled and nodded okay. She walked a little away from him and answered. It was Vincent and he said he was in Chamonix, waiting for her and there was an envelope with enough money in it for her to get to Chamonix. The envelope will be at the information booth at London City Airport. He said she should fly to Geneva then take the train to Chamonix.

Vincent asked her to meet him at the hotel Le Hameau Albert on Route du Boucet in the center of town. She said okay and would see him tomorrow. He asked her if she missed him. She said she missed him a bunch and they ended the call.

Schea came back to where Greg was waiting and said that the call was from her boss and she would be leaving tomorrow morning for France. He frowned and asked if she had to go so soon because he was going to be in London for another couple of days and would like to spend time with her, maybe take her to meet his friends. She smiled sadly and said she had to go. He shrugged and then said that they would at least be able to spend this last evening together. As they walked off, she reached over and took his hand - another first for Schea.

They were near Buckingham Palace, so they continued walking through Green Park and ended up on Piccadilly road. As they emerged from the park, they saw the Hard Rock Café a short walk away on the other side of the road. He smiled and said let's eat there. They did, and again, she enjoyed the brief history lesson that he gave her about Buckingham Palace and the Hard Rock Café, and they were indeed different stories.

They talked more about what he was planning to do, and about the places that she intended to visit on her trip. She had not given Vincent her last name or any information that he could use to track her, nor did she tell Greg. He seemed to accept this and didn't press her. He walked her out and accompanied her back to Greenwich.

She held hands with him as they walked the short distance to her hotel. They stopped in front of the Mitre hotel and turned to face each other. He thanked her for a pleasant time and she said the same. Then he leaned into her and kissed her on the lips. She was a little startled but recovered quickly and kissed him back. Finally, he pulled back, smiled and walked off. Another first for Schea - being kissed, kissing back and actually enjoying it.

Schea slept well, packed up her stuff the next morning and headed for the airport which wasn't far from Greenwich. She took the light rail system to the Westferry stop and switched to the train for London City Airport.

Schea entered the terminal and found the information booth. When she gave the guy her name, he nodded and handed her a large envelope. She then found a secluded section of seats in the lobby and sat. Inside the envelope was a large wad of euros and she counted out 3000 Euros. Vincent was obviously paying up front for not just the tickets but also for her services. She shook her head and smiled. She didn't need this much money but she would certainly use it wisely.

She went to the Ryan Air counter and purchased a ticket to Geneva. It cost her, actually Vincent, 500 Euros. She decided to keep another 500 for the train ticket and any just-in-case necessities. As she headed to the security check point, she saw a girl around her age holding a collection bucket and wearing a t-shirt with the word Charity on it. She walked over to her and asked, "What are you raising money for?" The girl said that the money would be used to help young girls in London who were on the streets.

Schea smiled and said, "Perfect." She deposited most of the remaining Euros into the girl's bucket. The girl watched the wad of money fall into the bucket and her eyes grew wide then she looked up to see Schea entering the security line, smiling.

Once Schea was through security and in the waiting area, she called Todd and explained what she was doing. He told her, "Go to the Visitor Information Office at the train station in Chamonix when you arrive. Tell the person there that you are Michele and you will be given an envelope. There will be a key in it and a locker number. You should find everything you need in the locker."

# 34 The Call

Todd did not have to wait long for someone to call about the event in Brighton, which didn't surprise him. After all, his employee had saved someone who was apparently very important. What did surprise him though was who had called. The caller said that he was calling from the office of the President of the United States and that the President and his wife wanted to personally thank Todd's employee for saving their son. *Oh boy*!

Todd did not expect that this was the client that Schea had saved and told the caller that he was sure that she would appreciate his thanks but that she was continuing with her job in Europe and might not be available for a few weeks. The caller said that was fine and they would make time whenever Ms. Tailor is available. Todd said he would tell her as soon as she was finished with her assignment.

He was thinking that they were done and was about to hang up when the caller said that the President would also like to talk to him when he is available. Now he was really surprised. He hesitated then said okay, and asked why the President wanted to talk to him? The caller told Todd that he did not know and was not privy to the details.

The caller asked when Todd would be available to come to the White House. Todd stammered and said, "Well, I guess I could come any time. Business is a little slow at the moment. However, I hope that White House security will allow me to keep my phone in case my employee needs me for something."

"I think that can be arranged." the caller said. "I will get back to you soon."

Todd set his phone down and sat staring across the room. Todd wondered. *What is this all about? Okay, it is a pretty big deal that Schea saved the President's son. I get that. And, I understand that they would want to thank her in person. Fine. I get that too. But, why would the President want to see me without Schea?*

He didn't have to wait long. He was called later that day by the same caller. The caller asked if he would be ready tomorrow morning and Todd said yes. The caller informed him that an army helicopter and pilot would leave Joint Base Lewis-McChord tomorrow morning and pick him up at around 7:00 am. It would then convey him back to JBLM and he would be escorted to an aircraft that would take him to Fort Monroe outside of Washington, DC.

He would be given a room in the VIP quarters for the evening, and the following morning, he would be met at his quarters at 8 am and flown by Marine One to the White House grounds. The caller asked if he had any questions. Todd said no and the call ended.

# 35 The Meeting

On the second morning after the call, Todd was escorted into the White House Situation Room. He was still in a state of confusion about all of this but tried to steel himself for his visit with President Jameson Bankcroft. True to the caller's word, he was searched but they did not take his phone from him. However, he was cautioned to carry the phone in his hand and keep it visible at all times while in the White House. Todd said he understood and would comply.

The agent escorted him to the Situation Room, opened the door, but did not follow him into the room. There were two men in the room - the President, whom he recognized, and someone he did not. The President stood immediately and came over to shake his hand. Bankcroft quickly said, "I am really looking forward to meeting Schea so that I can thank her for doing such a brave thing for my son."

Todd smiled. "I will contact your office as soon as she returns."

The other man introduced himself as Chuck Halverson and they all sat. The President started by saying, "I know you are probably wondering why you were asked to come to a meeting so quickly at the White House." Todd smiled, and the President continued, "I have been working with Mr. Halverson for about 6 months to form a unit that can be used for *special* missions. I have known Chuck since college and, although our career paths went in very different directions, we have remained best friends. I took the path of a politician and public servant, while Chuck went into the military. He has been in the Special Forces in Vietnam and the first Gulf War and retired after 30 years. I called Chuck and asked him to help me form this new unit."

Todd thought, *Okay, not much information there about why I am here.*

Bankcroft continued by saying that the types of people they want in this unit were the same as the ones that Todd had in his business. Now, Todd became wary, but Bankcroft smiled and held up his hand.

The President said that after he found out what Schea had done for his son, he wanted to check out where she worked. He said that his initial plan was to reward Todd's company with some government contracts. So he had his staff check into Todd's business and clients but couldn't find out much. Thus, he had had some additional research done and found that it seemed that Todd's company had some extremely unique talent working for him.

Bankcroft held up his hand again as Todd started to open his mouth. He quickly told Todd that all of this will remain classified and he had no intention of interfering with his work. Todd almost relaxed. Almost.

Bankcroft said Halvorson will take over from here. Halvorson started by saying that he too would keep all of the information about Todd's business classified. In fact, if Todd decided that he would prefer not to work with this new unit then he and the President would ensure that all of the information gathered would be destroyed and no further contact or action would be taken. Todd nodded.

Halvorson explained that this unit would be tasked with handling some of the most difficult rendition missions. The missions will be ones that could not be assigned to any of the other intelligence agencies, and the only high-level people involved would be the President and himself. They have been given approval by the heads of the congressional oversight committees and the intelligent agencies, and funding will come out of the Office of the President's discretionary budget.

He said that as far as he could tell, Todd's people handled the same kinds of missions they were thinking about assigning to this unit. Todd started to say something again but Halvorson raised his hand anticipating what he might say and told him that they were not interested in knowing about Todd's clients or any of his missions, past or present. He could continue operating as usual, but he would simply have one more client that might occasional ask for a resource. At this point, he fell silent and looked at Todd.

Todd sat quietly. He looked back and forth between both men trying to note any hint of deceit. He stayed quiet for half a minute and finally said, "Okay. I will be happy to have another client."

Bankcroft said he was grateful for Todd's trust in them and that it was not misplaced. "We have not assigned anyone as a resource to the unit yet because our requirements are so complex. We are still trying to find someone to be the first operative. When I heard about how Schea had handled herself in that dangerous and difficult situation, we wanted to talk to you."

"We figured that if your business has a teenage assistant who is as good as Schea, then you must have some pretty outstanding operatives doing field work. Would you mind setting up a meeting with us and your best operative? We want the first operative in our unit to be the best that you have to make sure the unit starts off with significant successes. We also want the first operative to be the model for subsequent operatives."

Todd smiled now. First, because if Schea were here, she would have gone off on these guys for assuming his best operative had to be a he! Second, because he knew that what he was going to tell them would *knock their socks off*.

The two men looked at him wondering why he had such a big smile. Todd continued smiling and said, "I do, in fact, have an operative in the field that is the best I have. The operative is on a mission but should probably be available for an interview in a couple of weeks."

Bankcroft asked, "How should we go about arranging for him to come in for a meeting when he finishes with his current mission?"

Todd smiled and said, "You have already begun the arrangements for the operative to come to the White House." He could tell they still didn't seem to understand. "You have asked to meet with Schea in a couple of weeks."

Now, they were really confused. The President said, "Yes. In order to thank her for what she did. Will the operative you will assign accompany her?"

Todd smiled. "Oh, I'm sorry for the confusion. I guess I didn't make it clear to you. Schea is my best operative."

Bankcroft and Halvorson stared at Todd as if waiting for him to laugh and say, just kidding. When he didn't and continued to look back at them, they turned and looked at each other. Finally, Bankcroft looked back at Todd and said slowly and seriously, "You're not kidding are you."

"Nope!"

Halvorson asked, "Todd, please give us some more background on Schea."

He told them all about the loss of her family, of Jenny, about how she came to him and about how she handled the training. He even told them about her match with Gus and the Wall Walk. He hesitated then said that due to confidentiality agreement with his clients, he could not tell them about his various clients or what Schea's assignments actually were.

"In terms of physical and mental qualifications, Schea is equal or better than anyone I have ever seen or trained. She could easily be a multiple sport Olympic athlete if she wanted to and her IQ was well above the genius level. That combination is what allows her brain to perfectly coordinate all of her physical and mental skills into a unique package for whatever she needs to do at any moment during a mission."

"But, her best and most powerful skill is her mission planning ability. At her age, most girls are trying to figure out boys, geometry and Shakespeare. But, Schea is determining the best approach alleys, weapons needs and escape routes in order to take down a target that has eluded all of the efforts of international and private organizations. Where they fail, she always succeeds and, often, by doing it alone. "

"All I can do is tell you that she has completed 2 missions and is on her third as we speak. She succeeded on her first two and I have no doubt that she will be successful on her current mission." He mentioned a couple of obstacles she had to overcome on each mission just to give them an idea that these were not easy assignments. "Both missions had up close and personal requirements and these were targets who were extremely bad and dangerous. Where other operatives and organizations had failed, Schea has succeeded. Her clients are never disappointed and often give her bonus payments for going above and beyond their expectations."

Todd stopped, looked at them and finished by telling them, "Schea is the real deal."

They both seemed to be impressed. Halvorson asked Todd if there wasn't someone else better suited to take on the types of missions he had described. Todd said that, at this time, based on what they had just told him, he didn't think so.

He told them there are missions that any of his operatives can handle. But, the up close and complex missions were Schea's specialty. He told them that her nickname at the training camp was *The Ghost*. She got that name because she had the ability to sneak up on any of the trainees and trainers without them knowing. But, he said, this particular Ghost skill went beyond that. Schea could sneak up on you while you watched her do it and you still wouldn't expect that you were her target.

He asked if they remembered the story he had told them about the match with Gus. They nodded. "Schea can make everyone around the target, as well as the target, think she is no threat. They always, and I mean always, underestimate her. They see a young girl in her teens and think. *What can she do?*" They smiled at that because they had both thought exactly that. "Schea is capable of getting into the personal space of any target. And when she strikes, she is very effective."

Todd finished by reminding them of the incident in Brighton. "None of the men in the Secret Service detail thought that she was a threat even as she moved closer to the President's son. The attacker didn't bother to worry about her either. And, even after she had taken the attacker out, no one assumed anything more about her than that she had been lucky. After all, she was just some teenage girl who worked as an assistant." Bankcroft and Halvorson smiled and shook their heads, knowing that is exactly what they all had thought.

Todd also decided to tell them that they could not second guess Schea's methods for getting close to her targets. They looked at him and said that was fine. He continued and told them, "You will keep thinking that she is a teenager, a young girl, going after some of the worst types of scum. The tendency, when you think of her that way, is to try to second guess the decision to send her. Schea will probably have to do things that no operative, let alone a teenage girl, should ever have to do."

"But," he said, "You cannot think that way. She knows exactly what she is doing and she never does anything she does not truly believe needs to be done to get to the target. However," he continued, "I do not believe that she would ever go so far as to let some pervert have his way with her. She probably does let them touch her and maybe see her unclothed but that's it."

Todd stopped and watched their reactions. Both men frowned and looked away. Todd knew that the President had a daughter not much older than Schea. Finally, they both seemed to accept what Todd had said, albeit reluctantly, and nodded.

He seemed finished, so Bankcroft glanced at Halvorson. Halvorson smiled, nodded his assent, and Bankcroft turned back to Todd. "We would like Schea as our first operative in the unit."

Todd smiled. "I thought you would. I will get back to you as soon as I can after she returns from her current mission."

He looked at both men, "But, the decision to join your unit will be completely Schea's. She, and only she, will decide if she wants to join or not. She will also have the final say as to whether she will take on a mission or not."

They smiled and Bankcroft said, "Of course. We wouldn't have it any other way." He finished by saying, "After all, we really don't want her to get mad at us for forcing her to do something she doesn't want to do."

Todd smiled. "No, you definitely do not want to piss Schea off."

# 36 Mission Three: Vincent (Part 3)

The flight to Geneva left at 7 am and Schea sat in first class thanks to Vincent's generosity. After it landed, she made her way to the train station by taxi, bought a ticket to Chamonix and arrived at 1 pm. She had wondered if Vincent was having her followed so she could not let them see her going to the locker.

She walked past the Visitor Office and the lockers, and entered the women's restroom. She found an empty stall and entered. She quickly opened her bag and changed her clothes. She also had small amounts of theater makeup in a plastic bag and used a small mirror to apply it. She had learned well from Alice. She pulled out a large canvas shopping bag that was folded up in her bag's side pocket, and deposited her travel bag into it.

She exited the restroom looking 30 years older, wearing a house dress and an awful looking sweater. She carried what looked like a bag of items from a grocery store. She had been in the restroom for about 5 minutes, so she had to hurry. She got the envelope from the guy at the Visitor Office and quickly retrieved the gym bag from the locker. She stuffed it into her shopping bag and re-entered the restroom.

She quickly wiped off all of the make-up, changed and walked out about 15 minutes after she had first entered. This time, she came out wearing a short white skirt, 2 inch heels, and a blue blouse under a short leather jacket. Her hair was down and fell across her shoulders. She looked hot. She hoped that, if someone was following her, they would simply think that she had been in the restroom so long in order to look her very best for Vincent.

She had told Vincent, when he called her in London, that she had to stay at a different hotel from his. She told him, "My parents will be calling me soon because it has been over a week since I left LA and I really don't want them to accidentally hear someone else's voice on the phone or in the background."

Vincent made a show of grudgingly agreeing knowing she wouldn't really need the room for long. He said he would book her into a hotel a short distance from his. "Besides," she told him, "you probably have very important business to conduct and you don't need me running in and out."

Of course, she knew exactly what that important business was. *Her*!

In the envelope she picked up in London, he indicated that he had booked her into the Hotel Le Faucigny, while he would be at the Grand Hotel Des Alpes. They were about 250 meters apart and close to many restaurants and bars. She proceeded to the hotel, checked in and called Vincent.

She told him that the hotel was beautiful and thanked him effusively for picking it and for bringing her to Chamonix. She told him that she had picked up a couple of brochures and had been reading about the area, and said she really wanted to go up onto Mont Blanc to watch the sunset. He suggested that they have dinner this evening, and they would definitely see the sunrise and the sunset from Mont Blanc over the next couple of days.

She knew what that meant and wasn't about to go to his room. She couldn't kill him there since she would have been seen with him. She could have done it in Brighton because Todd had arranged to have a *clean-up* crew sent after she was finished and no trace of Vincent would have been left there. But, they had not had time to arrange that in Chamonix.

She used her impatient teenage voice and pleaded to go this afternoon. "Besides," she said, "we will have time after the sun sets for dinner, and other things."

He finally relented and said to meet him at the Cimetiere du biolay in one hour. She screeched with excitement and said "thank you" over and over again until he finally told her that he had to go.

She hung up and got ready. It would be a little chilly so she knew she needed a sweater and, since they would be hiking, she needed a pair of sturdy shoes. But, she also knew that she needed to look good for Vincent. She stripped and put on a little red thong and a strapless thin bra. She wore her short white skirt, a wool sweater, and a pair of sturdy trail-running shoes.

Before she put on the sweater, she strapped her two knives to her upper body, one on each side of her chest. She secured them upside down under her armpits. They were thin but sturdy knives. Todd knew what she liked and, it seemed, he could also get whatever was needed anywhere in the world. *Cool!*

She checked a map of Chamonix and located the Cimetiere du biolay which was only a short walk away. She would be meeting Vincent at about 3:30 pm and they would have 2-3 hours of daylight before the sky started to darken and the sun set behind the western hills. She figured he would want to find a hiking trail that was secluded and led to a remote area, far away from any nosey tourists.

She also checked the map for trails that began near the Cimetiere. There seemed to be a number of them and they all looked pretty secluded to her but she really didn't know for sure. She had two maps, one that she had picked up as she left the train station and one that she was given by the overly friendly reservation clerk when she checked in. The clerk was a young guy who also checked her out as she walked away from the counter.

She thought of Greg. They didn't exchange contact information, since she could not do that but wondered if she should have asked him for his. *No. That would not have been a good idea. This was the life I have chosen, so there is no sense thinking about such things, at least for now.*

Schea left in time to make sure she was at the Cimetiere before Vincent. She wanted him to see an excited girl who couldn't wait to begin her little adventure in Chamonix. When he arrived, he hugged her tightly and gave her a squishy kiss on the lips. He also gave her butt a nice little squeeze. She giggled and kept saying, "Let's go. I don't want to miss the sunset." He smiled and took her hand.

Vincent led her away from the Cimetiere toward a narrow road that led towards the base of the mountain. Near the end of the road a trail branched off up the hillside. Vincent said he knew the area well, since his family used to come here in the summer for hiking and skiing in the winter. She said, "Cool," and kept telling him that they needed to go. She practically dragged him up the trail. After about 30 minutes, they reached a fork in the trail. The right trail was narrow and looked little used. The left one seemed to be the continuation of the trail that they were already on.

Schea started to pull him to the left but he said no, the right one would lead to a great spot to view the town and the sunset. She didn't argue. She just led him in that direction. If she had looked back, she would have seen a very satisfied Vincent. If he could have seen Schea from the front, he would have seen a very satisfied Schea.

Schea guessed that Vincent's plans would satisfy her plans quite nicely and, so far, they did. They continued for about 45 minutes and eventually came to a small clearing in the trees. There was a steep scrub area leading straight up to the left and a sharp drop-off to the right. On the way to the area they had had to cross a 4 foot wide stream and her left foot got wet as she jumped across.

She turned to look out over the valley in order to see the town and the sunset, but the view was blocked by a thick wall of trees and forest undergrowth. She turned back to Vincent and asked if this was the spot because she couldn't really see anything. Vincent smiled and said, "Yes, this is the perfect spot."

Schea knew, of course, what he meant by perfect spot, and it wasn't to see any of the town or of the sunset. It was to not be seen by anyone. But, she continued the charade and said, "But we can't see anything here." Schea asked innocently, "Did we come the wrong way?"

He smiled, "No. This is exactly where I want us to be."

What Vincent didn't know was that this was also exactly where Schea wanted them to be. Vincent moved a little to his left and backed away toward the steep hillside that headed up the mountain. Schea moved with him to her left and a little back from him. If someone could have seen them, they would have thought that they were about to have a gunfight in the old west. Well, it was going to be a fight but not with guns, at least, Schea hoped not since she didn't have one.

They finally stopped and Schea, smiling sheepishly asked, "Why are we stopping here?"

Vincent suggested, "You probably know why, especially if you'd just think about it a little."

She looked slightly away and asked quietly, "Couldn't we wait for that until this evening? That way, we could see the sunset, we could take a shower together, have dinner, and then, the other things."

Vincent smiled and said, "I really can't wait. You see, I will not be staying in Chamonix this evening since I have a very important meeting to get to in Moscow. So, we have to have our fun now before I leave."

154

Then, his smile vanished and he said, "I know what you did in Brighton. I know that you are a pretty tough little girl."

Schea had thought that he probably had her followed and knew about London and about Greg. She quickly said, "I was just lucky with that woman. I mean, I know a little about self-defense but the woman seemed to be crazy and really had no skills, so it was easy for me to knock her to the floor."

Vincent said, "Yes, my report seemed to indicate that the woman seemed to be a crazy woman. However, my report also said that you seemed to know more than just some simple self-defense skills. Anyway, I hope that you enjoyed Greenwich and the tour of the city because you won't get to see it again."

Schea's mind was reeling. *How could he know all of this? I must have been followed, but I am usually pretty careful about looking out for that.* Then, it hit her. *Greg! It had to be him!*

Suddenly, from behind her, Greg stepped out from the trees and said, "Hello, Michele."

She whirled around and stared at him. He was smiling and made a show of tipping an imaginary hat.

Schea had to think fast now. She looked at him and said, "Hello, Greg, or whatever your name is." She looked down and said, "I am so sad that you lied to me, especially after our kiss." She glanced at Vincent with an angry look.

Vincent simply stared at her with a smile on his face.

Schea couldn't let this turn-of-events affect her. After all, this is what she had trained for. She had to deal with it when things went sideways with Mendoza and the pirate, so why not here. She was lucky she always carried two knives in case one missed or didn't kill the target right away. She also figured that she knew what they were planning to do and she needed to play along in order to buy herself some time.

She had to become the *Ghost* for them. Even though they know what she did to the woman in Brighton, they probably thought that two strong men would be too great a match for a little girl, so she needed to feed that belief, and she needed to start right now.

She decided that they were looking for fun so she would give them some fun - for a little while anyway.

She moved a little to her left and turned her back to the trail that had brought them here. She kept looking back and forth between them with a totally scared look on her face. Finally, she started begging them not to hurt her.

She told them, "I was just lucky with that woman. I can't really do that kind of stuff with a man, let alone two men." She held her hands in front of her face and muffled a cry then looked at them again, pleadingly.

Vincent said, "Relax. I really do not want to hurt you. Greg is present just in case you get feisty while I'm doing you." He then glared at her. "So, don't get feisty and all will be fine."

"However, since Greg is here, well, he might want to have some fun too. Now, if you get feisty with Greg, well then, I will have to step in and help." Still glaring at her, he asked, "Do you understood what I just said."

Schea kept looking back and forth between them with a frightened look on her face, but she was actually calmly formulating her attack. She told Vincent, "I understand everything you said and I will not get feisty with either of you." She kept repeating that she would not fight at all. "You can do what you want with me, but please do not hurt me." She even generated tears for them.

While Schea was saying all of this she gave them a show. She slowly unzipped her skirt and let it slide down her legs to the ground. She stepped out of it and backed up about a foot. She watched them and kept repeating that they shouldn't hurt her and, she saw what she wanted to see. Both men were looking at her legs and, in particular, the tiny red thong that really left nothing to the imagination.

As they watched her with great expectations written on their faces, she kept talking and slowly reached under her sweater. She undid her bra and wiggled until it dropped out from under her sweater and landed on the ground. She stepped about 6 inches back from it. Now, they were torn between what they could see and what they couldn't wait to see. They desperately wanted to see it all.

Schea felt that she was far enough away from them to get her knives down, out and thrown without the guys being able to reach her. They were also paying lots of attention to her body parts except for the part above her neck, which was excellent. In her case, that is why she liked having those particular parts below her neck and the best part above it.

She reached under her sweater and moved her hands up enough to get the bottom of the sweater past her navel, then exposed the bottom of her breasts. Now they were hooked, so it was time to jerk the fishing line. She slowly grabbed the knives - her right hand grabbed her left knife and her left hand grabbed her right knife. Once she had them firmly in hand she whipped out both hands and threw.

The knife in her left hand entered Greg's chest. The knife in her right hand headed toward Vincent. Greg fell onto his back, dead. The knife had hit his chest dead center, literally and figuratively. His heart was pumping blood everywhere inside of him, but not where it was supposed to go.

But, when Schea snapped her head to her left, she saw that the knife that hit Vincent had indeed hit him in the chest but just to the right of his heart. He would die but not right away. Apparently, her strip tease had worked him up a little too quickly. He had already started reaching down to unbuckle his pants, which caused him to turn his body a little to the right.

Vincent wasn't dead but he was really, really mad. He grabbed Schea's knife, and pulled it free. This would accelerate his death but still not fast enough. He charged her.

She spun and went for the knife in Greg's chest. Just as she reached for it, Vincent managed to grab the back of her sweater. But, it was his left hand, so it had little strength given that the left side of his body was probably dead by now. She gave a jerk forward and he let go. However, this caused her to stumble toward Greg. As she fell, she twisted to her left and fell on her right side next to Greg.

As Schea hit the ground, she reached over, grabbed the knife in his chest and threw it at Vincent just as he started to fall onto her for the kill. Her throw would have been spectacular in a knife-throwing contest, but in this situation, it was dumb luck. The knife entered Vincent's right eye, continued into his brain, and he died instantly.

He fell on the pile of bodies. Schea had fallen in such a way that her butt was across Greg's crotch at about a ninety-degree angle. Vincent had fallen face-down onto Greg and his crotch was directly over Schea's. When Vincent fell he also had his arm in a position to strike at Schea. This caused his elbow to come down hard on Schea's chest which meant he got to feel her boobs without knowing it, but she sustained a deep bruise. She hoped she had no cracked ribs.

As she wiggled free of the ménage-a-trois, she smiled and thought that this is exactly the position that she would have been in, if the guys had gotten their way.

Schea did a quick check of the area to make sure no one was around, grabbed her knives and clothes then headed for the small stream they had crossed. She cleaned the knives and set them aside. She washed her hands and a few areas on her legs with splattered blood from the two bodies. Luckily, she had rolled to the side so there was no blood on her sweater or her hair. She put her bra and skirt back on and concealed the knives under her arms again.

She walked back to the bodies and did a search for anything that could identify her. When the authorities checked, they'd find some forensic matter and DNA but will only be able to determine that a female had been with the guys. The authorities might conclude that the men had had the same woman recently, and they would continue searching for some kind of hit man or group. The men were hardened, known criminals, so the authorities probably had lots of enemies to investigate.

# 37 Leaving the Alps

Schea walked back down the trail carefully observing the area in order to make sure she wasn't seen by anyone. She needn't have worried. Vincent knew what he was doing and she saw no one until she got back near the Cimetiere where there were a few mourners and maybe even some tourists.

She was not going back to the same hotel. After what had happened with Greg, she did not trust that Vincent did not have someone there watching for her. Schea walked to the area around the train station and found a nice-looking hotel called the Langley Hotel Gustavia. She walked in and asked for a single room for the night and told the clerk, "My bags are in a locker in the train station because I didn't want to carry them around while looking for a hotel."

The nice lady behind the desk nodded knowingly. As the lady got Schea a room key, she asked Schea if she was a tourist. Schea told her that she was an exchange student in London going to the London School of Economics where Mick Jagger went and was traveling on the continent this week on holiday. The woman smiled and thought that, as young as this girl was, she probably doesn't even know who Mick Jagger is. In fact, Schea did not, but only remembered reading somewhere that he had gone there.

Schea picked up another map at the train station and searched the area for a spot to deposit the knives. There was a small river running through town and a small lake just to the north. The lake was closer, so she thought she'd see it first. It was about a kilometer away, and only took 10 minutes to get there. It turned out to be a lovely spot to come and relax alone or with a friend. And, more importantly, it was also a great place to toss knives into it. Once she was sure no one was around, she reached under her sweater, pulled the knives out, and tossed them into the water.

Schea was not going to go back to the first hotel until late in the evening when she was sure that the clerk who had checked her in would be gone. She also did not want to go around to places where he might loiter and hang out. Schea stayed out of the central areas of town and wandered the long way around in order to look up at Mont Blanc. A series of gondolas climbed up the side of the mountain and continued all of the way to Italy. There was also a tram and a cable car that went up to the top of the mountain where you could look around at some pretty spectacular views. That all sounded so cool.

XXXXX

She finally went back to the first hotel at about 11 pm and entered through a side door. She by-passed the lobby area and headed up the stairs to her room. She grabbed her bag and changed into jeans, a blouse and a jacket. She also swung by the train station, picked up her other bag, and left the same way back to the Langley.

She went to her room, undressed, showered and called Todd. She briefed him on the results and her plans for returning. She had decided to take the gondola over the mountains, head to Milan, then fly home from there.

Todd told her he was glad the mission had gone well and told her that he would want the details when he sees her, but added that she needed to fly to Washington, DC and call him when she has her flight information. She asked why the change. Todd told her he needed to see her and would pick her up at the airport.

Schea slept soundly and decided to check out early in order to catch the gondola ride. The day was beautiful with blue skies and a warm sun. She went to the ticket booth and asked for one ticket to Italy. The older gentleman said, "You have chosen a wonderful day for the ride. The views will be spectacular. Head to the departure area where you will be guided to the next gondola available."

She walked over and a young guy called her over for the next gondola. When it arrived, he opened the small door on the side and gave her a short safety briefing. He told her things like, *stay in the gondola, don't throw anything out, and don't hang out of it.* She agreed to all and signed a waver that basically blames her if she died or got hurt. *Comforting!*

The gondola left the little covered shelter and headed up the mountain. It was so cool. As she passed over the tops of the mountains the views were, indeed, spectacular. She absolutely loved it, but it was over too soon. She couldn't even tell how long it took to get to the end of the ride because she was so engrossed in the sights and the quiet solitude. She hadn't thought about how quiet it would be, but then she realized that there wasn't a motor in the thing.

When she reached the end and the employee at the arrivals building opened the door, she was tempted to tell him to leave her in. But, she knew that she had to get going, so she thanked him for a wonderful ride and left.

XXXXX

Schea took the first train to Milan and then grabbed a cab to the airport. Once she booked her flight and passed through security, she called Todd to give him the flight details. He said he would meet her at the airport just outside at the curb.

She found the gate and sat until they started calling for her flight. Since they board first class first, she only had to sit for about 20 minutes. This was a non-stop flight to Washington's Dulles Airport and would take about 10 hours. The nice thing was that the first class seats could be turned into little beds. *Very nice! After what I had had to deal with, a little tender loving care was very welcome indeed!*

The flight took off and after an hour, the FA came back to Schea's seat, gave her a menu and told her that she'd be back to take her order in a few minutes. Schea said okay and the FA left. Schea looked through the menu and decided on the salmon. The meal was actually excellent and the salmon was cooked just the way that Schea liked it.

Memories of Vincent having her followed and Greg's betrayal saddened her. She had to be wary of anyone, boy or girl, who befriends her. She couldn't trust anyone it seemed and hated having to be that way. She even wondered if she could trust Todd's team or anyone outside of the group, like her

159

friends at the theater. This was a horrible feeling. *It truly sucked having to be so suspicious of people around me.* This is something she should talk to Todd about once they had some private time.

The other thing that this mission taught her was that she needed to keep her guard and awareness up even while she was working on tearing the target's awareness down. She should have at least become suspicious when both Vincent and Greg talked about admiring the young American singer. Also, Greg should never have been able to sneak up on her from the trees. That was a close call.

When the FA came to clear her tray away, Schea told her that she was probably going to sleep for the rest of the flight and asked for help getting the bed folded out. The FA came back as soon as she had put the tray in the galley, and helped Schea unfold the bed. She also brought some blankets. The FA asked her if she would like to be woken for breakfast. Schea said yes and thanked her for her help.

Schea slept until breakfast, ate and readied herself for the arrival. They arrived about 30 minutes early and pulled up to the gate. Schea grabbed her carry-on bag and headed off. As she passed the galley she thanked the FAs there and headed out onto the Jetway.

Once Schea cleared Customs and Immigration, she headed for the exit. She made her way outside, saw Todd, went over and said, "Hey."

"How was the flight?"

"It was great."

Only, it wasn't his car. It was a huge black limousine, and Todd directed her to it. She looked at Todd and he just smiled, opened the door for her, and motioned for her to get in. She did, and the limo pulled away. The driver was completely invisible on the other side of the window that separated the passenger area from the front seat area. The back area was huge, with big comfy seats all around and even a mini-bar.

As they pulled away, Todd smiled and looked over at her. "Would you like a drink?"

She looked at him and asked, "Do I need anything stronger than a Diet Coke?"

"Maybe." he said.

She sat back and thought. *What now?*

# 38 The President

Schea finished running the 20 miles along the Chesapeake Bay and felt really good. The trail had been perfect. It was relatively flat with a few small hills to give the runner a little challenge. It wound along the bay and passed through some patches of trees and fields. She had run to the 0 mile marker and turned to head back to the 10 mile marker where she had started. The run took about 2 and half hours.

She walked back to the hotel, showered and went down to check-out.

She decided to head west to visit Mount Vernon. She had never been there and had always felt that every *Red, White, and Blue* American should visit the home of George Washington, the first president of the United States, once in their life.

As she drove for the next couple of hours, she recalled visiting the home of the current President not that long ago.

XXXXX

Schea provided a detailed debriefing to Todd in the limo on the way to wherever they were going. After she finished, she was quiet for a bit, as was Todd. Finally, Schea said that she would like to talk with him when he had the time. She glanced over at him and Todd said, "Sure. We will have time later this evening." She nodded and they continued on in silence.

As they approached the central area of DC and the various famous buildings came into view, Schea looked over again at Todd and asked where they were going. He simply said to have patience. She figured that this was probably not going to be anything normal and asked if she needed to change. He smiled and said that she looked fine.

Todd was secretly glad that she was dressed the way she was. She looked like some teenage kid going out to a movie with her friends. This, of course, is what he wanted the people attending this meeting to see when they looked at Schea.

The limo turned and Schea saw the White House directly ahead of them. Now she was really nervous, and this time she demanded to know where they were going. Todd just pointed at the White House and said right there. Her mouth fell open and she stared out the window as they passed through the gate and around to the back of the White House where they finally stopped.

A few seconds later her door opened and a guy with dark glasses asked if she needed any help getting out. She nervously mumbled no thank you, slid over, and stepped out. She hadn't even noticed Todd getting out but suddenly he was by her side. She whispered to him, "What is going on?" He suggested, again, to be patient.

Another man in dark glasses joined the first and the small group headed through a side door and into the White House.

Schea's mind was a jumbled mess now. She didn't even know what to say or do, which was probably another first for her. Todd walked behind her while one man took the lead and the other brought up the rear. The procession proceeded down stairs, through hallways, and eventually came to an elevator. Schea's sense of direction was completely overloaded.

She kept thinking. *What the hell are we - am I - doing here. You do not go into the White House, especially through a back door.* She couldn't see Todd because he stayed behind her but, if she could, she would have seen a smile on his face and, if she could have read his mind, she would have heard him saying to himself that he was totally enjoying this and was so looking forward to seeing the look on Schea's face when she met the President.

The first man finally stopped and Schea almost slammed into his back. He knocked on a door, which quickly opened. The first man stepped aside and motioned for Schea to enter the room. If you had told Schea that she was going to prison right now she would have simply shrugged.

The man who opened the door asked Schea and Todd to take a seat. The room was sparsely furnished, but did have a table and 6 chairs. There were paintings on the wall of various outdoor scenes, a table along one wall with glasses of different shapes and a large pitcher. Schea and Todd sat at one end of the table. The man in dark glasses stood by the door. After a few minutes, the door opened againand several people started entering.

Schea noticed that Todd stood up immediately, so she followed his lead and stood up as well. As she watched the procession of people arrive, she recognized the first man as President Bankcroft. She also vaguely recognized the woman as his wife. The next man was young and she immediately recognized him as the guy she saved in the bar in Brighton. The last man was completely unfamiliar to her.

As she stared at them, she didn't notice that the President was heading straight for her. She leaned backward and thought about running away, but then thought. *Where would I go?* Besides, she now saw that Todd was looking at her with a huge smile on his face.

Suddenly, the President was only a few feet in front of her and was saying something. She couldn't seem to hear or speak but she did, at least, place a smile on her face. Finally, her brain seemed to clear and she heard the President say how grateful he and his wife were for what Schea had done for their son. *So that is who that guy is.*

Schea managed to mumble "You're welcome." as though he had thanked her for a muffin. Finally, he moved aside and his wife came over to her. Schea now put a big smile on and finally started to hear properly. His wife also thanked her and asked if she could give her a hug. Schea said, "Sure. I would like that." The President's wife wrapped her arms around Schea and Schea did the same. They held each other for several seconds then the President's wife pulled away.

Finally, the young man came over and extended his hand to Schea. Schea took it and the young man told her that he was grateful that she happened to be in the right place at the right time. Schea smiled, and said she was glad to have been able to help and it was really nothing. This made the President and the man that Schea did not know chuckle and look at Todd. Todd just raised his eyebrows and his shoulders as though saying, "See, what did I tell you."

The President still stood just to Schea's right and watched all of this. He could see that everything that Todd had said about Schea was true. All of the men, and even his wife, were taller than Schea. As a matter of fact, he, Todd, his son, and Halvorson had to be a foot taller. He began to find it hard to believe that Schea could do some of the things that Todd had told him. But, then again, the results speak for themselves.

He could also see the Ghost in her. She completely disarmed people. She was so sweet and cute and nice. She even acted like a teenage girl, and he knew all about teenage girls since he had one. Just looking at her, no one would ever fear her or think of her as a threat. But, the evidence of his son's almost fatal encounter in Brighton told him that she was exactly what Todd had said she was - a Ghost that can kill in a flash then disappear.

Finally, the President said, "I am so glad we had this chance to say thanks for what you did for our son." Schea just stood nervously, smiled, looked around and thought about running again.

That seemed to be the signal for everyone to leave. The President's wife and son left the room along with the man in dark glasses. Schea started to move with them toward the door.

*God I wish I had that drink in the limo, but I probably would have gotten sick, so it was just as well that I didn't. After all, throwing up all over oneself and then meeting the President would probably not have made a very good impression.*

Then she noticed that Todd wasn't moving and figured, *fine you stay and have a nice chat, but I gotta go.* However, as soon as the man with the dark glasses was through the door, it closed. The only people in the room now were Todd, the President, the man with no name, and Schea. Schea stopped moving, looked around and saw that they were all looking at her.

Finally, the President suggested that they all sit. The men sat, but Schea stood rigid as though her feet were cemented to the floor. Todd reached over and gently tugged her back to the seat next to him.

She whispered to Todd, "What's going on?"

The President must have heard her because he started talking while looking at her.

*Dammit, they are all looking at me.* She looked down at her shirt thinking that her blouse was open and they were looking at her boobs. *Oh God, I need a drink,* was all she could think.

She finally decided that she needed to get her head into whatever was going on and pay attention. *Don't get distracted. Remember what happened in Chamonix. Besides, she knew that this*

163

*must have something to do with her, which logically should matter to her. So, she told herself to listen and to pay attention.*

The President was finishing up another thank-you to her for what she did in Brighton. This time she just smiled. He continued. He told her, "Mr. Chuck Halvorson," whom he now introduced to her, "and I have been talking for several months about some of the sensitive issues that the government, and in particular, the intelligence agencies have to deal with around the world. We started to discuss the need for a unit made up of people who might be able to help with various strategies to deal with these issues, and we have been trying to find the right people to be part of this unit."

*Oh no,* Schea could see where this might be heading. *They are thinking of asking me to be in this unit so that I can sit around and think of ways to get the bad guys. And, then the big tough men will go off and execute her plan. Well, even though he is the President, I am going to tell him where he can stick that job offer.*

The President glanced at Halvorson, and Halvorson continued. "This unit needs to be completely secret, and the people in it must be the best of the best. They also must be able to handle any situation in the field that might come up. The people in this unit will never meet and will only receive their mission briefs from me. They will report the results to me, or someone that is assigned by me, and the operative will know who it is before they set off."

Schea was only half-listening now because she still hadn't heard what any of this had to do with her. She glanced at Todd, but he was just sitting, impassively listening as though he already knew all about this. She thought that if he had set her up for this job then, after she told the President where to shove the offer, she was going to give Todd a good thrashing.

Finally, Halvorson finished and the President started to talk. Schea was thinking, *Could someone just tell me what the heck I am doing here.* She sighed and continued to listen.

Bankcroft said, "So far we have not found anyone suitable for the mission planning and field-work. This is why we contacted Todd. We asked him if he knew someone that he thought was the best for these types of missions and field-work."

Schea rolled her eyes and thought *here it comes. He recommended me and they are going to ask me to be in their stupid unit sitting around making plans and, probably, sandwiches. Crap!*

The President finished by looking directly at Schea and asking her, "We want you to be the first field operative for this unit."

Schea was about to tell him where to shove his offer, but hesitated. She thought. *Did he just say field operative as in, I'm in the field running my own missions?* She kept staring at the President, and he, along with Todd and Halvorson, kept staring at her. Finally, Todd nudged her and whispered, "You might want to say something."

So, she did. She asked the President for clarification. "Will I be planning my own missions and going into the field as the operative?"

He said, "Yes, that is exactly what we would like you to do, Ms. Tailor."

She almost giggled. She couldn't remember ever being called Ms. Tailor. She decided that she should just smile and not giggle. She smiled, opened her mouth to say something, but ended up giggling.

You would have thought that she had been asked by the President to join his family for dinner. All three men stared at her in stunned silence. She realized what she had done and said, "I'm sorry, but I thought it was cool that the President called me Ms. Tailor. I have never been called that before, and it was just fun to hear it." They still continued to stare at her.

Then, she suddenly remembered the question the President had asked her. She shook her head, looked at him and said, "I would love to be the first mission operative in the unit." She smiled and said, "This is just so cool."

The President and Halvorson could still not stop staring at her.

Finally, Todd spoke. He looked at the men and said, "Isn't she everything that I told you she was?"

They still couldn't talk so they just nodded. Schea looked around then asked the President, "May I have a Diet Coke? I'm pretty thirsty."

This broke the silence, and the two men started laughing. The President finally got control of himself and told her, "Of course, you can have a Diet Coke."

He got up, went to the door, opened it, and said something to the man outside. About a minute later, there was a knock, and the door opened for a man who wheeled in a cart that had Diet Cokes on top along with an assortment of liquor and beer. The President got up immediately and grabbed a cold Diet Coke, filled a glass with ice, and poured the soda over it. He turned and handed the glass and can to Schea. He said, "Here you are Ms. Tailor and welcome to our one man, um, woman unit!"

Schea thanked the President and smiled. The President turned back to the tray and poured himself a scotch, while Todd and Halvorson each grabbed a beer.

They all sat back down again and the President said, "Let's have a toast to our first operative." They all raised their drinks to Schea and drank.

Halvorson started telling Schea, "You will not be getting your missions directly from me in this case, but from Todd. He knows you best. Todd will also be assigning his own missions to you. You will never be asked to discuss any of Todd's missions and should never volunteer anything either." She nodded.

"You can always refuse a mission if you do not think that you can handle it or if it just doesn't feel right. No questions asked. But when you accept a mission then you should complete it, if possible. Any debriefs will be handled by Todd and I. The President will no longer be involved unless he requests it for a very specific reason."

Halvorson stopped for a moment. The President, while looking at Schea, smiled and asked her age. He knew it because Todd had told them but he wanted to hear her say it. She said, "I am 17." The President looked at her warmly and thought. *Should they really be sending this young girl on the type of missions they had in mind? But then he remembered what Todd had told him about her successes. He also knew that the mission that she had just returned from a few hours ago had been a complete success.*

Schea sensed what the two men were thinking. She put her glass down and looked at the president and Halvorson. She stopped smiling. "I know what you are thinking. Here is this young teenage girl and you are going to put her into potentially horrible, life-threatening situations. But now, you are questioning that decision."

She looked at both men, one after the other, and with a calm but assured voice told them, "You need not worry about me. You will not be putting me in harms-way. I will listen to the mission details then I will decide to do it or not. As with Todd, and as you said yourselves, I will always have the right to refuse a mission. I haven't done so yet, but the knowledge that I can refuse is all that matters. As to the horrible people I go to kill and the shit I have to deal with," she looked over and asked Todd, "Did you tell them about my life prior to joining your unit?"

"I told them everything."

"Good." She looked back at the men.

Schea began again, "I have already been through horrible situations and nothing that I have seen or been through on my missions comes close. As for life-threatening, our lives are constantly under threat from storms, drivers on the highway, random acts of violence and more. There is nothing that I can do to protect anyone from those threats."

"But, rapists, terrorists, brutal world leaders, child traffickers, and mass murderers, well, that is a different story. I know exactly how to deal with them and have all of the skills needed to do so. And more importantly, I want to do it with all my heart and soul. As a matter of fact, I must do it or the deaths of my mother, father, brother and sister, and all of the other moms, dads and kids who've suffered at the hands of these brutes will not be avenged. I want to do it and will do it until as many of the bastards as possible are dead and rotting in hell."

She stopped talking, didn't smile, but simply looked hard at the two men. They were both stunned and couldn't think of anything to say. However, they both saw what Todd had meant about Schea's eyes. When she looked like this, you had better beware because she has just turned deadly serious, literally and figuratively.

Todd finally broke in and said, "Well do you gentleman have any more questions for me or Schea?"

Schea dropped her eyes off of the men and then looked back up at them. Both men were stunned again because her eyes were now warm and friendly. Schea was also smiling and turned to Todd. She asked, "Do you think you could top this visit to the White House when you take me on a tour of the rest of DC?"

Todd smiled. "I'll try."

The two men smiled at first then started jabbering away about how good it has been to finally meet her, and that if she needed anything to just ask Todd or Halvorson.

The President broke in at his point, looked at Schea, and said, "You can always come directly to me. If you ever need anything, all you need to do is call this White House number," he gave her a folded slip of paper, "tell them you are "the Ghost" and you will be passed right to me or Chuck if I am unavailable."

She thanked him and said, "I'm fine for now." Then she looked back at him and said, "Well, there is one thing. Can I have another Diet Coke? This one got all warm because of all this talking."

The President almost burst into tears but he calmly said, "You can have all of the Diet Coke you want." He got up, grabbed a couple of cold ones off of the table and handed them to her. He started to turn but then turned back and said, "In fact, you can call the White House for that too!"

Schea started giggling. "Now that's really cool. I can tell my friends that I get my Diet Coke from the White House. Of course, they won't believe me, but that's okay, I'll know."

They all stood with the President and shook hands all around. When it came to Schea, the President gave her a little hug then turned and left the room with everyone else just behind.

If they could have seen the President when he exited through a door at the end of the hall, they would have seen him leaning against the wall with his eyes closed. He was fighting back tears and thinking. *What have I done? She is just a kid.*

His wife appeared seemingly out of nowhere and held his hand until he opened his eyes. Of course, she did not know what had been discussed after she had left but she did know the President. They had been married for 30 years and she rarely saw him this troubled, so this meeting must have been hard for him. She simply told him to come along with her, and he did.

# 39 The Conversation

Todd, Schea and Halvorson finally exited the White House from a side entrance and Todd's car was waiting for them. Chuck thanked them for coming, and thanked Schea in particular for agreeing to join his unit.

Schea responded, "No problem. I am glad that I'll be able to help."

Halvorson went back inside while Todd and Schea got into his car to leave. As Schea got in, she asked, "What, no limo?"

Todd looked at her and said, "Next time, you can hire a limo."

She smiled. "Maybe I will."

They talked about the meeting and Todd's group. He told Schea that, "I have been leaving Lester in charge of the training more and more and he is a natural at it. He also seems to have found his calling and loves the additional responsibilities. I have also looked at 2 or 3 potential female recruits, but none have been suitable.

XXXXX

They arrived at a Holiday Inn just outside DC where Todd had already reserved two rooms. He showed Schea to her room and gave her the key card. It was already 7 pm and he knew that Schea would be hungry. "Would you like to get cleaned up and changed before we go someplace to eat? I took the liberty of going to your apartment in Boring to pack some clothes and things for you."

"Sure. Give me 30 minutes. I am starving."

He smiled. "Okay," and told her his room number. "Come get me when you are ready."

Schea went into her room, stripped and showered without checking on what Todd had brought for her. He did a good job. She came out of the bathroom wrapped in a towel and rooted through the suitcase he had left in her room. She put on underwear and a bra, grabbed a pair of jeans, and a blue t-shirt. She pulled her hair into a ponytail and put on a pair of running shoes. She knocked on Todd's door 22 minutes after he had left her. He opened the door and smiled. "You must be really hungry."

All she said was, "Pizza!"

There was a pizza restaurant down the street, so they walked to it. As they walked along, Todd asked, "So, what do you think of this new unit you just agreed to join?"

Schea didn't answer right away but finally said, "Well, I hope it will be successful. The two things I worry about are the potential for politics to get in the way, and whether or not the unit missions and resources will be protected from potential compromise."

Todd was impressed that she had picked up on these two points because he had been thinking the same thing. "I agree. I guess we will just have to see how it goes. The President and Chuck appear to be serious, so I hope they form a strong buffer between the politics and the unit which, at this moment, is just you. Remember, you can back out of this deal at any time."

Then, Todd stopped and turned to look at Schea. He had this serious look on his face so she stopped and waited. He pursed his lips and said, "You should never, ever, take a mission that doesn't seem right to you. I will always support your decisions regardless of what I think or Chuck wants or even what the President desires. I will always do whatever it takes to support you." She smiled, and thanked him.

They walked into the restaurant and went to the cashier. They ordered a large peperoni and mushroom with extra cheese. He got a Budweiser and she got a water. They found a booth and sat across from each other. They talked about the fact that she should consider moving to somewhere outside of the DC area. He also said that he planned to open an office and get an apartment in Baltimore, since he figured that he might be spending more time in the area.

"I spent time in Baltimore many years ago. I love baseball and am looking forward to being able to attend games at Camden Yard Stadium."

Schea was surprised by this and said so.

Todd smiled and said, "I think I am ready to devote less time to the business and more time to other things that I love to do, like baseball. Besides, Lester really loves managing the training and is happy to take it over. But, I'll still stay involved in the recruiting of trainees."

Their pizza arrived and they ordered another round of drinks. Schea attacked the food as though she hadn't eaten for weeks. At one point she said, "I've been craving some good pizza ever since I left for the last mission." Between bites, Schea mentioned, "I will start looking for a place out here soon after a visit to Richmond to see Jenny. It's been so long since we had a chance to hang out. I also want to go out to Bend to see Jim and Grace."

Todd smiled and said, "You should definitely go to both places. I don't expect a new mission for you from either me or Chuck for at least a couple of months."

After a bit, Schea looked at Todd and sheepishly said, "I might need some help doing more research on the boys. After my previous visits, I feel that I need to be more careful to not cause them to become wary that someone might be watching them."

Todd took a deep breath. "I thought you might ask for help at some point." They ate a bit more then Todd said, "Michael should be finished with his current mission in the next week or so. If he agrees, then I'll ask him to visit you in order to find out what you might want him to do." He cautioned her again about doing anything illegal.

Todd had 2 pieces of pizza and stopped, but Schea kept at it. Anyone watching them would have thought that she hadn't eaten in weeks. She finally stopped after 4 slices, which left 2 more. She looked at Todd and asked, "Are you going to eat those?"

"No. You take them." He smiled.

"Thanks."

They split the bill, paid, and got a box for the remaining slices then left. On the way, they stopped in a convenience store and bought some Diet Coke for Schea and some beer for Todd. He also got a bag of assorted nuts.

They arrived at the hotel and went to their rooms. Before Todd entered his, Schea asked. "Do you have time to talk about some stuff."

"Sure. Come to my room when you're ready."

Todd watched her go. He hoped that she would never grow out of having the hopes and dreams of a kid. Then, he frowned and thought. *What the hell am I thinking? She hasn't been a real kid for the past 7 years. Almost half of her young life has been spent dealing with things that no kid should ever have to deal with.*

Schea went to her room and put the pizza in the small refrigerator along with all but one Diet Coke. She took her t-shirt off, threw on a Seahawks sweatshirt, grabbed her coke and room key, then headed for Todd's room. She knocked and he opened the door. They sat in chairs by the window at a small table. Todd had a beer and opened the bag of nuts. He offered some to Schea, but she shook her head. After a few minutes of quiet, Schea began to talk.

She had told him about Greg during the debriefing, but only from when he appeared behind her on the mountain and that he had been following her since Brighton. She had not told him about actually meeting him in Greenwich and their time together in London. Now she did. She also told him about holding hands and the kiss.

Todd was really feeling like a parent now. It was like a daughter talking to her dad about her first boyfriend. This was a guess because he had never had kids. All he could do was listen to her as a friend and try to help her, as best as he could, with whatever she needed.

Schea finished by telling Todd how betrayed she had felt by Greg. She had liked him, even trusted him, and thought that he had liked her. She had been wrong on all accounts. "Should I have made the connection between them because of the singer? Should I have reacted to that coincidence?" She didn't wait for an answer. "Is this the way it is always going to be for me? Will I ever be able to trust people that I meet, especially boys? I'm worried about whether the friends I have made at the theater can be trusted? I wonder about the other trainees, the trainers, Jenny's new friends, everyone." She started to cry.

Todd had never seen her cry. He was frantic. His mind was going a billion miles an hour trying to come up with a proper statement, a workable scenario, a plan. Finally, he stopped and looked at Schea. She was crying real tears. She wasn't a client, she wasn't a trainee. She was a young girl, a friend, and that is exactly what she needed right now, not a plan. She needed a friend.

Todd got up from his chair and walked over to Schea. He got down on the floor in front of her and wrapped his arms around her. She fell into them like a ton of bricks and the tears came like a waterfall. Her sobbing was like nothing he had ever seen or heard. He said nothing. He just held her and let her get it all out. As he held her, he had the feeling that this wasn't just about Greg. These tears and sobs had been piling up inside of her for a long time.

He remembered when she had told him about her brother, her parents and her sister. Yes, she was extremely sad at their loss, but she talked about all of it in almost a clinical fashion. She described how she felt. She explained what she thought. She theorized how she could best handle it. But, she didn't cry. Not even one tear. These tears were old tears. These tears had been inside of her, waiting for years to be let out. Greg's betrayal had taken up the remaining capacity of her tear reservoir and the dam just burst from its weight.

Todd couldn't say how long she cried or how long he had held her. When she did finally stop, she still did not let go of him. He, of course, wasn't about to pull away on his own. His knees were throbbing and his hamstrings were screaming at him to stand but they would just have to deal with it.

Schea finally started to pull away slowly. She was sniffling and started wiping her nose on the sleeve of her sweatshirt. He got to his feet and somehow limped into the bathroom where he took the roll of toilet paper off and brought it to her. She mumbled thanks, started blowing her nose, and tossed crumpled wads of TP onto the floor.

Todd checked to see if she still had some soda left. He saw that there was very little left in her can so he asked for her room key and went to get some more. He came back, set it on the table in front of her and sat back down at the table across from her, waiting.

After a few minutes, Schea looked up with puffy eyes and a red nose. She said, "I'm sorry for all of that."

"Nonsense, there is nothing to be sorry about. You needed to do it and I am glad that I was here to help you in any way I could.

"I'm glad as well that you are here. I don't know what I would have done if you hadn't been."

Schea paused for a few minutes and took several deep breaths. She seemed to have finished the sniffling, but she kept the TP roll in her hand. He could see that she was gently stroking it, giving it soft squeezes. She seemed to be using it like a little kid would use a security blanket.

Todd thought he was going down that road again and thinking of her as a little kid. But, at this moment, she was a kid and needed to be. He would worry later about whether or not it had been such a good idea to recruit her but, right now, his job was to be a friend and let her be whoever she wanted to be.

Schea took several gulps of her drink. Todd finished his beer, grabbed another and sat back down. Schea began to talk. "I now recognize that this reaction isn't just about Greg. It is also about all of the years of loses, gains and loses. This is about always trying to get through and help others as well. This is about always feeling like I have to be strong and never be weak because, if you are weak, then you get hurt. The problem I'm having now is trying to figure out how to be strong and weak at the same time. How can I be strong in order to do my job, yet weak enough so that I can be a friend or maybe even love?"

At this point, she looked at Todd and said, "By the way, don't even think about whether you were right about taking me into your organization."

Todd just smiled and nodded.

Schea continued. "I want to do this. I'm glad that I am helping rid the world of scum like Mendoza and Vincent." She held his gaze until he smiled and nodded again. "I know how to be strong. It seems to come naturally to me. After all, I have had years of practice. But now? Now, I would also like to be weak. Not weak-weak, but open, maybe vulnerable towards feelings, and to the feelings of others. Most of the girls my age have had boyfriends for at least a year or two, some longer. Many have had sex, not that I want to go that far any time soon."

Todd didn't say anything, but inside he was saying *thank you* over and over. That would not have been a talk he could have handled.

"Even with my friends at the theater, I am not very open. When we get together at a restaurant or someone's apartment I listen to them, but rarely initiate conversations. Instead, I will often be thinking of the way some bad guy could surprise them, the best exit route, and who in the restaurant might be a robber or a killer. But, when I spent that little bit of time with Greg, I took my guard down and look what happened. I was almost killed because I had trusted him. How can I go through life never trusting people, with a few exceptions of course." She smiled at Todd and he smiled back at her.

Schea seemed finished, but Todd waited a minute, mostly thinking about what to say, then he remembered. *She just wants a friend to listen to her and to be her friend. I have never had a girl this young for a friend, but I have had many friends of both sexes over the years. So, talk to her as I would talk to any of them.*

Todd started. "On the one hand, you are right to be cautious when selecting a friend. People are people and some are nicer than others. Some can be mean. Some can be best friends for life. It can be hard to know any of this quickly. You already have a great ability to read people, but you should also remember that it is just that, a quick read. There will be errors, even if most of it is correct. Gut feelings are always to be trusted, but to a point. Knowing the difference comes with time and experience. Mistakes are learning opportunities and should be treated that way."

172

"However, I understand that in our business, a mistake, even a small one, can be deadly. So, yes, we have to be extra careful and cautious. I have no quick solutions for you. It is all a matter of time, experience and learning from the mistakes we have lived through. The hardest ones are the ones where your mistake gets someone killed."

"I remember reading one of Ian Fleming's Bond stories. In it, Bond is talking about a situation similar to the one you had with Greg and Vincent mentioning the same singer. He said. *Once is happenstance, twice is a coincidence and three times is enemy action.* Thus, you simply had a coincidence and should not have reacted to it."

He paused then looked back at Schea. "I have had 2 of those experiences where someone on my team got killed and they still bother me every single day. You never get over it." He looked hard at her now and said, "If you want to continue doing what you are doing, and I hope you do, then you have to prepare yourself for the day when that might happen. I hope it never does or that it won't happen for many years, but when and if it does, you need to be prepared to deal with it." She nodded.

"As far as our personal lives are concerned, the same basic ideas apply. You will have successes and failures. Follow your gut, take your time, and learn as much as you can about the person. Ask about how much they are like their parents and do they see them much? Ask about siblings and if they see them? I feel that I can get a pretty good read on someone by learning how they are with their family. I mean, if they hate their siblings, then maybe they aren't someone you would want to be close to."

Todd remembered something that his mother told him many years ago when they were talking about a girl that he thought might be the one for him. "My mom told me one time to try to find out as much as I could about how well the girl got along with her father. She said I should also find out how well her parents get along. And for a girl, she needs to look at how the boy's father treats his mate. That will be the role model for the boy growing up and it could be how he has learned to treat his own future mate."

Todd stopped and took a gulp of his beer.

Schea smiled. "Thanks. I feel much better. The crying, I now realize, had been necessary for me to do. I don't know what I would have done if I had been alone."

He smiled and told her no problem. He held his beer can towards her and she picked up her coke and they touched the cans together.

They sat for another hour talking about the next few weeks. "You should rent a car until you can get your own and your belongings shipped to your new place, once you find one."

She thought that was a good idea and would do it tomorrow. She asked, "Do you have an area in mind where I could settle?"

Todd thought a few moments and then suggested Annapolis.

Schea said, "I'll check it out. But first, I'll call Jenny tomorrow and discuss a visit."

"You might want to hire a good real estate broker to find you a place. They cost more but," and he smiled, "You can afford it."

She smiled back and said, "Yes I can." Schea planned to get a house this time.

Todd mentioned, "I will contact you as soon as Michael gets back and agrees to help you. Maybe, you can meet with him when you go out to visit Jim and Grace. Meanwhile, I will head to Baltimore and begin my own search for a place to live and an office to rent."

With all of that covered, they sat for a little longer talking about nothing in particular, weather, sports and the kind of extras they might get for their new homes. Finally, Schea yawned, and Todd said that she should get some rest. He looked over at the cheap hotel alarm clock and saw that it was already 1 am. He yawned as well and stood. He stretched and several joints clicked. He lamented and said, "Not as young as I used to be."

Schea smiled and said, "You appear to do just fine, for an old man."

He walked her to the door and turned to her before opening it door. He smiled and asked, "You okay?"

She smiled, looked at him and said that she was never better, and meant it. They hugged and Schea went to her room. She got into bed with her sweatshirt on, but took off her jeans. She was sound asleep within a few minutes.

XXXXX

When she awoke the next morning, she realized that she had not had any nightmares. That was the first time in years. She smiled and thought. *Maybe this crying thing isn't such a bad idea. I might try it again sometime, but not anytime soon. There is still work to do.*

# 40 Annapolis

Schea rented a car and headed for Annapolis. She drove out on Highway 50 then turned off on Route 70 which would take her to the center of the city. The only thing that she remembered learning about the city in school was that it was the Maryland state capital and that it was the home of the US Naval Academy. She figured that these two facts meant that she would potentially meet lots of politicians and lots of young men. She wasn't necessarily looking forward to either of these, but the latter sounded better than the former.

She found a public parking lot near the Naval Academy and began walking around the city. She liked what she saw. It had beautiful, old style architecture and lots of historical signs that she could read and learn more about the city's past. For example, the state house was begun in 1772 and is the oldest state house still in use. It is also the only state house to have served as the US capital, as well.

As she walked the area, she decided that she wanted to stay at least 2 nights, so she looked for someplace nice to stay. A short distance from the state house, she found the Loews Hotel. It had a nice exterior and a beautiful interior so she booked a room for 2 nights.

Her next task was to find a good realtor to handle the search for a place to live. She wanted to rent and would like to have a place near the water. She asked at the hotel reception desk if they had any recommendations. One of the reception staff, Joanna, said, "I know someone who used Annapolis Realty Inc. to find a nice home just west of town. The realtors there are very discrete and handle many upscale clients."

"Thanks. I'll check them out.

Schea found their office a few blocks up the street from the hotel and entered. The receptionist smiled and asked if she could help. Schea told her, "I would like to speak with someone about renting one of your listed properties."

The receptionist was about to tell her that she might want to try somewhere else when a woman who had come into the reception area to get a cup of coffee overheard the conversation. She came to the desk and asked, "Maybe I can help you." She led Schea back to her office.

The lady introduced herself as Maryanne James but told Schea to call her Anne. Schea introduced herself and they shook hands. Anne asked Schea, "What are you looking for?"

"I would like to rent a house somewhere near the water."

Anne said, "We only handle very expensive properties so rentals on the water will be very expensive."

Schea smiled. "I understand and that will not be a problem."

"Okay. Also, are you old enough to sign a contract?" Schea nodded. Anne sat back in her chair, saw how serious Schea was and said, "Okay, I'd be happy to show you some prospective properties and, if you see one that you like, you will need to provide money to hold the rental while a background check is completed. The owners are very careful about who rents their properties."

Schea smiled and said, "Sounds good to me. I like to be careful as well."

Anne shrugged and asked Schea to follow her. They went into a room that had pictures on the walls of many beautiful homes and a variety of large books on various tables. They walked by all of those to a large screen on the wall and sat in 2 comfy chairs. Anne picked up a remote control and hit a button. The screen came alive with the company's logo. She hit a few more buttons and began showing Schea beautiful properties along some of Annapolis's waterfront areas. She showed them one at a time and described some of their main selling points as she went along.

Anne didn't have any appointments that day and no paperwork to do. She had only been in the office to catch up on some emails and other correspondence. She had planned to stay for an hour or two then drive home for a relaxing day by the pool. When she saw Schea, she was reminded of her daughter who was just starting out as a lawyer in DC and felt the motherly instinct come over her. She didn't think Schea would be able to handle the costs of their properties, but she could at least help her to find more reasonable properties to look at. She knew of a few agents who had properties that might fit Schea's budget a little better.

They scrolled through a dozen properties when Schea suddenly told Anne to stop. She did and looked back at the screen. It was a beautiful four bedroom rental on Acton Cove and fully furnished. It included a separate office, a full kitchen and windows along one side of the living room, as well as two bedrooms that looked out over the cove. The living room had a small fireplace in one corner and sliding glass doors that led to a large deck. The deck looked towards the cove over a well-kept back yard that extended down to the water.

The description also said that there was an athletic club a few miles away which had a weight room and an Olympic-size swimming pool. There were also trails nearby and the house was located within a few blocks of the Annapolis City Dock area.

Schea turned to Anne with a huge smile on her face and said, "That's the one I want."

Anne gave her a motherly smile and told her, "I am not sure the rental cost will fit into your budget. Maybe we should continue looking?"

Schea looked at Anne, smiled and asked, "How much is the rent?"

Anne shrugged. "It is $10,000 per month."

"That's perfect. What's next?"

Anne stared for a moment then finally said, "Okay. Let's start the paperwork."

Schea got up and said she would like that because she still had lots to do. Anne walked Schea back to her desk, pulled out a stack of forms, and began helping Schea fill them out. When they finished, Schea got up and asked Anne when she would know if everything was a go or not. Anne said if there were no problems, and she looked directly at Schea, then they should know within a few weeks.

Anne asked Schea for $5000 down to hold the property while the background check was being completed. Schea agreed and handed her a credit card. Anne ran it through and handed Schea a receipt. They headed to the door. At the door, Anne told Schea, "I will be in touch."

Schea said "Okey-dokey," and left.

When Anne turned around, the receptionist said, "It sure took you a long time to let the kid know this was not the place for her."

Anne smiled, still looking at the door. "If this all works out, I just made my next quarter's commission, and then some."

XXXXX

Schea wandered around town and finally settled into a Starbucks coffee shop with an outdoor seating area overlooking the City Dock. She ordered a cup of green tea and watched the people coming and going. Eventually, she pulled out her phone and called Jenny. It went to her voice mail so Schea left a message that said she was back in the States and wanted to visit her. She also said she could be there the next day if that would work. She slipped the phone back in her pocket and hoped that Jenny would call back soon.

After about 10 minutes, a young man came over to her table and said hello. She looked up and said hi.

"Are you new to the area?" He asked.

"Yes." and looked away.

He stood there for a little bit and seemed to wonder what to do next. Finally, he shrugged and wandered off.

As he left, Schea had trouble shaking off the scene when Greg had done the same thing in Greenwich. She knew that she had to get over that and just move on. As Todd had said to her, these events are lessons they need to learn from, toss aside, and not store them up. She would have to try harder.

She wandered back to the hotel and changed into a knee-length dress and a light sweater. She left and wandered toward City Dock. As she passed a restaurant she stopped and looked at the name. It was The Chick and Ruth deli and they served crab cakes."

Schea had never had something like that, so she entered and ordered them. She was served and as she ate, she saw a sign that announced. *If you are here at 8:30 am during the week or at 9:30 am on weekends, then you will be asked to join everyone in reciting the Pledge of Allegiance.* She thought that was pretty cool.

As she walked back out to the street, her phone rang. She pulled it out and answered. It was Jenny. Schea stopped and started talking. At the end of their sometimes rambling conversation, she would now be heading down to see Jenny tomorrow afternoon.

As she headed back to the hotel, she thought. *The crab cakes were delicious, and knew she had just found a new treat for herself.*

Schea slept well again. This marked a couple of days now that she had had no nightmares. She threw on a pair of running shorts, t-shirt, running shoes and headed out. She had not seen a running, walking and biking trail near the water, so she headed out onto the streets. She found a trail about a mile from the hotel and took off. It wasn't crowded yet, so it was pretty easy to keep up a nice, easy 7 minute pace. She figured she'd run about 10 miles which would give her enough time to shower, pack, check out and get down to Jenny's place.

After about 2 miles she passed three young guys who were running at an easy pace and chatting. She went by them pretty smoothly and continued on. After about a minute, one of the three guys caught her and passed. Soon, the other two guys passed her. She smiled and thought, *Why not.* She picked up her pace and passed the three of them. She suspected that they attended the academy since they were young, fit and had buzz cuts. A few minutes later, they were next to her but didn't pass. They seemed to be content to just stay with her.

Schea decided to kick it up a notch and one of them dropped back right away. She estimated that she was now doing a 6 minute pace. She kicked it up a notch again and another one dropped back. She finally glanced at the one guy who remained. She was breathing pretty easily and so was he. She smiled at him and he smiled at her. Before long, he picked his pace up and she followed suit.

They kept this up for another 2 miles. She glanced at him again and smiled. This time, he didn't smile back and soon, he dropped back as well. She ran along for another mile, checked the time, and figured she needed to turn and head back to the hotel. She turned and headed back along the trail. As she went around a corner, she saw the 3 guys by the trail. Well, one was actually lying on the ground. As she went by, she slowed and said, "Thanks guys. It was fun to run with you." Then, she ran off.

She got back to the hotel, and an hour later, she was heading to Jenny's.

# 41 Jenny

After checking out of the Loews in Annapolis, Schea made the 4 hour trip to Jenny's place. The Kennedy's live in Colonial Heights, a very nice community located between Richmond to the north and Petersburg to the south. It is mostly rolling hills and forested areas. They lived close to Virginia State University and were within walking distance of the Amtrak Station, which is how Jeff got to and from his office in Richmond. Schea had visited her once and remembered thinking that it was a good place for Jenny to grow up.

Schea headed west then south on 95 which would take her all the way to Colonial Heights. It was a pretty drive through rolling hills and pretty farm areas. She knew that the main weather problems around here were severe storms in the spring, heat in the summer, and the potential for hurricanes in the late summer or early fall. It sounded horrible to her but maybe people thought that it was still preferable to the rainy Northwest. Schea didn't.

She arrived at a little before 3 pm, so she figured that Jenny would still be at school. She pulled into the driveway, got out and headed for the front door but only got a few steps before it opened and out flew Jenny. She screamed with joy and jumped into Schea's outstretched arms. Time wise, it hadn't been that long since they had seen each other but the lives of both girls had changed a great deal. Jenny was now 14 and becoming a stunning young woman as everyone knew she would. Schea, of course, had been working.

They finally let go of each other and stood about a foot apart before they simply locked into another embrace. It was as though they were trying to melt into each other and, in a way, they were. Finally, they did pull apart and appraise each other. Jenny was actually about as tall as Schea and very tan. Her Korean heritage had made her a little darker anyway, but now with the long sunny days, she was really dark. Her hair was long and a shiny ebony color. She was filling out in all the right places and looking beautiful. *Gosh*, Schea thought. *Ladies and gentlemen, let me introduce the next Miss Universe!*

Finally, Schea noticed that Mary was standing a few feet behind the girls. Schea looked over, smiled and Mary came forward to give her a hug. They all went into the house. Schea told Jenny, "I thought you would still be in school."

Before Jenny could respond, Mary laughed and said, "There was no way Jenny was going to go to school today. I think she would have locked herself in her room, if I had tried to send her." Schea smiled and gave Jenny a little finger wag and a "tsk-tsk" with a serious look on her face.

Mary laughed. "After your call, Jenny was beside herself, standing, sitting, talking, fixing up her room and giving orders to everyone, especially Archie. School would have been a waste of time today."

Jenny interrupted. "Oh Mom, I was not like that."

Mary smiled and asked Schea, "Would you like something to drink after your long drive?"

She asked for a Diet Coke and Mary went into the kitchen. Jenny led Schea into the living room and they sat next to each other on the sofa. They immediately started talking a mile a minute.

Mary came back with 2 sodas for the girls and a cup of coffee for herself. She sat and observed the 2 girls. She felt her heart warm. She could feel the immense love these 2 shared. She felt a little sad that they couldn't be together all of the time or, at least, more often. But, she knew that Schea was working on various important projects for Todd plus Jenny had school. She also knew from Todd that there was no one else who could do them, so Schea was critical to his work. Schea seemed to love her job, so the future for the girls looked like long absences, short intense visits and sad good-byes.

Mary finally got a chance to break into their rambling conversation and asked Schea, "How long will you be able to stay?"

"I can stay for a few days, if that is okay."

"That's perfectly fine with us. Archie and Izzy have missed you too, so they will be excited to see you once they got home from school." She excused herself and told Jenny, "You might want to help Schea get her stuff up to her room."

The girls jumped up hand-in-hand and went back out to the car. Schea grabbed the one bag she had and they bounded up the stairs to Jenny's room.

Jenny's room looked like a typical 14 year old girl's room. She had stuffed animals all over her bed, pictures and posters of stars, mostly boys, on the walls and a small desk piled high with school books, papers, and her computer. Jenny's bed was a queen-size, so it could accommodate both girls. Schea tossed her bag into the corner and climbed on the bed with Jenny.

Jenny knew she could not ask Schea what she had been doing, so she didn't. The only thing she asked was if Schea was happy and if she was okay everywhere. Schea smiled because she knew what Jenny meant by asking both of those questions. Schea told her that she was okay everywhere, meaning she was not hurt in any way on any part of her body. She also said she was very happy with her work and with her life.

Schea then looked at Jenny and asked the same thing. Jenny went on about how school was going great, she got all A's, was in several clubs, played tennis and field hockey, and had a bunch of neat friends. Schea listened patiently then she stopped smiling, looked seriously and sisterly at Jenny. Jenny saw the change and stopped in mid-sentence. At that point, Schea asked Jenny if she had a boyfriend. Jenny smiled and said that she did not, but she had gone to a couple of dances at the school and several boys had asked her to dance. She giggled and said that she thought that she might be popular with the boys.

Schea laughed and said, "Are you kidding me? You're gorgeous and I'll bet every guy at the school wants to date you."

Jenny slapped her arm and said, "Shut up," but she was laughing as she did.

They continued to talk for the next hour or so until they heard the front door bang open, then loud thumping on the stairs as though a herd of elephants was charging up. Suddenly, there was a loud and persistent knock at the door. Jenny cooed, and asked calmly, "Who is it?"

Archie yelled, "Come on Jenny, you know it's me."

Schea put her finger to her lips, and Jenny got quiet. Schea went over to the door and suddenly swung it open and yelled, "Who goes there?"

Archie tumbled backwards and fell against the far wall. Jenny and Schea howled with laughter until their sides ached. Archie mumbled, "I'm not scared." But he seemed close to tears.

Slowly, Schea turned to Jenny and asked, "Who is this very handsome young man?"

Jenny smiled and said, "Oh, him? That's just Archie."

Schea turned back to Archie and gave him an appraising look. "Are you indeed Archie?"

He stood straight and said, "Of course it's me."

"Well, you are becoming quite a handsome young man." She then grabbed him in a big hug.

Archie was shocked at first then he hugged Schea back and told her, "I really missed you."

He insisted the girls come to his room so that he could show Schea his new train set, his race cars, and his bug collection. After a few minutes, they heard the door open and close and another pair of feet ascending the stairs. But this time, they were quiet and unrushed. Izzy appeared at the top of the stairs and heard them all in Archie's room. She walked to the door and smiled at Schea. She was now 16 and had also become a very pretty girl. She was taller than Schea, but then who wasn't, and had long blond hair. She was, as they say, well-developed and put together. Schea came over to her and they hugged.

They all eventually made it downstairs and went out onto the deck. They sat and each updated Schea on what they had been doing. Izzy, of course, had a boyfriend and Archie had potentials he was checking out, which the girls knew meant that he was ogling them and wondering what to do, but they didn't say it.

Mary finally came out and told them, "Okay. Get cleaned up and ready for dinner. Your dad will be home soon and we'll be sitting down for dinner in an hour." Mary figured an hour should be plenty of time for them to avoid doing what she asked before she'd have to tell them to get ready for dinner again. She went back into the house smiling.

Jeff came home and all of the kids gave him a hug, except Archie. He shook hands with his dad. "That's what men do," he informed the girls. Jenny and Izzy each gently cuffed the back of his head.

Jeff gave Schea a hug, asked how she was doing and how long she would be able to stay. She said that she was doing well and that she'd like to stay for 3 or 4 days if that was okay. He smiled and said that she could stay as long as she liked.

It made Schea feel really good that she was treated as a part of this happy little family. Now that she would be living closer, she was looking forward to spending more time here, when possible of course.

The visit proceeded like the other visit. The kids spent a lot of time doing things together and just hanging out. Schea spent evenings sitting up late chatting with Jenny about all that Jenny was doing, and Schea also spent more time than usual chatting with Izzy.

They were so close in age that it was fun for Schea to get Izzy's perspective on things like boys and dating. After her fiasco with Greg, she figured that she could use some advice. She couldn't tell Izzy about Greg, but she could talk in a roundabout way about dating and boys in general. Izzy seemed to be very astute in this area and Schea got some great tips.

The family took fun day trips together on the weekend. There was much history in the area - from the first English settlement in North America at Jamestown, to the American Revolution and Civil War battlefields.

On one trip, they went to the Petersburg Battlefield, which was less than an hour away. It had been a pivotal battle during the Civil War. Neither side was a clear winner at the battle, but it did deplete the ever-dwindling Southern forces to the point where they surrendered a short time later up the river at Appomattox Courthouse. Jenny went on and on explaining what happened at the Battle of the Crater and Schea totally enjoyed it.

But, all good things must end and it soon came time for Schea to leave. As she was packing to leave, her phone rang. She worried that it was Todd with a mission, but it wasn't. It was Anne from the realtor's office. When Schea answered, Anne quickly told Schea how happy she was that she had been able to help her. She received all of the approvals back in record time and the approval from the bank specified that Ms. Tailor's credit was better than A+, so she could have any amount of money she felt she needed. Anne told Schea the rental was ready when she was, and asked Schea to call her on her personal number if she needed anything. Schea thanked her and told her she would be in touch as soon as she was ready to move in.

Jenny came in just as Schea hung up. She asked if that was one of those calls. Schea smiled and said, "No. It was a realtor. I will be moving to Annapolis and will be renting a house."

Jenny screamed and jumped on Schea then ran downstairs to tell the others. Schea smiled and thought that this was going to be a great move and life was getting so much better.

The Kennedys were all waiting downstairs as Schea came down. Jeff took Schea's bag out to the car while she said goodbye to everyone. Izzy told her to call anytime she wanted to talk then winked at her with a knowing smile.

Jenny walked her to the car and Jeff stepped back with the others. Schea and Jenny hugged each other and, just as with their other departures, there were no tears, because there was never a worry about seeing each other again. It was only a matter of when.

Schea whispered in Jenny's ear that she should always carry the bracelet and to remember to rub it whenever she needed her. Jenny surreptitiously opened the top of her shirt a little and showed Schea that it was still there hanging from a necklace that Jenny always wore. Schea smiled and said, "Good." Then, she got into her car and drove off.

XXXXX

Frank called his brother and told him, "I got it." Pause. "Okay. I will meet them there. Do you know when?" Pause. "Right. I'll go there and wait."

# 42 Doug

*Life was good!* Schea was thinking good thoughts as she drove to Dulles to catch a flight to Portland. She suddenly remembered the last time she had thought the same thing. That was the time Jenny went away. Well, that won't happen this time. Jeff and Mary were great parents, Jenny was happy and Schea would be living close soon.

Schea arrived at Dulles, turned in her rental, went to the flight departure display, and looked for the next flight to Portland. She didn't care about which airline. They were all the same as far as she was concerned. The next flight was in 2 hours. She went to the counter and asked if there were any seats left. The person behind the counter was a tall gray-haired lady who looked down at the little girl, smiled, and checked the flight for seats.

The woman eventually looked up and said she was sorry but the flight was already overbooked except for first class and, since Schea was not an elite traveler with them, she would probably not get on. Schea smiled as the woman said all of this then asked if she could buy a seat in first class. The lady raised her eyebrows and looked down at the screen. She said there was one seat but the price at this late hour would be over $2000.

Schea smiled and said, "I'll take it."

The lady looked at Schea as if to say, *yea right!* But, she played along and asked for her credit card and ID. Schea handed them to her, the lady ran the card, and it went through just fine. She smiled when she looked back at Schea and said, "I want to thank her for flying with us." She then gave Schea a complimentary pass into their VIP lounge. Schea thanked her and walked off.

Schea passed through security and went to the gate. As she passed people and groups, she saw a young mother trying to deal with a baby and a kid about 2 years old. They were being good but there was just a lot of stuff to try to keep track of. Schea walked over and helped her with one of the bags. The mother thanked her and Schea asked, "Where are you travelling to?"

The young woman said, "I am flying to San Diego to meet my husband. He is a captain in the Marine Corps and is returning from his 3rd tour in Afghanistan. I have been staying with my parents and they helped pay for my ticket to meet him, otherwise we would have had to wait until he caught a flight back here."

She frowned. "The only problem is that my flight just got delayed and won't be leaving for another 3 hours."

Schea asked, "Would you like to spend that time in the VIP lounge?"

"Oh, that would be nice but, unfortunately, I am not a member."

Schea handed her the free pass. "Well, you are now." The woman thanked her and Schea walked off smiling.

Schea's flight was not a non-stop, so she had to kill 2 hours in Denver. She took that time to call Jim to let him know that she was on her way. He said that would be fine and they would love to see her. Before she could ask about Grace, Jim said, "See you soon," and hung up.

Schea stared at the phone for a minute and wondered what that was about. Jim had never been that abrupt before. He was always cheerful and usually handed her off to Grace. Something was wrong. She hoped that Grace was okay. Maybe she was sick or hurt. Schea now became nervous and anxious. She still had a long way to go even after she landed since it was over a 3 hour drive to Bend.

The flight arrived in Portland and she proceeded to the taxi queue. She gave the driver her address and she was home 30 minutes later. She quickly dumped her stuff, and repacked her bag with clean clothes making sure she took warm clothes to shield her from the chilly nighttime temperatures. She grabbed a jacket, her keys and headed to her car.

Schea arrived at Jim's a little after midnight and saw that the lights were still on. As she came up the steps, both Jim and Grace came out onto the porch. At first, she was happy to see that Grace looked fine, but then she saw the looks on their faces. Something was definitely wrong. Maybe they were losing the business. Then she thought, *Oh God. Maybe Jeff called and something has happened to Jenny. No, that can't be it. Grace would be in pieces if that was it.*

They went into the living room, Jim grabbed a beer, got Schea a Diet Coke, and gave Grace a glass of wine then they all sat. Schea looked from Jim to Grace and asked, "Okay. What's wrong?" She had hoped they would have just started, but they hadn't. Grace looked at Jim and he started.

Jim told Schea, "We haven't seen Doug for several days now. We reported him missing, but since he is an adult from the area and single, the police said they really couldn't do much about it. He may have simply decided to go someplace else. Plus, there was no evidence of foul-play anywhere - his place, the ranch, nothing."

"We tried to reason with them and explained that Doug would not just leave. Doug would definitely not go off and leave his expensive gear, and he would not have left without telling us. But, the police said they still could not do anything."

"I and some of the other guides went to town and asked around, but no one has seen or heard from Doug in days. We went to his house. I have a backup key, so we let ourselves in. The place seems undisturbed. It did not look like he had been there in days, and it also didn't look like anything had been taken."

"The next day I and another guide packed up gear, and went out on horseback to search. We have done the same each of the last 2 days but still haven't found a sign of him. It is as though he just disappeared into thin air. I am at a loss as to what to do next."

Schea remembered Doug well. He was always good to her when she lived there and helped her when she struggled with a piece of equipment she was unfamiliar with. She wanted to help find him.

Schea told Jim, "I will help. I will call Todd and ask him if he can spare one of his trackers."

Jim looked down and commented, "It has been almost a week since anyone has seen him, and the trail must be compromised by now. I know you are one of the best trackers I know, but I am not sure even you can find the trail."

Schea assured him that Doug would be found. Jim saw the confidence she always had and it helped to reassure him. And, frankly, every time Schea said that something could be done, it was.

XXXXX

The next day, Schea went outside a little way from the house and called the number Todd had given her if she needed something. Todd answered and before wasting too much time on pleasantries, Schea told Todd what happened and that she needed help. He didn't hesitate for a second and simply asked what she needed?

She asked him who he thought was the group's best tracker and explained what they faced. He said that Kevin was the best he'd seen in a long time. She asked if he was available, and he said he would check with Lester and call back. Schea waited.

Five minutes later, her phone rang and she immediately answered. Todd quickly said Kevin will be there tomorrow morning. She said that was great and thanked him. Schea quickly told him about her new place and the visit with Jenny. He told her about his new office in Baltimore near the baseball field. Finally, she asked about Michael's status. Unfortunately, all Todd could say was *unknown*, which is the standard response when an operative was not finished with a mission, or has yet to report in.

Schea said thanks and went back into the house to tell Jim and Grace that an expert tracker would be coming to help tomorrow morning. They looked relieved and spent the rest of the day catching up. Jim gave Schea a tour of the changes that he had made to the property, showing off some repair work on several buildings, a new dock and a new boat that could hold more people.

They ate another one of Grace's delicious meals and started a fire in the fireplace. Schea told them all about Jenny and her move to Annapolis. When Schea finished, Grace gave her another hug and thanked her for filling them in. She said she missed her girls very much.

XXXXX

Kevin arrived at 9 am the next day. He and Schea knew each other, of course, which was why when he approached her, he only offered her his hand. Schea smiled and gave him a hug. He hadn't expected this. He remembered what would happen if anyone had tried that when she was in camp. The situation with Doug was explained to him, and they got down to business.

He briefly explained what he needed, so Jim went off and brought back everything he had asked for. Jim asked if he should get the other guides too. Kevin said that would not be necessary and, in fact, would be bad. "No. Only Schea and I will go out on the search. The more people who go out into the

186

areas where Doug might have been, then the higher probability the trail will become compromised. It might take a little longer this way, but I am sure we have a better chance of success if only the two of us go out."

Jim suggested that the trail might be too old. Kevin smiled. "A week is nothing. I once tracked a man who had wandered off 6 months before and found him in one day. But, unfortunately, he was dead from exposure."

He and Schea got ready and left. Jim and Grace watched them head off in the last direction that anyone had seen Doug go.

Kevin and Schea went on foot and he explained, "You can see obvious trails from a horse but not subtle ones. You need to be close to the ground for that. It doesn't sound like Doug had a horse when he left, so he had to have been on foot. People generally go missing in a remote area for several reasons - they are hurt, they are hurt in a fall then die, or they got lost. They also may go missing because they are trying to get away from someone or something, like a crazy girlfriend." He smiled at Schea.

Schea smiled back and said, "Or boyfriend."

"Yea. Or boyfriend."

Kevin continued, "The worst reason is because they did not have a choice. Someone took them for, probably, a deadly reason. The first three or four reasons tend to be fairly obvious because they do not try to cover their tracks. The last 2 can be more difficult because they do try to cover their tracks. Unless they are an excellent tracker themselves and know how to cover their trail, they can almost always be found. It doesn't sound like Doug was an excellent tracker, so I think he was taken." He stopped and looked at Schea.

She looked back and frowned. She was now resigned to not finding Doug alive.

"Since it is likely the last reason, we need to search for specific indicators. In this scenario, he could have been out on his own, but was ambushed for some reason. In that case, there would be a trail and then an ambush site. The ambush site would likely be a mess given what Jim had said about Doug. He would fight."

"He also could have been out and was somehow convinced or concerned enough to follow someone, or go in some direction other than where he wanted to go. In that case, he would have been lead away to a remote area and dealt with there. That can be a tough one because whoever did the taking would want to cover their trail. That often results in tracking to a dead end with no more indicators. Finally, he could have been out on his own, was surprised and couldn't fight for some reason."

Kevin thought for a bit then said, "I would guess that it was this last scenario. No one had reported a messy scene or body on the other searches, which would have been obvious even from a

187

horse. The second one could have happened but, I suspect that if something caused him to decide to go in a particular direction, he probably would have called Jim to report it before he continued. Besides, if it was that one, then we'd probably be wasting our time since we may not ever pick up the trail of the bad guys. So, we need to find his trail, follow it to where he was incapacitated, and see if we can pick up the trail to where he was taken."

They got started.

After a few hours, Kevin said, "I have Doug's trail." He showed Schea the markers, broken twigs on the ground and misshaped ground cover. They both followed this trail for about an hour. They were starting to lose light since they were in a valley and the sun had passed behind the Cascade Range. The sky would stay light for another few hours but it would not be shining on the ground where they were looking. They needed that sunlight.

"We better stop before we lose the trail and have to find it again tomorrow. Besides, we can start as soon as the sun is a little above the horizon because it will be on our side of the mountain range."

They set up their tents and made a small fire. They both continued to add layers of clothing and jackets as the sun set further in the western sky and it grew dark. They had MREs so they didn't need any pots or utensils and they had plenty of water, since there was a small stream nearby. They both had a handgun, a rifle and knives for protection in case a four, or two, legged creature came in to cause trouble.

Kevin knew he couldn't ask about Schea's missions, so he asked, "How have you been? Have you seen Todd? The camp is doing well under Lester, but they all kind of miss Todd's personality. Lester is more business-like, where Todd was, well goofy at times. We have not had any new female trainees since you left and well, we kind of missed you."

Schea smiled and said, "I miss all of the guys too. Say hi for me if you see anyone."

As it got colder and darker, they decided to crawl into their tents and sleeping bags. They decided on 2 hour shifts.

Schea was the last on shift so she was already up when Kevin crawled out of his tent at 5 am and went away to take care of business. When he came back Schea had already broken down her tent and packed everything away. She was munching on an energy bar and drinking some water when he walked back to his tent. They said "morning" to each other and after about 15 minutes, they set off on Doug's trail.

They followed it for another 2 hours when Schea said, "Wait. Kevin, come over and take a look at this." She pointed to a place on the ground cover that seemed new. She suggested that it had been disturbed, but then repaired and Kevin agreed. They began searching the area around it more closely. Suddenly Kevin called for Schea to take a look. He was on his hands and knees looking sideways at an area of low bushes and pointing underneath. Schea got down as well and looked. About 2 feet back and under the bush they could see a small orange object.

Kevin retrieved it and held it out. It was a piece of cloth and Schea instantly recognized it. It was the special type of cloth that Jim always had his vests made out of. They never became unreflective in water or snow or other severe conditions. Any type of precipitation seemed to just fall off of it, and it always had a bright shiny orange color. Schea suggested, "This must be part of the vest that Doug was wearing."

They now had the trail of the bad guys and it was easier for them to follow. It led to a small ravine that would have appeared hidden from above but, from ground level, you could clearly see the up-and-down slopes of the terrain.

They moved into the ravine and walked along the middle of it. Schea's foot suddenly struck something that didn't move. At first, she figured that it was a rock that was hidden in the grass and brush but she decided to bend down and make sure. She felt under the brush and her hand touched what felt like a person's leg. She called Kevin over, and they both got down and carefully started digging, which is when the smell hit them.

It was decomposing flesh. The body had apparently been buried about a foot under the ground and covered over with ground clutter that looked like the rest of the area. Some animal, perhaps a coyote, must have inspected the area and started digging. The animal probably heard them approach and was scared off. Otherwise, he, and his buddies, would have dragged Doug out and eaten him.

When they uncovered the head, Schea fell back and sat. It was Doug. She finally pulled out her phone and called Jim. She told him that they had found Doug, and that he was dead. They would leave it alone for now and wait for the authorities. She said she was sorry and Jim asked if she could tell how he died. She said she couldn't but that it was definitely foul play. She gave Jim their coordinates from Kevin's GPS locator so that he could call 911. Kevin and Schea went back up the slope to wait.

Both Kevin and Schea had seen dead bodies but Schea took this one a little hard because Doug had been a friend. Kevin stayed to the side and let her have some space. She didn't say anything and kept staring at the ground. Finally, she got up and walked away to a point about 30 yards down the way they had come. Kevin waited by Doug's body.

The police arrived by helicopter about 30 minutes after Jim's call. They landed a short distance away, made their way to where Schea and Kevin waited, and they told the police how they had tracked and found the body. The police told them they would need a written statement, and would fly them to the station in Bend. They grabbed their gear and headed for the helicopter. They arrived at the station a short time later, made their statements and were driven back to Jim's.

Jim was waiting when they got back and thanked Kevin for helping. Kevin said he was glad to have helped but he was sorry about the result. Jim nodded and went into the house.

Kevin told Schea that if she needed anything else, she should let Todd know and he will muster the necessary resources. She said thanks and gave him another hug.

As he walked to his car, he turned and told Schea, "You should know that everyone at the camp who was there while you were there was completely impressed with you. You should also know that any of us would do anything for you, so all you need to do is ask."

Schea smiled and couldn't really say anything because she had a catch in her throat. Kevin got in his car and drove away. Schea realized as she stood there that she has, in fact, made some great friends. She needed to forget about the scumbags she hunted.

# 43 Departing Boring

Schea stayed at Jim's for another week, but it was a somber visit because of the incident with Doug. The police forensics team found some evidence but not much. It was being sent to the Portland FBI lab for analysis. The autopsy showed that it appeared Doug had been tortured, and had eventually been shot in the back of his head. She passed all of this on to Todd once she had learned it.

Todd then said, "There are no drug labs or farms in the area as far as I know, so Doug probably hadn't stumbled on something like that. Besides, they would have just shot him and not tortured him. To me, it sounds like someone wanted information that Doug had refused to give them, at least initially. Apparently, he finally gave it to them when he couldn't take any more of what they were doing to him, and they shot him. But what information could he have had that would be valuable enough to send a team out to a remote area of Oregon? Schea, please caution Jim and Grace to be more vigilant. I will pass this on to Lester to make sure the camp increases its security as well."

"Schea, you should be careful too. If someone is looking for information, then they seem ready to do anything they have to do in order to get it. You knew Doug better than I did, so you and Jim need to try to think about what Doug would have known that someone would think was valuable enough to torture and kill for."

Schea told Todd, "I am heading to Portland and Boring for about a week in order to visit friends, say goodbye, and close down my apartment."

"Okay. I heard from Michael, and he will be back in a few days. I'll brief him on what little I know about what you want him to do then ask him to call you to set up a meeting." She thanked him for helping.

Schea said goodbye to Jim and Grace and was sorry about what happened to Doug. She asked Jim to relay anything he heard from the police, coroner or FBI lab. There were hugs all around as she got in her car and drove away. Jim and Grace watched her leave then wearily walked into the house.

Schea was at her apartment by late that afternoon. She changed and went for a quick run around the area, came back, showered and went to the local pizza place to eat. As she ate, she mulled over what Todd had said. They had tortured Doug for information that he had and then killed him, probably because he had given it to them.

*What information could that have been? What could Doug have known that was worth killing him for? She had to think this through logically. People know things about themselves, about others, about places, about skills they have, about things they've seen, about things they've done, and maybe about what others have done. What of this kind of information could have been in Doug's head that was important enough for someone to kill for it?*

*The only things she could think of that Doug might have known and someone else might have wanted from him were things about others, about what he's seen, and maybe about what others have done. Maybe the person Doug knew had known something or had done something that the bad guys wanted to know. But who could that be? Jim had served in the CIA with her dad, why not target him? She didn't know enough about the other guides to know whether they might know something important to a bunch of killers, but maybe they did.* She would pass on what she thought to Todd the next time they talked.

XXXXX

She had called Alice earlier and asked if she could meet up with her this evening. Alice told her the group was meeting at her place for some drinks, music and fun at 9 pm. Schea said she would be there.

Schea went back to her apartment, grabbed a jacket and headed out. On the way, she stopped by the manager's office and told her that she would be giving up the apartment in a couple of weeks. The manager said she was sorry she was leaving because she was such a good tenant. She told Schea that she would mail the balance of her advance payment to her new address, after deducting for cleaning and any necessary repairs.

She drove into Portland, went to Alice's apartment and arrived at 8 pm. Alice gave her a big hug when she came in and handed her a Diet Coke with a smile. Schea said thanks. They sat on Alice's worn sofa and Alice said, "I know you can't talk about your job but is there anything new in your life?

Schea smiled. "I visited my sister in Virginia then my friends Jim and Grace in Bend."

Alice said she wished she had family she could visit. Her parents were dead and her one sister refuses to talk to her. She smiled and said, "That's why we have friends."

Schea chuckled. "Well, I have some good news and some bad news." Alice said to tell her the good news first. "I am going to be able to see my sister more often now. But, the bad news is that I am moving to Annapolis. Of course, I'll come back from time to time to visit you, as well as Jim and Grace."

Alice said she would be sad to see her go and asked when it is happening? Schea told her that it would probably be within 1-2 weeks. Alice asked if it was for a better job. Schea thought of the President and said yes. Alice smiled and said she was happy for Schea.

As Alice went to the kitchen for a beer, Schea got an idea. When Alice came back, Schea asked her "Would you like to have all of my stuff?" Alice looked at her like she was crazy, but Schea quickly said, "It isn't worth it to me to have it shipped across the country. It would probably cost me more to do that than it is worth, so you would be doing me a favor if you took it off my hands." Alice smiled and said it would be a pleasure to do her a favor.

Then Schea got another idea. "Would you also like to have my apartment for the next year?" Before Alice could respond, Schea explained, "I paid a year's rent in advance because of my work schedule and would rather not deal with the small amount that the balance might be."

192

Alice looked at her wide-eyed and said, "I would love it, but I have no way to get back and forth to work."

Schea smiled. "Well, I am not taking my car either so you can have that too. It also isn't worth shipping or driving to the east coast."

Alice silently stared at Schea, which was the first time Schea had ever seen her speechless. Schea kept smiling and looking at her. Finally, Alice asked if she was serious and Schea said "Yes, but there is one condition."

Alice said, "It doesn't matter what it is. I'll do whatever you want."

"You need to wait until I clear up a few things then I'll need a ride to the airport."

Alice smiled. "Absolutely."

Alice's guests started to arrive about that time and Alice informed everyone as they entered, even before saying hi to them, that Schea was leaving. Everyone came over and gave her hugs and wished her well and asked tons of questions. Schea loved it.

Schea arrived home at midnight and, of course, she had left the party just as it was getting into full swing. She slept well, except that she awoke the next day thinking immediately about what happened to Doug and the possible reasons why. She went for a run and stopped by the manager's office when she got back.

Schea asked the manager how many months were left on her lease and the manager said she had 2 months left. Schea told her she would be back later to pay for another 12 months. The manager was happy with that and asked her if her plans had changed. Schea said no but she wanted to have her apartment available anytime she might be back in the area. She also informed the manager that a friend of hers would be using it while she was gone. The manager looked at her skeptically but Schea told her she was a good friend and would not be a bother. The manager nodded okay

After Schea showered she called the theater manager and told him she was moving but the donations would continue. He thanked her profusely and wished her well. She went to the bank and got a cashier's check for the next 12 months rent, gave it to the apartment manager and waited for a receipt.

When Alice took her to the airport, she gave her the receipt and told her that if she came back to the area, she might ask if she could stay with Alice for a little while.

XXXXX

She had a Subway sandwich for lunch and while she was eating it, Michael called. "I heard that you missed my charm and good looks."

Schea laughed and asked, "Doesn't every woman miss your charm and good looks? I figured I'd have to get in line in order to see you."

"Oh, you know you'll always move to the front of the line. Anyway, I hear you have a job for me."

"Yes. How long before you can meet me in Ocean Shores, Washington?"

"I can be there tomorrow afternoon."

"Good. Meet me at the Galway Bay Pub on Point Brown Road." He laughed and said good choice. "I thought you'd like it." She hung up and smiled. Michael's family had emigrated from Galway, Ireland.

Now for the boys.

# 44 Mission Six: The Boys (Part 3)

Ocean Shores is a pretty seaside community along Washington's Olympic Peninsula's Pacific Coast. It has beautiful long wide beaches that people can drive their cars on. Schea's family spent one July there many years ago. Schea was only 6 at the time but she remembered having lots of fun swimming and riding horses on the beach.

Schea left right after Michael's call. The drive was only about 3 hours and she arrived late that afternoon. She took a room at the Guesthouse Inn and Suites on Ocean Shores Boulevard. She had a nice view of the beach from her room and it was only about a mile walk to the Galway Bay. She ate at a pizza shop across the street from the hotel and took a walk along the beach.

The hotel served a full, hot breakfast in the morning until 9 am. Schea got up at 6 am and went for a 10 mile run along the beach. The hotel also had a pool, so she changed into her swimsuit and went to the pool for about an hour of lap swimming. After breakfast she went to the beach, and walked for a couple of hours then decided to have lunch at the Galway Bay.

The Galway Bay Bar, Restaurant and Shop is about 100 yards up from the intersection of Ocean Shores Blvd and Point Brown Road. It is a horseshoe-shaped building with a restaurant along one arm, a shop in the other, and a bar in between the two. The shop sells all kinds of gifts and souvenirs from Ireland. The bar has live Irish folk music every weekend, and can get pretty lively with people joining in whether asked to or not. One of the bartenders conducts karaoke on Friday nights.

Schea arrived shortly after 1 pm, sat at the bar and ordered a Diet Coke. She told the bartender that she was waiting for a friend before ordering lunch. As she was finishing her coke, she turned as Michael walked towards her through the restaurant. She got up and told the bartender that she and her friend were going to take a table. He said no problem and that he'd be by shortly to take their orders.

Michael and Schea sat at the table to the left of the fireplace near the window. The bartender took their orders of Irish stew for both, another Diet Coke for her and a Harp for him. Schea asked how the drive was. He said that it was fine and that he actually spent the night in Portland. Michael asked how she was doing and she told him about moving to Annapolis.

The food arrived and they chatted amiably while they ate. She talked about the house in Annapolis and her plans for her move. He told her, "I spent some time visiting with my mum, who was diagnosed with breast cancer 4 months ago. She is going through treatments and the cancer seems to be responding well to them." She said was happy to hear that his mom was getting better.

The bartender came over, cleared the table and Schea ordered another Diet Coke while Michael ordered a Harp beer. He looked around and smiled. "This is a pretty cool place. I love my Irish roots and enjoy seeing all of this Irish stuff."

Schea told him, "Take a look at the wall outside of the men's restroom when you go there. You'll like what you see."

He didn't even wait. He got up and walked around the corner to the restroom. On the wall, was a large map of Galway and the surrounding area. He stared at it for a few minutes and then returned to their table. "Thanks. The map is really cool." They touched their glasses and got down to business.

Schea told Michael about the boys and what they had done to her sister. She left nothing out. He had to know who he was going to be dealing with. When she finished telling him about what happened to Allison, she continued. "I found out that they have done similar things to other girls in the area. I don't think they have killed anyone else, but I really don't know. I also suspect that they may have help, probably from the police because investigations into allegations seem to get lost or covered up."

She also told him about her recon trips to town. He smiled when she told him about the disguise she used on the second trip.

"What is it you want me to do?"

"I am reluctant to go back again because I might begin to raise suspicion."

"I agree. Maybe I could go into town, pretend that I am new to the area and trying to get a job at the lumber yard. The boys are now in their twenties, so it will be easy to bond with them at a bar."

Schea said, "There is only one bar and they seem to go there often. It is the Pitchwood Taphouse located a few blocks from the lumber yard. The Golden Lion motel is a block up from the bar and would be a good place for you to stay. It is near the lumber yard and the bar. Also, here is the address of the Watson's house."

Schea excused herself and went to the restroom. When she got back, Michael was smiling.

Michael said, "I think I might have a way to handle your mission." He smiled at her and she smiled back. Yea, Schea's Mission!

"I have a friend who might work well in this situation. Her name was Kathleen and she is a gorgeous redhead from a little village just outside of Dublin. I helped her out of a jam some years back when I was in Dublin visiting family and friends. The jam necessitated a move and I suggested the US. She agreed and I helped her to get an accounting job back in Springfield, Massachusetts. She is a tough kid and might like a break from her dull accounting job."

Schea asked what he thought she might be able to do. "Well, she could easily play the hot, Irish, lass who is new in town. Maybe she could even pretend to be my girlfriend or just someone that wanders into town a week or so after me. Anyway, I will give her a call and see if she would like to have an all-expenses paid trip to beautiful Raymond, Washington."

Schea had to laugh at that. She also knew that she would be paying for Kathleen's free trip, which was fine with her.

Michael asked if she was sure she wanted to go through with this.

Schea was quiet for a while then said, "At this point, I am.  But, if I change my mind, I will call you."

He shrugged and said, "Okay.  Fair enough."

Just then, her phone rang.  It was Todd and he said she needed to come to Baltimore for a meeting.  She hung up and looked at Michael.  He knew that look.  She said thanks for helping.  He told her he was glad to help and wished her luck.

She left and went back to the hotel to check out.

# 45 Mission Four: Planning (Part 1)

Schea arrived at Todd's new office in Baltimore at 8 pm 2 days after she left Michael. She parked her rental in front and looked around. The area wasn't the best area of town, but it looked like it might be on the mend since she noticed new shops opening and people out enjoying some evening drinking and eating.

She went in the front door and found Todd sitting at a table with Randall King. Randall had gone through training with her, so they knew each other well. He was a big African American who could probably break you in two with his bare hands, but Schea also remembered an incident when they were on the same team. They lost the competition but no one cared.

The reason they lost was because as they were moving through a wooded area, Randy came across a tiny bird that seemed to have fallen out of its nest in a tree. He had stopped and gently picked up the tiny creature. Schea and Jack stopped and said, "Come on, we need to keep going." He glared at them but didn't say a thing. He just dropped his pack, held the little bird in one hand, and climbed the tree using his free hand until he reached the nest about 12 feet off the ground.

Schea and Jack could only watch as this gentle giant carefully put the little bird back in the nest, and pushed a little of the grass and twigs around it. He finally came down, picked up his pack and said, "Now we can go." Schea and Jack smiled at each other and took off with him.

Schea walked over and both men said hey. She did too, sat at the table opposite Randy, and asked, "What's up?"

"You have a hostage to recover." Todd informed them. "The hostage is a 14 year-old girl named Brandy and she is the daughter of a wealthy American software genius. They were on vacation in the Caribbean, staying on the small island of Mustique, which is one of many little islands that make up Saint Vincent and the Grenadines."

"The girl got bored and wanted to do something so she pestered her father until he finally relented. He and his new young wife had just had a baby boy, so they were probably spending more time with him than her. The dad told his wife that he was going to take Brandy over to Port Elizabeth on the island of Bequi to do some shopping."

"It was only about a 10 mile trip across the water and they would get to do some sight-seeing along the way. They could also stop along the way to swim. He asked Brandy if she'd like to do that, she said yes then ran off to put on her bathing suit and shorts. Her father walked down to the boat dock and told the captain of his yacht that he would be heading to Port Elizabeth in the sailboat. He was a qualified sailor, so the captain said that he'd make sure it was ready for the trip."

"The father called his security team and asked to have 2 men assigned to go with him and his daughter to Bequi. The men showed up at the sailboat at the same time as Brandy. She wore a bikini top, shorts over her bikini bottom and flip-flops. The security guys had a hard time not staring at her.

Her father wanted to tell her to go and put something more on, but he didn't. She was so willful and had wanted to get out of the house so bad that he was afraid she'd make a huge scene and ruin the rest of the vacation."

"They left for Bequi. The security men were also sailors, so they helped with rigging and other preparations for the excursion. They stopped half-way for a swim and Brandy pulled off her shorts, kicked off her flip-flops, and dove in, as did her dad. They swam for a while, got back on the boat and sailed on into Port Elizabeth."

"They dropped anchor, untied the small dinghy, climbed in and shoved off for the small harbor. They pulled up to the shore and dragged the tiny boat onto the beach. The father paid one of the beach boys to watch the boat then they all left to explore the shops along the small, but cute little harbor. They wandered through the shops for about an hour then Brandy asked if they could go into the café that was right at the end of the line of shops overlooking the small beach. They went in and ordered coffee and pastries."

"The café was also a bar and the owner told them that some years ago, Mick Jagger came in and started to jam with his guitar. Soon after, another man came in and started jamming with him. That man was David Bowie. The small crowd loved it. The dad was impressed but when he turned to his daughter and smiled, she looked bored and asked who those guys were. He just rolled his eyes."

"Brandy is a pretty but willful and careless teen. After about 20 minutes of sitting and sipping her coffee, Brandy said she had to go to the restroom. The father looked around and pointed to a door down a back hall. Brandy got up to go and the father told a guard to go and stand by the door."

"The dad continued to sip his coffee but after 15 minutes, he wondered if Brandy was okay. He got up with the other guard and headed back to the restroom. The dad knocked on the door and asked if she was okay. He heard nothing, so he knocked louder and asked again. Still nothing, so he went in. She was gone. He saw that the back window was open so he figured she must have climbed out."

"He and the guards searched the area for 30 minutes and found no sign of her. They asked people if they had seen her. They got conflicting answers. Some said she went toward the hill and others said she went toward the beach. He finally went to the small police station."

"Needless to say, she was not found."

"He stayed in a small hotel in Port Elizabeth for the next week searching and waiting in case she came back. The island is small, so they were able to search every house and square foot of land. There was a small airport, but they had no record of a plane coming or going that was carrying her or any girl near her age. There wasn't much they could do about the various parts of the coastline since any boat could have come and gone without anyone knowing."

Todd continued. "On the seventh day, the dad got a phone call. The man said that he had his daughter and demanded 2 million dollars if he wanted to see her again. He didn't hesitate and paid the money. She wasn't returned. He finally reported the incident to the FBI. They were sympathetic, but there wasn't much they could do outside the US borders. He contacted his various friends in high places and they tried to get him government help. They promised that if they heard of any sightings of the girl or any leads that might help, they would pass them on right away."

"The family finally returned to the states and decided to go a different route to find Brandy. He hired Private Investigators. He also knew some computer experts who could help track phone calls and emails. This all happened about 6 months ago. The father finally got a lead from an intercepted phone conversation that a friend in the state department passed on to him. Apparently, there was an auction to be held where the items were young girls. They were to be sold to the highest bidder and many would go to wealthy Middle-Eastern Arabs or Asians, as well as various other wealthy buyers. They followed that lead and found out where the sale would take place."

"They worked with local authorities and raided the event. They rescued most of the girls and learned that several had already been sold and moved. They also learned from a couple of the rescued girls, who came from a broker in French Guiana, that he had kept 3 girls. They didn't know why but they did say that one of the girls told them she came from a wealthy family. Maybe the broker wanted to get more money for her over the years, rather than to sell her to just one buyer. From their description of the girl, it sounded like Brandy."

"The problem is that none of the government agencies can act on this information due to the current agreements they have with Guiana. The father was pissed and yelled and screamed at them, but they were unmovable. He finally contacted me. And, that is why I have contacted you." He looked from Schea to Randy. They were focused and he knew they couldn't wait to get their hands on the scum bags that held the girls. He expected that Schea was ready to go right now, alone, but he had a plan.

He told them, "We think we have good intel on where the girls are being held. We believe they are being held at a large villa a few miles outside of Camopi on the Oiapoque River in the south of Guiana which also borders the Brazilian state of Amapa. Informants have observed three young girls walking around the grounds at night, always with a guard. They think that they fit the descriptions of the three girls mentioned by the rescued girls. That is where you are going."

"Randy speaks fluent French so which is why he is going and Schea is going to be his ticket into the villa. Randy will pretend to be a broker from Algeria who thinks he can get a better deal for Schea in Guiana. The villa is owned by a wealthy French industrialist named Henri Devoit who made his fortune making engines for cars all over Europe. He appears to have a taste for young girls so we should assume he has treated the girls badly."

"The informants indicate that he seems to have at least 20 guards around the place and about 10 staff members that come and go. The plan is for both Randy and Schea go to the capitol, Cayenne, and contact Henri's representative. Randy will tell him that he has a juicy product for sale and would like to offer it to Henri. You will need to convince him to let you come to his villa in order to show him the product. If not, then you will sell Schea to the broker, and he will take her to the villa. In that case, Randy will need to head there on his own then try to shadow Schea and the broker to make sure they got to the villa. We need at least one of you inside."

"Once inside, Schea needs to contact the girls, make them understand she is there to help and that they need to be ready. If things look bad" Todd got quiet and looked at Schea "then we must get Brandy out above all else. If we can only get one, it must be Brandy." He held Schea's gaze and asked, "Do you understood?"

She snarled back at him, "Yes. I understand."

"When you get out, head for the river. It is only half a mile away to the south and I will have an extraction team there for you. The country of Brazil hates the man because he has men crossing into Amapa stealing and selling girls, especially young tourists which, as you can imagine, is not good for the tourism business."

"They have not been able to stop him, but this might at least put a thorn in his side. They will not react to our presence, but they will not help either. Guiana doesn't really seem to care one way or the other what he does. We're sure that he has greased the right hands and told them to just stay away. This, of course, is also good for us. Questions?"

They discussed a few minor issues and, once everything was ironed out, they got up to leave.

Todd reiterated to Schea, "Brandy is the priority and the other 2 would simply be a bonus if we could get them out too."

She sighed and said, "Yes, I understood you the first time. But I will try, if possible, to get them all out."

He said, "Okay, but please bring our client's daughter out at all costs."

She nodded.

# 46 Mission Four: Meet the Rep (Part 2)

Randy and Schea arrived in Cayenne and took a room at a modest hotel near the tourist area. Schea would have to stay in the room at all times. She had to appear trapped. They agreed that when the rep came, she would need to be gagged and tied to the bed on the floor. She also needed to wear something sexy and a little revealing. In preparation, Schea had packed some things that she thought would work.

They had no trouble sneaking in their weapons. They bought the items in Surinam before they flew into Cayenne. Randy bought a silenced PPK and Schea bought two knives.

Randy wandered the streets until he found a place that might know how to contact Henri, *the guy knew a guy who knew a guy* sort of thing. After a day or so of guys who know guys calling other guys, Randy finally made contact with the rep, and he said that he would take a look at the girl.

Randy brought him up to the room and showed him Schea. She was disheveled but he could tell she was good material for his boss. She wore a see-through blouse with no bra and a short skirt that had slid up to mid-thigh. She was an impressive product.

The rep asked, "How much?"

"$50,000."

The rep laughed, "She wasn't worth that much. She's old."

Randy said, "Come on. She's 15."

"Exactly. Too old. My boss likes them to be 11-13 and preferably virgins, but that isn't a must."

Randy grumbled. "Make me an offer."

The rep said, "$15,000."

Now Randy laughed. They went back and forth until they agreed on $25,000.

"I insist that we go to the boss to make sure she is the right product and that, more importantly, I get my money." Randy demanded.

They now went back and forth on this issue. Randy finally had to agree that he would get $10,000 now and could accompany Schea to the town of Camopi, but not to the villa. They would leave the next day.

After Randy and the rep left to get the money, Schea untied herself and changed. Randy returned about an hour later with the money and they prepared for the trip to Camopi.

The rep arrived at 9 am the following morning. Schea was wearing jeans and a bulky sweatshirt. Randy explained to the rep, "It would raise a lot of attention if we dragged her out into the street with her hands tied."

The rep asked, "What if she tries to get away?"

Randy held up his gun and smiled. "I'm a crack shot. She won't get far. Besides, I pumped her with just enough dope to make her groggy, but still able to walk."

"Okay, we'll use my car to get there."

When they got downstairs, the car was waiting with a mean looking driver. The rep sat in back with Schea and Randy sat up front with the driver.

"It's about a 6 hour drive from here, but we will stop for some food and to use the toilet."

Schea stared out of the window during the whole drive to Camopi. The rep kept looking at her and would sometimes reach over and rub his hand up and down her thigh. He also liked to grab her breasts every so often. Schea never moved or even seemed to take notice. The rep finally stopped and just sat staring straight ahead.

It was a good thing that he couldn't read minds because if he could have read Schea's mind, he probably would have shit his pants. She was thinking very unpleasant thoughts about what she wanted to do to the asshole. Randy knew Schea could handle herself so he paid no attention to the back seat antics of the rep. Besides, he had his own thoughts about what he wanted to do to the rep.

They stopped a couple of times for food and toilet breaks. Schea had to sit with them but she did not eat. She just kept staring straight ahead. She did go to the bathroom once and the rep insisted he had to go with her. He actually watched her piss while she sat in the stall. When she finished, she wiped and pretended to accidentally drop the soiled tissue on his shoe. He annoyingly kicked it away.

They arrived at Camopi at 4 that afternoon. Randy was asked to get out and take a room at the boarding house next to the post office. The rest of the money would be brought to him there if the boss agreed with the rep's judgment about the girl. Randy got out and got a room. He knew that no one would come to see him unless it was to kill him and take back the $10,000. He snuck out the back and waited in a small copse of trees near where he had been dropped off.

The rep and Schea were driven through the gate of the villa and stopped in front of the main house. The rep got out along with the driver but Schea stayed seated. She was now alert. She was looking for ways to get out of the villa. She had been in a villa in Mexico when she went after Mendoza and she hoped that this one had a similar design. She figured there was an exit door of some type in a side or back wall.

She could also see that the walls were about 10 feet high with no guard towers. *That's good*, thought Schea. *The guards must be staying somewhere in the house*. She could see that the guards did go on regular patrols, or at least, they were doing so now. Two were outside patrolling together and 3 more were walking the interior perimeter. *It would be better to split them up or to have two separate patrols inside and outside. I will have to write a note for Henri before I leave so that he can make that correction to his security. But, then again, maybe I won't.*

Henri finally came out and the rep pulled Schea roughly from the car. Henri came over and looked at Schea from top to bottom. He also decided to feel the important parts, including her butt. He took the time to examine all of her very slowly and carefully with his eyes and his hands. He seemed satisfied at first, but he went through the process again to make sure.

Schea was thinking. *All right all ready. I'm getting tired of all this touchy feely stuff.* She decided right then and there that they were leaving tonight and she was definitely not going to leave a note for Henri about improvements to his security protocols. She wanted to get those girls out as soon as possible and planned on taking all 3 girls no matter what Todd wanted her to do. She also hoped, but knew this was secondary, that she would get a chance to pay back the rep and Henri for all of their touchy-feely attention.

Henri whispered something to the rep who nodded in understanding. The rep and three of the guards got back into the car and drove out the gate. Schea and Randy had figured this would happen. There is no way they would give him the additional money and let him go. They were going to kill him, take the 10 grand back and dump his body in the river where the crocs and piranhas would take care of it. Schea smiled inwardly because she knew how Randy would deal with these idiots.

*This is good. There are 2 guards outside already and 3 more going along with Mr. Touchy-Feely. That only left about 15 guards in the compound. Three would be outside the house and maybe 8 more in the house somewhere, possibly half would be on rest until the next shift change. This probably means that there might be 4 or 5 guarding the girls, and the rest in different parts of the house. She assumed that Henri would have the girls in the basement and he would be in an upstairs bedroom. There would probably be a couple of guards up there as well.*

Schea thought. *This is looking better and better in terms of the odds. This means I might only have to deal with 3 guards at a time.* She had her knives tightly tucked under each armpit already. If she weren't trying to act all bothered and scared, she would have started smiling, but that wouldn't do, at least for the moment.

Henri led the procession into the house and he appeared to be anxious for the show to start. *Man, he is really a horny little dork, isn't he.* They stopped in the foyer and he issued orders to 2 of the guards who disappeared downstairs. *This is getting even better. He is probably bringing one or more of the girls up to me.* She would have almost kissed Mr. T-F at this point, but she decided instead that she might kill him quickly so he didn't suffer too much. *Well, no, that was going a bit too far.*

Sure enough, about 5 minutes later, the three girls appeared at the top of the stairs and walked into the foyer. They were put in a line with Schea. She was yelling inside her head, *Please pick me.* He did. *Whew.* He also picked Brandy. *Okay, now I know I have to kill him quickly. He is being too kind to me.*

Mr. T-F barked at the guards and they led the remaining girls back downstairs. Brandy looked pretty bad - not beaten, but dirty, worn out, and ragged. Schea wondered if the guards had permission to have the girls too. Henri led them up the stairs and one guard followed.

XXXXX

After about an hour, Randy saw the car driving toward the small town. The night before, Schea told him, "I want this done as soon as possible and I plan to act tomorrow night if at all possible and you need to take out whoever comes for you then get your ass to the villa. I'll try to exit on the river or back side of the villa while you take out any guards you find outside as silently as possible then wait for me and the girls."

The car pulled up in front of the little boarding house, and two guards and the rep went inside. The other guard went around back. Randy moved in his direction. He crept to a position right behind the door that he had used earlier to exit the house. As the guard came around the side, he saw Randy standing with his back to him. He had been at the villa so he hadn't seen Randy. He got closer and asked him in French, "What are you doing?"

"I'm having a smoke." Randy replied in French while slowly turning toward the guard who had seemed to relax. Randy quickly covered the guard's mouth and snapped his neck.

Randy moved around the boarding house to the car. He started it then moved back to stand by the side of the front door. One of the guards came running out onto the porch. Randy grabbed him from behind and crushed his throat then dragged the body around the corner. Randy was lucky that they chose this part of town. There seemed to be no one around or people were used to this sort of thing and were just staying away until it was all over. He didn't care. He waited.

When the rep didn't find him in his room, the remaining guard and rep came out of the front door looking around. Randy was behind the last guard in a flash and killed him while the rep tried to run away. He was in the car and ready to drive away when Randy jumped in the passenger seat next to him. The rep looked at him, and Randy smiled and said, "Do you want to feel my boobs, asshole?"

The rep just kept staring at Randy. He was still doing that when Randy shoved the Rep's head into the dash several time. The rep screamed in pain the first few times then finally dropped against the door. Randy grabbed the guns from the guards, dragged the rep to the woods, put a bullet into the back of his head then headed for the villa.

# 47 Mission Four: Brandy Meets Schea (Part 3)

Henri led the girls into his bedroom. The guard that was behind them came in too and stood by the closed door. Apparently, Henri liked having an audience. He sat on his bed, while the girls stood about 3 feet away and two feet apart. Schea was nearest the door, and thus, nearest the guard. *That was good. He would be the first to die*.

After a minute of staring, Henri said, "Take off your clothes."

Brandy started right away. It appeared that she had been well trained by Henri. Schea imagined all of the things that he had done to her. Mr. T-F would die painfully.

Schea undid her jeans and pulled them down a little at a time. When they were around her knees, she began wiggling them down the rest of the way. Brandy was already naked. Schea could now see numerous bruises on her back, legs, and chest. Schea glanced at Henri with pure hatred in her eyes. Schea reached under her sweat shirt and undid her bra. It dropped to the floor. She slowly reached under again and found the knives. She gripped them tightly and took a breath.

Faster, than a striking cobra, Schea killed the guard. Henri was stunned into immobility. She pushed Brandy to the floor and leaped onto Henri. She was behind him before he could react to any of what was happening. His mouth was open as if ready to scream, but all that came out was a little gurgling sound as the knife sliced open his throat from ear to ear. Schea dropped him back on the bed and quickly went to Brandy.

Schea sat down beside Brandy and lightly touched her face. She grabbed Brandy's shirt and laid it gently in her lap. She leaned close to her and began whispering, "You're going be fine now. Some friends and I are here to take you home. Brandy, do you want to go home?"

She shook her head yes.

Schea told Brandy her name and asked hers, even though she knew it and had already said it. She wanted Brandy to say it and understand that she was going home. She told Schea that her name was Brandy. Schea thanked her and told her that she needed to do everything that Schea said, and asked, "Can you do that?"

"I can," replied Brandy.

Schea slowly helped her up and suggested, "We should get dressed now." They did. Schea told her, "We have to be very quiet now. Can you do that?"

"Yes. I can."

Schea moved toward the door. "Brandy, stay beside the door." Schea pulled her knife from the dead guard and wiped it on him. She also grabbed his AK47 and slung it over her shoulder. She stood in front of Brandy and smiled. "Did you like this place, Brandy?"

She shook her head no emphatically.

"Did you like anyone in this place?"

Brandy shook her head again.

"Good."

Schea put the knife that she had used to kill Mr. T-F into Brandy's hand. Schea looked at her again and asked, "Would you be able to use this on a bad guy if he tried to hurt you?"

She didn't respond for a moment and then nodded yes.

"Good." She explained the plan to Brandy. "We have to leave here and go to the other two girls to get them. We will then have to get out of the house and out of the compound. I have a friend on the other side of the wall who will help us. Do you understand all of this?"

"Yes."

"Good. Are you ready to go?"

Brandy smiled.

Shea smiled too and said. "Let's go." Schea turned to the door.

Schea motioned for Brandy to stay back then opened the door slowly. She looked through the small separation between the door and the frame but didn't see anyone. She motioned for Brandy to follow her. They stepped out into the hallway with Schea in the lead. Suddenly, Schea heard steps behind her. She pushed Brandy aside just as a guard appeared from around the far corner. He started to raise his gun but then fell backward with Schea's knife sticking out of his chest. Schea ran over, pulled it out, and came back to Brandy. Brandy couldn't help stare at Schea like she was some kind of apparition.

They moved to the top of the stairs, Schea looked down, didn't see anyone and they proceeded down. Luckily, all of the staff seemed to have gone home. *Maybe the guards cooked for themselves. Maybe Henri cooks for them.* They reached the bottom of the stairs and headed toward the door that the guards had used to take away the other two girls. They opened it and headed down to the basement.

XXXXX

Randy had arrived at the river side wall of the villa and waited for the guards to come around the corner. He pulled out his silenced PPK and watched. They finally came around the corner smoking and chatting amiably. He didn't feel bad about killing them. After all, smoking cigarettes can be deadly. As they came in front of his position, he stood and put a bullet into the head of each then walked over and put another into their chests.

He dragged the guards into the tree line and moved back into position to see if anymore came around or if he heard gunfire from inside the compound. If he heard gunfire, then he would enter the villa to help Schea and the girls. He knew that Schea would ignore Todd's warning and bring out all three. "You have to admire the little girl," he thought out loud. *Oops. I hope she didn't hear me say that. I can't be sure about her. She seems to have superhuman hearing as well.* He dropped down and waited.

Schea led Brandy down the stairs. She put her fingers to her lips and looked at Brandy. She pointed down, shrugged her shoulders, and then pointed both left and right. Brandy got the hint. She pointed to the right. Schea smiled.

They proceeded slowly down the stairs, stopping every few steps to see if anyone came around the corner or from behind them. As they reached the bottom, Schea noticed several rooms straight ahead. She figured those must be the guards' quarters. She moved to the right and had Brandy stop. She peeked around the corner and saw one guard in front of the door to what was probably the girl's room. She indicated for Brandy to stay where she was. Schea gave her the AK-47 to hold and hid her knife up her sleeve.

She hunched her shoulders and shuffled around the corner toward the guard. He looked up and moved toward her. He didn't look alarmed because he held his gun down. *Good.* Before he knew, Schea put a knife into his chest and he fell backwards with a loud thump. Schea went back and grabbed Brandy. Brandy was used to what Schea did so she didn't even glance at the guard.

Schea whispered to Brandy, "When I open the door, you need to go in first and talk to the girls. You need to convince them that help is here and that they are leaving. Can you do that?"

"I can." Brandy said.

Schea took the knife and gun from Brandy before she went in. She didn't want the girls to get scared of Brandy. Schea opened the door and stood back to let Brandy in. Brandy went in and began talking softly to the girls.

As Schea retrieved the knife from the dead guard, she suddenly heard footsteps. She stepped into the room, gave Brandy a knife and stepped back out. She looked back and put her fingers to her lips. Brandy nodded and Schea closed the door quietly. She moved toward the corner and just as she was about to peek around it, a guard appeared. She took him out with her knife and he fell to the floor. But then she heard door knobs rattling and doors opening. *Oh boy. This mission has just gone all to hell.* But, then she shrugged and thought. *When don't they?*

She pulled the AK47 off of her shoulder, made sure the safety was off, put it on semi-automatic, checked that the magazine was full, and stepped around the corner. She smiled at the first guard that she saw, and he looked startled to see one of the girls holding a machine gun. Then his eyes went wide. Too late. Schea put a few rounds into his chest and the shots drew the others out. She backed up against the wall until she saw that there were at least three more standing in the room looking around.

208

Schea stepped out and opened up on them. She kept moving to the left to make sure they couldn't just open up on her where she had stood. One of them got a few rounds off, but that was it. The guards fell in a heap. She waited to see if any more popped out of the rooms, but none did so she went back to the girls. She slowly opened the door and said, "It's me." She didn't want Brandy accidentally sticking her with her own knife. That wouldn't be good for her, but Randy would have a good story to tell Todd.

As Schea stepped into the room, Brandy came up to her and asked, "Are you okay?"

She smiled and said, "Sure, let's go."

Brandy still stared at her with concern.

Schea asked, "What's wrong? We gotta go."

Brandy pointed to a spot on her shirt near her left side. It was red. Schea had apparently been hit by one of the stray bullets from the guard who had gotten off a short burst before dying. Schea took a quick look, saw the bullet wound, and knew it had only passed through some soft tissue. The bleeding had already slowed to a trickle. She assured Brandy that she would be fine and encouraged her and the girls to start moving.

The girls all got up and proceeded out of the room. They followed Schea up the stairs with Brandy bringing up the rear. Schea had them stay back at the top of the stairs while Schea slowly opened the door and peeked around the corner. She couldn't figure out why no other guards had shown up. She waved the girls up and they moved towards the front door. Suddenly, she heard a noise behind the group. She turned to see a guard coming towards them from the side hallway. Before she could do anything, Brandy turned and started moving towards the guard.

Brandy was smiling and said, "Hey, Hector. Are we gonna do it tonight? You are the best of them all. You're so big." She put a huge smile on her face and started licking her lips. Schea and the rest of the girls stood still watching. Schea quietly took the safety off the gun.

Brandy was now only a foot away from Hector. He was smiling now and asked, "Where are you going?"

Brandy reached up and stroked his face softly. Just as Hector started to reach for Brandy's waist, she stuck the knife into his stomach as hard as she could. He growled and moved backward. He started to bring his gun up, but Schea was faster and blasted him with four shots to his chest. She put the gun over her shoulder again and moved past Brandy to Hector. She pulled the knife from his gut, wiped it off on his pants and handed it back to Brandy with a big smile. She leaned in and whispered, "Nice job." Brandy looked scared, but was also proud for thinking so quickly and taking action. She felt nothing for that sick bastard.

Schea moved back to the front of the girls and slowly opened the door. She worried because there were still likely 4 or 5 more guards somewhere, but she couldn't wait for them to do something.

They had to keep moving. She led them out the door, and to the right toward the river side wall of the compound, unfortunately, she did not see any doors in the wall. She motioned for them to get down and stay put while she ran to the back wall. No door there either.

Schea came back to the girls and told them to stay. She walked along the wall until she found what she needed. It was a large stone grinding wheel probably for grinding corn many years ago. Regardless, it was going to have a different use now. She motioned for the girls to come over to her. "I'm going to get on top of the wall, then lean over and pull each of you up and over. Brandy is the tallest, so she will help you two up. Brandy, go over to that stone, stand on it, and reach up for my hand after the girls are over. Do you all understand?"

They shook their heads yes, but then one asked, "How are you going to get to the top of that wall? It is too high and you're not even as tall as we are."

Schea smiled and said, "Watch." She handed the gun and knives to Brandy, and removed her shoes because they were leather and not suitable for what she had planned.

She moved away from the girls and stood at an angle to the stone then suddenly she took off at a sprint. The girls' eyes opened wide at how fast she was. When she got to the stone she stepped on it and leaped at the wall. They thought she was really nuts now. She was going to crush herself against the wall. Just as she was almost to the wall she twisted a little so that she was at a slight angle with it then literally continued running up the wall. When she was nearing the top, she planted her foot against the wall, leaped one last time, grabbed the top edge of the wall, and pulled herself on top. She spun around and crawled back to where the girls were at the rock. She looked down at them and said, "Okay. Come on over."

Brandy dropped the weapons and helped each of the girls up to Schea who pulled them to the top of the wall. Once there, she told them to hold on while she straddled the wall with her legs. When she felt secure on top of the wall, she leaned down and gently lowered the girls down on the outside of the compound. When they were at arm's length, she dropped them. They ended up falling about two feet onto their butts, but the ground was soft so they were unhurt.

Finally it was Brandy's turn. She stepped onto the rock and reached for Schea's hand. As she grabbed it, they both heard running feet and shouting. Gunshots started pinging off the wall several feet away. Schea was struggling to get Brandy up and over. Just as a guard seemed to be taking aim, he dropped to the ground, dead. Schea smiled and figured that Randy was around somewhere. Brandy was dropped over the side and Schea followed.

Schea herded the girls into the trees and squatted down. She indicated for them to be quiet and, after a few minutes, she got up, turned toward a tree and waited. Randy finally came out from behind it.

He shrugged his shoulders and said, "Damn, I can never sneak up on you."

She smiled and told him, "You're too big and noisy to be a sneak."

She introduced the girls to her friend. Randy saw the blood on Schea's shirt and asked if she was okay. She said it was just a flesh wound. Randy nodded and they headed for the river. This time Randy led and Schea brought up the rear.

They arrived at the water's edge and got down behind a group of bushes. After about 10 minutes they heard a whistle. That was the signal. Randy whistled back and the boat quietly came into view. They all climbed into the boat then it turned around, and headed for the open ocean. It took 3 days of constant driving at night, hiding during the day, and keeping quiet the whole time which was not easy for 4 teenage girls. But, they were all pretty tired, so they slept a lot, which was also a favorite pastime.

There were plenty of supplies on board, which made it even more cramped, but the girls didn't seem to mind. They cuddled up with each other and slept. Schea figured that is what they did back in their room too. Schea slept on and off, sharing the watch duties with Randy and the boat driver. No one introduced themselves, and Schea cautioned the girls to never use their names or anyone else's names for that matter. They were already amazed by this girl who didn't look any older than they were, so they obeyed her without question.

Late at night on the 3rd day they reached the inlet to the ocean. The driver pulled over to a small dock, pointed and they all got off. Randy lead the way to an old run-down shack, and they went in. Randy went back out and Schea stayed with the girls. They had to stay quiet.

After about 30 minutes, Randy came in and motioned for them to follow him. He led them to another small boat, they got in, and it headed toward the open water and a much bigger boat. When they got to the big yacht, they were helped on board from a low ramp in the back. Brandy smiled because it was similar to her father's.

They went to the main deck and were met by a tall man in boat shoes, shorts and white t-shirt. He welcomed them aboard and told them to follow another man to their rooms. He told them that they would each find new clothes, shoes, and toiletries. He suggested that they might want to take turns with the bathroom. He also suggested that they should probably sleep for a while. They had a long trip ahead of them.

Randy and Schea came over and shook hands with the man. He said that they have separate quarters in the aft area of the next deck below. The man noticed the blood on Schea's shirt and asked if she needed medical attention. Schea said she just needed a medical kit and that she would be fine. He told her that he would have one brought to her room. They thanked him and moved off to their rooms. The boat was crowded, so the small crew and the captain had to sleep in a small area in the dining area.

XXXXX

They made their way to Vila Velha where they caught a charter flight to Barbados. Randy called Todd when they were safely out on open water. He also passed on the names of the other two girls so Todd could contact their parents.

Schea hadn't carried a burner in case it rang during the operation so she was sitting on the deck in a two-piece bathing suit enjoying the warm sun and chatting with Brandy.

She glanced over at Randy as he talked to Todd on the phone and saw him look over at her at one point. He looked concerned about something. When he finished, she excused herself, went over to him and asked, "Is everything okay?"

He smiled and said, "Absolutely. Todd just wanted to be sure that we were all okay. He also told me that he congratulated us on getting all of the girls out. You can tell him about your wound when you see him."

Randy smiled and added, "Todd also needs to see you in his office in Baltimore when you get back. He'd like you to go there before going anywhere else." Schea figured that Todd wanted to give her a lecture for ignoring his order about Brandy being her highest priority.

Schea went back over to the girls and sat down on the deck next to Brandy. As Brandy talked about how amazed she was at the kinds of things that she could do, Schea kept having troubling feelings. She didn't get the idea that it was the phone call or that Todd wanted to see her. It was something else entirely, but she couldn't come up with anything. She eventually shook off the feeling and smiled at Brandy.

Schea thought that Brandy was a pretty girl and her figure reminded her of Jenny's. When she thought that, she got a sudden impulse to see Jenny. She decided to go see her as soon as Todd was done yelling at her.

They landed in Barbados and when the girls walked out into the reception area they all started to scream with joy because they saw their parents all standing there on the other side of the barrier waiting for them. The parents also started to scream. Schea and Randy smiled and moved off to the other side of the hall. Schea was thinking of how happy Brandy looked to see her parents. She wondered if this incident would rattle her cage a little and get her to settle down, or at least tone down her rebellious behavior.

Just as Schea was about to turn toward the next flight departure area, she felt a tug at the back of her shirt. She turned around to find Brandy standing there with her mom and dad. Her mom was holding the baby boy.

Brandy said, "This is …."

Schea immediately looked her in the eyes before she said any more.

Brandy stopped before she said any more, but then said, "She is a girl that I met on the plane." Her parents said hi as did Schea.

Schea smiled at Brandy. "It was fun talking to you on the long flight." Then she hugged her and whispered, "Remember, I do not exist." Brandy nodded while Schea whispered in her ear again, "Now please be a good girl."

Brandy stepped back, looked at her and said, "Oh I will, you can bet on that." Then they all turned and headed in opposite directions.

# 48 Mission Five: Jenny (Part 1)

Randy left Schea at the airport with a wave and a cryptic good luck comment. He said to be strong and smiled what looked more like a sad smile, than a happy one. She grabbed her carry-on and walked out into the bright sunshine. She found her car in the parking lot and headed to downtown Baltimore per Todd's instructions. She parked around the corner and walked into his office. She stopped in the middle of the floor.

There, around the table, were 3 of the 4 trainers that she knew, Kevin, Lenny and Andy, as well as 2 of her fellow trainees, Gus and Jack. There was also some guy she didn't know. She thought. *What is Todd going to do, rattle my cage in front of everyone in order to send a message? Well, so be it.* She continued over to the table and simply looked around and said, "Hello, gentlemen." They all gave her a nod. There was one seat open and it was next to Todd. *How appropriate.* He asked her to sit and she did.

Once she was seated, he turned his chair toward her and simply said, "Something terrible has happened."

Schea stared at him and, now that she was next to him, Todd looked like he hadn't slept for a week. Little did she know how close to the truth that was. She wondered what was really going on. She thought quickly and ran through some scenarios, like Michael was hurt or killed, but that wasn't possible. The boys can kill girls, but they'd never be able to take out Michael. Lester wasn't here, maybe it was him. Then she started to panic and thought maybe this is about Jim and Grace.

Todd could see what she was doing so he held his hand in front of her to get her attention. He looked at her then simply said, "Jenny has been kidnapped."

She kept staring at him. She must have heard wrong. He didn't say Jenny. He said Jerry or Larry or something else. And then she remembered Randy's call to Todd and how he had looked after hanging up. More importantly, she remembered the feelings that she started having after the mission. *Oh my God. This is true. He did say Jenny has been kidnapped. That is what he said.*

Todd could see that Schea's brain was trying to process what he'd said. He could see that she was trying to organize it into something other than what it was. Her eyes were swimming around and her body would tense and un-tense. He knew what was going to happen, and saw it right before it hit.

Schea exploded. She flew out of the chair and began screaming at the top of her lungs. She kept saying, "No, no, no" over and over again. Tears practically flew out of her eyes. No one moved. Frankly, they were all afraid. The new guy, Benny, had heard enough about Schea in the training camp so he was really scared.

Todd slowly stood and even more slowly moved towards her. She was screaming and crying and he could see that there was cold fury in her eyes. He had to do something before she hurt herself or someone else. He moved ever closer to her until he was next to her. She seemed to not even see him.

When he thought there was a slight lull in her rant, he engulfed her into his arms. She didn't resist. It was as though she had nothing left, she melted into his arms much like she did after talking about Greg's betrayal. He half walked and half carried her over to a sofa in the corner of the room. He held her tight as he helped her to sit next to him. He patted her hand and whispered to her that they will get her back. He said it over and over again. Finally, he felt her relax, and he slowly let go.

Schea quietly mumbled, "Where is she?"

"We don't know."

"Who has her?"

"We don't know."

"Is she okay?"

"We don't know."

"When was she taken?"

"It was a week ago."

She exploded again, only this time the fury was aimed at him.

"Why didn't you pull me out? What is wrong with you? Do you care about your crappy little group more than a little girl who is in danger and could be killed?" Then, she started to yell, "I hate you! I hate everyone in this room! I hate myself for not being here to protect Jenny! This is the second time I wasn't able to help a sister, and it will be the last!" She got up and moved towards the door. "I will find those bastards, and they will pay!"

Todd quickly ran to the door to block her exit. She stopped a few feet away and looked at him. Her eyes were telling him that he had better move or else, but he would not. "You have to stay and hear me out then, if you still want to go, so be it." He started to say more but she stopped him.

"You had better move or I will move you and you know I can do it."

He slowly opened his palms and said, "I know you can do it, but please listen for just a minute then if you want to leave, I will not try to stop you." He was speaking rapidly because he didn't want to give her time to react to her anger.

He quickly continued, "We do not have all of the answers but we have been working around the clock to find her." As he said this, he waved over toward the men sitting at the table. She glanced their way briefly and then looked back at him. "Those bastards have attacked one of our own and I, we, will move heaven and earth to get Jenny back safely."

215

"The President knows and he has told Chuck to give us whatever we need, short of troops on the ground. We have been working with the NSA and their tracking systems in order to find out where she may have been taken."

"We think we might know who one of them is. It is Frank. He searched my office while you were still at the camp. I didn't know it was him at the time but I am now sure of it. I think he wanted your contact information. All that I ever keep in those files is an emergency phone number for each trainee and, as you know, yours was Jim's. We think that it was he and some of his friends who killed Doug. They probably wanted to know where you were most vulnerable."

Todd looked at Schea and said, "They know you, Schea. Somehow they know a lot about you. They knew how to find you. They knew you were at my camp. How the hell would they know that kind of stuff? We think they tortured Doug and found out about Jenny. Doug knew Jenny and that she had left with the Kennedys."

"Whoever this is, they want to draw you out in the open for some reason. It wasn't good enough to just kill you or to kill Jim and anyone else close to you. They want you and they want you to suffer before they kill you. We need your help to figure this out, Schea. We need you. Jenny needs you to help us."

"Schea think about it. What would Jenny want you to do? She would want you to get help in order to help her. You know that, Schea, don't you? Think, Schea. If this had happened to someone else, what would you tell them? If Brandy's father had come to you for advice on the best way to get his daughter back, what would you have told him?"

"Please, Schea, we need you to help us find and get Jenny back to you and her family. Please help us, Schea. Will you help us?" He stopped there and stepped aside. He went to the sofa and collapsed onto it. He hated his job at that moment. He hated that Schea had to deal with this. He was going to get Jenny back safe and sound, with or without Schea's help if it was the last thing he ever did. But he desperately needed her help, and she needed their help. He had to make her see that.

Schea stood at the door with her back to the room for a long time. No one said anything. They just looked down or at Todd or at Schea's back.

She knew Todd was right. She could not do this alone. Jenny was too important for her to not use all of the resources at her disposal to get her back safely and, oh yes, kill every one of the bastards who took her.

She turned and walked over to the sofa. She sat down next to Todd. This time she wrapped her arms around Todd and whispered, "You are right. I do want to help and I need your help." He slowly turned to her and she could see that he had meant what he said. Someone had attacked one of their own and he would not rest until they had Jenny back safely. They sat for a minute together and then they both rose and went back to the table. They sat and looked at the group. Todd let Schea start.

Schea looked around the table and held each man's eyes with hers. They all saw what they had become familiar with at camp. Finally, she looked at them collectively and said, "Let's go get Jenny and make those bastards pay for what they have done."

# 49 Mission Five: Jenny (Part 2)

Todd reviewed for Schea and everyone at the table what they knew at this point. He told them that Jeff called him and told him that Jenny was missing. He reported it to the police and they were searching for her. They found her school backpack in a dumpster about a mile from school. They canvassed the area, and found out that Jenny had been seen walking home, and had even said hi to a couple of the people along the route she normally took. It was only about a half mile to her house from the school.

Part of the route passes by a vacant lot with overgrown grasses and bushes. People whose homes were along her route after the vacant lot had reported not seeing Jenny that day. The police searched the lot and found nothing. However, along the street next to the lot, they found some cigarette butts and some other litter that they are examining for prints and DNA.

The working theory is that she was probably taken in some van, so they have started searching all traffic cameras, home-security systems, and eyewitness accounts in a three-mile radius for any clues as to the presence of a van and the direction it may have been heading. Nothing has come to light yet.

"That is what we know." Then Todd said, "But this is what I think. I think that this has everything to do with Schea. I think that whoever took Jenny wants something from Schea. We need to try to figure out what that is. We need to go over all of Schea's missions to see if there are any connections to persons who might want some type of revenge. We also need you, Schea, to try to think back over your past to see if there might be someone who might want this kind of revenge."

"Finally, we need to investigate Schea's family history to see if there is anything in it that might provide a clue as to who might want to seek this kind of revenge."

"Schea and I are going to head to Jeff and Mary's to talk with them about what they remember. Schea will also search her past, as well as Jenny's, to try to see if there is anything there that provides a clue to this."

"I will search Schea's father and brother's past military and government service for anything there. I will ask Chuck to provide access to any records that might exist on them. I want Gus and Benny, who is an ex-cop and SWAT member, to go back to the police to check if they can see anything the police haven't. I will have Chuck contact the local police in order to assure that you get clearance for this."

"I want Kevin and Jack to go back to the scene and search it again. Talk to everyone along that route and beyond."

"Any Questions?" No one said anything. "Okay, let me say this once, this is our top priority from this moment until Jenny is safely returned to Schea and her family." As he looked around the table, he could see that everyone was completely on board with it.

Everyone left the table and moved out of the office to get started. They all gave Schea a quick glance and nod. Gus actually came over and squatted down next to Schea's chair. She glanced over at him. He gave her a small smile and told her, "I will personally give my life for you and Jenny. Don't worry, we will get Jenny back and kill all the bastards who had a part in this." She smiled and gave him a hug. He moved off and left with Benny.

Todd looked back at Schea and told her that he was glad that she decided to stay. She half smiled and told him, "You were right to stop me. Jenny is too important for me to go off half-cocked with no help."

XXXXX

As they drove to Colonial Heights, Todd told her that Michael and Lenny were actually going to be involved as well. He had asked them to develop several contingency plans for different parts of the states or world where they may have to go. He told them to make sure that resources were in place and ready to be moved at a moment's notice.

Todd said, "I will send them as an advance team as soon as we know where Jenny is. They will take only enough resources for them to get by until the rest of the team arrives. They were told not to take any action on their own unless, of course, they felt that Jenny was in imminent danger."

Schea stared at him but he did not look at her. He kept his eyes, and she suspected his mind, on the task at hand. She silently thanked him and all the guys for being there for her and Jenny.

They arrived at the Kennedys' home and the door opened immediately since he had called ahead to tell them that he and Schea were on the way. Schea got out of the car and ran to Jeff. She almost leaped into his arms and he held her tight, as she did him. He gradually released her and she told him that they were going to get Jenny back if it was the last thing that she ever did. He kept saying that he knew and was grateful. Mary appeared from behind Jeff, and Schea could see that her eyes were red and puffy. They hugged but didn't say a word, each knowing the other's feelings.

They all moved into the living room and sat. Schea helped Mary get some coffee and, while they were in the kitchen, Mary told Schea, "We sent Archie and Izzy to a trusted friend's house until we are sure they will be safe here."

Todd reviewed briefly for them what he and his team were doing and asked them if they wouldn't mind reviewing that day for him and Schea. They did. Todd asked about any suspicious activity prior to that day. He asked them if they had noticed anyone in the neighborhood that didn't seem to belong? Any strange vehicles? Had anyone reported seeing unknown people at or around the school? They answered no to all of these questions.

Todd asked them if the police had put a tap on their phone in order to trace any calls from the persons responsible for taking Jenny. They told him that they had. He said that the FBI will likely be involved soon since this is surely a kidnapping case. He looked at them and said that the authorities might not like him and his team being involved, so they should keep his team's activities quiet, if

219

possible. They will probably know that someone else is also looking into this, but not necessarily why. Todd instructed them if they get too nosy, have them give him a call. Jeff said they would and, if they did get a call from the kidnappers, they would call him as soon as they could. He told them that would be great. He also told them to try to write down, verbatim, everything that the kidnapper says.

Todd and Jeff wandered outside to the backyard after about an hour to check around the house for clues. Schea stayed with Mary. They were quiet for a few minutes and then Mary asked Schea how she was doing. Schea said she was good, except for what was happening now.

Mary nodded and told her that Jenny talked about her all the time. She was always telling her friends that her big sister had a really important job that let her travel all over the world. When her friends ask about what you did, Jenny would put on a serious face and tell them that she doesn't know and that her sister's job required lots of secrecy. Mary turned now to look Schea in the face, smiled and said that Jenny was very proud of her.

Schea struggled to hold it all together as she heard this. She told Mary that she was proud of Jenny too. She then told Mary that they will bring Jenny home safely. Mary could only nod. She remembered all too well, the many bombings and kidnappings that she saw and heard about growing up in her native England. Almost none of them turned out well, but she managed to turn to Schea and tell her that she trusted her and Todd completely.

XXXXX

Todd and Schea eventually left and headed back to Baltimore. Schea had not been home since she returned from Guiana, so Todd dropped her at her car and told her that he will keep in touch. As she was about to leave his car, he reached over and grabbed her hand. She turned back and he was suddenly at a loss for words, but she knew what he wanted to tell her, so she smiled and told him that she trusted him and the guys. He let go, and she headed for Annapolis a few minutes later.

XXXXX

Frank called his brother and told him, "The shipment is on the way."

# 50 Mission Five: Jenny (Part 3)

Schea got back to her place and tried to get back into some type of routine. She unpacked her small bag of stuff and went for a 15 mile run. This time, as she passed some of the guys from the academy, they didn't try to keep up with her. There were a few who could keep up or even go faster, but most seemed to want to follow her from behind. She figured that she knew why they thought behind was better than in front. Closer to her behind was even better.

She slept fitfully the first night, but collapsed the second night into a deep sleep as soon as her head hit the pillow. Unfortunately, she dreamt that she was too late to save Jenny and watched her being stabbed to death. She woke up screaming. She barely even dozed the rest of the evening.

Todd came by the day after the dream in order to give her an update on all they had found out. Gus and Benny didn't find out anything new from the police but Kevin and Jack, the trackers, had considerable success. Kevin suggested that he and Jack walk along as many streets around the area as they could to try to get a sense of what might have played out that day. They talked to hundreds of people over the first 2 days.

Then, yesterday afternoon they got a lead. A retired gentleman who spends a lot of time outside in his yard cutting the grass, trimming, weeding, tending flowers, et cetera happened to remember seeing a dark blue van about 2 weeks ago, give or take a few days. He remembered it because he had never seen it before. He remembered seeing a man in the passenger side, so that meant at least two men were in front. He had no idea what was in the back. He also did not remember any distinguishing markings or writings on the van, nor did he remember a plate number.

They checked the archives of traffic cameras in the area and found it again, heading in the direction of Hopewell. They called Gus, who came by with Benny to pick them up. They drove to Hopewell and on a hunch, went down to the marina. They split up and canvased the marina workers, boat owners and boat rental companies. Benny called the rest of them over after an hour and took them to an owner's boat.

The owner said that he remembered a boat berthed there a couple of weeks ago that was new to him. He didn't pay much attention until near the date that Benny had been asking him about. He said that he remembered seeing a blue van drive up and park. Two men had gotten out, opened the back of the van and hauled out a large crate they loaded onto the boat. There had been another man in the back of the van.

The owner recalled that he went over at that point and said hi. They were pleasant and returned the greeting. So, he asked them if they needed any help and they said no thanks. He asked what they were heading out to do. They didn't look like they were going fishing since there didn't seem to be any fishing gear anywhere. One of the men said that they were just heading out to do some sightseeing. As he told the owner this, the two men finished loading the crate, started up the boat's engine, and slowly moved out into the channel. The owner remembered the third man smiled, and said

221

that he had to get back to work and left in the van. When he turned, he saw the boat heading down river.

Todd called Chuck immediately and asked if he could get any Coast Guard or satellite surveillance on the area. He said that he'd try. Yesterday, the Coast Guard reported that one of its routine patrols had spotted a boat near First Colony off-loading something onto a small dock. As they approached to investigate they saw a crate being loaded onto a small van. By the time they got to the area, the van was gone, and the boat had moved down the river. They found the boat docked and deserted about 2 miles away. They reported the van to the local police and said that it appeared to be suspicious. The van was found 20 miles away near an abandoned airfield by Queens Lake. They did not find anything to trace on the boat or in the van.

Todd was smiling when he got to this point. Schea drew her eyebrows together, stared at him and said, "There's more right?"

He nodded. "The FAA had picked up a small plane in the area and followed its flight path. It landed on a small island airfield in the mouth of the Chesapeake and, a short time later, another larger plane took off. It headed to Bermuda and landed in Hamilton. The authorities there were notified and arrived just as another plane took off from a private area of the airfield. They monitored the flight to the east but it soon disappeared from their scopes."

He was still smiling, so Schea waited. "A flight that seemed to match the speed, direction, and markings was spotted by an Alitalia flight heading to Naples. Several other country Traffic Control Systems followed it to Sofia, Bulgaria."

Now Schea smiled. "So now we know where they took Jenny."

Todd shook his head and said, "We only know that, and the info doesn't have a 100% probability, but we are pretty sure that it is accurate. Unfortunately, we do not know where they went after arriving or how they may have transported Jenny - truck, van, plane."

"Now would be a good time to check again on what connections anyone in your family has with that part of the world, but logic would tell him that it is your dad. I worked in the area a few times myself and know that Jason had been on at least one mission that I remember. I have no idea what the mission was, but I have already placed a call to Chuck to see if he can find any information on missions by Jason in the area."

"I have sent Michael and Lenny into the area. Lenny is fluent in Russian and can probably speak Bulgarian well enough. The good thing is that most Bulgarians still speak Russian since, under the Soviet occupation, everyone had to learn it in school. Michael's cover will be as an Irish businessman looking to start a company in Bulgaria that makes parts for high-tech smartphones. He will tell people that he is confident that Bulgaria has a very tech-savvy bunch of young engineers."

"I have brought Gus, Benny, Jack and Kevin back to the office and told them to get ready to deploy to the area."

Schea asked, "Why can't we head there right now?"

Todd said, "We could but what would we do if Jenny has been taken someplace else and we are all stuck in Bulgaria."

Schea thought about it and understood his logic. But, she was so anxious to get going, she could hardly contain herself. Todd knew this and told her that they should at least wait for Chuck to get back to them. She nodded sullenly.

XXXXX

Todd stayed that evening in her extra bedroom. They both kept looking at his phone thinking that it would ring any second. It did, at 2 am in the morning. Schea was in his room like a shot. Todd was sitting on the edge of the bed nodding and asking questions. The call lasted for about 10 minutes and Schea was about to snatch the phone away when he hung up. He set the phone aside and looked at Schea with sadness in his eyes.

After a few seconds, he said, "We are 99% sure that this all has to do with Jason's mission in Bulgaria 25 years ago. The mission happened near the seaside city of Varna, Bulgaria. The country was just coming out of communist rule and crime was rampant. A local Bulgarian living near Varna had set up a Mafia-style organization that dealt in weapons and prostitution. They were not afraid to use force and had eventually expanded their business interests all over Eastern Europe. The newly emerging Western style governments were trying to wipe these elements out but didn't really have the structure or the muscle to do so, and asked for help from the west."

Todd continued, "Most of the countries provided monetary and some high level support. A few with well-developed entities that could operate against these types of organizations did try to help, and France, Britain and the USA were primary sources for this support. Several Eastern European countries asked the US to do something about the Varna Organization and we said that we would look into it. Jason was eventually assigned to the mission."

"Information that was provided to Jason by the Bulgarians, Romanians and Chechs indicated that it was run by a man named Nicholai Kolchenko. He had smaller organizations in the countries of Romania and Yugoslavia, but he operated all over the region. He sold guns to anyone who could pay his prices and he provided girls to many countries, especially those in the Middle East and North Africa."

"The information indicated where he lived and several agencies put eyes on his house around the clock. One country even had someone on the inside of his organization. Jason also learned that Nicolai had a wife, mistress and 5 children, 2 girls and 3 boys. He figured that the best way to take him out was to get above his home, put a laser on it, and call in a strike after he was sure the family was out. Jason went to the area and waited."

"Their man inside found out that the family was going to be out visiting an uncle in Burgas, about 150 kms south along the coast. Jason decided that it would be a go once it was confirmed the family was off the premises. On the date given to Jason by the informant, Jason hid, watched, and

223

waited. A launch was readied from a friendly country and Jason would light up the target as soon as it was confirmed that the family was gone."

"The following morning the insider confirmed that the family had left. Jason but a laser on the target's last known position in the house and the missile was launched. It struck, and the house went up in flames and debris. Jason exited the area."

"It was thought to have been a successful mission. Yes, they got Nicolai, but all of the family had not gone to Burgas. The boys had, but the mother and girls had stayed behind. The insider left before confirming this because he saw the family vehicle leave and figured they were all in it. Jason felt horrible and left the CIA a year later."

Schea stared at the floor during this explanation. Now she knew why her dad would get melancholy sometimes and wander off to be alone. Her mom would just tell the kids that dad did his best thinking when he was alone. She probably knew most of the real reason, if not all of it.

"Chuck told me that the oldest son, Stefan, was now in charge of the organization. It had been temporarily in chaos, but an uncle held enough of it together to keep it going. Once the oldest was in his 20s and had learned enough about the organization to run it himself, he took over. He had learned well and was even more ruthless than his father had been. His youngest brother disappeared soon after the tragedy and the next oldest brother, Petre, became head of a supposed legitimate company based in the UK. He was watched by the British, but they could never make a connection between him and what his older brother was doing."

At that point, Schea said, "Now we know where the youngest son went. He came to the states and took the name Frank."

Todd nodded. "Of course. Frank was sent to keep an eye on your family once Stefan figured out who had killed his parents and sisters. How he found that out we may never know."

"Chuck said that Stefan moved his house and headquarters to Dragovishtitsa in the far southwest corner of Bulgaria. It was close enough to Sofia for business trips and transportation needs, yet far away from prying eyes. The intelligence agencies had no one inside, but there were people watching the place from the outside most of the time." Todd finished and said, "We should try to get some sleep."

Schea nodded and went back to her room.

When Todd finally got up and went to the kitchen to make coffee, he found Schea was already there. She sat at the kitchen table looking sullen. She was struggling to take in what she had learned about her dad's mission. He must have felt terribly guilty for all of those years. The girls had only been 7 and 9 when they were suddenly killed. They were innocent of nothing more than being little girls whose father was a horrible man, but they only saw him as their dad. It made Schea wonder if we can ever truly know the people we love.

Todd sat and set a cup of tea in front of Schea. She seemed to see it but not recognize what it was. He finally asked her what she was thinking about. She was about to tell him, when Todd's phone rang. Todd quickly answered it. He didn't say anything for a minute and then asked, "How good is this?" A minute later he hung up and told Schea, "We know where Jenny is."

He told her that one of the people watching the house saw a car drive up to the compound and through the gate. He had a good view of the front of the house and was able to see the occupants of the vehicle as they got out and entered the house. He saw a man get out of the driver side door and go to the rear door. He opened that door and reached in. The watcher then saw him pull a girl out who fit Jenny's description. She was blindfolded and needed help walking. They entered the house but he didn't see her through any of the windows that were in his view.

Schea's eyes became intense, and she started to head for the door. Todd went after her and got in front of her just as she was about to exit in her baggy shorts, old sweatshirt and bare feet. He asked her where she thought she was going. She said that she was going after Jenny. Todd held up his hands and told her to wait and think about this. He told her to remember that we are part of a team and she needed the guys and they needed her. She stopped trying to leave and just stood.

Todd said they needed time to get into place. "I will call the office and tell the guys there to get ready to deploy. I'll meet them and we'll head to the American forces unit in Kosovo. The President has authorized them to help us. The President has also called the leaders of Bulgaria and Serbia. He called in a few favors which they were glad to give him. They don't like Stefan and his family anyway and will not intervene, but they will not help either."

"Once we get to Kosovo, we will move out on our own and cover the 120 kms in trucks to the border, then cross into Bulgaria. The house is just to the west of Dragovititsa. Michael and Lenny will meet us at a designated spot. I will also contact an old acquaintance from my days working in the area. He owes me a favor for saving his life a couple of times, so he'll gladly help and provide men. No one seems to like Stefan or his operation."

He took a breath and said, "Schea, you need to stay here." She almost exploded again, but Todd knew it would come so he quickly started to explain why she had to stay. "You need to give us time to get in place. Stefan is most likely to call you and you need to wait for the call." She almost asked why call her, but Todd started again quickly. "Remember, Jenny's kidnapping is all about getting you to go over there. Stefan will call and threaten Jenny if you do not come to meet him. You need to do everything you can to stall and give us time to get into position. You must make it look like you have no idea why he has taken Jenny."

She seemed to understand as he talked. Her shoulders sank, but she finally said he was right, and she would stay and wait for Stephan's call. "When he calls, I will ask to talk to Jenny then tell him I will leave as soon as I can book a flight."

Todd relaxed and told her that would probably work well. Although he cautioned that Stefan was probably not a patient man. He may have already bought her a one-way ticket on a flight he had specifically chosen. She should try to delay but not push it. He might try to demonstrate the urgency by doing something to Jenny. Schea nodded in agreement, but looked even angrier. Todd reminded her that she may be watched during all or part of her trip there. She should act accordingly, worried, yes, but not too stressed or rushed.

Todd sighed and told her, "I understand how you feel but this is the right way to do this if we are going to save Jenny. You will probably be met by someone when you arrive, and he, or they, will take you to Stefan. Stefan will be waiting and he will have armed men around him. He will know about your skills. You should not underestimate his resolve for getting revenge. He is a mean and ruthless bastard, who seems to enjoy hurting people."

At this, Schea looked up at Todd and half smiled. "Well, he will soon find out that I also know how to hurt someone and that sometimes I even enjoy it."

Todd smiled as well and put his hand on her shoulder. He gave it a little squeeze. But, he added, "No matter how angry you got, stay alert and be aware of your surroundings. You need to rely on your training and experience."

Todd left at that point and Schea slumped into the cushions of her sofa. It faced the window and the bay. The sun was well up by now and it was going to be a beautiful day. Even if it had been a lousy day, she would have felt exactly the same. She was angry and sad and lost and hopeful.

XXXXX

She spent the whole day wandering from room to room. She would sit for a while, stand, then look out a window, then sit, then move to another room, then go through the same routine. She tried to eat but nothing tasted good, so she gave up, put it all back into the refrigerator or in the garbage.

She also kept looking at the clock on the stove. It would show 10 am and, when she looked again, it would show 10:05 am. This routine went on and on and on all day long. She kept thinking. *Why has Stefan not called?* Then, she remembered Todd's words. *They need time and this was giving them time.* Schea also reasoned that Stefan would not hurt Jenny, at least not horribly, she hoped, because he wanted Schea there, probably to see it happen. This gave her hope, but it also made her extremely mad. She had to stay focused, give Todd time to get into place, stall Stefan if she could, and get proof that he has Jenny, and that she is okay. Remain alert. Remember her skills and experience.

At 10 pm, she was now on the sofa leaning back into the cushions. Her eyes were finally closed. She was exhausted and hadn't slept much in the past week. Her body was sleeping, but her mind was active.

The phone rang and she bolted for it. *Where was it?* She couldn't remember where she had last had it. She was frantic. She tried to calm herself and focus on the ring. She followed it into her bedroom and answered.

226

She heard what she figured was Stefan's voice. "Is this Schea Tailor?" She said, yes, and asked, who is this? He didn't answer her question and asked, "Would you like to visit Jenny Kennedy?"

*Give Todd time*, she thought. She waited for him to ask again.

He warned, "You should really answer my question if you ever want to see Jenny again."

She paused then asked, "How do I know Jenny is with you?"

He asked someone something nearby but she couldn't hear what was said.

Then, she heard the voice that she had been craving to hear. It was Jenny. Jenny simply said, "Hello."

Schea almost started to cry but stopped herself. She had to reassure Jenny that she would be safe. "Hi, Jenny. Are you okay?"

"Yea, I'm okay."

"Good, good. Please try to stay calm. I'll be there as soon as possible then we will be able to go home."

"I would like that and …." She never finished. The next voice was Stefan's.

"That was all very touching and I can tell how much you pretend sisters love each other."

Schea wanted to strangle him right then and there. *Stay calm. Give Todd time. Think of what you learned in training.* Schea calmly responded, "Yes, we do love each other. When can Jenny come home?" Stefan laughed, of course, and Schea rolled her eyes and waited.

Stefan began, "Well, that will probably not happen for a very long time. It all depends on what you do from now on. You need to come to me then we'll see. You will catch the flight to Sofia tomorrow at 8 am from Dulles airport. Go to the information booth in the lower level near the international arrivals. There will be a package there that will contain your pre-paid ticket and all other instructions you need." Before she could ask for more time, the call went dead.

She stood still for a few minutes staring at the phone and thinking of Jenny's voice. She was trying so hard to replay it in her mind over and over. She so wanted to have Jenny here now with her. Tears started to well up, but she got control of herself. *Stay calm. Remember the training. Stay focused.*

She packed whatever she thought she might need, although she didn't figure that she'd be doing much other than killing a few bastards and bringing Jenny home. She left her backpack on the bedroom floor.

At that thought, she ran back into her bedroom and searched in her dressing table for the little stuffed Panda bear that Jenny had given to her on her last visit. Jenny had bought it for her on a visit to the Smithsonian's National Zoo, where they have the Pandas. She stuffed the little bear into her pocket. Then, she thought about the little bear and moved it into her underwear. She knew that she would be searched pretty thoroughly and didn't want them to take it away. Hopefully, they won't dig too deeply, and rolled her eyes.

She had plenty of time to get to the airport since it was only 11:30 pm. She would use this time to review the plans that Todd and she had worked out before he left. The drive would take about 1 hour and 30 minutes so she figured she'd leave around 4 am.

She moved back to the sofa and sat with her legs curled up under her. She closed her eyes and pictured Jenny. That made her smile.

XXXXX

She saw her as she had been on her last visit when they sat in her room on the floor across from each other. They had been chatting about music and movies that Jenny had seen with her friends. Schea didn't listen to much music or go to many movies, but she loved hearing Jenny tell her all about them.

At one point during their floor-chat, Jenny smiled sheepishly and asked if Schea had a boyfriend yet. Schea gave her a false frown and said that, sadly, she did not. Jenny looked at her seriously and told her that she was lying. Schea was startled and said she really did not have a boyfriend.

Jenny harrumphed and said she didn't mean that was a lie. Of course, Schea didn't have a boyfriend. Jenny said the lie was that she pretends to care that she doesn't.

Schea couldn't help it. She burst out laughing and pretended to start wrestling with Jenny. Jenny started laughing as well and the two girls rolled around on the floor grunting and doing all kinds of pretend wrestling holds.

After they became exhausted, they went back to their respective corners across from one another. They were still giggling and Schea asked Jenny if she had a boyfriend. At this, Jenny's cheeks got a little pink and she said no, but that there was this one really cute boy that she thought might like her.

XXXXX

Suddenly, Schea's internal alarm clock went off and she woke up. She quickly glanced at the phone and saw that it was 3:30 am. She rushed into the bathroom, showered, brushed her teeth, and went into the bedroom to dress. As she pulled on her underwear, she remembered the bear and ran back into the bathroom. She retrieved it from the clothes piled on the floor, gently brushed him off and put him back into her panties. Before she went out the door, she stood and took one last look around. She loved this place, but she knew she might never see it again. With that, she headed to her car and to Jenny.

# 51 Mission Five: Bringing Jenny Home (Part 4)

Todd arrived in Kosovo at 6 am local time the following day. He figured that he had between 12 to 24 hours to get set up on site before Schea got there. He didn't know when Stefan would call but he knew that he would not give Schea any extra time. He hoped that he had closer to 24 hours but, if not, his plan was to be ready in 12. He would not let Schea and Jenny down.

The President, through Chuck, had authorized a direct military airlift flight into Kosovo for Todd. Chuck told Todd that the President would secretly do all he could to help but, if asked openly, he would explain that this operation was to rescue an American citizen, a little girl, who had done nothing to deserve this. She was also the daughter and niece of brother, who are decorated American soldiers.

The President had no qualms helping them to get her back. Diplomacy would not work because this was not government to government. This was a known criminal who sold guns, drugs and girls. Chuck said he was sure that no one would question the President on his use of such limited government resources. He also said the President didn't really care if this caused blow-back on him. He could take it.

Todd contacted his friend in Bulgaria on the way over and told him where to meet up with Michael and Lenny. He said they were expecting them, so please don't start shooting each other. After landing, he, Gus, Benny, Kevin and Jack headed in an old Volvo truck for the border. It would be about a 3 hour drive, if the truck held up over their poorly maintained roads. Many of them had still not been repaired after the Balkan conflict many years ago.

Once Jenny and Schea were safe, they would need to use the truck to get as close as possible to the border in order to radio for the Black Hawks to come and extract them.

Something could go wrong during operations, especially ones as complex as this. However, he knew that whatever happened, it would not stop them from getting the girls out safely. He was not very religious, but he did believe that God existed somewhere and he hoped He was with them now.

XXXXX

Schea arrived in Sofia well-rested. For some reason, as soon as she got on the plane at Dulles, she went sound asleep. She figured that maybe it was because she was now finally doing something to get Jenny back. She also figured it was because there was a plan, and she trusted the plan, and more importantly, she trusted Todd and the men with him. There was a flight change in Vienna and another in Sofia so she used this time to review the plan, and remind herself to stay focused, calm and alert.

As she exited from international arrivals, she walked out among the waiting families, friends and tour guides. She knew what to look for, so she didn't linger. She walked to the exit door marked Taxis and went to the last taxi in the queue. A man got out and came around to her. She had no bag, so he simply pulled her around to the back of the vehicle and roughly searched her for weapons. He groped a little here and there, but Schea didn't notice. If he felt the bear, he didn't say or do anything. He pulled open the trunk and pushed her in.

She knew the drive would be around 3-4 hours over some pretty rough roads. The countryside in this area was supposed to be scenic with rolling hills and lots of nice views of the Rila mountain range, but she only saw darkness and flashes of light, which were usually the result of a head bump into something in the trunk.

They finally seemed to have arrived since the vehicle had stopped and hadn't moved for about 5 minutes. She heard voices outside during that time but didn't understand anything that was said. Finally, the trunk was opened, and Schea had to blink hard in the bright light. She figured it was probably early morning on the day after she left. Before she could see clearly, she was grabbed by a couple of large guys and hauled towards the front of the house. Another guy opened the door from the inside and Schea was pushed into the large entry hall.

There were three guards, one in front and one on each side of her with their guns pointed directly at her. The guard who let her in the door searched and groped her again, while the other guards smirked at her. She stared directly back at each of them until they stopped smirking.

The guard in front pulled her roughly to a door directly across from the entrance and the other guards lined up behind her. When the guy got to the door, he stopped and knocked. Schea heard Stefan say something from inside and the guy opened the door. He moved behind her and pushed her into the room. He pulled her to a stop near the middle of the room. He then moved a short distance to her right. He had his gun out and pointed at her, and she figured the other two did the same behind her.

She saw Jenny as she came into the room. She was to her left and a man was standing behind her. Jenny looked like she was sedated. Her eyes were open but she seemed to have a hard time focusing them. She had a couple of bruises on her cheeks and was pretty dirty. She wore a t-shirt, a pair of jeans, but no shoes. Her feet were dirty and looked like they had been made to walk on some very rough surfaces. She could see several scratches along the sides of both feet.

Straight in front of her was a man in his mid-to-late 40s. He must be Stefan. He was sitting behind a large desk that looked to be made of heavy oak. The room was probably an office since it had bookshelves and a few chairs set in front of the desk. As she looked to her right she saw a wall with a bookcase and an ugly painting.

Schea turned back to look at Stefan and her eyes screamed venom and no mercy. He saw it and smiled. At that, she heard the door behind her open and close. Someone walked quietly in and stood several feet behind her. She didn't need to turn to know who it was. Schea smiled and said, "It's nice to see you again, Frank." Frank had been smiling because he wanted to surprise her but he had forgotten just how perceptive she could be. He held his position.

Stefan started talking. "Welcome to my humble home and I hope that you enjoy your short stay here. Actually, you will only enjoy it if you follow one rule. That rule is that you do not move from where you are standing. If you move even a centimeter, then I will kill Jenny right here so you can watch. Then, I'll kill you. If you stay still, I will still kill you, but I will let Jenny live. However, I will have to sell her since she will no longer be of any use to me. Do you understood this rule?"

Schea didn't say anything, so Stefan nodded to the guard behind Jenny and he pressed his gun into her neck.

Schea immediately said, "Yes, I understood the rule."

Stefan then asked, "Will you abide by it?"

"Yes, I will."

"Good." The guard behind Jenny lowered his weapon.

Stefan started again. "Do you know why you are here?" By her reaction, he smiled and said, "You do know." He continued. "My sisters were only 7 and 9 when your father brutally slaughtered them."

Schea continued to stare at him. She had to focus, stay calm, stay alert.

"My mother wasn't much of a loss, and frankly, my dad was kind of a brute to me and my brothers. But my sisters were different. They were sweet and caring and loving. They wouldn't even let anyone kill a spider that got into the house. They would capture it in a box or jar and take it back outside to set it free. Their deaths must be avenged."

"After the murder of my family, I and my brothers were cared for by an uncle. The uncle started the search for the murderer. One of the guards patrolling the grounds when the murderer struck saw him as he left. He got a limited view of his face, but he could describe his height, weight, and a few other physical characteristics well enough. He knew he was Caucasian, that he had dark brown hair and blue eyes. The murderer had removed his dark glasses right after the attack to rub something from his eyes."

"We figured he was CIA or SEAL, so a series of bribes, a little torture, a kidnapping or two finally got us a name. The rest was easy. The name led us to the man, which led to a home, which led to a family. We observed this family for several years until we were ready to act. Then, we learned that the boy had joined the army. We also found out that he was going to be in Afghanistan, which served us very well."

"We paid off one of the Taliban leaders in the area where he was located. The bribe required them to capture, torture, and murder the soldier. We had to stipulate that it be filmed so that we could be assured that he got the right guy and not some other dumb GI. We didn't care what they did with the video after we had our proof."

Schea interrupted him and asked, "Who was the Taliban leader?

"Why do you want to know?"

231

Schea looked at him and said, "I just want to make sure that I have the right man when I kill him."

He paused and thought. *Wow, she is pretty brazen. I like it. But, she really isn't leaving so why not tell her.* "His name is Muhammad Shefara."

Schea nodded and said, "Thanks."

Stefan shrugged and continued. "The next goal was the parents. We felt that they had to go together since ours did. My brother, Petre, who is outside with a large group of armed men waiting for your friends to show up, conducted that operation." Schea gave a slight reaction and Stefan caught it. He smiled and told her, "Yes, we knew that your friends would come to help, but they are few and Petre has many men, so they won't live long."

"Anyway, Petre hired two dumbass suicide bombers in the US and told them what he wanted them to do. He said that the targets were brutal murderers of many innocent woman and children in the Middle East. We may have exaggerated a little but it worked, and they were convinced. We helped them plan it, and when we learned of the NYC Marathon that the parents were doing to honor their murderer son, we chose that venue for the attack. It worked out very nicely."

Schea was getting sick of hearing this and almost said so, but Stefan seemed to know already what she was thinking. He said, "I know that this troubles you to hear all of this, but I felt it only fair that you know the entire truth before you die." Schea shrugged.

He continued and said, "The next goal was to kill both you and your whoring sister."

Schea really had to block this soliloquy from her mind. *Stay focused, stay calm, stay alert, think of Jenny.*

Stefan said, "When she was killed by her 2 boyfriends that was just dumb luck for us. Unfortunately, you moved away and we had trouble keeping up with where you were. Finally, we learned that you were in the *murder-for-hire* camp."

"Don't get me wrong. I admire your resolve to avenge your family, and I really admire how skilled you are. Frank, of course, filled us in on much of it. But, there were also rumors from people in my line of work about a girl who had extraordinary killing skills. I always figured that it would be you. And, I am really glad that I have finally met you and that I will be able to get you out of this line of work, and away from those hard working businessmen."

"Frank also mentioned that, once you finished your training, you could be extra hard to find and corner. You'll have fake names, accounts and other documentation. You could also be in disguise. It would probably take a while to locate you each time you moved. And of course, when you are on a job, we'd never be able to find you. But then Frank heard about your fake sister," he glanced at Jenny.

"Frank secretly got into Todd's office and found your contact number and quit the camp soon after you left. He tracked down the contact and, after some searching, found out that one of the employees knew a good bit about you. And, as they say, the rest is history. But, most important of all, here you are."

Schea just continued to stare at him. She knew that he would not underestimate her, so she had to come up with an approach to get him out of his comfort zone. The staring seemed to be doing the trick, and she could see that it annoyed him. When she didn't respond or say anything, he began to scowl.

A few minutes earlier, Schea began to hear what sounded like gunfire, and it had now increased in volume and frequency. It also seemed to be getting closer. She could tell that the guard to her right and the one behind Jenny seemed to be getting nervous. They kept making quick glances toward the doors. As Stefan started to say something more, a large bang was heard outside of the door and gunfire could be heard. The fighting had to be really close. The two guards behind her headed out to the hall behind her.

The guard to her right started for the door but stopped and looked back at Stefan. Stefan motioned him out and he left through the door to follow the others. There was another large explosion in the hallway behind the guard with Jenny and it startled him. Stefan told him to check the hallway. As he opened the door, there was another loud crash and Schea heard Frank start to move towards the door behind him where the guards had gone. Stefan seemed to be ready to yell for him to stop.

It was time. Schea felt that Frank was close enough behind for her to hit him pretty solidly. She swung around and caught him in the throat with her forearm. He gasped and fell. Stefan looked like he was going for a gun, so Schea ran and dragged Jenny from the room into the hallway.

Schea heard several shots hit the doorjamb as she went through. She quickly saw that the guard who'd been holding Jenny was gone. She pulled Jenny to her feet and made her move to the left down a hallway away from Stefan. She turned to the left again at the first opportunity but had no idea what the layout of the house was like. She was just moving on instinct. She turned right next and saw a door ahead of her. She kept moving and heard more gunshots behind her. She went through the door and found herself outside.

It looked like the back of the house. There was a wall but it had a door. As she moved toward it she passed a dead guard. She leaned down and quickly retrieved his gun and pulled a knife out of his side. She shot the door lock and went through. She was now 10 yards from a wooded area and headed there.

After about 20 yards, she stopped and sat Jenny down against a tree. She quietly told her that she was safe. She was going to get to go home. She was going to see Jeff and Mary and Izzy and Archie. Jenny slowly let a small smile form. Suddenly, Schea heard a noise behind her, spun and was about to shoot, when Gus held up his hands in surrender.

Schea threw herself into his arms. She almost cried. Almost. This was not over by a longshot. She pulled back and pointed at Jenny. Gus was with 2 men she didn't know. She told Gus, "Please protect Jenny and get her out of here." He said he would. He watched as Schea went back towards the house and didn't say anything. He smiled, picked Jenny up and carried her to safety with the two other guys.

Schea made her way back to the house. The gunfire was becoming less and less, but she had no idea who was winning. She didn't care at this point. Jenny was safe, but she still had two more tasks to complete. As she moved toward the door that she had just come out of, she saw a body behind a tree. She cautiously approached it with her gun raised. As she peeked around the tree, she saw that it was Frank. He had a gunshot wound in the stomach and had lost a lot of blood, but was still alive.

She walked over and stood in front of Frank. He looked at her and his eyes pleaded with her to help him. So she did. She shot him in the forehead and whispered, "That is for Doug." She moved on.

She entered the house and heard noises but no gunfire. Most of the noises were groans and moans. She made her way back to the office, but as she passed a hallway, she heard a voice that she recognized. She smiled and approached the voice. It was coming from another room at the end of the halfway. She left her shoes outside so that she could move silently - like a Ghost.

She got to the door and listened. It was Stefan and another man. They spoke Bulgarian so she had no idea what they were saying, but Stefan sounded mad. *Good. He will be distracted.* She peeked in and saw that Stefan was pulling stuff out of a safe. He had his back to her and was across the room while the other man was standing a little behind and to his left. There was a bed to her left about 3 feet inside the door. She moved.

As she entered the room, she put a bullet in the back of the other man's head. But, Stefan was fast. There must have been a gun in the safe because he whipped around and fired at her. She was hit in the leg and went down behind the bed. She wiggled up close to the bed and pushed herself as close to the floor as possible. Stefan fired several more shots into the bed just above where she was hiding. She moved slightly under the edge of the bed. As she peeked under the bed, she saw his feet come into view. She aimed and hit his left foot. He went to the floor on his knees. She shot his right kneecap and he fell to the right.

He still had his gun and tried to aim it at her under the bed, but he was in too much pain, and his shot hit behind her. Before he could get another shot off, she shot him in the chest. He groaned and rolled onto his back. She scrambled to her feet and limped cautiously to where he lay. She kicked his gun away and stood over him. He looked at her with complete disdain and hatred. She smiled, bent a little so he could see her face better, and pointed the gun right at his nose. She held that position so that he could take it all in. She said, "This is for my family," and fired. She put one more into the messy glob that used to be Stefan's head. With that, she sat on the bed.

She heard heavy footsteps in the hall and aimed her gun at the doorway. But she heard another familiar voice and said, "Oh, it's you. You're too late, but please come in and join me."

Todd walked in, looked at her, then at Stefan. He sat next to her and put his arm around her. He helped her to her feet and they walked out together. As they did, he told her, "We overwhelmed Stefan's men because they only estimated there would be 4 or 5 guys with you." He smiled and said, "Everyone always does that with you."

Todd told her that Petre was killed, and she told him that Frank was dead. She also told him that it was Frank who killed Doug, and that Petre had hired the suicide bombers that killed her parents. Then she told him that Stefan had paid a Taliban leader, Muhammad Shefara, to capture, torture and kill her brother. Todd only nodded and walked quietly with her to the point in the nearby forest where everyone was gathering.

Todd told her, "My Bulgarian friend brought 30 guys with him, and they were all very well trained. I found Gus back at the rally point with Jenny and Gus told me you had gone back to the house. I knew you would, of course, so I came to find you."

She said, "Thanks for everything." At this point, he could feel her slipping down a little on her wounded leg. So he carried her to Jenny.

Once there, a guy with medical training patched up Schea's leg. He told her, "You'll be fine since the bullet went through cleanly. Jenny will be fine too. She has some bumps and bruises and her feet are in bad shape, but all of that will heal up once she gets some medical care. By the way, one of the men went to a nearby village, and procured a pair of shoes and thick socks for Jenny to wear."

Todd's Bulgarian friend came over and shook Todd's hand. He also looked at Schea, smiled, said something to Todd in Russian then he and his men disappeared into the forest.

Schea looked at Todd and asked, "What did he say to you?"

He smiled and said, "He told me that if he had men as tough as you then he would be able to cut his staff, save money and still be able to handle any work that came his way." Schea just grunted.

Once they were ready to go, the girls said, "We need to go take a pee."

Todd walked with them, and checked the area to make sure it was safe then he walked a discrete distance away and waited.

After Todd left, Schea reached into her pants and pulled out the Panda bear. She told Jenny, "I used it to make sure that I kept focused on what I had to do in order to save you."

At that, Jenny reached into her pants and pulled out the bracelet that Schea had given to her those many years ago. She told Schea, "I was 100% positive that you would come to rescue me because I rubbed the bracelet every time I had a chance."

Schea smiled and they hugged.

Pretty soon they walked back to Todd holding hands and smiling. They walked right by and headed back to the group of men who had helped with the rescue. Todd watched them pass. He smiled because they walking away like they had just had a fun time exploring a bird in a tree or some other cute little woodland creature.

# 52 Home

They made their way to the extraction point. Todd told Schea as they were leaving that Jack had been killed in the assault, and Benny and Kevin had been shot but would be fine once they got them to a medical facility. He also told her that his Bulgarian friend had lost two men and several others had flesh wounds.

Schea felt really bad about Jack. He and she had worked well in training and he had been one of the first to befriend her when she started. She figured she might have to get used to the loss of operatives and friends.

Jenny walked side by side with Schea and would not let go of her hand. They went to each man and thanked them for what they had done. They all smiled and said that they were just happy that the two of them had made it through okay. Gus was the last they went to. They both gave him big hugs. It was the only time that Jenny let go of Schea's hand. Gus didn't even try to hide the tears that appeared in his eyes. He hugged Schea tight because he knew she wouldn't break, but he was very gentle with Jenny.

They reached the extraction point and the Black Hawks showed up within 15 minutes. They had been hovering across the border waiting for Todd's second call letting them know they had arrived. The wounded and Jack's body were loaded into the first Black Hawk, which took off right away. The remaining people got into the second one and headed back to the UN base camp where the Americans were positioned.

Once they landed, they were all checked out by the medical team and released. Only Benny and Kevin stayed since they needed further attention before they could be taken to Ramstein Air Base in Germany. Todd, Schea and Jenny were not going there. They were taking a commercial flight from Pristina to Vienna then on to Dulles. Jeff and Mary would meet them there.

Before everyone went off in their respective directions, Michael came over to Schea and told her that he was happy that they were able to get Jenny back safely. She thanked him again. "When you are ready, Kathleen and I have a plan for the boys I'd like to discuss it with you."

Jenny and Schea sat next to each other in the first class cabin from Vienna to Dulles. They talked quietly and would giggle every once in a while. They held hands during the whole flight. Todd sat across the aisle from them and marveled at how resilient they seemed to be, especially Jenny.

After all that they had just been through, they could still giggle about silly things or about something that one girl joked about to the other. He found it amazing. Of course he also knew that when they did finally separate, the dreams and fears might set in. He was more concerned with Jenny since she was not used to the things that she had had to endure. Schea would likely do better.

XXXXX

They arrived and made their way to the waiting area outside of international arrivals. As soon as they walked out, Schea heard two screams, one was from Mary and the other was from Izzy. She also saw Archie just standing stock still like he was cemented to the floor. He could only keep staring at Jenny and then he started to cry big tears. Jeff also had tears in his eyes as he moved to Jenny and Schea. This was the second time they let go of each other. Jenny rushed to her parents, Archie and Izzy. They all competed to give Jenny the biggest hug and the most kisses. When she hugged Archie, it seemed like he would never let her go.

Then it was Schea's turn and they all gave her big hugs. They had noticed Schea limping a little but did not say anything. As soon as they were done with Schea, the girl's hands, like some magic wand had been waved over them, were back together. Neither girl had to look for the other's hand. It was just there as they reached out.

Todd was thanked and got hugs from Mary and Izzy. He got a very manly handshake from Archie.

Jeff gave Todd a firm handshake and said, "Thank you."

Todd could see that he was at a loss for what else to say, so Todd quickly said, "I'm glad to have been able to help." He leaned into Jeff a little and quietly said, "The actual rescue of Jenny was done by Schea." By the look on Todd's face, Jeff knew what he meant.

At this point, Todd took his leave and said, "I'm glad that it had all turned out well." He turned to leave, but before he took his second step, he witnessed the third parting of the hands because both girls wrapped their arms around him at the same time. Once they let him go, he smiled at Jenny then pulled Schea aside before the girls hands found each other again.

He told Schea to stay as long as she liked. "When you are ready, we can meet at your place to discuss what you want to do. There are no missions coming your way from me or Chuck until you are ready."

He started to move away but Shea hugged him again and whispered, "Thank you." When she let go, she looked at Todd and told him, "All of the costs for this mission, including what the President and Chuck provided will be paid for by me." He started to protest, but she grabbed his arm tightly and said, "No. This was my mission. And, I have every right to take responsibility for its costs."

He could tell there was nothing he could say or do to persuade her otherwise so he sighed and said, "Okay." Then he smiled and said, "You will be receiving a bill in about a week or so."

Todd looked over at the little group and waved to everyone as he walked away. Schea went right back to Jenny and they all walked away together. If she could have read Todd's thoughts as he walked away, she would have heard him saying to himself, *Now I'm even more positive that we are doing the right thing in our work. It's to help put families back together and punish the people who try to tear them apart.*

Jenny and Schea sat in the back as they drove the 3 hours to Colonial Heights. Jeff had an 8 passenger SUV, so Izzy and Archie were in the middle seats with Jeff and Mary in front. Jenny and Schea were in the back, holding hands of course, but all of the kids took turns chatting about school, TV shows they watched recently, movies and, of course, boys.

Neither Jenny nor Schea had any baggage, so they simply went to their room. They decided to shower and change before heading back downstairs. Schea had some clothes in Jenny's room that she had been leaving there over the months of visits.

They walked hand in hand into the kitchen where everyone was sitting around the table talking about the fun things they were planning to do over the weekend. The girls sat down and joined in.

Schea stayed with the Kennedys for 2 weeks and limped a lot less by the time she left. Jeff had taken a leave of absence from his job as soon as Jenny had been taken, but he had to start back to work after a week. The kids and Mary mostly hung out around the house playing games, watching movies or playing video games. Jenny could still beat Schea almost all of the time and even Archie about half the time that they played. Izzy was more like Schea in that she wasn't very good at video games and really didn't care.

At the end of the second week, Schea decided that she needed to get back to her place. Everyone understood, even Jenny. The night before Schea left, she and Jenny sat up most of the night talking about when Schea would visit next, when Jenny could come up to DC where they would be able to hang out, and when they might be able to take an extended trip somewhere with the family, maybe to see Jim and Grace. Jenny knew she could never visit Schea's place because of Schea's work and was fine with that.

XXXXX

They dropped Schea off at the train station the following morning. There were hugs, kisses, and tears all around then lots of arm waving as the train pulled out of the station. The train ride to DC would take just over 3 hours and Schea spent that time thinking about Jenny's rescue and how scared she had been during the whole assault. She knew that she had had to contain it in order to stay focused and calm but it had been really tough. She wasn't really scared for herself. She had conquered that a long time ago. She was scared that she would screw the rescue up and Jenny would be hurt or worse.

She also thought about Frank. *How could he have been so nice while at the camp and then turn on me so easily? He had really seemed to like spending time with me. Maybe he actually had. Who knows?* She certainly didn't have the experience to know what all of that meant.

She had also been duped by Greg, so maybe she did need to figure this out at some point, but not now. She had to schedule a meeting with the boys.

Todd met her at Union Station and they drove to her place. As they drove, he told her that he had debriefed Chuck on the mission. He had also asked Chuck if there was anything that they might be able to do to get the Taliban leader that Stefan had used to kill her brother.  Chuck said that he would look into it but that it was doubtful anything could be done.

"I also told Chuck to send you the bill for all of the costs that were provided for the rescue.  At first he tried to say that was not necessary, but I insisted that you wanted to cover them since it was your mission and, therefore, your responsibility.  Chuck started to ask me if that was something that you could afford, but then he remembered your introduction interview and said "Never mind."  He said that he'd put the figures together and would forward them to me then I will include them with my bill."

As they pulled up to her place, Todd told her, "Michael is not on any missions so he will be available whenever you are ready.  Give me a call and I will know how to get hold of him."  He gave her a hug, and she got out of the car.

Schea entered her place and stopped in the middle of the living room.  She dropped her small bag and just looked around.  She took it all in.  She was home and could just be herself, well not exactly, but pretty close.  She changed and went for an easy run then spent an hour in the pool near her place. It felt so good just to do these things with no one shooting at her.

# 53 Mission Six: The Boys (Part 4)

A month after she got home from Bulgaria, Schea flew to Portland and got a room at the Hilton. She called Alice and asked if they could meet up. Alice was excited that Schea was back and wanted to show her what she had done with her old apartment.

Schea drove to Boring, went to her old front door and knocked. Alice opened the door, grabbed Schea and dragged her into the apartment. "I am so happy to see you. Come in, come in!"

Once Alice let go of Schea and she was able to walk on her own, she looked around the living room. There were lovely paintings on the walls, beautiful art pieces on the various tables and hutches, and the carpet was new. Everything was color coordinated and in a perfect spot.

"Alice, this is absolutely beautiful." She looked at Alice, "Alice, you are amazing. This is wonderful. You should be an interior designer."

Alice shrugged. "I've always loved doing stuff like this, but I've never had a place of my own. The other apartments where I have lived were either shared with someone or the landlord had strict rules about what you could do in them. This is the first place that I have lived where I could actually make it my own. I've also always loved art and designing things so this was an opportunity to experiment and see how it looked."

"Well, I still think you should go into interior design as a profession."

Alice laughed. "Maybe someday, when I can afford it. Come on. Sit down. The usual order, I assume."

Schea smiled and nodded. Alice was such a sweetheart. Schea filed away the idea of an interior design business for Alice.

They had a fun time and Schea ended up staying in the spare bedroom that night instead of the Hilton. Alice told her about some of the plays she had worked on and what the other members of their little theater group had been up to. She also admitted having met a guy but wasn't sure if he was the right one. Alice, of course, asked Schea if she had met someone.

"No, not yet."

Alice looked at her with a serious face and told her that she needed to get on with that. "You know honey, you're not getting any younger and time is just frittering away for you."

Schea looked at her wide-eyed then Alice broke out in laughter. She lightly punched Schea's arm and told her that she was kidding. "Look, you're still a teenager and there is absolutely no need to rush to find some guy."

XXXXX

Schea headed back to Portland and, before she left, she told Alice that she would try to come back for another visit soon or to maybe meet up with her downtown. Alice said that she would love that, and the gang would be thrilled to see her again.

When Schea got back to the hotel room, she called Todd. She asked him to contact Michael and ask him to fly to Portland. She asked him to pass on his flight information and she would pick him up.

XXXXX

Michael arrived 2 days later.

Schea met him at the airport and drove back to her hotel. As she drove, they talked about things like the weather, the fun she had with Jenny and her friend Alice. Michael told her about a girl he had met a few months ago. He said that she was pretty nice but he didn't know how it might work in the long run because of his job.

Schea nodded. "I have wondered about that too. As far as I can tell, none of the guys working for Todd are married. I know we are never told any private information about each other but I would think that there would have been hints every now and then about a personal life." Michael said he wasn't aware of anyone being married either.

They walked into her hotel room and went over to the two chairs and table that sat near the window. She had a small refrigerator in her room and asked Michael if he'd like a beer. Michael looked at her sternly and said, "You are too young to be buying alcohol."

She looked back at him, "I didn't ask you if I could buy or not buy you a beer. I asked if you wanted a beer."

He threw up his hands in surrender, smiled and said, "Sure."

She got him a beer and she got herself a Diet Coke.

Once they had their drinks, Michael started. "Okay, I spent two weeks hanging out with the boys at the Pitchwood. I took your suggestion and stayed at the Golden Lion Inn. By the way, that place is really a dump but at least it was clean. The boys took to me easily. I made up a couple of stories about the girls I had known over the years. I even made up a story about raping a girl in Ireland when I was 17. I laughed when I told them the story. I told them, I guess I won't be going back to Ireland any time soon. The boys then admitted that they had done that too but they didn't give any names, dates, or places."

"The boys even had me come over to their house for beers. That house makes the inn seem like the Hilton. It is dirty and smelly and so run-down it should be condemned. I looked around when I first walked in and made a face. Hank had seen the look, cuffed me on the shoulder, and said that this place was just temporary. He said they were about to come into a large inheritance and would be out of this crappy backwater town soon. He said that maybe they'd move to Reno or Vegas."

242

"At the beginning of the second week, I asked Kathleen to show up in town. I told her to get a room at the inn and come into the Pitchwood later that evening. The boys and I were there when she walked in. She has wild red hair that she never ties up. It simply flies around her head every time she moves it. She wore a tight short skirt with a tight t-shirt. She did not wear a bra, so there was nothing to leave to the imagination and her boobs were constantly struggling to pop out of her top. When the boys saw her walk in, their eyes nearly popped out of their heads. Actually, all of the guys in the bar were staring at her."

"Kathleen went up to the bar and ordered a scotch on the rocks. She can drink any man that I know, including me, under the table so she knew that if any of these locals started buying her drinks, she would probably set their bank accounts back quite a bit. She moved to a vacant table, sat and slowly crossed her beautiful long legs. You could have heard a pin drop by now. I broke the ice and whispered to Hank, watch this. I walked over to the table, sat down with my beer and said hi."

"Kathleen and I had worked out what we wanted them to see so she said hi, and we started an amiable discussion. We would laugh every so often, whisper something up close then laugh again. We really had the boys drooling now. About an hour later, I pretended to say something she didn't like. She smacked me across the face, got up, told me that I could pay her tab, and walked out."

"The boys rushed over to sit with me and Hank asked what happened. I laughed and shrugged it off. I told them that I only asked for a feel, and I guess maybe I was moving too fast for the bitch. I told them she and I had a history so we acted like that all the time, but she'll come around and winked at them. The boys would have given me anything after that. Kathleen came in each night for the next 4 nights then left town."

"On the second night, the boys got brave and sat with her. She would joke with them and, if they said racy stuff to her, she would only laugh along with them. We wanted them to think that they were getting somewhere with her because they were such a fun couple of guys. But, then she was gone and I left a few days later. I told them my mom was very ill, and lived in Boston, so I had to fly back to be with her. They put on sad faces for me and hoped that she would get better. I told them I'd be back as soon as I could."

Schea told Michael that she really liked what he and Kathleen had put together. She asked, "Do you think Kathleen will mind being the bait to draw the boys out?"

"Are you kidding? She is anxious to do it. I told her about what they have been doing and she was mad as hell. She wanted to get them right then, but I told her that you would be the one to take them down."

Michael outlined a plan for Schea to consider. "I will go back to town in a day or two and get back into the swing of things with the boys. Kathleen will come back to town 4 days later and we will both stay at the inn. She will come to the bar 2 days in a row alone and play the hottie again. On the third night, she and I will walk in together. We will be all buddy-buddy and do some kissing."

"I will invite the boys over to sit with us. She'll say something like, she remembers the boys as being so nice on her last visit, and they will gush over her. After a few hours, she and I will get up to leave. She'll head out first, and I'll pretend that I forgot something. She'll head to the inn and I'll go back to the table and sit. The boys will be too curious not to ask me if I am sleeping with her. When they do, I'll wink and nod. Then I'll quickly run out the door and back to the inn."

"Kathleen and I will stay in the same room in case the boys get curious. The following night I will come in alone. The boys will, of course, ask me where Kathleen is and I'll tell them that she had to go down to Portland for the day but will be back tomorrow. They'll ask me all kinds of raunchy questions and I'll answer some, laugh at others and smile at still others."

"As things seem to be winding down, I'll pretend to be a little drunk and conspire with the boys to meet Kathleen tomorrow evening and bring her to their house for drinks and fun. They will, of course, agree. I'll also warn them that they cannot tell anyone about the party. After all, we don't want any others there to take away some of our fun."

"I'll tell them that I'll bring her to the bar tomorrow evening. The boys will be there, of course, and we will all hang out as we did before. After a couple of hours, Kathleen will start acting like she is getting a little too drunk. The boys will take my cue, excuse themselves and head to their house. I'll whisper to the boys that I'll talk Kathleen into going with me to meet at their place after about 30 minutes. They will love it."

"You will be in the house when they get there and will do what you do so well, and Kathleen and I will head out of town. After you are finished talking with the boys about old times, you can go back to your car then head wherever." He stopped and waited.

Schea asked a few questions but overall she loved it and thought that it would work quite well. At that, they finished their drinks and went out for a walk down by the waterfront. As they walked along, she brought up the topic of having a mate while doing this kind of work. Michael thought for a minute and said, "It might be possible, but the person would have to be pretty special and have to have a ton of trust. I mean, they would have to watch their partner in life leave, knowing they may never return or how long they might be away."

They were both quiet for a few minutes then Michael said, "I really don't think I would want to put someone through all of that. It would simply not be fair to them."

Schea nodded and just said, "Yea, probably not."

Michael stayed the night in Schea's room on the other double bed and headed to Raymond in the morning. "I will not see you there and hope it all goes well. Those boys are true bastards and admitted to me that they had, what they called, fun with a lot of girls. I'm glad that you let me be a part of your plan."

She thanked him and wished him luck too.

He reminded her, "You should be in their house in four days at around 10 pm."

"I wouldn't miss it for the world." Schea said.

"I wish I could watch you and the boys get reacquainted but know that is impossible." They drove to the airport car rental lot. As he walked to his rental, he thought about the boys and said to himself. *They are in for a really big surprise.*

Schea now had no qualms about what she planned to do to the boys. Even if the authorities found out about what the boys had been doing, how many girls would come forward? Not many. The boys would probably get convicted, but they'd be out after a few years on good behavior and then they would start again. She was not going to allow that to happen. They deserved punishment for what they had done to Allison, to all of those other girls, and for what they would do to more girls in the future. She was positive they would never stop.

# 54 Mission Six: The Boys Meet Schea (Part 5)

Schea made her way to Raymond on the night that Michael had said he would get the boys to the house. She arrived at 9 pm and parked along Henkle Street, which ran along the south side of the town. She pulled off the road and parked amongst some trees. When she got out of her car, she made sure that her car was not visible from the road and headed toward the town. She had about a half mile to cover in order to reach the back of their house. She was dressed entirely in black and had on black nylon gloves. Her shoes were black and the soles were sturdy leather with hardened heels and toes.

She knew the area well from the time she and Allison had lived there. She would stay in the tree line all the way to the back of the house. She skirted by the Willapa River on the right and the High School Athletic field on the left. It was slow going because the underbrush in the tree line was thick and there was no trail. She also wanted to move slowly so as not to make any noise, plus she was constantly checking around her for any late-night lovers or prowlers. She arrived at the back of the house at 9:20 pm.

She moved cautiously through the broken-down part of the backyard fence and up to the back door. She listened just to make sure no one was inside or in the area. The left side of the house had a dead-end street, and the right side bordered on the yard for the house next door. The owners of that house, as she remembered, were an elderly couple that went to bed early.

She entered the house and moved quickly to the living room and closed the blinds. She then moved down the hall, found the fuse box, and pulled all of the fuses. She was confident in her ability to move and see in the dim light provided by the street-lamp across the street but figured the boys would not be good in the dark. She'd put the fuses back before leaving. She moved back to the living room, scanned it for large objects or anything that could be used as a weapon, and hid them behind the sofa. She would also put them back before leaving.

Schea went to the kitchen and gathered up a dozen or so empty beer and whiskey bottles from the trash bins. It was nice of the boys to never take out the trash. She put them in a paper bag and hid them behind the sofa too. She fixed up some kindling and placed small logs in the fireplace in order to set a fire after the boys arrived. It would make a pleasant setting for their reunion.

She next went over to the matching chair and sofa, sat in the chair, and pushed down hard on the arms and into the back of the chair. It was a hefty and sturdy piece of furniture, although the upholstery could use some help. She moved it a little so that it faced the entryway to the living room.

Michael said he'd call once the boys left the bar so Schea sat in the chair and waited. After about 20 minutes, Michael called. The boys were on the way and he and Kathleen were heading out of town. He wished her luck. Schea said thanks and turned off her phone.

Schea heard the car pull up in front of the house then footsteps as the boys walked up the front steps. She heard them talking and laughing about what a good time they were going to have when

Michael and Kathleen finally arrived at the house. As they entered, they tried to turn on the lights, but nothing happened.

Hank cursed and moved into the living room in order to check the fuses down the hallway. He entered and stopped short, causing Rod to bump into his back. They both stared. Hank finally smiled when he saw that he was looking at a girl but he couldn't tell exactly who she was.

Hank asked with a lascivious grin, "Who are you, sweetie?"

Schea answered by saying, "Hi, don't you remember me, Hank?"

"No, why should I?" said Hank.

"Well, you should remember me because my sister and I used to live here and you said you really wanted to have fun with me."

Recognition finally spread across Hank's face. He smiled. "Right, you're the little sister of the dead girl. Such a tragedy." He frowned.

Schea smiled and said, "Yes, it was a terrible tragedy. Anyway, I happened to be in town and wanted to come back to see how you boys were doing." She sat with her arms laying on the armrests and her legs crossed under her.

Hank also smiled, grinned at her, and said, "Wow, I figured you'd turn out to be pretty, and I was right. But you're kind of small."

He turned to Rod and asked, "Do you remember our little friend here?"

Rod smiled and said, "Oh yes, I remember her well."

Hank turned back and told Schea, "Your sister had much better boobs, but yours are probably pretty nice too. I am really looking forward to some fun with you tonight, but we must be quick since we will be having some company soon." He paused then said, "Wait, hey, I have a great idea. Why don't you stay and be part of the party too? Would you like that?"

Schea looked at Hank sadly, "Well, I do thank you for the compliment, but I must decline the party invitation. As a matter of fact, you will not be having company tonight, so it will be just the three of us."

She still hadn't moved. Rod was looking nervous and started shifting from foot to foot. His eyes were scanning from side to side.

Hank was oblivious. He shrugged and said, "Okay, I think that three can still be a lot of fun, and it just means that I'll get to spend more time with you. You know, get to know you better."

Schea continued to sit and look at him.

He finally said, "I am really going to enjoy this."

She countered, "I seriously doubt that you will enjoy this, but I know I will."

Hank scowled and started to move toward her but Schea sat quietly and watched. When he got about 2 feet away and began to lean in toward her, she pushed up with her hands pressed down on the arms of the chair, struck out with both legs, and slammed her feet into his gut. She continued moving and launched into him, knocking him backward. She landed on top of him and hit him hard three times in the jaw then twice in the neck.

Before Rod could react, Schea moved off of Hank and slammed her foot up into his crotch and, when he bent over moaning, she hit him with a quick hard uppercut to the left side of his face. As his head turned with the punch, she came down hard with her elbow into the base of his skull. He went down with a heavy thud. He was out.

She turned her attention back to Hank who was still lying on his back, moaning. She walked to him, looked down then kicked him hard in the balls then his side, and finally his head. She squatted next to his face so that he could see her. He looked at her, horrified. She smiled and asked, "Are you having as much fun as you had with my sister all those years ago?"

Hanks mouth started to move to form what looked like a *"Ple..."* but Schea punched him hard in the throat and he went still.

Schea checked both of them and noted that they were still alive but probably in a great deal of pain. They were both out cold. *Good.* She slid the sofa over to the front of the fireplace and dragged both boys to it. She hauled Rod onto it and arranged him into a sitting position. She left Hank on the floor near the opening of the fireplace.

She returned the heavy objects to where they were originally and spread the empty bottles around the sofa and on the floor near the boys. She checked to make sure the fireplace flue was closed and started a fire. She went down the hall and replaced the fuses then came back to the living room. She pulled out a thin nylon mask and covered her mouth with it. If she stayed too long then she could choke on the smoke that was building up, but she had no plans to overstay her *unwelcome*.

When the room had a good bit of smoke built up, she gingerly pulled out a small burning stick from the fireplace and placed it on the sofa. Next, she pulled another one out and laid it next to the interior wall. She watched and waited until she saw that the sofa and the interior wall were fully engulfed in flames. At that point, she left through the back door and headed for the tree-line.

By the time she got about 100 yards from the house, it was a blazing inferno. The boys should have been better stewards of their property.

When she reached her car, she heard the sirens of the fire engines responding to the blaze. She knew it was too late to save the boys or the house, so the firemen might let it burn and try to protect the homes nearby. She stripped off her clothes and shoes and put them in a plastic bag. She put on the spare clothes she had brought along and a pair of running shoes. She moved to the road, checked for traffic, saw none, so she went back to her car, drove out onto the road, and headed south toward Portland.

She stopped just to the west of Vancouver, Washington, got out and took the bag of clothes with her. She walked a short way to the shore of the Columbia River and found an area with a lot of large rocks. She put about half a dozen rocks into the plastic bag and tied it securely. She poked a few holes into it so that the air would escape then tossed it into the fast flowing river. It sank almost immediately. She went to the little hotel just outside of Vancouver and into the room she had reserved earlier in the day.

She slept well and, in the morning after a quick shower, she packed up her little bag and headed for the airport. She checked in for her flight and went to the food court for a bite to eat. She flew back to DC, picked up her car, and went home.

The following day, she searched the Internet for news about a fire in Raymond. She found a brief article that said the fire looked like an accident. It seemed that the occupants had been drinking heavily, started a fire in the fireplace, but forgot to open the flue. It looked like once they realized their mistake, they tried to close it but their efforts caused the fire to spread out of the fireplace.

Schea smiled, and thought. *The mission has been successfully completed.*

# 55 Missions Five and Six: Good News

The following day, Schea got a call from Michael. He asked, "How are you doing?"

"All went well and I am doing great."

"Hey, I am in Baltimore. Can you meet me in Todd's office this afternoon?"

"Sure."

When Schea walked into the office, she saw Todd and Michael sitting at the table, each with a cup of coffee. She grabbed a Diet Coke and joined them. "What's up?"

Michael smiled. "I have some additional news about Raymond. Kathleen went after the deputy before I got there on my trip. She had watched him on the previous trip and got a feel for his daily routine. She knew that between 1 and 3 in the afternoon, he sat by the highway checking for speeders. She dressed in her hottest outfit and passed him going 15 miles over the speed limit. He put on his lights and pulled her over a few minutes later. By then, she made sure that they were a good bit out of town."

"When the deputy walked up to her window, she gave him a whole lot of cleavage to look at and had her skirt hitched up just enough to show a good bit of her thighs. She told me that the deputy could hardly talk, so she helped him along. She told him that she was extremely sorry. She said she was in a hurry for a photo shoot in Portland and did not want to be late."

"She told him that if he could let her go this time then the next time she was in town, they could have dinner together. She begged him not to tell anyone since she did not want to get into trouble and lose her day job. The deputy apparently remembered the boys talking about a really hot redhead and what they wanted to do to her. He appeared to get jealous and decided that he would not tell them about his encounter with her."

"The deputy finally took his eyes off of her boobs and smiled at her. He gave her a stern warning about safe driving and told her to give him a call when she got back in town. He gave her his card, she thanked him and even stroked his hand and arm as he handed her the card."

"She went back to Raymond two days later and stayed clear of the Pitchwood and the inn. She had called the deputy on the way and had agreed to meet him at a picnic area just outside of town. She told him that it would be a nice day for a picnic so they could be outside together and she would pack a lunch."

"They met just after noon, ate and talked for about an hour. She started out by sitting across from him but then moved and sat next to him. She had on a pair of shorts and a tight t-shirt. When they finished, he walked her to her car. She told him that he was such a nice guy, and that most of the other guys she meets are only after one thing. They say disgusting things to her, and she just can't stand it anymore. She wants to meet a nice guy like him sometime."

"She told me that he fell all over himself, telling her he agreed, and that he hated how guys act around pretty girls. He said he would never be that way toward her. She gave him a sweet kiss on the cheek and got into her car. Before she pulled away, he asked if he could see her again and she said sure. Maybe he could meet her in Portland for the weekend, and she would show him around town. He said he was free the following weekend so she told for him to call her."

"He did, and they met in Portland on Friday afternoon. They stayed in separate rooms at a little hotel near the airport, went into town, walked around, ate dinner, and even saw a play. When they got back to the hotel, she kissed him on the lips, and they went to their rooms. They did the same thing on Saturday, but did not go to a play."

"They came back to the hotel to watch a pay-per-view movie. He bought some beer, and they sat in his room on his bed since there was only one chair. The movie was a comedy so they laughed a bit, and she kept leaning into him, brushing her hair on him, and letting her boobs hit his arm. He finally leaned in and tried to kiss her."

"She told me that she pulled away quickly and said that she is not that kind of girl and she hoped he would not try anything. He was horrified and said no repeatedly, and would not try anything. He said that he knows boys who are like that and hates them. She patted his arm and moved close again. She called him by name and sweetly asked him what he meant by other boys. He hesitated but she kept coaxing him to tell her."

"Finally, he told her all about *the boys* and how they used him to help find girls. They also made him cover up any police reports. At this point, he got tears in his eyes and confessed that they would beat him if he didn't. He said that he never did anything himself but would just suggest a girl that was new in town. And, if any complaints were filed, then he made sure they were lost, misplaced, or incomplete."

"Kathleen said she patted him on the back as though consoling him. Then she said she had better go to her room. He mumbled okay, and she left."

"What he did not know is that hidden in those beautiful boobs of hers was a recording device that captured his confession to her. When she got back to her room, she pulled it out, and made a copy of it. She wrote a note that said that if he ever showed his face in Raymond again, then this was going to be sent to the Washington State Patrol (WSP) for investigation. She put all of this in an envelope and left it at the front desk for him. She went to the airport and flew to New York to wait for my call about your mission."

When Michael finished, Schea looked at him and said, "I knew I liked Kathleen! She's amazing."

Michael smiled and continued. "Kathleen is mailing a copy of the recording to the WSP in 3 days. I wanted you to know this because the investigation will likely end up looking into Allison's death. They may also wonder if any of the girls might have maintained enough of a grudge to have conspired to kill the boys."

Schea looked at him aghast and said, "Oh, my, my, that would be a horrible thing to have happen."

Todd rolled his eyes and Michael said, "Yes, well, you need to be ready for a possible phone call from the authorities in the near future."

Schea nodded and said, "Thanks for the heads-up."

Todd thought a moment and said, "If they call me, I'll tell them that you were working on an assignment for me during the time the boys died, and that the assignment is for a confidential client. If he ends up needing a name, then I have plenty of people who will say whatever I ask them to say. I suggest you tell them the same thing."

Four days later, both Schea and Todd each got a call, and they told the investigator the same story about working on a confidential project.

XXXXX

A week after that, Schea received the bills from Todd and Chuck. When she opened them, she got angry and called Todd. When he answered, she asked, "What is going on? This was my mission. I am paying for it. I want you to...."

Before she could go on, Todd yelled, "Hey, stop. Let me explain."

She sighed, stopped and waited.

Todd explained, "A senator got wind of the use of some military assets for some secret operation in Europe and demanded to know about it. He wanted to know what was done and why, and started making a huge issue out of it. The President decided that he had to do something. He had Chuck call Jeff to tell him about the problem. He said he would not allow any interviews or press to come to his house or bother Jenny."

"He would place guards around his house and Jenny 24/7 if it came down to it. But he told Jeff the President wanted to tell this senator that they had sent a secret team in to rescue a kidnapped little girl. They would only use her first name and asked if Jeff could send him a recent picture of Jenny, with her face away from the camera, doing something fun so people would see that she was a complete innocent in all of this. He agreed."

"Jeff sent the photo and the White House Press Secretary was given the story and the photo. A press conference was called 2 days later. The story was that a little girl, whose father and uncle are decorated veterans, had been kidnapped. She was kidnapped for no other reason than that she had been in the wrong place at the wrong time. She was taken by a ruthless gun and drug dealer who also sold young girls to the highest bidder."

"The government had no means to rescue her, and diplomatic approaches had yet to achieve any results. Time was short because he would sell her as soon as he got a high-enough bid. The

252

President suggested that a private security team make the rescue. The only support the US provided was air support to get them there and to bring them home. We also provided some satellite support, if there was no strategic need for the bird at the time."

Todd said, "The room buzzed with questions. They wanted to know the girl's name. They were told that Jenny was her name. No address will be given. No information whatsoever will ever be given out which would cause this poor family's privacy to be compromised again. The private security team paid all of their own expenses. The questioning continued for 30 minutes."

Todd smiled and looked at Schea.

"Brandy happened to see the press coverage and recognized someone in the photo. You, Schea, she recognized you. Jeff had apparently sent a picture from an old visit where you guys must have gone to a zoo. You were well in the background, but Brandy recognized you. She went to her father and told him what she theorized, which was that you somehow helped out another kidnapped little girl. She had no idea that Jenny was your sister."

"Brandy's dad called me and asked if this was true. I told him that I had no comment. I guess he figured that it was true, and he deposited 5 million dollars into our account to cover any expenses for the rescue. He also sent me a letter that said he would fund any future kidnapping rescues if the family could not afford it."

"His letter told me that he was so thankful to have Brandy home again. As he thought about her rescue, he felt so happy that he had been able to afford the steep price to get her back. As he thought about it, he decided he could not live with himself if he didn't do all he could to help others to get their kids back."

"He also said he was extremely grateful to the female member of the team. Brandy would not tell him that you were the one she saw in the picture or your name. He is not even sure she knows the name but this person must have said something to Brandy that changed her life. Brandy helps around the house, volunteers in the food bank, and is a youth leader at church. She stays home with the family and plays with her baby brother most of the time. He can only say that it was a magical transformation, and he wants that person to know what she has done for his family."

Todd stopped and waited for Schea to say something. He finally said, "Schea?"

She sighed and said, "Okay. I do understand why he did it, and I am very grateful to him for wanting to help others. I feel like people who can do something for others, should do whatever they can."

Todd said, "I agree. I'll call you if I hear anything more about the news story and the exposure."

XXXXX

Todd called Schea again about 3 weeks later. When Schea answered, Todd immediately started talking. "Turn on the TV."

She thought, *Man, will this never end?* Todd was so insistent that she said okay.

He said that he'd call back in 10 minutes and she said fine.

Schea turned on the TV and began to watch a news story that was interrupting the local broadcast. The news anchor said, "... Repeating, a suicide bomb has gone off in a noted Taliban terrorist's camp. Preliminary reports are that at least 2 dozen men were killed including several high ranking Taliban leaders. One of the highest ranking leaders was Mohammad Shefara." Schea heard nothing after that. She just stared at the TV and cried. They were tears of sadness for what had happened to Rob and tears of happiness that the bastard who had done it was now dead.

Several minutes later, Todd called. Schea answered and quickly asked, "How?"

"The US really could not have done anything about Shefara, mainly because they have such a small presence there and second, because anything that could be tried by remote devices only has a 50/50 chance of success with a high probability of killing civilians. So, I called your Arab buddy and asked if he could help and he said he would try."

"Your friend told me that there were plenty of dumbass suicide bombers for hire in the area so he would have one of his men recruit one and ensure that he does the job right. He sent his man in with the bomber to make sure. The mission started about 6 weeks ago. It took that long getting close enough and trusted enough for the bomber to get into a position, and to make sure he got the right man. He was getting antsy and nervous, until one day, Shefara showed up at the camp and stayed for 2 days. This was the bomber's opportunity so he took it."

All Schea could say was, "Please thank our friend."

Todd said he would and hung up.

Schea couldn't believe it. All of the people who had wiped out her family were now gone. She wondered. *What will be my obsession now? This revenge thing has occupied my life for so long that it's became something for me to hold on to each day, especially while I am on a mission.* She always envisioned her mission targets as people who may have done to others what was done to her family, and knew that what she was doing would help protect other families. *Now, how should I begin to feel each day?* She knew she would always miss her family but she just wondered if having no revenge to seek would change her.

# 56 A New Start

It had been two months since Muhammad was killed and one month since her Rahim mission. She began to notice changes in herself. She felt more contented, had fewer dark thoughts, and happier. She hoped she also exhibited a happier persona.

She had been to visit Jenny several times and Jenny had met her for a weekend in DC. Jenny seemed to be completely over the kidnapping. They never talked about it or their feelings about it or really anything about it. Jenny also had a boyfriend. Actually, she hung out with a boy who is a friend because Jeff said that she couldn't have a true boyfriend until she was 16. She and Jenny laughed about the arbitrary age of 16.

Schea started attending a church nearby. It was the First Presbyterian Church, and was a short walk from her place. She didn't go every Sunday, and didn't participate in any of the groups especially the youth group. *Goodness, what could I talk about regarding my work and my life?* She went because she liked the music and the serenity of the place. She liked the messages that focused on love, forgiveness, and lots of good stuff. They may have sounded cliché to some but she found them a welcome contrast to what she saw in her job.

XXXXX

Schea had gone to a service this morning and, as she was leaving the service, she saw a young man approaching her.

He came up to her and said, "Hello."

She smiled and said, "Hey." She remembered seeing him a few times before.

He asked, "Would you like to get a cup of coffee?"

She almost blew him off, but then said, "Sure." They headed to the Starbucks coffee shop at City Dock. On the way, Schea remembered Greg and Frank. Suddenly, it was like someone had slapped her face. She told herself, *Stop thinking about them. This is a new and happier you.*

After a short time, she realized that he was chatting amiably about the weather, the town, and other small talk. She reminded herself that she had plenty of evidence of really good guys. She thought about Michael, Jack, Todd, Kevin and Gus. *Think about the guys in the theater group back in Portland, especially the one that she ran with who invited her to join the relay team. They are all cool, fun, respectful guys who would never hurt anyone.*

Suddenly, she heard the guy next to her asking, "Did you hear me?"

She smiled and said, "Sorry, what did you say?"

"I asked your name."

"It's Schea. It is spelled S-c-h-e-a and the "c" is silent, so it's pronounced Shay!" She smiled.

"Nice to meet you, Schea. I am Colin."

"Nice to meet you too, Colin."

At the Starbucks, they placed their orders and sat outside. Their order was announced and Colin went in to retrieve it.

As he drank his coffee and she drank her tea, Colin told Schea, "I am a second-year midshipman at the Naval Academy and am 21. I have seen you out on your runs when I've been on one myself. You are really good and I'm usually well behind you."

She chuckled. He smiled and asked, "What?"

"Nothing. Thanks for the compliment."

"I am studying nuclear physics at the academy and will probably spend my 6 commitment years on a nuclear sub. I am not sure if I'll stay in or get out of the Navy at the end of my commitment because I might try to finish a doctorate." He paused and asked, "So what are you up to? School? Work?"

"Oh, I am a research assistant at a security company based in Baltimore. Most of what I do is confidential. Security obligations, you know. I often travel ahead of a project to set up meetings and stuff. It's not all that exciting, but our clients almost always demand a high level of secrecy." Schea smiled and shrugged.

"Yea, I understand security stuff being at the academy myself and all." He paused and then continued, "My father was in the military, so there were a lot of things that we didn't know regarding his work. We now live in Manitou Springs, Colorado. It's a small town, but the area is very beautiful. It sits at the base of Pikes Peak. Have you ever been there?" She shook her head no. "I also have an older sister and a younger sister. How about you? Where is your family from? Do you have any brothers or sisters?"

This caught her off guard. When asked about family, she usually said, "No, they are all dead." But that was because she was mostly dealing with other operatives or people who didn't matter. This seemed different. *How do I say no, and then what if he asks how they had died?* She saw that he was looking at her expectantly.

She sighed and said, "I am from Bend, Oregon and my parents passed away some years ago. I do have a younger sister who lives near Richmond, Virginia. "

He sighed and said, "I am so sorry about your parents." He was polite enough to drop the topic, so he asked, "Do you see your sister often?"

"I see her every month or so depending on my work and travel schedule. She is living with a relative now, and they have a wonderful family. We always have a great time when we get together."

They stayed and talked about random things over the next couple of hours.

They finally got up to leave. Colin walked with her back to the church and didn't ask to walk her home.

As they arrived at the church, Colin said, "I had a really nice time. Would you like to go out sometime for dinner or maybe a movie? I am free this weekend, if you are."

Schea must have looked startled because, after an awkward silence, Colin fumbled a little then said, "That's okay, maybe another time." He turned to walk away.

Schea quickly called to him and said, "Yes, I would like to go out this Saturday. Just give me a call Saturday morning with the details." She gave him her phone number.

He said, "Great. I'll do that."

It seemed to her that he walked away with a little spring in his step.

As she walked toward her place, she thought, *Maybe I have a little spring in my step too. I hope that the date goes well. I have never really been out on a date before. Maybe I should call Izzy to get some tips.*

She actually wasn't sure that she would be able to go. She had called Todd a week ago and told him that she was ready to get back to work but now she was hoping that he wouldn't call until after Saturday.

XXXXX

Todd called Sunday. "Hey, you have a mission for Chuck to Malta."

Schea sighed but was still happy. She and Colin had a fun time last night at dinner and they talked easily with each other. He walked her back to her place and, this time, they kissed.

*This is good for me. I like having a guy around who isn't trying to kill me.* She smiled, and headed for her car, and to Malta.

# Also by Greg Judge

*Schea's Revenge*

Schea Tailor takes personal interest in her missions. She lost her entire family at the hands of brutal killers and now wants all killers and abusers of innocent people gone so that others do not have to go through what she did.

Eighteen year old Schea has a job to do. She teaches the worst of the worst criminals around the world they cannot hide, nor escape, from her.

While on a mission to terminate the head or an organization dealing in the trafficking of young girls, the bad guys plot to kill someone close to her and succeed. As they celebrate their success, they do not realize their problems have just begun.

Schea has close ties to people in high places and to her employer, an operator of a 'private security company'. They have all used her skills on a variety of special missions and have promised they will provide whatever resources she needs to find the killers of her friend.

It will take time but the killer must pay.


*Voyages To Secrets*

Willa and her dad, Dan, put off a world sailing trip after losing Willa's mother and brother in a boating accident. Ten years later, Dan is now a successful investigator and business owner and Willa, at 15, is an accomplished runner, archer and speaks 4 languages. Willa feels they are now ready for their trip.

In the beginning they have wonderful experiences while the time at sea gives them the opportunity to talk about what could have been and what is possible.

A mysterious phone call near Africa takes them on a different voyage. It is a voyage for truth across the United States and eventually Russia. They uncover enemies they never knew they had and find danger and death at every turn. Willa eventually finds herself alone in Russia running from a deadly enemy and her skills are put to the extreme test in order to survive.

Made in the USA
Monee, IL
23 January 2020

20778936R00142